HONOR AMONG THIEVES

HONOR

AMONG

THIEVES

RACHEL CAINE & ANN AGUIRRE

KT KATHERINE TEGEN BOOKS
An Imprint of HarperCollins Publishers

Katherine Tegen Books is an imprint of HarperCollins Publishers.

Honor Among Thieves

Text copyright © 2018 by Rachel Caine LLC and Ann Aguirre
Frontispiece art copyright © 2018 by Patrick Arrasmith
All rights reserved. Printed in the United States of America.
No part of this book may be used or reproduced in any manner whatsoever
without written permission except in the case of brief quotations embodied in
critical articles and reviews. For information address
HarperCollins Children's Books, a division of HarperCollins Publishers, 195
Broadway, New York, NY 10007.
www.epicreads.com

Library of Congress Control Number: 2017943387
ISBN 978-0-06-257099-4

Typography by Katie Klimowicz
18 19 20 21 22   PC/LSCH   10 9 8 7 6 5 4 3 2 1
❖
First Edition

For everyone who marches to the beat
of a different drummer.

HONOR AMONG THIEVES

Prelude: Nadim

I feel the stars.

Energy pulses against my skin, murmuring secrets about this small galaxy, about orbits and alignments and asteroids streaming in space. Impulse makes me want to dive and cruise those currents, but I control these urges.

I shift my attention to the flutters of life within my skin.

Marko glows orange with crimson streaks. He is warm, always the easiest to find. Just now, he stands and stares at the blue-green orb swirling below us. I cannot swim down to see what he remembers of this place. The planet's gravitational pull would break my bones. But he shows me flashes: smiling faces, a field of flowers, an old woman with eyes like slices of sky.

"I'll miss you," I tell him.

He flinches a little, surprised to hear me, as if he's ever truly alone. "Me too. It was a good run."

He once told me that it's strange when we talk; he thinks I should find him as insignificant as he does the bacteria in his stomach. But I have had time to acclimate to the strangers in my system. I safeguard the small voices, as is my privilege and duty. There will be more to my life, but only when I've proven myself.

The stars sing again, this time in sleek, seductive harmony. I resist their melody, but the call is growing stronger.

Despite my passengers, I am empty in a way I cannot name. Marko tells me it is because our voyage is over; he calls this sadness. Perhaps I have learned this feeling from him. My first Honor gave me a human name, *Nadim,* and I have kept it safe, along with the other words and shapes and colors that shade my new existence. Like sadness.

I do not like this low orbit, but I must wait. I have been ordered to wait.

My new Honors will come.

Will they be warm and orange like Marko, or crisp and gray like Chao-Xing? She is harder to find, a shadow in my skin, and her silence feels like scraping. Yet her thoughts tap at me endlessly, asking questions I am not permitted to answer. Some answers have not even been given to me, so she can scratch as deep as she wishes. There will be no sudden brightness at the bottom. She is an itch I cannot shake out and I will not be sorry to see her leave. Marko touches where my skin is thin. Such gentleness, I should not feel it, but his feelings amplify at the point of contact. Warmth rolls through me, through layers of muscle and bone, until there's a happy shiver in my depths.

"Please take care," I say in his native language.

"You too. Bye, Nadim." With a final pat on the surface near him, he turns.

A mechanical ship buzzes about me; I check the urge to play. Their constructs are fragile, they have no instinct, and a nudge from me would destroy the craft. I must be docile. I must comply to complete my training. I'm close now. I've learned so much.

To my other Honor, Chao-Xing, I say nothing. She has no words for me, no spare feelings either. Only questions, still, questions that I can't answer. I open so the shuttle can land. There is a burst of cold, swirling energy, which compensates for the minor discomfort. I think this is what yawning must feel like. The humans speak, but not to me. And then they go.

For the first time in one solar year, I am alone. No warmth. No shadows, either.

The elder makes contact, stern and determined. *Be mindful. Stay alert. Now, we wait.*

Yes, Typhon.

I am ready.

PART I

Transcript from **Good Day, New Detroit**, *with hosts Kephana Washington and Saladin Al-Masih, August 12, 2142*

WASHINGTON: Welcome to today's show! We've got news from the Honors Selection Committee about upcoming picks, footage of the Leviathan arrival in the solar system and Mars flyby, the latest on that new *Heart of Fire* release...

AL-MASIH: . . . Plus, a fantastic, fresh, local-grown farming co-op right in the city center, the Kanda School choir, a special profile on returning Honor Marko Dunajski, and a cat who might be the next Pawcasso. So let's get to it!

WASHINGTON: Our first guests this morning are Sarah Simms and Ivor Johanssen–that's right, we've got two of your favorite Honors!– who are going to walk us all through the exciting process inside the notification and training of this year's new set of those chosen to represent humanity with the Leviathan. Sarah and Ivor, hello and welcome. You were both chosen four years ago. Can you each tell me, what did you think would happen, and how did it differ from the reality of going out aboard one of the Leviathan ships?

SIMMS: Well, for my part, I'd been training for this my entire life. Hoping for a chance, I should say, but working for it too. I had pursued a doctorate in biology, and I was really hoping that if I was lucky enough to be chosen, I'd get a chance to study the inner workings of these living ships in a way no one had before.

JOHANSSEN: [laughs] How did that work for you?

SIMMS: [laughs] Not very well, I admit. But the experience was breathtaking! These creatures truly are beyond classification, beyond anything that I can describe, especially once you're close to them and living within their bodies. I'm a little chagrined to admit I didn't get too far with my research. There's too much to keep you busy with assigned duties, and once you're out there seeing other worlds, experiencing what these Leviathan do . . . It changes your perspective.

AL-MASIH: And you, Mr. Johanssen?

JOHANSSEN: Sarah and I were aboard different ships, of course, but I would say my experience was similar. There is a certain . . . wonder to being on board a living ship that is so hard to describe. It makes you feel both very privileged and also very insignificant at the same time.

WASHINGTON: And your favorite things?

JOHANSSEN: Setting foot on another world. I know, we can do that on Mars, and colonization of Io isn't far off now, but the feeling of being quite alone on an alien world is overwhelming. It makes our own differences here on Earth seem very petty.

SIMMS: Absolutely. I suppose also the idea that the Leviathan sing to each other . . . that was truly something that captivated me too. We have a love of music in common.

WASHINGTON: I know this might be a touchy question, but it's something so many people have messaged in that I have to ask: neither of you continued after your Honors year, going on the Journey farther out into the universe. Can I ask why?

SIMMS: For me, I knew from the beginning I would not go on the Journey. It was a family decision. I couldn't leave my parents and my brothers and sisters behind, not for a lifetime. It was just too much to ask. [laughs] It was quite an honor to be chosen for the year, and quite enough for me.

WASHINGTON: And were you asked to continue?

JOHANSSEN: I would rather not answer this question. It was a very personal decision.

SIMMS: I was not, but I was happy with not being asked.

WASHINGTON: Sarah, can you explain why?

SIMMS: No, not really.

WASHINGTON: But I think our viewers really want to know–

JOHANSSEN: This isn't what we came to discuss. Let's go on to what happens once the selected names are received at the Selection Committee HQ. Of course, the Elder Leviathan choose the names from the database we send them once a year, but once the names arrive, the prior-year Honors are dispatched to do the formal notification–

WASHINGTON: I'd really like to return to this question of the Journey, about which we still, a hundred years in, know so little. Can either of you shed any light at all on–

AL-MASIH: [interrupting] Unfortunately, we're just flat out of time for these fascinating questions, Kephana! Thanks to the biotech supplied by these amazing living ships, humans have not only survived a global crisis that threatened to destroy us, but we now have clean energy, safe food and water, and incredible advancements in medical care. We continue to be grateful to them, and excited about the annual Honors selection process.

WASHINGTON: Across the board technological gains have led to the booming space program and the shining beacon of hope that is Mars colony. And speaking of Mars colony, let's get the latest gossip on what's hot in the dome! [offline] What was that? You cut me off!

AL-MASIH: [offline] What did you think you were doing, Keph? You can't go off script like that! Look, Ms. Simms, Mr. Johanssen, I'm sorry on behalf of my colleague–

WASHINGTON: [offline] Don't apologize for me, you jerk. I was asking what everyone wants to know!

SIMMS: [offline] All right. You want something off the record? I wouldn't go on the Journey even if I had been asked. And you wouldn't either.

WASHINGTON: Why–

[recording ends]

CHAPTER ONE

Breaking Point

New Detroit

The Lower Eight

MY MARK MOVED with an expensive, high-heeled strut, the kind that said she'd grown up fed with a silver spoon. That tracked with the haircut and outfit that tried to look edgy but just looked money instead. Not much older than I was—eighteen, max. I'd been trailing her for blocks, but she'd never once looked around for trouble.

Dumbass.

This one, she belonged in Paradise on the other side of the invisible wall, where the suckers thrived—full of brand-name merch and clean, wide streets. Full of polite *good mornings* and *how are yous*.

But she was in the Zone, *my* Zone: gritty, dirty, the shops full of knockoffs and people Paradise didn't fit. Like me.

My mark swaggered down the cracked sidewalk and clearly expected others to make way and . . . they did. An old lady hobbling on a walking stick flinched to avoid a shoulder check, and my target didn't even break stride. The street, she felt, was hers. With a designer bag dangling, she looked like the tastiest score I'd seen in months. She deserved this. Plus, she had to be up to no good, slumming in *my* neighborhood: the Lower Eight, the only blight still remaining on the ripe peach of New Detroit. We could see the graceful old lines of downtown, preserved and refined, from where I stood. That didn't mean we were part of it.

Moneygirl seemed to be aiming for a dive a block down. I moved faster, got closer, and before she could dodge inside, I flicked the knife open that I'd been holding ready in my hand. I quickly reached out and sliced the strap on her purse. Hardly a hiss of resistance, and no security cable in it at all. The prize fell into my hands like a ripe fruit, and I kicked off the broken sidewalk to a run.

I raced around the corner and pushed against the side of the building.

"Thief! You're dead when they catch you!" Good luck with that. Enforcement drones were hard to come by in the Zone because people were always trapping and scrapping. She'd have even less luck finding a human patrol officer.

Her shrill cries faded as I bounded over a fence and cut through an alley, high on success.

With this haul, Derry and I could eat and drink for a week. One more week of freedom. I crouched in the shadow of the VR porn studio and wedged myself in to take a quick inventory. It was every bit as lush as I'd hoped—all kinds of tech, some meds that would sell high, and . . .

I pulled out a metallic box. It had a thumb lock on the lid, but that was a fancy's ignorant precaution; I popped the hinges and got the thing open within seconds. Inside, there was a single clear pack that quickened my pulse. Glittering crystals, flashing multicolored in the weak sun. Some kind of chem. Definitely nothing I'd seen on the street before, but new ones showed up all the time. Might be worth coin. Under that, a slender little data tab. Only a right fool would take traceable tech, so I stuck the chem in my pocket, stashed the metal box with the data tab still in it under some bricks, and bolted.

I crisscrossed twice and backtracked once before darting down a crumbling set of concrete stairs. Constantly glancing over my shoulder, I knocked on a rusted metal door in code reserved for Conde's clients. A bony hand reached out and dragged me into the den, but I'd done this before, so I just shrugged out of Conde's grasp and offered him the heavy embossed bag. The leather—real leather!—rippled like silk. Buttery soft. Cash in every inch.

"Make it quick, man. It's warm," I said.

Conde didn't like to be told what to do. He was a skeletal old fence, pale as spoiled milk, gray hair ratty around his shoulders, but he was smart, and he didn't argue. He shuffled to the counter, which looked like it had been ripped out of a kitchen. That was the only homey touch, though, as electronic guts, glowing screens, and dangling wires covered every square centimeter. His den swam with shadows and smelled vaguely of piss and rodent droppings, but Conde was the best in the Lower Eight, we all knew it.

"Nice," he grunted. Not a big talker, Conde.

As he unpacked the bag's contents, one of the wired-up screens on the bench lit with a broadcast, and a woman as flash as the one I'd ripped off smiled at me from the screen. The holo title pulled out and expanded into the room so you couldn't miss the thing as it spelled out *HONORS* in spinning, swirling gold. *Damn*. It was that time again. This was Countdown Season, close to Honors Return.

Ugh. The Honors. I was already sick of hearing about them, and the season had only just started. Sure, when I was little, I believed all the hype about the arrival of the live ships; unlike SF invasion vids, these aliens were good, helped us out with discoveries and knowledge, and healed the planet that we'd screwed up. But one thing I'd realized about the histories they fed me in school: they weren't the real story. They were polished and half-true at the best.

Earth was still spilling over its banks, Mars could only take so many, and there was a waiting list for the moon, which had basically become a country club. While the Leviathan had solved a lot of problems for humanity, they couldn't create additional landmass.

The planet was all nice again, thanks to their tech, but it wasn't like we'd earned our redemption. The Leviathan showed up out of the blue, offering salvation, and asking for volunteers in exchange; they picked a hundred humans a year to ride along in some alleged cultural and scientific exchange. The way the media spun it, it sounded like the Honors spent their year abroad riding unicorns and farting rainbows, and I was sick of the whole spectacle.

Right then, the announcer was offering a boring retrospective. "Thanks to the biotech supplied by these amazing living ships, humans have not only survived a global crisis that threatened to destroy us, but we now have clean energy, safe food and water, and incredible advancements in medical care. We continue to be grateful to them, and excited about the annual Honors selection process."

His costar added, "Across the board, technological gains have led to the booming space program and the shining beacon of hope that is Mars colony. And speaking of Mars colony, let's get the latest gossip on what's hot in the dome!"

And off they went, to another segment that I immediately

tuned out. I'd always wondered why nobody back in the day questioned the Leviathan's motives, but the world was so screwed that it must've been like dying slowly in a pit; you don't ask questions of somebody tossing down a rope. In my world, there was no free lunch, and eventually the bill for saving our world would come due. I could feel it.

Not that it mattered to me. Those were Paradise problems. I'd never seen an Honor except on the vids, and I didn't care about their magical lives and media-friendly adventures. Let the rest of the world throw parties and consume every bite of the media crap. I just wanted some food and maybe a drink and a place to sleep. I'd lived in their picture-perfect world and I turned my back on it. I'd rather be cold and hungry than trapped and steeped in propaganda.

Not that it was easy to escape it, even here where people rejected most of the alien-driven advancements that made living on the other side of the fence so *nice*.

I hated nice.

Conde growled and yanked wires to short out the holo. He wasn't a fan of the show either, I guessed. I could see him tallying the value of each item he pulled out of the bag I'd brought—a brand-new H2, tricked out with shimmery crystals. Damn, I'd never had anything but an old tablet; this was next-gen holo-tech. There was also a nice case of nanotech makeup and some device too new for me to even recognize. When he finished, he named a figure that seemed a little low.

"Are you kidding me? You'll get twice that just from components."

"I'm taking all the risks here, kid."

"I could offer this haul to Gert instead." That was Conde's primary competition.

With a little growl, he upped his offer. "Final bid, take it or leave it."

"Deal." I hid my smirk. Haggling was just one of the charms the Zone had to offer. Before paying me, he popped open the H2 and snapped the tracking chip. He'd also strip and crack the other devices before resale, but that didn't concern me. He paid in old money, no longer minted but still accepted by vendors in the Lower Eight. The other roamers would be convening in the squat by now, and I pictured Derry's grin when I showed up flush. We didn't mess with e-money in the Zone: too easy to track, and we'd worked out our own system, different values than anywhere else.

Maybe I'll buy a fifth of something fun before I go home. . . . After all, it was Honors Countdown, right? The Flash were partying. Why shouldn't we? Better alcohol than chems. Maybe if I got to him fast enough, I could convince Derry to have a drink with me instead.

Three blocks over, an entrepreneur sold rough

homebrew out of a leaky still, and it would blur the edges. Waving to Conde, who was already working on the unit to break it down, I let myself out. It was second nature to scan my surroundings to make sure nobody had tracked me, but I'd been doing this a while, and the coast seemed clear. Tucking my pay into my undervest, I sauntered down to Moonshine Charlene's. As usual, she was sitting on her front stoop in her housecoat, which was more than a little grimy. Came from using her bathroom for business instead of hygiene, I suspected. Her hands were filthy, but the process of fermentation would kill any bacteria, so I didn't let it trouble me.

"Got anything good?"

"You know it, cookie." She rose with an audible pop. "You want sour mash, dirty gin, or dry lightning?"

"Surprise me."

While she went inside to fill a plastic bottle with cloudy amber goodness, I extracted exactly enough coin to get the crew buzzed.

"You look like a dry lightning girl to me. Enjoy." Moonshine Charlene settled on her porch with a grunt.

Deal made, I hid my contraband in a milky old-days plastic bag. Wasn't especially worried anybody would try to jump me for it, but I knew better than to tempt fate . . . or other crims. People who preferred life in the Zone to Paradise also tended to make their own rules. Me included.

Ever since I was little, my personal file had been marked with judgments like "violent tendencies," "impulse control issues," and "serious problems with authority." My family had been fractured a long time—my mother and sister had tried hard, but I hadn't been right with living in Paradise, not like they were. Now they were gone, off to a new life on Mars, and all I had left—if you could call it that—was my father.

Better to think of myself as an orphan.

Currently I was supposed to be banged up in a reform facility learning to be an upstanding member of society, but like all the other group homes, Parkview couldn't keep me for more than a couple of days. Derry always came, and when Derry appeared outside my window, he meant freedom. And freedom was pretty much all I wanted.

I stopped at a street stall and bought a bag of steamed meat buns to go with the homebrew, and there was still a reassuring jingle of coins in my pouch. *More good stuff tomorrow*, it promised. My belly growled, reminding me that I'd had nothing but a handful of sticky rice sometime yesterday, but going hungry sometimes was a proper tradeoff since I no longer had people telling me when to run, read, eat, shower, shit, and sleep.

I also no longer had anyone whispering that I was bent and wrong, a failure and a burden. Humming a few bars of a song that had been playing in Conde's shop, I turned down the cul-de-sac half-barricaded by rubbish bins that led to our little corner of the world.

Something was very wrong in our world. I'd walked up on a face-off.

Derry held a broken board, his pretty mouth curled back in a snarl. His coppery hair shimmered like nanotech magic, and his pale skin was smooth, despite rough living and the chems he couldn't give up. I knew him, down to the shadows in his eyes, the shake in his hands. He'd scored something while I was gone.

And it was wearing off hard.

A man in a suit stood facing him. Facing *them*. The rest of our crew—Lo, Timo, JJ—had bottles or blades, but they all seemed wary. Odd, since it was only the one guy. But he wore an expensive Paradise suit, custom-tailored, and I made out the telltale bulge of concealed weapons under the fabric.

One knife too, and maybe a second shoulder holster. This is not good. What was he doing here? He wasn't slumming it. He hadn't just stumbled on us, either.

The stranger had deep-set eyes, a prominent brow, and jaw that could crack open a beer. Not a handsome face but a strong one, fearless even. He half turned at my quiet approach. His smile chilled my blood.

"Ah," he said. "There you are. I've been waiting."

I put the booze and food down; no sense in having it

get in the way. As I did, I let the folded knife drop from my sleeve into my palm. Not open yet. I didn't want him expecting it. "You don't know me."

"Zara Cole. You made a mistake today." The gentle tone contrasted completely with the promise of violence in the man's flexing hands. "Your last, gutter rat. Where's the box?"

He took a step toward me.

I didn't back off. I'd learned fear made you weak if you paid mind to it. But he'd said *the box*, not the purse. And I was thinking about the broken metal case I'd hidden in the alley, and the shimmering chem in my pocket.

"Get away from her," Derry growled.

He might as well have been talking to the wind for all the attention the suit gave him. "Do you know what you did wrong?" the man asked me softly.

"It's a long list," I said.

The man laughed. "Did you think we wouldn't come looking? It was easy to ID you. Witnesses tend to be cooperative when you mention Torian Deluca's daughter."

Oh shit.

Even I'd heard of the legendary Deluca. In the rush to rebuild on the ruins of Old Detroit, he'd come up hungry and ruthless. He'd made billions from strong-arm deals, but these days, he was a legit businessman with a lingering reputation for cruelty. People said he was rich and crazy, but never within the big man's earshot.

And I robbed his daughter.

I should have known that strutting bitch had never felt afraid a day in her life—for good reason. Daddy's rep was an invisible shield. But this? It still seemed like an overreaction.

"Yeah? Better call the cops," I said, and squared my shoulders. Finger on the switch to open the knife.

"Mr. Deluca prefers private justice."

That didn't sound so good. I pictured myself tied to a chair, beaten to a pulp. Days later he'd hide my corpse in the foundation of some real estate development. *My ass. I'm not going out like that.*

It's five against one. We can fight it out.

This ugly suit was reading my mind, because he smiled even wider and drew his gun. "Drop the knife."

"Run!" I shouted, and took my own advice, but I wasn't fast enough.

Deluca's strongman ignored the rest of the crew as they scattered and was on me before I took three steps. He twisted my arm behind my back, and I went with it, rolling my shoulder so it popped out of the socket. This wasn't the first time I'd used that trick, and the flash of pain didn't slow me down. I kicked hard at his knee but couldn't get the right angle, so my foot raked down his shin. Painful, but he didn't seem to care.

The guy laughed, digging his fingers with intent to bruise. "I guess you already know how this turns out."

From behind him, Derry said, "Yeah? You don't." He slammed the board upside the guy's head, hard enough to stun. His face was set like one of the Paradise statues.

The suit let go of me, and I lurched forward, tumbling into a rubbish heap a few meters away. Glass broke my fall and sliced into the skin above my elbow. The stink of rotten food mingled with the coppery tang of my blood. As I stumbled to my feet, the thug charged, and at the last second, I used the wet garbage to skid aside, narrowly avoiding a hit that would've dropped me. Rebounding on the wall, I kicked off to a better defensive position while the goon rounded on me.

Derry booted him toward me as I searched for something—anything—to use as a weapon. There was a pile of broken pipes nearby, so I grabbed one and swung for the fences. The impact toppled him sideways and he landed hard on a metal cylinder that speared right through his fine suit. He coughed, tried to breathe, flailed . . . and went still.

He was dead. Really, really dead. The shakes set in.

I won't panic. I can't.

The others had already disappeared. It didn't matter that we'd been together for six months. Survival and freedom at any cost, right? Only Derry didn't leave. He dropped the board and wrapped his arms around me, not saying a word about how I should've known better, even though it was true. I held him hard, listening to his heart.

Stroking my back in soothing sweeps, he whispered, "We'll hide the body and disappear. Nobody will ever know."

HONORS, THE: A program administered by the Worldwide Honors Selection Committee (WHSC, see topic) under the direction of the nonhuman race collectively known as the Leviathan.

Program announced on September 1, 2042, following humanity's first encounter with the Leviathan at the International Space Station, where the Leviathan rescued ten doomed astronauts (see topic, film, documentaries).

The Honors program a) provides a worldwide database of humans between the ages of sixteen and forty and b) contacts, transports, and trains those selected as Honors each year. Selection of one hundred Honors per year is done by a representative Elder Leviathan. It is unknown what process they use to select these individuals, but statistically, a higher proportion of scientists and musicians have been chosen than would seem probable (see the Lao Formula for detailed calculations). Recently, the Lao Formula has been amended with a new weighting variable to account for an increasing number of outlier selections from nontraditional areas and specialties, including two selections last year of military specialists.

Of the Honors chosen to travel with the Leviathan each year, most— an average of 92 percent—retire from the program after carrying word to their replacement Honors of their selection. The remaining average 8 percent is chosen to, and agrees to, take the Journey (see topic), a lifetime commitment to travel as part of a Leviathan crew.

Although no one knows what occurs on the Journey, some experts speculate that the Leviathan are learning as much from humanity as humanity is from them, and that this may pose a potential security issue for the future. [citation needed] [unattributed] [marked for deletion]

CHAPTER TWO

Breaking In

POPPING MY SHOULDER back into place wasn't pretty. I managed not to yelp as Derry twisted and pressed. Once the bone slipped back into the socket, the pain gave me a hard, electric jolt and then subsided. I breathed through it. Like always.

"Good," Derry said, but I could tell his attention was on the dead man impaled on the pipes a few meters away. "Help me get him off there?"

"Tarp first."

I was the practical one, the planner, and Derry went to salvage some scrap of plastic big enough to wrap the body. I walked over to stare at the corpse. Didn't bother me, though it was gruesome.

He provoked us, I reassured myself. *Who sends a kill order over a stolen purse?*

That made no kind of sense . . . except to a narcissistic sociopath like Torian Deluca. The box might have held his daughter's personal chem stash or maybe it went deeper, but this was also about his stung ego. By exterminating me, he'd wipe off the stain to his pride and send a message to anyone who might be thinking of messing with his property.

This wouldn't end like he wanted. I wouldn't go out that way.

That was what I tried to tell myself. But despite Derry's apparent coolness, he was still shaky, coming off whatever he'd scored while I was out hunting up our lunch money. I wondered how much he'd spent on his high. And where he'd gotten the coin.

While Derry was gone, I rifled the corpse's pockets and came up with an H2, late-model thing, encrypted. It didn't have a simple fingerprint unlock; I tried pressing the dead thumb to it, to no effect. Deluca bought next-level stuff. *We can take it to Conde*, I thought, but then realized that wouldn't be smart; Deluca would have real-time tracking on his men, and finding this device would be child's play. Conde would kill me if I left him exposed like that, and he'd never touch this if he knew how bloody it was. He was probably pissed enough that I'd sold him stuff stolen off a Deluca.

I'd seen him crack enough cases to know the basics, so I grabbed a thin piece of metal—had been a fork once, maybe—and pried the thing open. The chip sat nestled in the center of all those tiny connections, gleaming lush gold. I yanked it out, put it on the cracked pavement, and used a brick to bash it to pieces.

Then I pocketed the device. What Conde didn't know wouldn't hurt him, and it'd be a waste to destroy such a pretty piece of work. I could sell it later, probably.

The dead man had a fat pouch of old currency coins instead of an e-money card, which I guess wasn't a surprise; he was a crim, after all. Funny. I was making more off his death than I got off Deluca's daughter. *You killed somebody. You should feel bad about it.*

But I didn't. He'd been a dick, and now he was dead, and that was that.

Derry came back with a tattered but sturdy length of plastic from the dump nearby, and together we lifted the body off the pipes with a nasty squelch. It leaked, but the tarp took care of the mess. I tied it closed around his neck, waist, and feet with scrounged bits of wire and cord.

Swiping the sweat from my face left a smear; I felt the stickiness of blood, breathed in the copper. I'd forgotten about the gash on my arm. *If enforcement scans the scene, they'll find it's lousy with my DNA.* Not that enforcement spent a minute more than they had to out here in the Lower Eight anyway.

"Z," Derry said then, as I secured the last bit, and I looked up at him. His face was set and pale, and there was a bad tremor in his hands. "They'll kill us for this."

"Deluca won't call in the cops," I said.

"Doesn't matter. He sent this snake for you, and he'll keep coming."

"Then we run."

"Where? Where does Deluca not get us?" Derry's eyes shone bright amber with fear. He'd comforted me at the start, but reaction must be setting in, and he was starting to think about his own chances. Plus, he was coming down; he'd been on and off the stuff as long as I'd known him. For some, that was how they coped with life in the Zone. I never asked why, because in the Zone, the past was a minefield, and some borders shouldn't be crossed.

I hesitated, considering the chem in my pocket, rich-girl goodies, probably potent as hell. *I should give it to him.* But I'd been trying to keep Derry off the stuff. *But it might keep him focused. You need him steady.*

It surprised me a little to be so calm as I analyzed our odds of escape. *Damn. Derry's right.* Torian Deluca had a worldwide reach. He was absurdly rich, ruthless, and dedicated. You didn't get to stand where he did without being willing to commit to the body count.

"I didn't *kill* his kid, I just stole her purse! He might let it go."

"Now?" Derry tilted his head at the body. "You think? That guy sure acted like this was bigger than a snatch and grab."

He was right. Getting rid of the suit had been necessary, one way or another, but his death opened up a whole new barrel of shit. "We sell his device and use the cash to get out," I said. "Way out. We're not on the net anyway. He'll have a shit time tracking us once we're off our usual turf."

Derry didn't look convinced. I wasn't either, but it was our best hope.

At last he nodded. "We'll bury him in the dump. Let's go."

Quickly, I found a tattered, filthy rug that someone had set out for garbage collection. While the Zone might not be as surveillance-hot as Paradise, we'd still draw unwanted eyes hauling a bloody, person-shaped plastic package. I rolled the body up in it and then doused the area with the grog I'd bought earlier. If I was lucky, the cheap booze would degrade the evidence.

Since when have you ever been lucky, Z?

"Ready?" I asked.

In answer, he shouldered half the burden. The suit had been a big guy, and dead, he seemed to weigh twice as much. Derry was shaking, pasty, unsteady, but he managed.

Wasn't pleasant, but we did it, sweating, mouths and noses covered against the stench as we carved out a deep trench in the mountains of trash—we called it Mount Olympus—and dumped the rolled body into it. I'd have scavenged the nice suit, but the pipes had ruined it, along with the blood. I shoved trash over his makeshift grave. In less than half an hour, he'd vanished without a trace.

Time for us to do the same.

Our friends hadn't come back, but attachments were flexible around here. They could smell danger a mile off, and I didn't blame them for scrambling. This place would be blown for a while as Deluca sent thugs to search for his man. They might find him in the dump. They might not. But they'd rip apart anybody they found in the area to ask questions.

Better if our crew found new friends. Other holes to hide in.

We were three blocks from Conde's when I saw the black tail of smoke rising, and a cold feeling crawled up my spine. *It can't be Conde. Everybody deals with Conde. He's got protection.*

Some sinister whisper in the back of my mind said, *From Deluca? Nobody does.*

Derry didn't say anything, but we exchanged a look and broke into a run. The streets were strangely bare now; the rats of the Lower Eight knew when to go underground, and they must have sensed real trouble.

Real trouble they had. The entire block of Conde's shop was deserted, not a single face in a window. The acrid smell of smoke hung everywhere, and something worse.

Burned flesh.

Derry and I turned the corner and stopped. We just stared at the smoldering hole where Conde's building had been. Deluca had tracked the purse. He'd probably raided the place, searched it, and not found what he was looking for.

Then he'd sent a drone to make a public statement.

With a shuddering breath, I grabbed Derry and dragged him into the shadows under an overhang. Everybody was off the streets because they'd seen what happened. Somewhere up there, in the low-hanging clouds, the drone might be circling, looking for another target.

Looking for *us.*

I dug the dead man's device out of my pocket and threw it hard. My aching shoulder twinged, but the thing flipped end over end, catching the brief glitter of sunlight, and plunged into the inferno that had been Conde's shop.

Before today, I'd never seen Derry shaken; hungover, high, coming down, strung out, all that, but *scared?* No. He'd always been cocky and assured, a smooth criminal, confident he could go anywhere and do anything. But looking at this, he knew better. So did I. The problem was, he'd stay. We'd met in my first forced rehab, separated when I got released ahead of him, but when they let him go, he found my house and persuaded me away. Then they sent me to reconditioning, and he came for me again. And again, until finally the last time I'd left, my family had too. For Mars.

The past few years, Derry—flying or falling, chemmed or sober—had been my one constant. He wouldn't leave me now. Not unless I made him.

I had to make him.

"Derry," I said. His eyes were dark and bleak, and I took his hands in mine to get his full attention. "*D.* Time to split up."

"No." He said it quietly, but he meant it.

"Listen. You *can't* stay with me. Not this time. Maybe this will cool off, but it won't do it soon." I squeezed his hands hard, contrasting the chilly pallor of his to the warm brown of mine.

He pulled me close, wrapping his arms around me. We both reeked, but I didn't care. There was only his trembling body, the fast rhythm of his breathing. He was on the verge of breaking.

"He's not after you," I said.

"I helped you kill his goon, Z!"

"He doesn't know that. All he knows is he sent a guy

for *me*, and the guy died. Derry. It's on me. I'll handle it."

He shook his head. His hair brushed my face, soft as feathers, and I pulled in a deep breath. I had concrete in my soul, but he had a way of breaking it. "You can't just leave me on my own, Z. It's *Deluca*. I need something to cool me out. Get me something?" There was a pleading note in his voice. A bite of desperation under it.

"I can't," I said, which was a lie; I had a sweet little bag of chem burning a hole in my pocket. "They'll have people on the streets, and it's my face they're scanning for."

He pushed me away and paced. I knew the harsh, fast way he moved, the jerky steps, the tic in his cheek. Sometimes, the chem's burndown left him angry. Now, he was pissed and scared. Bad combination. "I need something. Right now. You did this. *You* did." It was rare his anger turned on me, but it had happened before. I'd learned to back off when I saw the flash of it.

"I'm going back," I said. "To Parkview. They'll send me to lockup this time. And lockup is way safer."

I was right, and he knew it. Derry was a street kid; he'd grown up fighting. But this death, it was an important one, life-changing. And he must've parsed that before me, back in the alley. Layering that on top of his natural coming-down paranoia . . . It was bad.

Bad enough that I worried he'd make a mistake. Do something we'd both regret.

"I'll get you out of there," he said. "Don't I always, Z?" He hadn't let me go yet, but he would. He had to.

"Not this time," I told him softly. "Don't look for me. Just look after yourself."

"I will," he said. When I turned to go, he moved. He grabbed my arm and spun me hard toward him, and kissed me. That melted me, but then he whispered, "You have to find something to get me through. I can't—without . . . Get it for me. Please."

For months, I'd tried to keep him off the chems; it had worked, sometimes. But never when he was like this.

I silently reached into my pocket and pulled out the chem I'd taken from Deluca's daughter and pressed it into his hand. "Careful," I whispered. "I don't know how strong it is. Hell, I don't know *what* it is. Just a taste, okay? Only when you need it."

He took in a gasping breath and pressed his forehead to mine, then kissed me again. Sweet, this time, but it still left a bitter taste in my mouth.

I might never see him again. It hurt like pulling bones out of sockets. Hearts out of chests. But neither one of us were the type to say that or let it show. He lifted his head at a whisper-whir in the clouds; the drone would be one of the quiet models, stealthy. A murder drone. And it was scanning for us. No. For *me*.

He didn't let me go. I opened my hands and stepped back. Leaning in, I kissed him fiercely, and ran.

Heart burning like Conde's building, I kept to the rat's maze—covered walkways, tunnels, camouflaged nets that flapped overhead. The Zone residents were always wary of drones, though mostly they were trying to protect themselves from enforcement models, not murderbots. I had military-grade heat on me, so I moved fast.

Parkview Rehabilitation Home was technically in the Paradise part of New Detroit, but barely. It was on the outskirts, within sight of the thick fences of the Zone. You could tell the difference at a glance, a sharp divide between the haves and have-nots. Money and suffocating conformity versus cheap, dirty freedom. The world was largely sparkling these days, orderly and gentrified, but most cities had an underbelly, full of those who wouldn't—or couldn't—follow the rules.

Even Parkview, scruffy by Paradise standards, had a cleanly manicured look, with soft grass and trimmed bushes and new paint on the old bones of the house. Sunny yellow and deep black accents on the window and door frames. It looked like luxury to someone like me who dossed in damp ruins and ate sticky, day-old ration rice from street cookers.

Luxury was a trap.

I checked the sky. No sign of the drone; it was probably circling the area near Conde's shop, and I'd left that a mile back. I was probably okay. I hoped Derry was. *He is*, I told myself. *Derry's a survivor. He knows how to dodge.*

Somebody had repaired the braided-wire fence where I'd cut my way out last time, and judging by the warning sign, the voltage was working again. Closer to the heart of Paradise, there was tighter security and human sentries. Here on the ragged border, we had drones, robo-patrols, and lightning gates.

At first I just hid beneath a sprawling old tree and counted, timing the sweep of the robo-patrol from inside the perimeter. *Four minutes, okay.* I could work with that.

When the first raindrop hit me, I swore. The deluge splashed the leaves overhead and trickled down to hit cold on my head. I pulled my gray hood up to conceal my face, tucked in my dark curls, and hoped the drone didn't have DNA sniffing; some did, especially the newer military models.

When the next four-minute interval started, I left the tree and slid into the beating curtain of rain. The air smelled sharp with it, spiced with the earthy tang of mud, and I moved faster as the downpour started to soak through my hood. Parkview's lights had switched on, and the house glowed warm gold in the gloom.

But I was still on the wrong side of the lightning gate.

Keeping low, I circled the property until I found the drainage ditch. Dirty water poured from the narrow pipe. It wasn't big enough for me to crawl through, but the earth was soft and sunken. I buried all ten fingers in the soil, hauling it away in muddy scoops. Between the dark and the driving rain, it felt like I was digging my own grave. If I didn't get inside—to the relative safety of the system—I might have to do just that.

Every four minutes, I flattened and froze. The robo-patrol wasn't programmed for nuances, and I needed to be sent to the right facility when I was caught. I trusted Mrs. Witham enough to arrange that.

No telling how long I burrowed, but eventually I had enough room to crawl under. Probably. If I'd miscalculated, I'd fry. *Best to count it down.*

As soon as the bot passed, I squirmed forward, pulling myself with palms and elbows. There was a spark as I drew my feet out, and I dropped, avoiding the patrol for the last time. When the light passed, I got up and sprinted for the house.

I vaulted the steps onto the porch. It was mostly dry, though there was a leak near the corner that drizzled a silvery stream; it snaked across the concrete and under the welcome mat at the door. It was all sickeningly familiar. I hadn't spent a lot of time at Parkview, but the smell of the place, the feel of it, was like every other rehab stop.

No, not quite the same. I caught another scent as I raised my hand toward the bell. Vanilla, butter, something light and warm and sweet.

They were making cookies.

The smell sparked memories in an uncontrollable rush.

I saw my mother's face. I hadn't wanted to think about what this was going to do to her, but there it was. In her last message, she'd looked so tired, and though she'd never admit it, I was the one who'd put those years on her face. She'd fought so hard for me—at university hospitals and research clinics, in and out of rehab. They fined her every time I ran away, and she still hadn't let go. I was the oldest. I should have been helping her, not constantly adding to her burden.

I closed my eyes for a second, and there it was, the memory of me shattering my family forever. Mom had held my hand, anxious, staring at a document that already had my father's signature on it. Shaking her head. "I don't want to do this. Kiz and I, we're making a fresh start on Mars. There's a place for you, baby. Come with us. Away from here. Away from *him*!"

She meant my father, or Derry, or both, and it did sound tempting. New Detroit offered a lottery to all citizens, and the ones picked to join the Mars colony were guaranteed food, housing, job training if they needed it. They'd won the shot. But if I felt confined on Earth, imagine how it would be, living forever inside a snow globe. No amount of security would let me breathe right in that life.

I didn't tell her about my fears. I just said, "Sign the form."

She'd wept as she wrote her name, dressed in her Sunday

best and a fine hat with silk flowers and delicate lace. She'd given me the freedom I wanted, and walked away, because I hadn't given her any choice. I'd watched until I couldn't even see her shadow anymore. Most of my good memories had gone with her. Before the pain, before my family fractured under me, there was Mom and singing and *butter cookies* and—

Shivering, I shoved away that old weight. I already felt trapped, and I hadn't even stepped inside. I rang the bell and yanked back my hood as the locks clicked and alarms beeped. Then Mrs. Witham opened the door and looked me over with a cool gaze shaded by cat's-eye reading glasses. She didn't need them, really. She just liked how they looked. Like the apron she wore over her clothes, and the way she put her graying hair up in a bun. She thought those touches made her seem grandmotherly.

"Zara," she said without a smile. "It's an ocean out there. Come in."

No *where have you been* or threats or punishments. Not yet. I stepped in, and it felt like a cage door slamming. I felt short of breath and shaking, and it wasn't just from the cold and wet that had soaked into my hoodie. Mrs. Witham shut the door and turned toward me. With the dim light, it was hard to read her expression, but I didn't imagine it would be friendly.

At least she's not working for Deluca. That was why I'd

chosen to be processed by someone who played by the rules. Mrs. Witham might push my buttons with her adherence to rehab policies, but hopefully, that meant she wouldn't sell me out, either. At the police station there would be more tech, more chances for Deluca to spot me and have me hauled off to his private compound under the aegis of a bogus transfer order.

I could hear other kids—younger kids, kids who deserved a break—talking and laughing as they made cookies. Parkview had a nice kitchen. Warm. Dry. The food wasn't bad, even if it was cheap and processed. Not like I hadn't eaten worse. Or not at all.

I said, "Look, you need to send me to Camp Kuna."

That surprised her, and she stepped forward into the glow of the cheap hall light. It revealed widened eyes behind the cat's-eye glasses, but nothing else changed in her expression. Not even a frown marred her smooth, dark skin.

"We can talk about this, Zara."

"I'm trying to keep you safe. Somebody's after me. Somebody bad. They'll find me soon and—" *And I can't have this place ending up like Conde's. I can't carry that too.* "Safer if you get me to rehab. For me and the other kids too."

The reminder that her other charges were in danger got Mrs. Witham focused. She studied my face for a few seconds, then reached in the pocket of her shirt and pulled out her H2. Punched the emergency alert and put it on the table.

She didn't even hesitate, and I wasn't sure if I felt good about that or not. Didn't really matter. It was what I'd needed her to do.

"Better smash something," she said. "They'll need evidence of violence to take you."

I looked around. She had plenty of nice things here, probably old. I picked up a big vase and looked at her. She said nothing, but I saw a muscle twitch on the side of her face. I put it back and picked up something else, a fragile china plate with flowers etched on it, and saw the minuscule nod.

Then I smashed it into bits against the table it had been sitting on. Sharp fragments skittered all over the floor.

"That enough?" I asked.

She nodded and sat down. From the other rooms, voices had gone to quiet whispers, and I saw a face looking around the corner. Couldn't remember her name. She'd only been there a couple of days when I left, and I never really cared about their names anyway.

"You okay?" the girl asked Mrs. Witham.

"Keep everybody calm," the woman replied. "Everything's fine. Zara will be leaving soon."

"Thought she already skipped." The girl had a Lower Eight accent, I realized. Maybe she was a charity case. Or maybe her family had clawed their way up to Paradise before being thrown back on the dumping ground, and she'd hung around.

"Never mind, just do what I told you."

The girl disappeared, and the door into the other rooms shut, locking us in together.

We waited in silence two minutes or so, until sirens flared and enforcement bots scanned the situation. Then human agents from Camp Kuna arrived to take me into custody.

"Zara," Mrs. Witham murmured as they fastened my restraints. "Take care of yourself."

It was the nicest thing anybody who wasn't Derry had said to me in a while.

BREAKING NEWS REPORT:

Dateline New Detroit

August 21, 2142

Honors Countdown week continues on our twenty-four-hour coverage, with hour-long special features on each of 2141's Honors as we welcome them back home for their triumphant return. Each of these heroes will complete their assigned duties with the Selection Committee upon landing, which we're told include rigorous debriefing, medical and mental health checkups, and of course, their assignments to welcome this year's new Honors. We can't wait for the dramatic reveals!

Today we've already noted the scheduled arrivals of twelve of last year's Honors, including fan-fave Marko Dunajski and his flight partner, Zhang Chao-Xing. They'll be restricted from interviews until after the new Honors are delivered back to the New York training facility, but we're burning to ask: Are they going on the Journey?

Stay tuned to our nonstop coverage to discover the answers, and don't forget to take our neural test. . . . Are you suited to be an Honor?

CHAPTER THREE

Breaking Free

PROCESSING WAS DONE in a ten-by-ten room with white-block walls and aluminum benches. Two prisoners sprawled there already, one on a bench and the other on the floor. I perched on the edge of one of the benches, ready to move as soon as I was called. This was Camp Kuna, designed for *problems,* for people in need of socialization and reconditioning. People who'd failed the system. I'd never been here, but I knew the type well.

It was safe. Safe, clean, secure, and boring. Exactly what I needed right now.

I watched my cellies closely for any sign that Deluca had

infiltrated the place ahead of me, but they were dead to the world, and eventually tedium took over. My spine sagged. I relaxed and finally paid attention to the screen on the wall outside the bars. Honors Countdown frenzy was still in full swing, and now they were showing an agonizingly in-depth retrospective of each of the hundred people chosen last year. They were only in hour twelve.

Worst part of the year, Honors season. In Paradise, nobody watched, talked, or dreamed about anything else. At least back on the other side of the fence I could have avoided most of it. Here? The only escape came through sleep.

This particular hour was about one of the seventeen Honors picked out of China last year—Zhang Chao-Xing, a severe-looking woman who had a degree in something complicated. The show took us to her home, which had all the comforts, including a proud, smiling family. Just like me, minus the proud part.

Just like me, except I was sitting my ass on a cold aluminum bench, waiting to be given a boring uniform and boring job and boring classes. Again. Though the thought didn't escape me that maybe I did deserve it. *You stole the purse. You killed a guy.*

I didn't even feel that guilty, really. It wasn't like I took anything from people who had less than me.

In hour fourteen of the retrospective, someone finally

came, but she wasn't there for me. The woman in uniform nudged the pasty guy on the floor in the ribs to wake him up.

"Let's go. Your room is ready."

The boy got to his feet without protest. He probably weighed fifty kilos max. His dead gaze met mine, and I shivered, wishing that look came from some kind of chemical numb. But I'd seen the expression before, hopelessness creeping in like mice behind the walls. He'd get treatment here from painfully sincere staffers; maybe he'd even get well. That was the goal, anyway.

The guard had woken up my other cellmate too, and she sat up on the other bench, yawned, and shoved the lank hair away from her face. I had no taste for conversation, but my fellow inmate looked chatty and it'd be dumb as shit to shut my eyes until I knew something about her. While there was a camera above us in the corner, nobody could come fast enough to save me if she turned out to be dangerous, not just antisocial.

"What're you in for?" she asked, in the middle of a yawn.

I met her challenging stare with a half smile. "Jacked a mobster's daughter and killed one of his guys."

Laughter nearly doubled her over—loud, contagious bursts that made me almost join in. Almost. When she could breathe well enough to speak, she wheezed, "Sure, and I robbed the old coin exchange!"

"Where'd you hide the loot?"

"Look, don't tell me and I won't tell you. Fair deal." She hesitated, then leaned over and extended an open hand. "Clarice."

I shook it. "Zara."

Evidently she took that as proof that I wouldn't tear her throat out with my teeth, because she went back to sleep. I didn't. Well, not until we'd covered another hour of an Honor who came from the Seychelles and liked to water-ski. I finally dropped off in sheer boredom.

"Zara Cole?" I woke up with a start and found that I'd somehow missed the door opening. Across from me stood a new guard, thick with muscle. She didn't look like she'd take any crap, either. Her gray uniform was crisp, hinting that she'd just come on duty.

"Yes, ma'am." I'd learned to feign respect. People who wore uniforms seemed to like that.

"You have quite a file."

"Aww, thanks!"

"And a sense of humor, I see. You'll find we have zero tolerance for bullshit here. Understand?"

"Sure."

"Then follow me."

I looked back as she led the way and realized that somehow I'd managed to sleep through Clarice being taken out.

The vid was in hour twenty of the Honors marathon.

I really needed to work on my alertness. This place—this kind of place, anyway, with its signature peaceful scent being sprayed into the air, with the just barely audible calm music—lulled me into a sense of security I couldn't afford.

She took me to a windowless room and shut the door. "You know the drill, Miss Cole. Strip, shower, and scan, please."

Maybe it was the politeness that grated on me. Here we were, walls and bars, and she was still saying *please*. What a joke. But she was right: I knew the drill. Once she'd shut the door, I stripped off my kit and folded it up, then stood under the lukewarm shower. It was both bath and decontamination, and had a sharp, lemony scent to it that left a bitter, medicinal aftertaste. My curls started off cute, but I couldn't look after them in the Zone, so they were fried from lack of conditioning, and this all-purpose cleaner wouldn't do my hair any favors. Good behavior would get me toiletry upgrades; that was how they trained people to play nice in places like this.

I came away clean, dried off, and stood with arms and legs spread for the scan. The mechanical voice that told me when it was over was polite.

I'll get tired of that quick.

When the all-clear sounded, I went to the shelves and took out a thin undershirt, simple panties, baggy yellow pants with an elastic waist, a loose white shirt without buttons or ties, and flip-flops. There was also a thicker shirt that could be layered over the lighter one and a warm sweater in an ugly hot color too. Forget drones; I'd be visible from space.

The guard opened the door and gave me a quick nod. "Thanks for your compliance."

"Thanks for not cavity searching," I said brightly.

She didn't quite know how to take that, because she said, very seriously, "Your scan was clean. I didn't need to."

We walked down a hall with doors spaced equidistant. They were all closed. My room was more of a cell once the door shut behind me: single bed, sink, toilet, small screen built into the wall. They'd given me slippers, though. I hadn't worn slippers since I was six. They were the same color orange as the sweater. At least I'd match.

"You have an hour before breakfast," the guard said. "Welcome to Camp Kuna. You'll be provided with your activity schedule after chow. You'll be expected to complete all required socialization classes, exercise, therapy sessions, and work details. This isn't punishment, this is—"

"Preparation, yeah, I read the brochures," I said. "Got it."

She gave me a long, level look, and I could tell she really *had* read my file. "Zara. We don't give up on people. You understand that, right?"

"Maybe you should," I said, and sat down. The mattress

was respectable, if not luxurious. I'd slept on piles of rags, by choice, but I had to admit mattresses were a comfort I wouldn't turn down. Suddenly, despite the napping in the holding cell, I felt exhausted. "You said I have an hour?"

She nodded. "Rest. I'll come get you."

After she locked the door, I tried to detangle my short curls with my fingers. Helped some, but I needed products and a trim, stat. Giving up temporarily, I rolled onto my side and fell asleep in record time. I dreamed of flying. It was probably because of those damn Honor vids, but it felt . . . good. Free.

When the guard roused me for breakfast, I came back to Earth hard, and it felt like the weight of gravity might suffocate me.

My routine commenced exactly as the guard had described it: food, class, exercise, therapy, work. It lasted from sunrise to sunset, but the evenings were free, and we weren't locked up in our rooms. Camp Kuna had a big common room filled with games and screens, though the games were all multiplayer; no zoning out on your own. If you wanted that, you had to read.

I chose books, but that didn't mean I got left alone. I was paging through a space fantasy that had started life as Honors fanfic before the author changed the names when someone plumped down in the chair beside me, put up her feet, and said, "I see you're fitting in."

It was the girl from holding. She seemed cheerful, though she couldn't have looked worse in these neon colors. Her light-brown hair was a wispy mess, and she brushed the flyaway strands back with a move that had to be automatic. "Clarice, remember?"

"I remember," I said. "And I'm still reading."

"You've got an A on your ID tag."

"So?"

"Third-strike antisocial is what it means. They're watching, you know. Seeing if you can make friends. So make one."

Clarice had an A at the start of the string of numbers that IDed her, too. We gave each other smiles that meant nothing, and she asked me about my book. We talked about how sick we were of seeing the Honors countdown, which was now winding down to the big week of announcements.

"It's bullshit," Clarice said. "I think it's all rigged anyway. Who gets picked? Rich folks, that's who. You ever see somebody from the Lower Eight in there?"

"Never. So you're probably right."

"Besides, who'd want to go live on some ship and give all *this* up?" she deadpanned. "Three hots a day, fancy clothes . . ."

"Education," I put in.

"And learning a trade? We don't call this side of Detroit

55

Paradise for nothing. So . . . you want to play a game?"

"Want to read my book," I said, though truthfully, I was skimming it because the Leviathan were pretty fascinating. "Are we done making friends now?"

Friendship by appointment, for mutual benefit; the docs watched for loners and signed them up for special programs. Socialization. Neither of us needed that noise. Might have been screwed up, being fake friends, but at least it kept us in the middle of the road, rehab-wise.

"Guess so," she said. "Same time tomorrow?"

"It's a date."

I was really unlucky because my assigned mandatory therapist hadn't burned out yet. I was used to overworked drones, but instead, when I stepped into the warm, friendly office he kept on the nicer side of Camp Kuna, I knew I was in for it. My therapist—Dr. Yu—was a youngish man who dressed casual without making it look like he was trying too hard, and he didn't look up as I walked in. He was too busy scanning records.

"Yeah, no hurry, I'll wait." I kicked back with a thump on the soft cushions of his sofa. It smelled of something floral, probably aromatherapy. Not relaxers, I was interested to notice. Most therapists I'd seen sprayed that stuff like it was oxygen. "Word of advice, it took the last guy a couple of months to get through all that. Want me to come back?"

Silence. I shifted on the couch. I wished I had a headband for my curls, but they'd turned me down, figuring I might try to choke somebody with it. They'd trimmed the knots at least, and my spirals looked better since I'd sweet-talked the provisions officer into slipping me some products on credit. I had plenty of time in here, enough to develop a good wash-and-go style.

"I've got the gist," Yu said, and put the H2 down. He sat back in his chair and gave me the standard assessing look. His was a little sharper than I was used to. "Good morning, Zara. I'm not going to insult you by asking if you know why you're here."

"Nice," I said. "Ten points. I'm here to tell you my trauma so I can become a useful member of society. Bring up the music, credits roll, we both feel good about ourselves."

"You use sarcasm as a shield," he said. "That's fine. We all need armor. The world wounds people. My job is to help them get better."

"I'm fine," I muttered.

"You choose to *voluntarily* live in dangerous conditions in the Lower Eight, where there's no reliable enforcement, next to no medical care, and among criminals. Why do you think that is?"

"Because at least they're not lying assholes who glide along in life never *doing* anything! They're real. The world's real out there, doc. You should try it."

"I have," he said. "I helped build Benny's. I was on staff there for four years. I just rotated out six months ago."

I went still. I think I actually sat up, in fact. Benny's—St. Benedict's Medical Facility—was the shining light of the Lower Eight. It had been built by hand, by charity workers, from the ruins of an old hospital; it charged nobody, ever, and it ran on donations from Paradise. I'd gotten fixed up at Benny's more than once. So had Derry.

If he'd worked at Benny's, he'd been out in the real world. *Well, shit.* That made it harder to ignore him.

"So," I said. "Go on, then. Psych me."

Yu laughed and sat back. Crossed his legs. I closed my eyes. The sofa was damn comfy; I could wait him out.

He let me get good and cozy before he said, "Your mother sent a message from Mars on your behalf. Do you want me to tell you what it said?"

Mom. I kept my eyes closed and said nothing. I tried to feel nothing, but there it was, that eager little bump. "Nope," I said. "No point. I know what she told you."

"I don't think you do. She explained about your headaches. How difficult they were for you to handle at such a young age. How the pain caused you to act out, and how nothing seemed to help. True?"

I'd started getting the headaches around age five, though my memory was fuzzy on details. I just remembered the pain, the screaming, lashing out because nobody, nothing could *help.* Including all of the Paradise docs, for all their skill. I'd spent the better part of a year feeling like I was dying. Not something you handle well as a little kid.

"Yeah," I finally said. "That's true. But they fixed me."

Thanks to the Leviathan, their tech, and eventually, a little dose of their DNA. Being a lab rat was not my favorite thing to remember, either.

"Eventually," he said. "But your anger issues remained. They worsened. Why was that, Zara?"

"Don't know. Don't really care. C'mon, Saint Yu, do you really think what happened when I was *six* is going to fix all my shit?"

"Your mother clearly loves you," he said. "And she's very worried about you. So let's talk about your father."

Let's not.

"My mom and dad separated a long time ago," I said. "Neither one of them has anything to do with me, anyway. I got emancipated, remember?"

"Yes. Your mother regrets that choice, but—and I'm sure you know this—she had to make a change for your sister's sake. Your father was a terrible influence, and they were afraid of him. Just as you were."

"I'm *not* afraid of him!"

"Even when he dragged you off to that faith healer?"

Time slowed down, and for a second I couldn't comprehend what he'd just said, because I'd never told *anyone* about that. It wasn't in my records, how could he know . . .

He spoke to Mom, of course. She told him.

I covered, badly, with a fierce smile. "Faith healers are fakes."

"Then why did he take you?"

I shrugged. "He was sure enough prayer would stop the headaches. Didn't want me seeing the docs. Only God, all that. Mom's the one who insisted on going to the hospitals." And it had cost her, standing up to my old man. I remembered that too.

"Tell me about the faith healer."

"What about it?" My throat had gone very dry, and my hands were cold. I wished I had a blanket. The room had seemed warm before, comforting, but now it felt icy. I was surprised my breath didn't puff white. "Like I said. Fake."

"All right. Just tell me what it was like. I'm interested."

"He took me to a church," I said. "Some little weird place. I think it's gone now. This fake healer pretended she was pulling evil spirits from my head, he paid her, the end. I had a screaming headache the next morning. I guess it cured him of that obsession."

Dr. Yu studied me, but he didn't say anything, and I wished he would. The world felt soft around me. I didn't want to think about this. Didn't want to remember it, but I couldn't *stop* now.

The woman went by the name of Angela, which was

probably made up; she had brassy hair and big blue eyes and her skin was so pale you could see veins underneath. Creepy. She wore white, all white. And her voice . . .

"She said the headaches came from all the sins bottled up inside me," I said. "She said she'd suffered from them too, and prayed and prayed until one day, God told her to take her sins out. So she grabbed a kitchen knife and slashed herself open and sure enough, she reached in and grabbed a big, black bag full of sins and pulled it out. It broke open and black spiders crawled into her, and she had to vomit them back out. Black goo. Then she passed out." I swallowed hard, tasting vomit. "When she woke up, she had a healed scar on her side just where Jesus had been stabbed with the spear, and all her headaches and sins were gone."

"That sounds terrifying," Yu said. "Especially for a six-year-old hearing it."

"She showed us the scar," I said. "And then she said she'd take *my* sins out, but mine were in my head." Yu said nothing to that. He leaned forward a little, eyes intent on me, and for no reason at all, I went on. "My dad helped her tie me down on the altar. He put his belt around my head to hold it still. And they prayed for a long time, and I kept screaming and screaming, and finally, somebody heard, just before she cut my head open. The police showed up, but Angela untied me and acted like they'd just been praying over me, and I made it all up. Nobody believed me." I looked hard at Yu. "She was going to cut into my skull and *take out my sins* and my dad believed her. He'd have let her. He'd have *helped*. I was *six*."

I heard the anguish in my own voice, and I hated it. This was a long damn time ago. I was over it. Past it. I'd survived everything they'd thrown at me. I couldn't feel anything about it, not anymore.

Yu said, very quietly, "Then sending you to the religious camp afterward must have felt like a complete betrayal."

That hit me like a slap. I'd never connected those two things before, the faith healer, the wilderness camp that had finally destroyed my trust; Dad had always been heavily religious, Mom mildly so, and years lay between those two things happening. Years of Mom trying to keep me safe and help me get better.

But he was probably right. That camp had been the last straw. The last time I'd trusted either of them, even though the faith healer hadn't been Mom's fault, she hadn't even known about it. She'd thought the Bible camp would help me.

Not shove me off the cliff.

I looked at Yu directly and said, "You're really good at this."

"I'm only good at it if it helps," he said. "But I think you're starting to understand something about yourself."

Yeah. I understood why I craved freedom so much now. Hated being tied down to rules and regs and conventions. It wasn't about any of those things. It went back to being six, tied hand and foot to an altar, with my father's belt holding my head still, and being *powerless*.

"I don't know how the hell that helps," I said. "Understanding something doesn't change what happened."

"It helps you decide whether or not you want to keep making the same decisions, once you understand why you made them."

Huh.

Yu offered me a bottle of water, which I accepted. It helped wash the dry, vomity taste from my throat. I felt . . . cleaner. "Do you want to talk about the camp?" he asked me.

Turns out, I did.

The next week my schedule shifted around, so immediately after breakfast I went to work detail: the laundry. It was where all the newbies started, and I'd been on this rotation before. I knew all about sorting, treating, loading, unloading, folding. It was soothing, mindless work, and in my spare moments I daydreamed about being out in the world, free and clear.

The routine, the boring familiarity of fresh-smelling clothes and the tang of detergent, made me careless.

I was at the folding table, making sure the edges of a

sheet were crisp and even, when something brushed my curls on both sides. Weird sensation, like a breeze, but I felt no puff of air . . . and then a blur skimmed over my vision.

It took me a second to realize something had just gone over my head, and then it was too late.

The thin cord pulled tight.

I had just enough time to jam my fingers under the garrote, which hurt, but saved me from immediately choking. Only one thing to do: I threw myself backward on my attacker. We hit the floor, and the cord slackened for a second—long enough for me to yank it loose—and as I dropped it, I twisted like a cat. The floor was smooth concrete, nothing I could use to my advantage, kind of a problem since I specialized in environmental fighting and the folding table was solidly bolted to the floor.

The sheets weren't. I kicked my leg up, hitting the metal hard enough to make the folded stack topple, and grabbed a handful of cloth. The first thing I did was shove some in her open mouth to muffle her, and then I pushed the stringy hair back from her forehead to look into her eyes.

"Got to do better than that, Clarice," I said. She'd been trying to fight, but now she stilled, signaling surrender. Or biding her time, whichever. Didn't matter. "I'm taking away the gag. You yell, I punch you in the throat. Nod if you understand."

She nodded. I pulled saliva-slick cloth out of her mouth, and Clarice sucked in a deep breath—but when I raised my clenched fist, she let it out again, quick. One of my fingers registered a sharp stab of pain—broken, I realized, from the force of her garrote. She really had meant to kill me. If she'd gotten me facedown and put her weight into it, I'd have been unconscious in thirty seconds, dead in no more than three minutes. Which she knew. I looked at the cord I'd kicked away; it wasn't just cord. It had solid little handles tied on to it, the better to strangle with. Professional.

Clarice had earned the A on her ID tag.

Shit. I thought it was safe here.

Close up, she reeked of adrenaline sweat, her eyes bloodshot, but she still smiled. "Sorry, Z. Just business."

"Got to step up your game. You know how long people have been trying to kill me?"

"Relax. I give."

"Who sent you?"

She managed to shrug. "It's just cash in my commissary account. Going after you got me a deluxe movie package, gourmet meals, and a bunk upgrade."

Deluca. Of course. I figured he would find me, but I'd been hoping Camp Kuna was beyond his reach. They featured this place on the vids a lot, highest success rate in the nation, so I'd thought maybe that meant extra protection. Money always made way, though, and people like him didn't let things go. For him, this hit hadn't been expensive at all.

Wasn't in my nature to let things go, either. As I looked

at Clarice, I thought about how I could never turn my back on her again, and I had to sleep sometime. Killing her would be as easy as using that garrote she'd brought, or stuffing a sheet down her throat and holding her still until she choked to death. But where did that put me? I was already third-strike antisocial. I'd go to one of the max houses for sure, and I couldn't deal with that. No rehab, just prison, with hard-time crims. Way harder than Clarice, or anyone else in here. Surviving max was for monsters.

"You going to kill me?" Clarice asked as if she could read my mind. I sat back, still watching her. I also saw the red alarm light flashing on the camera, which meant security had been alerted that we were out of view. They'd be coming to check. Any minute.

"Not right now," I said. "I've got to rewash all these sheets."

She blinked. "Why? You can't trust me."

"It'll take Deluca a while to catch on. So enjoy the hell out of those movies, eat all the special meals. Once he figures it out, he'll cash out your account balance and bribe somebody else."

"Might pay somebody to come after me too."

"He might," I agreed. "Chance you take, *friend.*"

She gave me a look I couldn't read, and I stood up and offered her a hand. After a long hesitation, she took it, bent, and picked up the cord.

I grabbed it from her and tucked it away in a pocket.

She grinned. "Can't blame a girl for trying."

Right on cue, a guard walked in the door, trying to look casual. We both turned toward him, and I had a moment's doubt what Clarice would do.

But she winked, picked up an armload of sheets, and said, "Let's get busy."

After making sure Clarice understood that she wouldn't get a second chance, I got a medical bot to see to my broken finger. Didn't even hurt. I was coming out of therapy when the same guard who'd escorted me on arrival—the polite, muscular one—found me and pulled me aside. "Miss Cole," she said. "Come with me."

"Why?"

Wariness crawled over me. Clarice had gone after me in a blind spot, so nobody else had seen, but maybe she'd ratted about the fight. No, that didn't make sense. She wasn't the type, and she had more to lose.

"You'll see," the guard said with an inscrutable look.

There was something odd about all this. About her too. She was still polite, but there was something else going on. She stood farther away, almost . . . reverent in her regard. *Maybe they did see the fight. Maybe this is how they treat badasses at Camp Kuna.*

I spotted Clarice as we strode down the hall; she gave

me a startled look, eyes widening, and I decided she had no idea what was going on, either. So, not about the attack. Something else.

As we approached the common room, the hot buzz of conversation swelled. Lots of voices, all of them excited. *What the hell?*

Everything went quiet as I walked in, and I felt disoriented, like a security hi-beam had hit me in the face. I wasn't used to being stared at.

Belatedly I noticed that the common room was filled with prisoner neon, plus new arrivals in designer suits. I focused on a small woman with the fixed expression of someone who'd had too many cosmetic tweaks. Her platinum blond hair didn't suit her; neither did the bloodred lipstick. While some might find her attractive, she scared the hell out of me. She wore a Camp Kuna ID tag that read *KAMRYN KOSTLITZ, CEO.*

The boss.

When she stepped forward and smiled, the rest of her face didn't move. She extended her hand, and I ignored it. "What is all this?"

Kostlitz somehow turned the fact that I'd refused her greeting into a gesture of presentation to the people standing nearby. "Zara Cole, ladies and gentlemen!" As if I was some star coming onstage.

Then I realized that was exactly what was going down.

The other inmates displayed a full range of emotional response: shock, anger, and delight. Drone cameras hovered all around, catching me from three different angles, and there were delegates in expensively tailored royal blue, with white patches on the breast. I knew that logo. Hell, everyone knew that logo. It was playing on every screen in the world right now: an elliptical shape that mirrored the Leviathan's shape, etched in silver and gold, set on a stylized star, with a tricky H hidden in the design.

The man in the center of the group stepped forward, and some folks skipped a breath.

Marko Dunajski.

I didn't follow the Honors, but hell if you could avoid knowing who he was. Pretty as a movie star. Tall. Dark haired. Fair skinned, with a Slavic point to his chin and broad, strong cheekbones. He looked like every hero fantasy come to life, right in the common room of Camp Kuna, and none of the kids here would ever forget it.

A year ago, he'd been plucked from university (Cambridge. I'd unwillingly watched his bio in hour forty-six of the Honors retrospective) and sent out to space. Now he was back to meet his successor.

"Zara Cole," he said, and walked forward to extend his hand. "I'm Marko Dunajski. Welcome to the Honors."

Interlude: Nadim

I am waiting.

Chastened.

Typhon calls me weak and easily swayed. Not only by the stars but by those we study, searching for the answer to a question the Elders do not allow us to ask. Compliance is required to pass the trials and continue on the Journey.

Many of my cousins have gone ahead. I should have proceeded already, but I . . . I cannot stop the questions. And I cannot deny that even in my failures, I find satisfaction.

Impossible to kill the spark of anticipation, because this waiting means everything begins anew, and the ones who come offer a chance for me to make it right. I have their names, but I cannot yet know their colors or why the Elders chose them until they arrive.

I tell myself that this time will be different.

This time I will succeed. I will complete the test and then, finally, I can follow the song that I am not supposed to hear, a song of pain, and loss, and death. It rings over me in ebbing waves, sad as parting, deep as gravity. These are secrets I am not meant to know, questions I am not supposed to ask. My cousins vanish into the black, and their songs go quiet. The stars sing on.

This time will be different.

Closing voiceover by Garry Moscowitz, director of the banned documentary **Shadows in the Sky***:*

Since the arrival of the Leviathan on that fateful and historic day, we've gained so much perspective. Humanity is not alone in the universe. After generations of exposure to science fiction stories, that might not have come as a shock, but it still had a profound effect ... but what effect? Did we feel less important, less special? In a way, that seems to be true. But there's an argument that this was not a bad thing.

Humanity's hubris had, by that time, led us into a mire that was slowly, steadily drowning us, and for all that we saw the signposts, we kept on walking right into the mud, the rising tide. Arguing over whether the mud was just temporary, whether the tide would continue to rise. Why did we do it? In part, because we thought that humanity was implicitly special. That we had been chosen.

The arrival of the Leviathan, timed to save us from our own last, gasping folly, might have reinforced that belief; in some people, it did. Some religions became more convinced than ever that humanity had a destiny greater than any other species. But for many people, it became the moment that the opposite came clear: that humanity, for all its cleverness, was not unique. And what is not unique can be replaced.

Maybe the loss of that certainty did some good. It refocused our energy away from our greed and toward what we objectively identified, as a species, as good: caring for one another. Caring for our world, as good stewards.

In return, the Leviathan, who some see as angels, and a few as devils . . . the Leviathan gave us a true path to the stars. To touch, as the old poem says, the face of God.

But what did we find there, in the black? The Honors chosen to go return with wonderful stories; yet the ones who Journey never come back, never send us word. We're told there are reasons, that they've gone so far that communication is impractical, and maybe that's true. But maybe, just maybe, these angels, these creatures, these shadows that pass across our skies and into the dark . . . maybe they aren't telling us everything.

And maybe we need to ask that question before we send more of our best, our brightest, out into the black. Ancient Greece sent its children as tributes to the Minotaur.

If there is a monster waiting out there among the stars, we deserve to know.

CHAPTER FOUR

Breaking Big

MY FIRST IMPULSE was to hit Marko Dunajski on his perfect chin.

I didn't, mostly because I'd get punished, and besides, there were a *lot* of cameras staring in my direction. The usual code of silence wouldn't apply here.

But I *wanted* to hit him, because I was afraid, and I hated being afraid. I already knew—however impossible it was—why Marko Dunajski was here. If I couldn't go to Mars with my mom, I sure couldn't commit to living inside of a sentient alien, where I'd be trapped in the weirdest way possible. Claustrophobia didn't begin to describe my issues, because it wasn't just enclosed spaces. The idea of being locked down for a whole year? Hard pass.

I defaulted to the philosophy that had served me my whole life. *When in doubt, attack first.* It made people back off, provided a moment to plan the next move or get a head start on an exit strategy.

I wasn't supposed to be staring into the cameras, but I couldn't help that; I didn't want to look at Marko, because he shouldn't be here, saying my name. Had to look at him, though, because he was talking to me again.

"I'm sorry for the surprise, but that's the way it's done," he was saying. He spoke English, but with an eastern European accent, and it took a second for me to realize he was trying to apologize. To me. I wanted to leave, but I could feel the guards hovering back there, blocking my retreat. "Are you all right?"

"Push off." As comebacks go, it wasn't my best. "I don't want any part of this mess. Leave me alone."

He hadn't expected that, for sure, and the shock on his face almost made me laugh. *What's the matter, pretty boy? No one ever said no to you before?*

I turned around, and sure enough, the gate was shut, with two guards standing between me and the way to my cell. They were staring at me like I'd grown another head. Kamryn Kostlitz, CEO, looked like she might have a stroke. Her sweet PR opportunity was turning into a disaster.

Someone stepped close to me from my right, and I snapped my head in that direction to stare at her. Clarice held up both hands and wiggled her fingers to show she wasn't carrying. "Hey," she said. "Come here."

I didn't want to, but she took my arm and pulled me toward her, and before I could put an elbow in her face, she whispered, "Play nice! You don't spit on a golden ticket. You *cash in*."

"I'm not some damn Honors pick!"

Clarice's mouth set in a hard line. "Say yes. You walk away from this, you think we're not going to kick the fool out of you?" She suddenly grinned, but her eyes stayed mean. "Besides. Makes a good excuse for why I couldn't kill your ass. Might save my life."

I yanked free of her grip, but she had a point. If I was dressed in a shiny Honors uniform, I didn't have to be afraid of drones or slick monsters in suits. Deluca would have to give up; there'd be too much splash if anything happened to me. I wasn't safe in here like I'd hoped. I wouldn't be safe out there in the Zone, either.

But I'd be safe as an Honor.

Plus, there were undeniable perks, including compensation for my family. I didn't give a shit about my dad, but Mom and Kiz . . . Yeah, they deserved this payout; I'd cost Mom plenty with fines, court costs, rehab fees. I almost laughed. I couldn't picture myself standing by some podium with the bands playing, shaking hands with the World Union President. I could barely exist for a few days in the sterile bubble most people called the world; the grit of the Zone was where I belonged.

As I wavered, weighing the pros and cons, Kamryn Kostlitz sidled up to me. "Say yes. Say it now. If you humiliate me, I'll send you to Barraga."

That was the bogeyman of institutions, where they stuck the no-hopers. It wasn't a place you went to be fixed, only caged.

My jaw clenched. I'd been on the verge of accepting, but I didn't like being pushed. "You got no cause."

"Don't I?" She had shark eyes, now that I was looking at her up close. "But I can think of a million reasons, and an . . . interesting offer just came in."

I could easily imagine her selling me out to Deluca. There would be documentation on my transfer to Barraga, but I wouldn't end up there. Having Kostlitz's hand out to Deluca meant that my time was up here at Camp Kuna, no matter what.

Time to make the best of the bad.

Pinning on a smile, I spun and walked back to Marko Dunajski. He seemed slightly amused, which made my knuckles ache with wanting to punch him. I controlled the urge and managed to force something like a smile. "Sorry," I said. "It's a shock."

"I imagine," he said, and leaned a little forward, like we were friends. "I don't think they ever sent for anyone from rehab before."

"Why the hell do they want me?"

Marko's smile looked genuine. He'd probably practiced it for the cameras. "We all have value, Zara. And we all come from different circumstances. They don't choose us for what we've done, but for what we can do." When I didn't answer, because I didn't know what to say to *that* bullshit, he lost some of the shine. "Are you really turning down the offer? Because that would be . . ."

"Unprecedented," said one of the sharply dressed media clones standing nearby. She looked like she'd been turned out in a doll factory. An expensive one. "Nobody's ever declined. Millions of people would kill for a chance!"

Being chosen was like winning the lottery, but I'd never even bought a ticket. On the other hand, since they were offering, I'd be a fool not to sign on. In a year, this would all be over and I'd be back with a permanent celebrity sheen. Harder for Deluca to get me then.

I looked right into her bio-grafted head-cam, that hungry, beady third eye that never blinked, and gave it my best, brightest smile. "I'm not turning it down," I said. "That would be foolish." I turned to Marko and held out my hand. "I'm very pleased to be, uh, Honored."

He had a firm grip, but his hands had the smooth,

pampered feel of a man who'd never picked through garbage or curled up cold in the ruins. He'd had a perfect life in a perfect home with a perfect family, and when he'd gotten picked as an Honor, it had probably just seemed inevitable.

"Congratulations," Marko said, and this time, his grin was real. I could see it in his eyes. "You won't be sorry. You're traveling with Nadim, and I like him very much."

"Who's Nadim?"

His eyebrows rose, just a little. "Our ship. Sorry, *your* ship now. We will move on, Zhang Chao-Xing and I, to a ship traveling farther. We have been accepted for the Journey."

Sure. "The Journey." It was a bigger thrill than being an Honor, or so they said. Sounded like a terrible idea. But I nodded and smiled anyway. *Ship. My ship.* I felt a little sick.

The Camp Kuna inmates were whispering to each other, wide-eyed and lovestruck . . . if not with Marko, then with the whole idea of being plucked from the ashes, like the old Cinderella stories, to go to the stars. Only the Honors and the lucky few chosen for Mars colony ever left Earth. I was giving these people *hope*.

Marko took my hand, raised it high, and we turned to face the head-cams as they broadcast this out to everybody on Earth. I was the feel-good story of the year. My fellow inmates started clapping and hooting and yelling, some through tears of joy. Like I'd earned something.

Accomplished something.

Like I wasn't a person anymore, just some empty space where they saw themselves, someday.

Marko had brought me a uniform. I guessed I shouldn't have been too surprised about that; after all, the Honors Committee found me, arranged for all the media coverage. They'd know my size too.

It fit almost *too* well. The trousers were tailored perfectly in nu-silk, light and warm at once. The dark blue jacket buttoned over a nu-silk white shell, and my name was embossed in gold on the plate just above my left breast. Oh, they'd included new underwear too. Comfortable boots. *Nice.*

Part of me had to wonder if Deluca was behind this, somehow. To the best of my knowledge, the Honors program was inviolable, but that bastard had a long reach. Maybe Kostlitz had pushed me toward this because of him.

Probably not, though? She wanted the free PR for Camp Kuna. Plus, I had to be tougher to get to, now that all the cameras were aimed at me.

Still, I didn't relax. As I came out of the changing room, I got another spontaneous round of applause, this time from the guards and Camp Kuna administration, who'd gathered to shake my hand on the way out. The same people who'd stared at me with a cool, assessing air, who'd marked my files and assigned me to menial work, now looked at me with stars in their eyes.

Kostlitz posed for a holo with me. I shook hands because it was the only way to get through them, and beyond the wall of Camp Kuna uniforms, I glimpsed Marko's blue and white. It felt like a relief when I made it to his side. He shook hands with as many as he could and signed personal H2s on the way out.

The media ate it up.

Since Clarice was on record as my friend, I hugged her. "Stay out of trouble."

"Here? Not a challenge. Shit, you just made me special."

I had to laugh as I turned away. I whispered to Marko, "Is it okay if I say good-bye to Dr. Yu?"

After some juggling, we found my head doctor in the crowd. "Already wishing you well, Zara. Take care of yourself." His sincerity touched me, but I couldn't show it.

That's it. I'm out of here. We walked out into the large, grassy exercise yard and headed for the gates. They cranked open. The guards actually *clapped.*

Once we were outside, Marko turned and held up his hands as the camera drones pressed in closer. "Okay, okay, enough," he said. "Let Zara have a little time, all right? You know how much of a shock it can be. You remember me when I was picked?"

He gave them a slack-jawed expression of surprise, and

some of the media types behind us laughed. The drones hissed away, nearly silent in the open air. I was sure at least one or two were still tagging us from a distance, and the people with head-cams were probably taking long-range vid, but it felt like I had some privacy again.

Marko tapped the door of a long, sleek e-car parked nearby, and it opened for us. "Get in," he told me.

"Where are we going?"

"The terminal," he said. "We have a rail car standing by to New York. You're the last one on the list. The official announcement is tomorrow. I thought the train would be best. You can rest, and it's . . . private, don't worry."

Like he understood how exposed I felt, how turned inside out. Maybe he really did. I sank into the luxury of the e-car; the seats adjusted to my body, and the safety straps clicked in as a rush of warmth came over me. Commercial relaxers—not enough to get me high, enough to take the edge off. The car must have read my blood pressure and heart rate.

Biotech from the stars. Gift from the Leviathan—they'd changed the world, a hundred years ago, way before my time. I lived in the pretty, sterile bubble of the After, but every chance I got, I ran to the old-school struggle of the Lower Eight. Flaw in my code; that was what I always thought. Only Yu now had me thinking it was something different, the way my old man made me instead of faulty

DNA. Not that it *changed* anything, but it did lighten the load a little.

Marko got in the other side and approved the route, and the car set out smoothly on the drive. I paid attention, because being in an e-car this nice was a whole new experience. Self-drivers were common, but this was top-model stuff. *Conde would drool all over himself for the parts*, I thought, but then I remembered that Conde was a brittle tangle of bones in a smoking hole.

"You all right?" Marko asked me again. I nodded slowly. "It is hard to take in, I know. I felt wrong for days, after."

The laugh that got away from me had buzz-saw edges. "Look, *Marko*, we don't have anything in common."

"Don't we?"

"I saw your special. You're not like me."

"No. And I don't know why the Leviathan asked for you. I've read your file. You have brains, but no control. Thief, vandal, troublemaker—"

"Is this how you chat up girls? Because I've heard better." He could've added *killer* to the list. But that wasn't in the file.

I could almost see him considering saying something rude, but he just shook his head. "Sorry," he said. "It's just that you are . . . so unexpected, for an Honor." I was used to being checked out, but Marko wasn't doing that. He appraised me with curious, unemotional eyes.

I was the first Honors pick straight out of rehab. Maybe I'll be the first to disappear too. Until we left Earth, I'd be seeing Deluca in every shadow.

"Why do you think they chose me?"

Marko shrugged. "They are Leviathan. A hundred years after the arrival, we still don't understand them entirely. Don't doubt that there is a reason, though."

"If you say so." I wriggled in my seat to get my spine relaxed. My pulse was slow and lazy now, and I felt ever so light in my skin. Good stuff, what these e-cars pushed. I must have needed it.

"You're the youngest Honor ever chosen. The media will make much of that."

"Let 'em," I said. "Don't care."

"You don't care about much, I can see that," he said.

He wasn't wrong.

Marko faced forward as the e-car took a left turn and accelerated into a lane, along with a smoothly flowing river of vehicles. The city rose up around us, vast and resurrected and full of wonders. Beyond the edges I glimpsed the darker, jagged line of the Lower Eight, with the outline of the dump, a harsh feature in the middle. Not so many lights out there. And not many wonders.

"I don't have anybody," I blurted. I didn't mean to say it, but there it was, out in the open, before I could think better. Damn relaxers. "I mean, for the ceremony."

Watching the lead-up coverage, I'd seen last year's ceremony, and Marko standing with the happy, proud circle of his family. All the Honors had family, seemed like. Derry couldn't afford a ticket, Mom and Kiz were on Mars, and I'd rather not see my old man.

"You do, actually. Your mother and sister will be landing tomorrow. They were both so excited when I spoke to them."

The smile cracked my face wide open before I could stop it. "Really?"

It wasn't that I didn't love my mom, even though I'd cut formal ties when I'd had her sign me into adulthood. No, that was exactly why I did it. I didn't want her weighed down with me anymore. If she'd known I felt that way, she would've fought even harder for me. But she'd suffered enough for me, and I wanted her to live in peace while I handled my own business. She had to get Kiz raised right. Away from him. And me.

Marko seemed to take my silence for concern. "Don't worry, the full trip is covered by the Honors program. They won't have to pay exorbitant shuttle fees to go home."

"Good." Hell, maybe I'd made Mom happy and proud, for once.

Then Marko dumped a bucket of ice on my joy. "Your father will be there too."

"*What?*" I curled my hand into a fist.

"He will meet us in New York tomorrow, before the ceremony. I'm sorry there won't be more time for you to spend with him."

I wasn't sorry. I didn't know what I was going to say to that asshole, who'd taken a belt to me because I couldn't stop screaming with the headaches, right up until the Paradise operation that had finally fixed it. Way too late.

"Well," I said, and turned to look out the window at the city gliding past. "There are probably financial perks for having an Honors daughter, right? Makes sense he'd show up."

Marko elaborated, thinking that was an actual question, not rhetorical, but I tuned him out. I made noncommittal noises until we reached the terminal. I slid out of the e-car and saw that more media coverage awaited; I had no interest in giving interviews. Marko clued in to my mood and bypassed the circus with an oh-so-photogenic smile and wave. That didn't mean they gave up, so I resigned myself to having my face splashed all over the holo. If looks could have exploded drones and head-cams, I'd have been charged with a capital offense.

Inside, the terminal shone with chrome and polish, people in suits hurrying to catch their trains, families huddled together around their luggage. An enormous antique clock was all that remained from the historic station the terminal had replaced twenty years back. I stared up at it for a few seconds as my new reality gradually sank in.

"We're this way," Marko said, and pointed to a part of the terminal cordoned off with barriers and police. More press.

And an actual *red carpet*.

"No," I said, and laughed, because that just couldn't be right.

"Ready?" Marko asked.

Obviously not. "Can I use the bathroom first?"

He hesitated. "You won't disappear?"

"I swear. You can let me pee in peace."

"I'll keep watch on the hall. For your protection, the press can be a little aggressive," he said, and there was a little bit of color flushing his cheeks now. He was probably cursing the luck that had landed him with the worst Honors recruit in history.

But he didn't argue. He escorted me to the facilities and waited just beyond the hallway. I suspected he was standing guard more to keep me from bolting than to keep reporters and drone cams at bay. I did go, and washed my hands after, but I needed the quiet pause more than anything. The relaxing chems from the e-car had started to fade, so my nerves jolted hard as questions boiled over in my brain. *What am I doing? Can I really do this? Should I?*

I stared at myself, seeing a thin, brown-skinned girl with dark, scared eyes and a heart-shaped face, crowned with a pile of curls that still needed work. I didn't look polished or prepared. Reading the advertisements scrolling at the bottom of the mirror, I tried to tell myself I was doing the right thing.

But I wanted to run. I'd never wanted to run so much in my whole life.

CHAPTER FIVE

Breaking Orbit

AS SOON AS Marko spotted me coming out of the restroom, he wasted no time dragging me off to board.

The rail car shivered as it powered up, and music blared from terminal speakers outside. We glided out of the private area into the main terminal, and through the darkened windows I saw that people had congregated in huge numbers to watch our departure. Some carried handmade signs, hastily fashioned, with my name on them, and with a shock, I even recognized the old woman who sold my favorite steamed pork buns in the Zone; she was holding a painstakingly lettered placard that read, GO, ZARA!

LOWER EIGHT REPRESENT!

At that moment, it hit me how major this was.

"You ready for this?" Marko asked me, and I nodded. He hit a control, and the window cleared, so they could see us.

I raised my hand to wave, and the crowd went nuts. I could feel the emotion rushing out of them, into me, like sunlight. I stood by the window until the crowd rolled by, until the city disappeared into a tangle of wires overhead and weeds that grew under the elevated tracks. With nothing left to see, I adjusted the tint on the window so it showed me only my bemused reflection.

I flinched when a handheld hit the wood table beside me. "Required. There's a lot to get through. We have four hours on the direct route—try to read and absorb as much of it as you can. Believe me, there will be a lot more once we get to New York."

I shoved it back toward him. "I'm not into homework." He gave me a look I recognized from every disappointed teacher. "Look, I said I'd accept. I didn't say I'd study on it, did I?"

"You'd better try," he told me. "If you fail orientation, you'll be eliminated, and an alternate selected."

"So I go on my way. Big deal."

"No," he said, and it sounded like real regret. "You go back where we found you."

Back to Camp Kuna, where the CEO was ready to check-mark me right into the hands of Torian Deluca . . . or max prison. Either way, my life would be over.

I said nothing. If he'd threatened me, I probably would have smashed the H2 to make a point, but that apologetic tone disarmed me, a little.

Hell, I thought. *It's just some reading.*

I sat down and picked up the H2. Data skimming at light speed through the legal disclaimers and warnings, I scrawled my signature with a fingertip. When the legal stuff was out of the way, a new file opened.

It showed footage of a Leviathan in space, lazily unfurling its dorsal sails to catch the sun, and I guess I was supposed to be impressed, but that was pretty difficult when I'd already been subjected to a numbing array of Honors season vids.

But after that was real intel. Not the glistening, polished docudramas, but uncensored details about First Contact—recordings of the astronauts a hundred years back aboard the International Space Station. Of the alarms going off as one of the sections blew. Of the controlled urgency of their communications back and forth with Earth. Listening to those long-dead people recording their last messages to families, I couldn't help it. Hearing *them* was different from actors saying the same words. It was raw and real and—even now, even with the low-quality vid—I couldn't look away.

And then, the Leviathan. Two of them, appearing out of the shadow of the moon, swimming toward the ISS like space was ocean. Circling it.

The message appeared simultaneously on every computer screen aboard the human station: *WE HELP*.

"I know," Marko said, and I jerked out of my trance. "I try to imagine how those men and women must have felt, in that moment. On the one hand, this . . . entirely alien creature, with unknown motives. And on the other hand . . . a chance to live. It required extraordinary trust, I think, to choose to believe them."

Or just desperation, I thought.

I dove into the reading, which included technical specs about the interior areas of the Leviathan, descriptions of crew quarters and amenities provided, and an overview of what would happen in my week-long training and PR sessions. It was a lot. Way too much, in fact.

"We're nearly there," he said eventually, which came as a surprise.

I'd almost forgotten I wasn't alone, but when I looked up, Marko had cleared the window, and beyond it . . . beyond it lay New York City.

The newest of the towers reached above the clouds, and they *moved*, constantly, slowly shifting like clock parts, so that residents had a panoramic view of the city. I couldn't look away as we sped closer, closer, swallowed up by the tiered streets before we dipped down into a tunnel beneath them. The train emerged from the rushing darkness and glided into the station, to a smooth and perfectly controlled stop. A pretty tone sounded, and the latch on the door went green. Gazing at what awaited us, Marko looked tired too. And resigned. I recognized his press face.

"Does this ever stop?" I asked.

"The crowds? Eventually. You get used to it," he replied with a half smile. "It's like the Mars lottery—everyone dreams of being chosen. So they'll be obsessed at first, but then someone else hits the jackpot, and you're old news."

That was a lie. He'd been holoed and followed every second since he'd been picked, and now, so would I. But there was currently no better choice.

A girl around fourteen shrieked when the door opened and begged him to sign her H2. With a smile and wave, he shook his head, escorting me through the throng gathered on either side of the cordoned-off red carpet to the street, where another e-car idled.

But I stopped cold because somebody I hadn't seen in years was waiting in front of us. Time hadn't been kind to him. His brown hair was mostly gray, and his pasty skin had both wrinkles and rosacea. The din faded and I felt like a spotlight might as well be shining on the two of us.

Dad.

He came toward me with a huge smile and hugged me like he'd never said I was worthless, like he'd never been a monster bellowing at me to *stop complaining*. "Zara, I'm proud of you."

Proud. Of. You.

I couldn't believe those words had just come out of his mouth. When I remembered the coldness in his eyes when he'd "disciplined" me, determined to drive the devil out, I swallowed a scream. Over the years, he'd made it clear that I disappointed him in every possible way and that his love had to be earned.

Now it seemed like getting picked as an Honor made me worthy, at least for the cameras.

I clenched my teeth and held it in. I didn't return his hug, but I didn't shove him away either. My father stepped back after a long, awkward moment and looked at me with what I realized was . . . uncertainty. "Zara? How have you been?"

How have I been? I thought about the Zone, going hungry, all the nights I'd huddled in the cold with Derry. I couldn't speak or I would have shouted in his face. I might've chosen life in the Zone over dealing with him, but if he'd been different—patient with me and good to Mom—then *maybe* . . . Well, no point wasting my energy on what-ifs.

I glimpsed flashes of my "inspiring" story (a word they actually used) playing giant-sized on buildings around us. My scowl looked impressive on that scale. They were calling me a "wild card pick" on the news, speculating on the mystery of exactly why the Leviathan wanted me. Dad's picture flashed up, smiling just as he was now.

"Aren't you going to talk to me?" I couldn't shut out his voice, especially when he was in my face like this. I smelled day-old garlic. "Sharon says—"

I turned toward him so suddenly he pulled back. "Keep my mother's name out of your mouth. If I have to smile and shake your hand, I will. But there's nothing else, right? I will *never* forgive you."

That was as blunt as I could make it. I didn't miss a flare of anger in him, the way his fist curled, like he wanted to smack the defiance out of me. Some things didn't change.

Marko glanced between us and then murmured something into the mini-H2 on his wrist. "I think it would be better for you to make your own way to the hotel, Mr. Cole. I'll send a separate vehicle for you."

A surge of gratitude almost made me smile. "Let's get out of here."

The e-car was posh inside, and I liked it even more when we left my old man standing on the curb. The giant holos shimmering on the buildings flashed my picture up again, noting my arrival. Asking the question I was curious about right now: *Why her?* Apparently, experts were weighing in. I was glad I didn't have to listen to them break me down into tasty pieces for public consumption.

We reached a flash hotel, a tower of gold with obsidian

accents that was famous for hosting the Honors when New York won the bid, along with more drone cams and reporters eager for a glimpse of our party. Marko skated us past, an old pro at dodging unwanted attention.

At that point I had to say, unwillingly, "Thanks."

Marko nodded. "I understand. It's overwhelming."

As we reached the front doors, my old man climbed out of his e-car and waved to the crowd. I quickened my step to avoid sharing the impromptu spotlight with him.

"I'm sorry," Marko said. "But it's common for family members to participate, even estranged ones. This makes for a better media event. The Honors program promotes global unity, and they like the idea of facilitating reconciliation. No borders, no limits . . . remember that slogan?"

"It's fine," I told him. "I can take care of myself."

He nodded. "You'll need to answer some questions inside. He'll expect to stand with you."

"I don't want him talking."

"Then I'll make sure he doesn't," Marko said.

He seemed to be acting as a protector. Marko wasn't my brother or my friend, though. I barely knew him, except the story from the holos. But if he could keep my dad's mouth shut, I'd take that as a gift.

Sure enough, inside in the lobby, there was a crush of reporters sporting grafted-in cameras and enough drones whirring overhead to create a breeze. The hotel's atrium was an extravagant place, with vast holo walls that currently displayed . . . space. It felt like floating, with the nano-tinted carpet shimmering black with little points and sparks of light appearing and burning at random.

The vast shape of a Leviathan swam slowly around the walls of the room. Its skin glimmered like burnished metal where light touched it. *Like a fish in a bowl*, I thought.

Took me a minute to realize that Marko was clearing a path for us.

So many reporters shouting for my attention. I didn't hear the voices I wanted most, so I scanned the crowd until I spotted my mom and sister. Amid the media frenzy, Kiz nearly flattened me with a hug.

I jumped excitedly with her and then stepped back to *really* look at her. Almost as tall as me, now. A shower of thick, springy curls all the way down to her shoulders. Vivid light-brown eyes and the dark-ochre skin tone we shared. Kiz was wearing an orange shirt and loose flower-patterned skirt, and—

"You're grown," I said.

I hugged her; she grabbed me back, bouncing. She couldn't restrain a squeak of excitement, though I wasn't sure if it was the reunion or all the press coverage. Hard to believe this polished young woman was the same kid who'd cried when I wouldn't let her tag after me.

"Missed you," Kiz whispered.

"Me too."

Mom stepped up then, smoothing down her dress like it might fly away, and I saw tears gleaming in her eyes. I got my height from her, and my shoulders. Kiz and I both inherited her lovely hair, though my mother kept hers in tight, natural curls close to her scalp. She opened her arms, and I forgot about press junkets and clamoring reporters. I'd never been the daughter she wanted and she hadn't always been the mother I needed, but there was no question that I loved her and Kiz. Or that she loved me.

I just didn't know how to *live* with them. My father had carved a hole in all three of us, and we'd each filled that space as best we could.

"I'm so proud of you," Mom said. My dad had claimed that too. But Mom meant it.

I smiled. "It's good to see you both. Was the trip okay?"

Kiz grabbed my hand. "Z, it was *amazing*, you could see the Leviathan all up in orbit. . . . We don't see stars through the dome, but there are so many, it's just so beautiful!"

I gave her a grin that felt real. "Guess I'll see for myself pretty soon," I said.

"Oh, good, you're here!" A professionally attractive woman joined us, wearing an ice-white suit and high heels. Everything about her screamed money. "I'm Gidra Valdez, your press liaison."

She gave some introduction I only half listened to

because I was worried that my dad was about to step forward and start running his mouth. I made sure Mom and Kiz stood on either side of me—with my old man forced to the back row with Marko and Ms. Valdez.

"Is it true that Zara is your replacement aboard Nadim?"

Marko had an easy, holo-friendly smile. I'd never be able to do that. "Yes, it's true," he said. "Chao-Xing is coming with her own replacement today as well."

A tall, goofy-looking reporter waved until he caught my eye. "Zara, Zara! Are you a musician as well?"

I swallowed and managed to croak, "No."

"Then what are your talents?"

I shrugged. "Take a look. Figure it out."

My old man had had enough of being ignored, and he pushed forward, trying to join our family lineup by force. "I'm Zara's father," he said, "and—"

Marko gestured; his mic cut out. Mom smiled for the cameras. "I always knew Zara was special. She's strong, and she's always been *very* independent."

Kiz beamed and waved; she was *so* photogenic on the holo that it hurt in a good way. Like, it was worth all this nonsense to see my baby sister this happy.

Mom and Kiz took a few questions about life on Mars, but it was me the press wanted to hear, so I answered as best I could, hating every minute of it and not saying much beyond bare facts, but it kept Dear Old Dad from spewing whatever lies he had rehearsed.

Eventually, Ms. Valdez signaled the crowd. "That's all the time we have today, everyone! Please meet me in the briefing room in Ballroom B for downloads of Honor Cole's biography and highlights."

Someone shouted, "Will Zara's family be available to answer some questions?"

I glanced at Mom, who shook her head slightly.

"No," I said, at the same time my old man, of course, said, "Yes," and I glared at Marko. He went to instruct Ms. Valdez, who nodded briskly, as if herding and muzzling the families of Honors was just another part of her job. Which it probably was.

"This way." Marko guided us off the dais, and I held on to my mom and sister as we moved through the crowd. "I'll show you to your room."

Kiz smiled at Marko, so cute that his expression warmed up by ten degrees. "We've got ours already. Some Honors rep said we're in an adjoining suite."

Finally, a bright spot to this circus.

Just then, a side door opened, disgorging a disheveled guy in his twenties. He had a look straight out of the Zone—unshaved, pallid, shaky, wearing a stained Honors uniform. His eyes locked on mine, and I recognized the look in them. Equal parts desperate and haunted. Saw a lot of both on the streets, and it didn't look any different in a fancy hotel.

Kiz let out a little cry and moved back. Marko instantly tapped his H2, and a security notice flashed on the wall beside us. Guards would be on the way, fast.

The guy grabbed my arm, and I moved to free myself with instinctive violence, but he was strong. *Really* strong. "It's a lie." His breath smelled sickly sweet. "Ask them about the weapons. *Ask them.* I think . . . I think I remember—"

"Who are you?" I blurted that back just to keep him talking instead of twisting, but all I could think of was how much I was going to have to hurt him to get rid of him.

He didn't seem to hear me, too panicked or lost in memories. His intensity gave me the shivers. "Don't go out there with them, they lie, they all lie. I think—they told me—" He let go of me and slapped his head with both hands, hard enough to hurt. Kept doing it. "No, no, that's not right, I know I saw—I know—" His voice was rising in pitch and panic now, but I was already backing off. He grabbed for me again. "Please *listen*! Don't go!"

"Step away from my daughter!" Mom charged forward, and with a strength that surprised me and shocked him, she wrenched his hand away and twisted it until his knees buckled. I'd never seen all that much resemblance between us, but *damn*, that expression? I'd felt that on my own face. Pure, righteous fury.

She didn't let go until security charged in to take control. And then she turned on Marko. "What the hell was *that*?"

"I'm sorry." His eyes were bleak as he watched the intruder being rushed out. "Valenzuela was a year ahead of us. He . . . didn't adapt well on the ship, and had to be removed midyear. I thought he was in treatment."

That sounded like a prepared explanation, and I had a good ear for bullshit. "He seemed fine in the interviews he gave before he shipped out last year." I'd listened with half an ear while I was stuck in Camp Kuna, but I still remembered Valenzuela. He'd been relaxed, confident, eager to start his trip. No sign of the shambling wreck he was now.

"That's not always an indicator of how well someone integrates."

"If you say so," I muttered. Didn't believe a word. *Don't go*, Valenzuela had said. He had to mean, *Don't go up to the Leviathan.* Why not? What did he know?

Tense silence reigned until the elevator doors dinged open. We got in.

Kiz asked softly, "What did he mean, telling Zara not to go? Is there some kind of danger?"

"Of course not," Marko said, and distracted her by talking about all the celebrities who would be attending various events. I didn't miss that slick diversion.

Ever polite, he walked us down a long, empty hallway. The carpet was black, with nano-stars and slowly swirling galaxies. We were walking on space, and on either side, doors showed pulsing designs of nebulas, Oort clouds, and thick star fields. We stopped in front of one that shifted from a spinning galaxy to *Welcome Honor Cole* at our approach. Marko handed me a thin, clear card, and as I touched it, the door clicked open.

"You won't need it again," he told me. "It's keyed to your DNA. Just keep it on your person. Get some rest."

As he walked off, Mom opened the door to their room, pausing long enough to say, "They gave us a copy of your schedule. It's rough. You feel like a late dinner tonight?"

"Yeah. I'd like that."

After my mom and sister went to their room, I inspected the posh suite I'd been assigned. The closet held a full week of Honors uniforms stacked on the bed. The nu-silk didn't wrinkle, no matter how I twisted it up. When I wandered into the bathroom, I found an array of sponsor-provided toiletries and nano-cosmetics on the counter, and a shower big enough to lie down in, if I wanted. I didn't, but it was gorgeous to rinse off the travel, co-wash my hair, deep condition, and use the luxe products to finish my curls. The finger-styling went much easier than it had at Camp Kuna.

Time to get dressed.

Afterward, though I was definitely hungry, I checked out the schedule my mom had mentioned. No joke, but it was *packed.* Orientation, lectures, sim training, press junkets, luncheons, fittings, and specialized classes.

Yet I hadn't forgotten that weird moment in the hall,

earlier. *Valenzuela* . . . When I checked the net, I pulled up a ton of results for Gregory Valenzuela, all glowing profiles. Not one of them mentioned him being pulled from a Leviathan midyear. They'd just stopped reporting on him.

Cover-up, or just respecting his privacy? Hard to tell, but I hadn't noticed the newshounds out there respecting privacy much. It was too juicy a story not to splash out, unless someone had a very tight lid on it.

I wanted to follow the trail, but Mom and Kiz were waiting on me. My head was all over the place; it was great to see them, but their faces reminded me of what I put them through, so it was a cycle of gladness and guilt, longing to be back with them and a never-quite-gone urge to bolt. I pushed all the distractions away with an effort. I really did want to make the most of our time together.

Once I got ready, I knocked on the connecting door. It took about five seconds for the locks to click back and the door to slide open. "Set?"

Kiz had touched up her lipstick, and Mom had swapped her fancy shoes for pretty but still-comfortable ones. "I hear the hotel restaurant is something," Mom said.

On the way to the elevator, Kiz started naming all the things she was going to eat that were hard to get on Mars.

Which made me wonder, "How is dome life, anyway?"

She thought for a minute. "Structured. But my school is awesome. We take field trips outside for science sometimes, and I thought *that* was a big deal. Can't believe you're going to space, Z. But then you always did want to run as far as you could."

That stung, because she was right. I'd always been about running away. Once, I'd seen some gorgeous street art in the Lower Eight: the words *INERTIA=DEATH*, surrounded by exquisite color and Leviathan-inspired patterns. It had made a lasting impression, and I'd been living by that principle ever since. So, maybe taking them up on this Honors thing *was* as far as I could ever go. If I looked at it that way, I might warm up to the idea. In time.

Early the next morning, I woke up because my door made a soft, respectful chime, but when I put it in view mode, there was nobody there. Just a fancy arrangement of flowers, and a card stuck on it. I opened the door and brought it inside.

The card said, *Give it back, and I'll let everything go.*

Deluca.

All of a sudden, the purples and reds of the arrangement looked like bruises and bloodstains. I ripped up the card and stepped away for a second with my heart pounding. The room read my anxiety, and I smelled lavender as the relaxers were pumped in.

I dumped everything in the disposal unit, along with the ripped-up card, and hit the *delete* control. It took about two minutes to incinerate everything, but when the container opened again, there was no trace of Deluca's message.

The hotel has anti-terrorism scans, I told myself. It was standard for these fancy places.

Fear couldn't be eradicated so easily, though. It haunted me the whole week, through all the lessons and drills, all the interviews and info sessions. I learned about Leviathan biology, including a very basic (and mostly theoretical) analysis of how their bodies processed energy gathered from starlight and used it to drive their propulsive systems, which were strong enough to overcome the speed of light, when they chose to use them. Not a lot of info about the Leviathan's social structure; there were Elders who accompanied the younger ships we'd be traveling with. They seemed to be larger and stronger and generally more badass. I approved.

More classes. Virtual navigation, which I hated. Hands-on console repairs, which I didn't. We were introduced to a variety of sims that we'd be expected to use aboard the ship, partly to keep us in good mental and physical shape. My favorite, to no one's surprise, was the fighting sim, where I got to kick ass for cardio benefits. Perfect scores.

Second favorite unit? The crash Leviathan MD course. I had a thousand questions about the emergency procedures, how we might be called on for medical intervention, and a more in-depth study of biosystems. When it came time to choose my elective seminar, I picked Leviathan physiology over navigation.

But worrying about Deluca cost me when I took the final tests; I couldn't focus on the higher math and I choked on the chemical formulas. Thankfully, I leveled out on tech and rocked the unit on biomechanics. End result? With my cumulative total, I passed by two points.

Yep. Bottom of my class. I was certain that was just what they expected. But deep inside—very deep—I was still disappointed, before I put on the brassy armor of self-confidence and pretended that coasting just above fail was my survival strategy.

The send-off gala the night before our departure was the social ticket of the year, and my mom and sister were beyond thrilled to be going; they'd gotten free fancy dresses and makeovers, while I stuck to my uniform. I *had* gone for a haircut, though—trimming my curls on top, undercut, with a fade on each side, so I looked sharp and tailored as I threaded through the crowd.

I headed for Kiz, who was chatting up a famous Nigerian pop star. With his dark skin, well-trimmed goatee, and white suit edged in silver, Obari was *fine*. I could see why my sister was glowing. A hand wrapped around my arm, stopping me. When I turned, I was facing a tall white man in a crisply tailored black evening suit. His smile was all shark teeth and cold, dead eyes, and even though I didn't recognize him in that second, I knew his type.

"Nice to finally meet you, Miss Cole. Congratulations are clearly in order. The first Honor chosen from the Lower Eight." He was still holding on to me with his left hand, but now he extended his right. A giant ring with a red stone—ruby?—glinted on one of his fingers. "Torian Deluca."

My mouth went dry, and my pulse stuttered, then sped up. I wanted to pull free and bolt, but you don't run from a dangerous beast. "So?"

He wrapped both hands around mine, approximating a congratulatory gesture, but it ground my knuckles together so hard my eyes watered. I didn't flinch, holding his gaze until he tipped his head like a curious predator deciding what to bite first.

Deluca leaned in. "You have something I want."

"I hope it's a smile. I give those for free . . . Oh, wait. Fresh out."

"Didn't you get my card? *I want the data.*"

"Well, I don't have it. What are you going to do? Kill me here in the ballroom?"

"I'd kill every Honor in this place if I had to," he said. "I don't have to. You've got a weakness. If you want to see him alive again, you're going to hand the data tab over."

Him?

Derry. I'd given Derry the chem.

Horror paralyzed me for a second, and then Deluca pulled an H2 from his pocket. He turned it to show me the screen. The sound was off, but the picture was right there in vivid color: Derry, screaming. Bloody.

I wanted to grab something, *anything* to use as a weapon and kill this man right here. Instead, I raised my gaze back to Deluca's and said, "Don't know him."

"No?" He shook the H2 back and forth a little. "Doesn't ring a bell? Derry McKinnon?"

"Nope."

"Funny. He went looking for more of this." From the same pocket, Deluca produced a small bag with just a dusting of shimmering crystals. "Derry said a lot, like how you killed my man Enzo and forced him to bury the body. Look, kid. If you think you can bootleg my designer formula, well." He drew his finger across his throat. "Don't even try. Hand over the data and I'll . . . let it go."

That was a lie. I saw it in the icy smile that came after.

"And Derry?" Numbness trickled in. The rest of the ballroom had faded out. *Derry talked. Not just about the chem, but he straight-up rolled on me.*

I had been making excuses for Derry for years, and it stopped now. No matter what, he shouldn't have given me up. Not with everything I'd done for him.

Fucking asshole.

"Let him go, and I'll tell you where to find the tab. It's still in the box." I took a wild guess, because it didn't really matter if I was wrong. "You had the formula on that data tab inside, right? What'd you do, kill the chemist and wipe his records?"

Deluca was smooth. He hardly reacted at all, but I saw the little creases at the corners of his eyes, the nearly invisible twitch in his jaw. That box I'd grabbed hadn't been his daughter's personal stash; it had been Deluca's production order, and she'd been taking it to his street lab. That formula he'd stored on the data tab, the one I'd ditched? That was worth billions.

But not to me. The only thing it was worth to me was Derry's life.

When he didn't respond, I said, "Do we have a deal?"

"I don't work on credit. He's dead if you don't cooperate."

No choice. I had no other leverage, so I called up a map and marked the alley where I'd dropped it, next to the VR porn studio. "Here," I said. "I stuck it under some fallen bricks. Probably still there, unless somebody found and scrapped it."

I killed twenty agonizing minutes at his side while he dispatched goons to check the site, and after his men retrieved the data tab, he pulled out his H2 and jabbed the screen. Then he held it out to me, a live feed; I could see the clock off to the side, set to Detroit time. A guy in a mask stepped up and slashed Derry's ropes away. Derry got up, staggered, and ran. The guy in the mask shook his head and said something I couldn't hear to the camera, and then he picked up the H2 on the other end and turned it around. I saw Derry darting out a broken doorway.

"What guarantee do I have that you're not just going to hunt him down now and kill him?" I asked.

"None. But why would I bother?" He took in a breath, all too aware of the drones, the head-cams, the other people around us. Forced a smile. "Besides, people like him are leverage. Go ahead, run to the stars. I'll be waiting when you get back. Maybe we'll do some more business, kid. I still haven't paid you back for the disrespect to my daughter."

I watched him go, unable to focus on the event at all.

It was late by the time all the new Honors had their big moment, beamed live all over the world: two in the morning. I had no false excitement left, just fear. Fear of Deluca's long reach, fear of the unknown. Whatever, at least Derry was alive and we were quits.

I couldn't sleep. Instead, I paced, watching the clock, feeling everything around me shift, change, and crumble. I packed the few things I owned. I watched some coverage of the upcoming launch event. . . . The reporters, at least, weren't sleeping any more than I was. I got surprised by an

111

interview with my father, who popped up out of nowhere; I shut it off rather than hear him say my name.

As the few hours passed, things compressed into flashes. *Flash*, and I was eating breakfast from a fancy tray while Marko updated me on what would happen today. *Flash*, and I was in an e-car with Marko, Mom, and Kiz, heading for the launch site.

Flash, and I stood in the early morning light, surrounded by paparazzi, while my mother held me tight and whispered, "Love you, Zara. You're gonna do great things."

Kiz got in on the hug. "Don't screw it up."

I took pleasure in knowing that my old man wasn't sharing this public family farewell. Like he did me, I wrote him out, now that *I* had the power.

Time stopped moving so quickly then, as if my brain had decided to take it all in. In a few moments, I'd be leaving Earth. Leaving everything I'd ever known. Amid a flurry of photo ops and terse mini-interviews, I finally boarded the shuttle. *I'm about to meet an alien.* Not a metal ship. A *living creature* that traveled in space, taking me along for the ride. That scared the hell out of me, now that it was more than just some holo, some abstract concept.

Valenzuela's warning echoed in my head. *Don't go.* Maybe this was a bad idea, worse than staying to face off with Deluca. My stomach knotted.

Somehow I lifted a hand to wave to Mom and Kiz. Mom

put her hand to her heart, and I did the same. Then I was inside the shuttle.

Marko made sure I was strapped in and settled beside me. Across the aisle, a dark-haired girl that I vaguely recalled as Beatriz, the other new recruit, was breathing hard and blinking back tears while Zhang Chao-Xing—imposing and very stiff in the flesh—ignored her distress.

"It's okay," I said to the other girl, but really to myself.

The engines engaged and started to spin up, and the strangest thing happened: a wave surged inside me, almost new to me. Anticipation. This felt like running, all right, running away from my past and everything in it. Racing full speed toward the unknown.

I was good at running.

When the shuttle shot up, the roar blanked everything else as we left the Earth and flung ourselves out toward the stars.

Interlude: Nadim

Below, the planet spins. It is a beautiful world, lush in hues and energy, filled to bursting with life in fascinating shapes. I wish I could visit it, but skimming the thick atmosphere is as close as I dare. I am with the others, my year-mates, and we circle the globe in a weightless flock.

We are all empty.

It is a strange thing to feel the hollow spaces and the silence again. Peaceful, but sad. I miss Marko's calm, whispering presence. I wonder what new humans will bring me. Chao-Xing taught me a chill kind of patience. Marko taught me to listen. Each of them teaches, each of them learns. This is the way.

Elder Typhon hovers higher, hidden in starshadow, adrift on dark currents. His sails are furled as he waits. I can feel his eagerness to be done and traveling again, but I don't know what drives him on. I feel no such need, at least at the moment; the song of stars whispers far, far away. I could stay caught in the glow of these humans for ages and feel content. This is what drew us to them, this energy. Many forms of life exist in the vast, black ocean between suns, but few burn so brightly. Sing so clearly.

My new crew is coming. I feel the hot pulse of the shuttles—poor, inert things, driven by machines and not life—bringing them up from their drowning-heavy ground to the cool surface where I drift. Fifty vessels, each bearing guests. As mine nears, it gives me golden, sweet joy to feel Marko on board, less to feel Chao-Xing, but she is familiar all the same.

The other two are different, as different to each other as to me. One burns with a nervous, brittle brown chatter of fear; the other has a red edge of something else. Harder, but . . . sweeter too. Something I have never known.

Something new.

PART II

CHAPTER SIX

Breaking Through

THE UPWARD RUSH felt like the purest freedom I'd ever known.

Though I'd hated almost everything that led up to this moment, exaltation shot through my veins. I watched the Earth fall away, along with all constraints and restrictions. Whoever I'd been dirtside, this was a fresh start. This was a new me, this uniform, this slick haircut, this *possibility*.

Inside, though. Inside, I was the same old Zara. I didn't know if that would ever change.

I'd never flown on a plane, let alone a shuttle. For a small craft, this thing had a lot of thrust. We rocketed up, and a final boost pushed us, shuddering, past the atmosphere, and the revelation hit me hard, watching that shifting sky. The universe opened up like a darkly blooming flower to reveal a black sea full of Leviathan.

My breath caught.

Even at this distance, they still looked big, so they must be enormous up close. I'd seen the holo at orientation, of course, but nothing could do justice to the silvery, flickering sheen of them, contrasted against surrounding darkness. Their hulls gleamed with a sort of incandescent starlight, and I thought of the silver moonfish I'd once seen in an aquarium. I wondered how their skin felt to touch. Awe crept over me when I processed the fact that I was looking at a living creature with such magnificent lines. The nearest Leviathan was broadest across the center, with graceful curves from head to tail. The tail stretched out into a tapered point, and solar sails stretched out like fans, iridescent as butterfly wings.

Holy shit. I'll be living inside *someone.*

That was a bizarre thought, kind of reminiscent of Jonah and the whale. That wilderness Bible camp had made sure I knew lots of pointless stories. I leaned forward, straining my harness for a better glimpse. The shuttle nosed close, and the creature . . . opened.

Staring into the maw of our new reality, the other girl had a panic attack. Her big brown eyes went wide, her breath starting to shorten and grow harsh. I'd seen it before on the streets. Sometimes, if people had asthma, we had to find a med bot and get them on a breather. But she didn't seem asthmatic. Just scared to death.

"You're Beatriz, right?" I'd met her during training week, but we hadn't spent much time together. She didn't answer. The shuttle lurched to a stop, and a strange, syrupy gravity drew us back down into our chairs. Chao-Xing ignored Beatriz's distress. She was entirely occupied with her personal H2. Reading her own coverage, I guessed.

"Hey!" I said sharply, leaning forward. "Ms. Zhang. Give her a hand or something."

"Excuse me?" she said without looking up.

"You. Isn't she kind of your responsibility?"

"Not anymore. We've docked."

"Chao-Xing," Marko said, in a patient, resigned tone, like he'd developed it over a thousand uses. "Come on. Give her a relaxer. She needs it."

The woman looked irritated as hell, but she dug around in a bag by her seat, broke open a medkit, and snapped a vial under Beatriz's nose. The girl's breathing evened out, and her eyelids fluttered, like she might pass out. "There," Chao-Xing said. "Happy?"

"Delighted," Marko said in a voice that was anything but. Wow. These two . . . didn't really get along.

I didn't wait for an invitation and unfastened my straps. Once Beatriz calmed a bit, Marko disengaged the doors, and we stepped out into what seemed like a kind of docking bay. But the floor felt strange and spongy beneath my feet. I bounced a little. The ship carried a faint smell that the others didn't seem to notice, but it swirled around me like a smoky, caramelized sweetness. I drew it in deeply as I spun in a circle, trying to wrap my head around the fact that I was *inside* a living creature. Though I didn't like anyone bossing me around, I waited for Marko, because he had the scoop on what our next move should be.

"I'll give them the tour," he said to Chao-Xing.

It didn't seem like she intended to even leave the shuttle. "Make it quick. We're expected soon."

Marko stepped out with a smile that wasn't directed at either of us. "Nadim, these are your new partners, Beatriz Teixeira and Zara Cole."

I was trying to figure out how to greet a *ship* when I heard a sweet, low voice, somehow both in my head and outside of it, vocalized in subharmonics that vibrated pleasantly down my spine. "I'm so happy you're here."

The classes had spelled out that the Leviathan would communicate with us directly by voice, but this felt like the ship was talking to me—and *only* to me. The sincerity rolled over me so hard, it made the top of my head tingle. For a few seconds, I stood speechless, and I felt squirmy, for *no* logical reason. I got my breathing under control and shifted, feeling the give beneath my feet.

"Uh . . . hi," I mumbled. My cheeks felt hot. No. I did *not* blush. I hadn't blushed since I was eight.

Beatriz let out a squeak and grabbed my arm; Nadim's greeting hadn't made her feel any better, clearly. Marko led us through the docking bay and deeper into the Leviathan. *Into Nadim*, I corrected mentally. It always used to piss me off when people dismissed me, so I couldn't deny this ship's personhood, which sounded weird even in my head. We passed a kind of membrane that drifted over my skin—not unpleasant, just strange—but Beatriz was shivering by the time we stepped into a corridor that might have been a nerve pathway. The walls this deep shone an ivory pink, and on instinct, I reached out, then remembered how much I hated people touching me without permission.

"Go ahead," Nadim said. "It's all right."

That startled me, but I put my hand on the wall. Carefully.

Marko smiled. "Warmer than you expected?"

Definitely. Warm and silky too. "It doesn't hurt when I touch him?" I asked.

Nadim answered, not Marko. "It feels nice."

Carefully I drew my hand away and followed Marko into what I recognized from the orientation classes as our common room. The furnishings were lush and human-made, and I wondered if all this human-added stuff felt uncomfortable for the ship, like a human wearing braces on his teeth.

There was also a familiar data console—again, like the

one I'd used in orientation week classes, with all its inputs. Marko recapped how to use it while I stared up at the curves and hollows of the ceiling; it reminded me first of a church, and then of the top of a human mouth. It was impossible not to feel a little overwhelmed by the collision of the familiar and the strange.

"Zara? Are you listening?" Marko sounded just a touch impatient. I quickly pulled my attention back to him.

"Sure," I lied, and I could see he knew it.

"For the first day, you'll be free to relax a bit. Then Nadim will take you on a short trip. By which I mean, within the Sol system. After that, the second phase of your training begins. The console has all the information regarding your schedule and the goals you must achieve."

"Question," I said. "What if we don't? Achieve. Do you bring us back to Earth?" Not that I was intending to fail, but better to be prepared. Next to me, Beatriz still seemed blurry from the relaxers. I couldn't tell if she was going to be able to handle this.

Nadim answered me. "I'm certain you will do fine," he offered, "and I will be of assistance in any way I can. The projects you will be working on are of benefit to both of our species. If you fail, then I fail too."

He absolutely had a mind of his own, though I should ask about pronouns. Regardless, it sounded like he intended to be a partner. In a way, that was great because there were three of us here, not just two. But it also meant that if Nadim had his own goals, and his own agendas . . . then we could be at odds.

That put me on edge, again. Because as soon as we left orbit, there would be nowhere left to run. My breath went in a sudden rush. Maybe space wasn't freedom after all. What if it was a wasteland, and I was in a lifeboat that could turn on me at any time? Something clearly went wrong for Gregory Valenzuela. Maybe that was just his own latent problems that bubbled up, or maybe it was something more. *Stay alert.*

Marko wasn't paying attention to me; he was talking to Beatriz, who'd finally focused enough to ask some questions. I stood there frozen, heart pounding, wondering if I could make a break for the shuttle. Go home.

Home to what? Derry sold you out. Deluca will be waiting.

I closed my eyes, and I was surprised to hear Nadim say, very quietly, "Are you all right, Zara Cole?"

I looked at Beatriz and Marko, who stood a short distance away; neither of them acted like they'd heard a thing. It was incredible that a ship could manage the equivalent of a whisper. It was in my head, but it *sounded* like someone standing a respectful distance away, speaking quietly.

It was in my head. That should have felt weird, but . . . it didn't. Sounds, after all, were just vibrations that got interpreted in the brain; he was just cutting out the step and tapping directly in. It didn't feel strange at all.

Which was strange, in itself.

"I'm only speaking to you," he said helpfully. "How may I help you feel more at home? The first day, I know, can be difficult."

I turned my back on the others and walked a little distance off, so they couldn't overhear. I lowered my voice to a whisper. "Look, I don't know—I thought this was a good idea, but now . . ."

I felt . . . something. Not my own emotion. It was like a shadow had brushed over me, but a shadow on my soul, not on my skin. Took me a second to identify what it was, but I recognized the feeling instinctively: Nadim. And Nadim was *sad*. There had been some talk of possibly perceiving a ship's emotions in training, but damned Deluca had kept me from absorbing as much as I should during my Earthside sessions.

It felt weird. And at the same time, it felt like something I'd always, unconsciously, needed—sound, where there'd only been silence. Presence, where there'd been loneliness. I didn't know why. In the training they'd talked about it as some kind of thing to be avoided. Why would anyone avoid this? Was it dangerous?

"I would be unhappy to lose you so quickly," he told me. "You are . . ." He hesitated, as if he didn't quite know how to put it. "Bright."

"Bottom of my class," I muttered. "Sure. I'm bright."

"That is not what I—"

Nadim's voice got cut off midsentence as Marko turned toward me and said, "Zara? Beatriz and I were discussing meals. Nadim has more than enough food stores, so you can eat well during your Tour. They're prepack, vacuum-seal meals, but . . ." Marko lifted his hands. "You get used to it. The WHSC tried to stock things you like."

A shiver of amusement ran down my back. *Nadim's feeling, not mine.* I was going to have to figure out how to push that away, if I wanted to keep my distance. "Hey!" I said, and turned around, not sure where to face him. "Food's important to us. What do *you* eat?"

"Starlight," he said, in that calm, warm voice. "Your sun is quite young and has a spice to it. Very strong."

"That's not weird at all," I said.

"I find your ways strange sometimes too. But interesting."

"This way," Marko said, and led us on. "Let me show you the library and the entertainment room."

We were midway through the tour when his comm buzzed. "Are you almost done? We're already forty minutes behind schedule." Chao-Xing. The tone was just short of rude.

He sighed. "Give me five minutes. I'll be there soon." Turning to us, he added, "That's just her nature. Okay, we'd better wrap this up. Remember: relax today. Tomorrow, start focusing on your goals."

That wasn't nearly enough information. "But why do we have to—"

"Understand this, Zara. I can't address your curiosity right now. One day, you'll see. But please accept for now that there are reasons for everything we do in the program."

"There's usually a shitty reason for secrecy," I said, and was a little surprised when Beatriz nodded. "It just seems strange that we're being dumped so fast, okay? I haven't forgotten what that dude said at the hotel. Or how you brushed it off."

Marko hesitated as his H2 flashed. "I told you, he had problems. They should have been caught earlier, but that's why you're going through this shakedown period," he said. "Candidates need to be quick to learn, quick to adapt, from the jump. There won't be anyone to hold your hand later, so if you can't handle it, we need to know that fast, before we leave the Sol system. We'll check on you at the end of the week."

Damn. I was probably safe from Deluca, but all kinds of things could likely go wrong out here. Maybe this week was a kind of extreme personality test; they needed pioneer or hermit types, who wouldn't crack halfway through the Tour.

Unlike Gregory Valenzuela. I instinctively *liked* Marko, but I wasn't sure I could trust him; still, my options on Earth weren't better. Assuming he was on the level, it wasn't like I had a lot to give up. Now that Derry had sold me out, I only gave a damn about Mom and Kiz. They were fine on Mars—out of my old man's reach—and Derry had gotten the last favor he could expect from me. I was less sure of what Deluca could do to my mom and sister, but they would be semi-celebrities for a while. That would help protect them.

Besides, I liked a challenge.

"All right, we got the gist," I muttered. "Take off, then."

"You'll do fine," Marko said. "Nadim can answer any other questions you have. Good luck, you two."

Beatriz tightened her grip on my arm as Marko strode away and vanished down the corridor. I didn't move for a while, not sure what to do.

"Did they leave?" Beatriz asked.

"Not yet." There was a pause of about a minute . . . and then a little shiver in the thick, strange gravity that I felt through the soles of my boots. Beatriz squeaked, closed her eyes, and clung tighter. "Now they have gone. Do you want to see their departure?"

"Sure," I said, before Beatriz could say she didn't, and a broad patch of skin in Nadim's wall just . . . disappeared. "Holy shit!" I couldn't hold that back, and I felt a rush of two things at once: disorientation and exhilaration. Like falling toward infinity. It was so beautiful. Velvet black, shot with colors that I'd never imagined, and below, the bright spinning ball of home. The silvery flash of Leviathan.

And the tiny, insignificant shape of the shuttle moving from Nadim off into the distance, heading for another ship farther out.

I stepped forward to rest my hands against the transparent skin, staring. Nadim still felt warm and silky, but I was looking out at the cold vastness of *the universe*. It almost felt like I was moving outside, drifting into the beauty. It was wrong to feel both small and *home* at the same time, but it felt like I was *meant* to be here. I'd never felt that way before. I'd always been restless, looking for something I couldn't find.

Here it was. A strange kind of home.

"I think Beatriz needs you," Nadim said apologetically, and I jolted back into my body, stepped away, and the window disappeared. He was right. Beatriz had collapsed into a chair with her hands covering her face, not quite crying, but close.

I claimed the chair beside her and touched her shoulder. She flinched. "Hey," I said. "You all right?"

"I'm fine," she said, very faintly. "I'm sorry. It's just—"

"Strange? Check to that. They dragged me out of rehab for this." I leaned forward. "Tell me what you need right now."

She gave a hitching little laugh and dropped her hands to her lap. "Home?"

I didn't know what home meant to her. A place? People? A view? I couldn't help with any of that. Maybe a distraction would work. "So you're giving up. That fast."

She looked up at me—confused for a second, and then heat building behind those eyes. "No."

"Then quit hiding in a corner. We're in space. You knew this was coming."

"Knowing something isn't the same as experiencing it!"

"Serious question," I said. "Because if we're going to be depending on each other, I need to know: you going to freak out on me when I need you?"

Her lips parted. She formed an answer, then swallowed it. Then stood up. A little wobbly, but she steadied it. "It was just a surprise," she said. "I'm fine. Nadim? I'm fine. You can—open the window."

He did. I loved the view. I knew Beatriz still hated it, but she stared out like she was facing down a wild animal. Back straight. Okay, then.

"Why do you think the Leviathan saved those astronauts back in the day?" I asked.

She lifted a startled gaze to mine. "You mean, the ones aboard the ISS?"

"Yeah. Seems weird, that timing. Humanity was about to destroy itself, right? And then there's this space disaster tailor-made for miraculous intervention, and heroes right there, ready to zoom in and save everybody."

Beatriz stared at me with a focus she hadn't had before. And a little indignant lift to her chin. "Are you implying there was some kind of conspiracy? That the Leviathan had something to do with the ISS accident?"

I shrugged. "It's a well-oiled con back where I'm from. Make somebody sick, then sell them the medicine they need to get well."

"You're not a Space Truther, are you?"

"Well, some of them have good points." I was playing. I didn't believe any of what Space Truthers spewed, but this was doing good things for her mood. Distractions worked.

"The Leviathan had nothing to do with the mess we made of Earth!" Beatriz sounded completely sure about it. "We got ourselves into it, haven't you read the histories? How we just ignored all our problems until they were too big to be fixed?"

I did remember. How fools in power argued against scientific fact and brought in phony experts to keep doing nothing. I blamed them for it too. But I needed to keep her stirred up, more anger, less fear. It was a kind of emotional-energy exchange.

"Maybe. But sure seems like they caught us right when we couldn't afford to ask any hard questions, you know?" I grinned at her. "Anyway, I'm Zara, straight out of the Lower Eight in New Detroit. We saw each other at orientation, but I figured I'd make it official."

She seemed torn between continuing the argument and being polite. Civility won. "Beatriz Teixeira," she said. "Rio. Although I also lived in São Paulo for a while."

"At least you're not looking like you might pass out anymore, either. See? Arguing is good for you. Let me make some coffee."

She gave me a reluctant smile. "I'll do it. I have a recipe."

Beatriz had a flair for mixing it with steamed milk and cinnamon, and that was heavenly. We sat at the round white table and drank, and she looked like a different girl. Relaxed, she had an open sweetness about her. We talked about Rio, a place that existed only in stories for me, but was real enough to her, with all its shops and busy streets and white sandy beaches.

When we finished our drinks, and she seemed okay, I said, "So, we're going to take a short cruise in the shallow end, right?"

I don't know how he knew I was talking to him, but Nadim answered. "Within this system. Where would you like to go?"

Beatriz appeared to be at a loss; that left it to me to decide. Nobody had ever asked me to pick a destination before, let alone on this scale. It felt like he'd just offered me the Sol system on a silver platter. I gave the first answer that popped into my head.

"Mars. I'd like to see Mars."

I'd never walked in the domed city where my mother

and sister lived, but I'd studied up on it. Now I could admire the view from orbit, where everything was red magic, mountains and valleys blurred into shadows and squiggles. It would be good to see it and imagine my mom and Kiz, going about their lives there. Some of the old pain had softened into a bittersweet sting. Mostly, I was glad I'd managed to leave them smiling this time.

Everything shifted as energy rippled through us, and Beatriz let out a surprised cry and grabbed at the table edge. I pictured a dolphin leaping in the sea, a kind of joyful burst of unleashed motion. I'd expected there would be more ceremony, like I'd have to be at the helm or input coordinates, but for a Leviathan, this jaunt was probably like a trip down the block to buy steamed pork buns.

Beatriz nearly fell over as the forward motion increased, so maybe we should've been strapped in. His exuberance clearly scared her.

I went back to Nadim's skin and reached out. He must have known exactly what I wanted, because this time, he didn't just open a window, he gave me a huge expanse of transparency. The first glimpse stole my breath. Earth retreated beneath us, along with the last sliver of blue sky. The darkness bloomed with stars. We sling-shotted around the moon, enormous on our left as it whirled past. Then he dove deeper, so that the patch of galaxy in the distance swirled in smoky, sparking colors.

"Can—can you slow down, please?" Beatriz asked. She sounded shaken. I turned away, and the transparency closed. She'd gotten up from the table, but she looked sick again. "I'm sorry. I'm trying."

She was. I couldn't bust her for having vertigo problems. Hopefully, she'd learn to kick them. "Maybe you should lie down awhile?"

Nadim didn't speak to us, but glowing pulses shot across one wall, and following the lights led us back to our quarters. We had separate rooms, though they were next door to each other. The furniture had been built into the walls, probably to keep things from shifting during transit. Beatriz fell onto her bunk and closed her eyes with a soft whimper. "I'll be all right," she said. "I trained for this, I swear I did. I just need . . . I need rest."

I left her and went back to watch our progress. I was still fascinated with the view. It didn't seem possible that he could travel so fast, but in the time it had taken me to get her settled, I could already see Mars as a small orange orb, growing as we raced closer. He slowed as the red planet deepened before us, and without meaning to, I pressed my palms to the port-skin.

Mom and Kiz are probably there by now. Maybe just getting off their own shuttle. Thinking about me. Sometimes I'd wondered how it must feel, just seeing a milky dome above them when they looked up, no stars or sky. The whole universe lay before me, and part of me wished I could share this breathtaking vision with them.

It occurred to me that I missed them. Really missed them. I'd been holding that back a long time, pretending that I didn't need them, didn't need *anybody*. But up here, it was safe to admit I still loved them.

"This made you sad," Nadim said. "I didn't expect that. I'm sorry. Why do you feel that way?"

My head jerked up. *Right, I'm not alone here. But . . .* "How do you know?"

"I can . . . *see* is not the right word. Neither is *feel*. It's somewhere in between?"

I tried to imagine what the bacteria in my system might be feeling and failed utterly. In orientation, they'd warned us off of feeling *his* emotions; I wasn't sure they'd ever even mentioned him picking up on ours. I wasn't sure how I felt about this development. Cautiously I ran my hand down the wall, and a jolt of . . . *something* tingled through my fingers. I quickly pulled back. "What was that?"

After a pause, Nadim said, "I'm not sure," and he sounded surprised too.

I tried it again. Same tingle. It wasn't like I'd got an electric shock; rather, it felt sort of good, like positive feedback. It faded. When I tried again, nothing.

"Do you want to stay here awhile?" he asked me. "It is a lovely planet. I can remain in orbit if you wish."

"I guess," I said. "What's all this like for you? Is it strange, having us with you?"

A pause. "Nobody's asked that before," he said.

"Really? Out of how many . . . uh, Honors?"

"I've partnered with twenty different sets," he said.

"So forty people, and nobody's ever asked how you feel about it until now?"

"No."

That struck me as weirdly human-centric. Hadn't they thought of him as . . . real? Having his own feelings and life? Not even Marko? *Way to be ambassadors, people.*

"You shouldn't feel sorry for me," Nadim said. "I'm very used to human behavior."

He'd read me, again. Effortlessly. I was used to being a closed book, and now I felt . . . open. That worried me and brought up the old fears. I didn't like being vulnerable. "Okay, now, hang on," I said. "How are you reading my mind?"

"I'm not," he said, and sounded startled about it. "I wouldn't. But you . . . you feel like colors, and the colors are made of emotions. You were purple, but you're brightening to red now. And that feels . . . warm. Like the taste of a star."

"I . . . what?" My stomach lurched in the most unexpected way, not seasick, but that pleasurable shiver rolled over me in waves again. People didn't just say things like that, certainly not about me. "Okay. Sure."

"Did I explain it badly?" He seemed concerned.

"No, it's fine. Just—it's pretty personal. They told us back on Earth we might feel stuff on board, but—"

"You already do, don't you? Don't I have texture?"

Belatedly I realized I was still resting my hand against the wall. I wondered if all new Honors felt this strange when they first came aboard. I wondered if that was what had so badly damaged Valenzuela, not slamming this door and locking it up. I stepped back and fixed my eyes on Mars again. "That's not what I'm talking about. There's feeling with my fingertips and . . . feeling with feelings." That sounded complicated, but I couldn't phrase it better. "Look, are you sure you can't read my mind?"

"Not read it, no. I've never had that deep a relationship with any of my Honors. I can see moods, but it's rare that I connect any more deeply. Of course, I'm still learning."

"You're in training too?"

"Yes. But I'm near the end. Soon, I'll be ready for the Journey."

"Yeah, I got some questions about that—"

"Perhaps later. Beatriz isn't feeling well. You should probably check on her. It might help if she had something to eat." I had the unmistakable sense he was trying to ditch my question. Nice try, but I didn't get distracted that easy.

"Yeah, well, I'm not the chef on this cruise. She'll have

to get it herself." I meant it, but then I reconsidered enough to ask, "Is she sick? For real?"

His lovely voice radiated regret. "Just disoriented. This happens sometimes. I hope she can adjust to me. Not everyone can." He sounded . . . a little wounded.

Until this moment it never occurred to me that we could hurt the feelings of a ship, even if it *was* intelligent. This was all so new. So odd. And once again, I remembered Valenzuela. Maybe he couldn't deal with all this . . . sharing. Felt weird to me too.

I didn't want to admit it also felt . . . good.

"Did Marko and Chao-Xing have trouble adapting?" I asked, and headed for the kitchen. He was right. Food probably was an ace idea.

He didn't answer the question, and I decided not to try it again. Could he get mad? I wasn't sure I wanted to find out, not this fast. I pulled out drawers and examined the neatly ranked packages. Apparently, they were specially branded to us—I spotted some things in the drawers marked with my name that made my stomach growl. I chose a meat-pie pack and read the instructions on the back. It only took a half a minute to warm it in the reheater.

Oh, hell. Maybe I ought to take the girl something after all.

Beatriz's drawer had a lot of dishes—some I recognized and a lot that I didn't. *"Feijoada,"* I mumbled. Sounded tasty. I took it out, cracked it open, heated it up, and then stacked it on top of my meal. After grabbing two packaged waters, I went to Bea's quarters. Nadim had to give me a helping pulse of direction along the way, but I didn't mind. Already I was warming to the idea that no matter where I went on board, he'd always be there if I needed help. That was . . . comforting. It shouldn't have been. I should have been freaked out, trapped, wanting my freedom. Being on this ship was the opposite of *alone*.

But it also felt good for someone to be looking out for *me* for a change. When I'd been out there in the Zone with Derry, I'd spent so much of the time watching for the danger signs with him . . . keeping him away from the chems, helping him through it when I failed. Now that I thought about it, that hadn't been much like freedom at all. In the rear view, it was starting to look a lot like being manipulated.

Maybe it had been easier to focus on Derry's needs than try to sort out my own shit. I shouldn't make that mistake up here, but I couldn't be rude, either. Which reminded me of things I was used to doing back on the ground as regular politeness. My crash course on Earth had told me that Leviathan didn't have gender, which made Nadim nonbinary, though his voice sounded male. So I said, "I'm wondering how I should refer to you. Pronoun-wise."

"*He* is fine, since that is how I register to you. I have no preference. But I appreciate you for asking." The warmth of his tone made me glad I'd taken the time.

"Don't tell me, this is another first?"

"No, others have asked, probably because it's covered in orientation."

He seemed in a good-enough mood, so I risked it. "You never answered me, by the way. Is there some reason you don't want to talk about Marko and Chao-Xing?"

"I was trying to decide whether or not my answer would violate their privacy, but after consideration, I think I may address the question in general terms. Marko missed his family regularly—more at first, when we left, of course. But he liked to talk to me, and that seemed to help, and he often sent back messages home. Chao-Xing did not miss anyone particularly, and I suppose in many ways she adapted very well to being in partnership with a Leviathan. She loved the exploration, but in terms of emotional adjustment . . . she never warmed to me. In her eyes, I always remained a vessel. Not a friend. Separate."

"That's messed up." I paused in the hall and patted the first organic part of him I could reach, and it happened again: warmth pulsed down my palm and into my wrist. Leaving my hand in place while balancing trays and boxes of water with the other, I sensed something deep in my bones, almost like a purr radiating from Nadim's depths. It could be his pulse or a subharmonic communication I couldn't quite understand. It made me want to keep touching him.

Especially when he said, "I'm very glad you're here, Zara."

Elder Typhon greets you, Earth people of the WHSC. In response to the standard inquiry, two hundred and seventy-one individuals of Earth who have been sent on the Journey have not returned within communication range, but the greetings of their families have been sent out in hopes that they will be received. I am aware, through the songs of my people, of the natural death of seventeen human crew members, which is in keeping with the lifespan of your species. Their bodies have been committed to the stars, as is our custom. The names of those so honored are at the end of this message.

The remaining humans engaged in the Journey continue, as do the Leviathan to whom they are matched.

We thank you for the gift of these new Honors, whom we will watch and test upon this year's small voyage. We will train them in our technology, and they will teach us the way your species approaches science and the solving of problems, as well as the history and culture of the people of Earth, which we honor and value as well. The discoveries that result from our joint experiments benefit both our species. We will continue the research requested by your scientists, as has been agreed.

This covers the specific questions we have agreed to answer for this Honors cycle. Any others must be submitted for the next year.

CHAPTER SEVEN

Breaking Up

AFTER THE FOOD, Beatriz felt comfortable enough to start exploring; Nadim gave us a walk-through of places that were accessible to us—a tiny fraction of his actual size, I realized. But still huge for two people.

We'd already toured the highlights with Marko, including the library—almost a hundred shelves of real paper books and a vast collection of e-media, new and old. There was even a theater next to it, with a stage and an area where media could be beamed.

But as we opened room after room—many of them self-sustaining experiments and lab facilities—we finally stepped into mystery.

It made no sense to me when I walked into that vast space. It was the last thing I expected to find—a glittering sea, lit from below in slow, rolling pulses of iridescent light.

"I—" My voice failed, and I looked at Bea. "What the hell is this?" The room was dark, warm, and humid. "Please tell me it's not your stomach."

"I don't eat food," Nadim reminded me. "I eat starlight."

"Then tell us it isn't your bladder," Bea said, which made me nearly choke on a laugh.

"I understand what you mean, but it doesn't apply."

"Then back to my original question," I said. "What the hell is this place?"

Nadim seemed amused. "Zhang Chao-Xing was an Olympic athlete, did you know that?"

Of course I did. I'd been subjected to the brain-numbing retrospective vids in rehab. She'd been an Olympic . . . swimmer.

"It's a pool," I said faintly. "But how . . ."

"She had a special request. I arranged it. Don't worry, the water is exactly like what is found on Earth. I can make it fresh or salt. She preferred fresh water for the pool."

I went to the edge, crouched down, and dipped my fingers in the water. It was warm as a bath.

"Do you swim, Beatriz?" he asked.

"Yes," she said, and sounded brighter now. She knelt next to me and touched the water. "I used to swim in the ocean. We would pack up the whole family, bring lunch, and I'd bodysurf with my brothers while my mother and grandmother slept in the sun. It's been years since I've been. This is so beautiful!"

Nadim said, "It can be much more so. Beatriz, is it all right if I show you the stars?"

She took in a deep breath. "Not yet. I just need a little time." She let out a shaky laugh. "So stupid! I studied for this. And yet when I look out there, I feel so . . . so lost."

"You aren't," Nadim said. "I can navigate a very long way. Even if I can't see the stars, I can hear them. Does that make you feel better?"

"I . . . suppose," she said. "I'll try tomorrow. Okay?"

"Yes, Beatriz. Do you mind if I show them to Zara?"

"Go ahead," she said. "I'll . . . be in the hall."

She retreated, and I stood. "You already showed me the stars," I told Nadim.

"Not like this." He sounded smug and a little delighted. "Look up."

I did.

The entire vast roof seemed to vanish. It was just me, the glimmer of the water, and . . . depthless black shot with stars. I should have felt dizzy, I suppose; I should have felt overwhelmed and terrified.

It was the most magical thing I'd ever seen. I sat down, then sank flat on my back to stare. The joy that moved through me felt like the purest thing I'd ever known.

"That's my home," Nadim whispered, and I felt *how he felt*. What had he said about me? Warmth and the taste of stars? Like that. I could almost hear those stars now, a high singing that pulled at me, pulled. . . .

Nadim's voice came again, sharper. "Zara?"

"Yes?" I felt dreamy. Floating. Everything was warm and wonderful and perfect. The stars were closer. Louder. Echoing in my head and my blood.

"Stop!"

That snapped me back to reality, in a hurry. I sat up, and now I did feel dizzy, and small, and incredibly insignificant. Cold. I felt cold.

"Stop *what*?" I demanded. I had an edge in my voice too. Something that wasn't quite a word whispered through the air between us. "I don't understand!"

"That was . . ." He didn't seem to quite know how to say it. "You were . . . you saw . . ."

"It's okay when you pick at our feelings, but not when I do it to you?"

"Yes." Nadim still sounded very odd. "I realize that's wrong, but—no one has ever done that before. Reached so deep. I'm not sure—"

"You're not sure you like it," I finished. "Fine. I'll stay out of your head, you stay the hell out of mine. Deal?"

"Yes." His voice had no emotion to it at all. Just sound.

The stars vanished overhead, and it was just a room, just water, just the taste of my own disappointment.

I stalked out into the corridor and found Beatriz. She looked at me funny. "What?" I snapped.

"You had a fight," she said, and smiled. "With an *alien*. That's quite a first day."

I shrugged like it didn't matter. The truth was, I was still reeling from that rejection; it shouldn't bother me since I'd been looking at people's backs for as long as I could remember.

"Yeah, well. Pissing people off is kind of my super-power." Nothing in my training had prepared me for wriggling into a Leviathan's thoughts. I didn't know how I felt about it— Wrong? Ashamed? Afraid? Maybe all of that, and yet it had felt so *right* at the time. Beatriz didn't seem to get to Nadim like I did, so why . . . *Maybe it's the surgery that fixed my headaches. That little piece of Leviathan DNA.* I might be tuned to Leviathan frequency now or something. It would explain a lot. That was . . . terrifying and exciting in equal measure. Did it make me strong in this place, or weaker than ever?

Beatriz suddenly yawned, and I caught it too, and we both laughed. "Is it night?" she asked. "I don't even know what time it is. But it feels like I've been up too long."

That was an excellent question. How did time zones even work out here? That was something nobody had asked in our informative sessions, but to keep a schedule, we had to operate on a clock. I led the way back toward the data hub, which seemed like the central point of our useful space.

Nadim, I noticed, didn't light our way for us in helpful pulses on the walls. Maybe he was still offended. In training, the instructors had explained how the Leviathan kept track of us, and essentially, it was like we were always on his alien GPS. Ghosts inside his skin he could feel moving, breathing, existing.

The interface obligingly told us the time, and Bea was right. It was late. Somehow, time had slipped by, and I hadn't even noticed. After skimming some historical facts about how near-Earth space used to be set on Texas time, but now was international, I realized we were living on Icelandic time. Until we decided mutually what sleep/wake schedule to use.

It dawned on me with a rush that we could soon be so far away that time would have no real meaning, no sunrises and sunsets to regulate our days. Just schedules. We weren't going to be bound to even those ancient rules. We could make our own.

Maybe hours would have more than sixty minutes. A week could be ten days. It was like all the rules that bit at me like barbed wire, my whole life, might soon drop away, and I wanted to stomp my feet and shout in exultation.

No limits.

"That's a happy look," Beatriz said. "Why?"

There was no point in trying to explain. She seemed like someone who had colored inside the lines in school while I was out back spraying my incomprehensible art all over the walls. *Maybe that's why they paired us up, checks and balances.* More to the point, I could at least answer her other question.

"That's because I can tell you, it's ten thirty at night in Rio right now. Twelve thirty in the morning, ship time."

"You should rest," Nadim said then. "Your alarms will sound in six hours."

Nadim wasn't kidding about the wake-up call. It started as a quiet, respectful chime. When I rolled over, groaned, and pulled a pillow over my head, it got louder. Louder. Became a gong, relentless and metallically pounding next to my head.

I yanked myself away from the wall and off the bed. They'd walked us through mock-ups of the crew quarters during our orientation week in New York, and I knew where to find the pull-out toilet, the slide-open shower.

Clean, uniformed, and still cranky at the early start, I headed straight for the canteen, where I found Beatriz finishing up her breakfast. She gave me a cheery smile.

"So what the hell did we have to get up for?" I meant

the ask for her or Nadim, whoever wanted to answer. Beatriz's smile pulled a cute dimple in her cheek this time.

"You didn't check your H2?"

"I don't have one."

"It's in your quarters," Nadim said. "It contains your assignments for the day, and you must track and enter progress. Please get it."

I gave Beatriz a pleading look, and she shook her head, but she got up, left at a run, and came back with the device. She handed it to me, and I opened it with a tap. "Oh, seriously, *come on.*"

Beatriz turned her device on, and we turned them side by side. We had exactly two things in common today: lunch and dinner. Apart from that, we'd be working on our own until nearly seven Iceland time. Twelve hours, minus two for meal times. From my uninformed, quick view of her schedule, it looked like Beatriz was going to be doing some programming work, database updates, and various math-y tasks. A few things in the lab.

I checked mine. "You're kidding me," I muttered.

"You will be assisting with assembly of upgrade equipment," Nadim said.

Beatriz finished her coffee and carried her plate and cup to the small disinfecting unit, then came back to pluck her H2 out of my hand. "See you at lunch, Zara."

I glared at the handheld left to me, put it down, and

defiantly drank a cup of coffee before I got to work.

I ended up in a room I hadn't been in before, a space built out as some kind of storage and workroom; I wondered which of the former two Honors had been in here using the tools, which ranged from blunt sledgehammers to fine-pointed, delicate circuitry points. I knew my way around most of them—time in the Zone would do that—but I'd never seen so many together or in such careful order.

The handheld showed a bin to pull, and I walked down a long row of closed storage containers; the one they wanted me to access was enormous. It was also on wheels. When I touched it, it glided out and followed me like a pet back to the workbench, then obligingly opened to reveal . . . something. My first impression was that it was an engine of some kind, but it was massive. Not a design that looked totally human-inspired, either, though it had some familiar aspects. I looked through the notes. Lots of information about putting thing A into slot B, but nothing much about what it was supposed to actually *do*.

And that bothered me. A lot. The knowledge the Leviathan had shared with humanity was mostly biological or biotech in nature—including genetic cures, like the DNA patch that had ultimately fixed the headaches I'd endured through my childhood. I had a tiny little piece of Leviathan DNA in there, fixing what was broken. Everything they'd given us had an organic root to it, a *grown* kind of technology.

Was this what they were getting from *us*? Human labor and mechanical ingenuity? Somehow, the PR had all been about "cultural exchange" and such. Like the Leviathan delighted in learning things—which might actually be true. But this machine . . . this was something else entirely.

"Nadim," I said. "Can you hear me?"

"Yes," he said as if he was standing right next to me. "How can I help you?"

I jumped a little. That, I thought, was going to take some getting used to. "What is this thing?"

"An upgrade," he said. "For me."

"I mean, what does it do?"

"Its purpose is classified."

I dropped the handheld onto the workbench with a bang. "Not doing it."

"Zara, if you don't do your work—"

"What, you'll fire me? Bounce me back to Earth?" I didn't want that, I really didn't, but I wasn't about to let him know it. I was careful to keep my anger up front. "Look, I don't like secrets. I want to know what this is, or I don't touch it. Understood?"

Silence. A lot of it. I could feel something rippling through the air, but I couldn't tell what it was, and though I was tempted to put my hand on his wall and try to figure it out, that seemed . . . intrusive. So I crossed my arms and waited.

Finally, Nadim said, "You're being difficult."

"Is that a disqualification?"

"Not doing the work will disqualify you," he said. "Zara, *please*. I don't want you to be expelled from the program. Can't you—"

"Take somebody's word for it that what I'm doing is a good thing? No way in hell. That's why I hated Paradise—I mean, New Detroit. It was twenty-four-seven rules for our own good and nobody could tell me why. And this?" I gestured around the workroom. At him too. "This is all secrets too."

"Secrets are necessary sometimes," he said. "You must have a few."

"Yeah, well, I'm not asking you to work on mine, am I?"

More silence. I was aware that there were time limits, progress reports to be filed; I was aware that I was flunking out, *again*, on what might be the biggest test of my lifetime.

"Screw this, I'd rather—"

"All right," Nadim cut in. "I'll tell you what I can. Is that acceptable?"

"Depends on what you say."

"That is part of an alarm clock."

I couldn't help it. I laughed out loud, a burst of shock that turned into genuine amusement. "I'm *sorry*? An *alarm clock*?" Nadim, I realized, wasn't laughing. At all. I didn't get any sense of amusement from him, and his silence was telling. "Okay, apparently I'm wrong, it isn't funny. Explain?"

"I shouldn't," he said. "I could get in trouble."

"With who, exactly?" Because everything I'd ever seen about the Leviathan, on all the holo documentaries and in the orientation classes, had classed them as loners . . . born in space, separated almost immediately from their parents to travel the universe and grow as sentient beings on their own. They learned by doing and listening. They weren't social, exactly, and I didn't think they had a reporting structure—at least, none that anyone had ever talked about. But he'd referred to an elder. Maybe that was who he was worried about.

Nadim didn't shed any light on it. Instead, he brought up a vid that shimmered in the air a meter in front of me.

I didn't recognize the face of the young woman. She spoke in what sounded like Russian, but in the next second, it switched to English. Nadim automatically translating it, maybe.

The woman—the Honor—looked sick and scared half to death. "I don't know what happened," she said, and glanced over her shoulder. What was in view appeared to be the data console room, though there was something wrong with the color of Nadim's wall-skin; it seemed purplish, bruised, wrong. I thought the picture was out of focus. Then I realized what I was seeing was smoke, or at least some kind of visible fog obscuring it. The Honor tried to wave it away, coughed, and then bent off to the side to spit out a thin trail of blood. "We should have followed the course that was recommended, but he said the alternate route was fine when we proposed it. Now we can't wake him up, we can't—"

"Another one's coming!" someone shouted, this time in Mandarin, offscreen. I recognized two words of it from chatter in the Zone, and the translation provided the grammar. The Russian girl looked down at the data console and frantically tried to do something. It must not have worked, because she let out a helpless cry. A blur, a shudder, and she fell away.

Then the wall behind her shattered open, a sucking, gaping hole into space, and the smoke that had been hanging in the air vented out in a thick, twisting rope that snaked out and left nothing behind.

The air, I thought, and gripped the edges of the workbench tight enough I felt a sting. *The air just got sucked out.* And though I hadn't seen her disappear, she must have been pulled out with it. There was no movement, no sound. The hole slowly closed up. It took long, silent minutes.

The vid stopped. I felt hollow and sick.

Nadim finally said, "I fell asleep."

I spun around and faced the wall, as if he was standing there. As if he wasn't all around me. "What *happened*?"

"We were in the black," he said. "The black between stars. Off the course we should have followed, but I thought—I thought that the alternate route would be more interesting. I was very young, and it was too far between stars. I . . . I could not ration my energy so far. I fell asleep."

Trying to understand, I asked, "What's so bad about sleeping?"

"For you, it's a quiet period, but for us, it can be more. Deeper."

"Like hibernation?'

He considered the word before answering, "Like that, yes. That was the first time I fell into a very deep, unplanned sleep; it is a failing that is rare among my kind. I never realized it could be dangerous until then. But my Honors didn't know how to wake me, and . . . several meteorites pierced my skin. By the time I'd healed and woken, it was—it was too late. The system that provided them with air had been damaged and took too long to heal."

"When . . . when was this?"

"My third voyage," he said quietly. "I am very careful now to stay to the approved routes, where I know I will receive enough light. On the Tour, I don't stray too far into the black. But I am graduating soon, so I have asked for this device. You must complete it. Before I take the Journey, it will be installed, and when I fall asleep, it will shock me awake. An alarm, to protect my Honors."

A wave of grief swelled, crashing down, closing on me from all sides—Nadim's guilt. It was easier to sense his emotions when I touched him, but this was powerful enough that even without contact, it felt like being coated in ashes, in a thick, choking pall of utter sadness. This story hadn't been circulated by the media; that was damn sure. The Honors program must have compensated the families for the loss and quietly swept the tragedy under the rug. Way before my time.

"I was so *young*," he said. "And I will never let it happen again. That's why this is important, Zara. That's why you *must* do the work. Please."

I could hardly breathe under that crushing burden. Nadim's guilt hadn't faded, though this must have happened decades ago.

I put a hand against the wall. Not a conscious decision. Comfort. One wasn't enough. I put both hands there, leaning toward him. His emotions came through even more clearly, and it was everything I could do not to weep for him. "It wasn't your fault. Everybody sleeps. Even Leviathan, right?"

"I should only go into a dark sleep when it is safe to do so. It was my responsibility. I can't fail again," he said.

I didn't even know why I did it. Maybe just because I needed to. But I bent forward and rested my cheek against the wall. I felt a pulse of something like surprise, then relief, then a rush of something very complicated bolt through me and through him too.

The choking grief slowly eased away, replaced by something like . . . wonder.

"It's . . . less. You made it *less*."

I didn't ask if he meant the grief or the guilt, mostly because I was basking in the unique pleasure of making things better with just a touch. With just *caring*. For a few seconds, we floated together, just streaming that inexplicable connection. Quietly I pushed off, out of—what was that? An embrace?—and picked up my H2.

Sometimes I wasn't sure what questions would bother him. "Is it some kind of genetic condition? I mean, with all your advances—"

"Yes, it is linked to a mutation. Because of it, when I am awake, I am much better at channeling energy in a crisis than most of my kind. Everyone has strengths and weaknesses. You probably don't know why Beatriz is good at math and you prefer more practical concepts."

He had a point. "Well, she's studied more, and I *do* have a knack with gadgets."

"Among my kind, having this . . . mutation can be seen as something that could disqualify me from taking the Journey. But if I make this modification, it should convince the Elder that I can manage my condition appropriately." Nadim paused, like maybe this was a gray area.

"I've got it." The way I read it, this sleep issue was along the lines of a disability. So this was an accommodation, not a fix.

"I need this to keep you safe," he said. "Will you do as I ask now?"

"Depends."

"Zara!"

"Is there an off switch?"

He sighed. "Yes, because all Leviathan must enter the dark sleep at least a few times in their life. The device is built with a code that will allow it to be disabled under certain conditions of safety. It must only be used when I am bathed in starlight, and there are no other risk factors. I will place this code in the records. Is that acceptable?"

"Then absolutely."

It was grueling work, requiring both technical comprehension and physical dexterity, but I was in my wheelhouse. I blazed through the assembly, and I found a few things to add on as I went, including a second, hidden off switch—a mechanical one. I didn't always trust beamed code. If Nadim needed to enter that deeper sleep state, and the damn shock collar wouldn't let him, then there needed to be a backup.

But I didn't tell him, because I knew he'd object to me modding the design. I skipped lunch and kept working, flying through progress steps, all the way to the testing phase.

I left the diagnostics running and went to dinner, feeling sweaty, exhausted, and exhilarated all at once. I'd finished *two days* ahead of schedule.

Take that, bottom of the class.

※

After dinner, since I was done with my to-do list, I sat down in front of the data console and absently said, "Hey, Nadim? Are you tied in to this device?"

"Of course," he said. "I provide it with power."

"Yeah, I mean . . . can you read the data on it?"

"I can, but I don't normally. It is for your use, organized in human structures."

"Okay. Mind if I poke around a little in past records?"

"I don't mind. The recordings are there to help you. There is nothing in there forbidden to you."

Digging around in the data proved to be fun. I was no Conde, but I'd rehabbed enough times to understand how to find the stuff people buried in their data sets. Which was how I unearthed the coded personal journal of one Marko Dunajski. Recording our thoughts was encouraged "for posterity" but not mandatory, which was good, because I was pretty sure I didn't want to have my thoughts out there for anyone to see.

I figured Marko's entry would be gold from the beginning, because he looked *grumpy*. "I'm going to record, please ignore me," he said, which I thought was a strange way to start, until I heard Nadim's voice on the recording say, "Of course, Marko." Marko chugged more coffee and set the cup aside. Rubbed his face like he might scrape his features off.

"I thought . . . I don't know what I thought." His tone surprised me. When he had me on the recruitment trail, he'd seemed so confident that I figured these would play like propaganda films. Instead I had Marko, uncut and unkempt. "Okay, let me start again. When I was chosen as an Honor, it was the happiest day of my life. I thought I was prepared. Before getting on the shuttle, I read all the previous Honor biographies and interviews with people who were alone on space stations, and I watched vids about the first settlers on Mars. I understood that we're partners with our Leviathan in training during the Tour. But once the fanfare and celebration stops, it's . . . a sobering responsibility. How does it make sense that somebody like me has been sent on a mission like this? I'm not a scientist. I am a *musician*."

Somebody like me. The words caught my attention and tugged because I'd been wondering the same thing.

"What we've seen out here, it's marvelous. Unbelievable. So many civilizations that no longer exist, because they've destroyed themselves. Nadim doesn't say it, but I think the reason they show these places to us is to explain why they take such an interest in humans. We're here now. We *exist*. And we were going to destroy ourselves when they first met us and end up another cautionary tale on the Tour. I suspect the Leviathan couldn't stand to see it happen again. He says that the two who made contact were on their own, responding because they couldn't ignore the cries of the wounded in the dark. That has a certain . . .

beauty." Marko's voice changed. Grew darker and rougher. "And I'm sure Nadim believes the story. But I'm not sure I do any longer. There are things that don't make sense out here. Things he avoids talking about, or can't tell us. There are mysteries in the dark too."

So, like me, Marko wasn't all sunshine and flowers. He had an edge I'd never suspected. Good. It made me like him better. And his words put me more on my guard too. *Mysteries in the dark.*

"Still, for all that . . . This is going to sound stupid, but I'm just talking to myself, aren't I? There are people who study the stars their whole lives and never get to soar among them. I can't help feeling that I didn't deserve this chance, but I intend to make the most of this experience. I'm going to learn everything I can and make my family proud. And maybe . . . maybe I will go on the Journey, if the Leviathan give me a chance. Solve the real mysteries. Finally explain once and for all what the Leviathan want from us . . . or want us to learn from them."

Maybe it wasn't meant for me at all, but that message arrowed straight into my heart. *Make my family proud,* he'd said, and I realized that I desperately wanted that. My family and I, we were like passengers on trains heading in the same direction but on parallel tracks. I loved my mother and Kiz. Maybe we'd never be like a regular family, but if I could make them proud of me, of something I accomplished—that would be . . . good.

But I also had to take Marko's doubts seriously. I'd come on board thinking about Valenzuela and his incoherent warning; Nadim had soothed that jitter out of me, but this made me think, again, about what we weren't being told. What *mysteries* the Leviathan kept.

"The thing is," Marko continued, "I'm not sure I'll be chosen. Nadim seems to need more interaction than he gets from me. Certainly he's not getting it from Chao-Xing. It helps when I play for him. The Leviathan are musical from their core; I think that's one thing that fascinates them about us, our ability to summon up our own songs, even though we aren't born from the same culture. Even though we can't hear what they do. I like Nadim, but I feel we're not . . . not a good fit. He has just one more try at finding someone who fits with him before he goes out into the black. I hope—I hope someone next year works. If they don't, he'll either be matched for a long time with someone who isn't on his frequency, or he'll be alone out there. I don't like to imagine that."

I wasn't sure exactly what Marko was talking about, but it was sad to consider Nadim setting off on the Journey unhappy. He had a real yearning to bond with people, or at least, that was what I sensed in him. He was lonely. More lonely than anybody I'd ever met.

It occurred to me that this was pretty rude, listening

to Marko talk about Nadim and his shortcomings when Nadim was bound to have heard all of it. Marko, after all, had made a point of asking Nadim not to listen when he was recording. Leaning back in my chair, I said, "Um, Nadim?"

No answer. I had an awful thought that he was so bothered by Marko's observations that he didn't want to talk to me at all . . . but then I reached out and touched the wall and tried again. "Nadim?"

"I'm here," he said.

"Were you listening?"

"No," he said. "It was a private record. I don't listen to those. It isn't polite." There was a certain precision to his response that made me smile.

"Let me guess. Somebody yelled at you before for spying on them."

"I've had dozens of Honors aboard. Most of them have yelled at me when they became frustrated or felt they had no privacy. I don't take that personally, most of the time."

Most of the time. That got me curious, made me want to ask.

I didn't.

From a transcript of a research interview between **Dr. Elacio Camacho** *and* **Leviathan Moira,** *conducted aboard the Leviathan, 2112*

CAMACHO: May I play you a sample of how we interpret the sounds that stars make, Moira?

MOIRA: I would like that.

CAMACHO plays a recording.

MOIRA: That is a very limited interpretation, Dr. Camacho. It is only sound. There is no life in it.

CAMACHO: It's only a digital interpolation based on the shifts of light frequencies. We find it useful for various calculations.

MOIRA: It makes the stars sound very stupid.

CAMACHO: [pause] Are . . . you saying that the stars are intelligent?

MOIRA: Creatures of your planet sing. I sing. The stars sing. Who am I to believe they are not singing on purpose?

CHAPTER EIGHT

Breaking the Peace

THE SILENCE THAT followed as I hovered near the data console might have been awkward. I supposed that our connection let him sense my lingering curiosity. "Did you . . . want something else?" Nadim asked me. "There are more recordings. I could leave you to play them in private."

"No, I'm done." I yawned. "Maybe I should just go to bed."

"If you prefer. Or you could proceed to the media room. Beatriz is singing."

"She's what?"

"Singing. She is quite accomplished, though I believe she underestimates her talent."

"Did she say it's okay to listen?"

Instead of answering, Nadim lit up a pulse on the corridor wall for me to follow.

Halfway there, I heard her, a quiet voice, then louder, stronger. I didn't know the song. I didn't go into the media room, but I peeked in and saw Bea standing on the stage, her eyes shut, her face lit with transcendent joy as she sang and sang, the notes soaring with pure and perfect beauty.

It was like the starlight. Like the dizzying black beauty of space. It was free and fierce and full of longing. It was so far beyond me I felt lifted on it, taken out of myself.

Nadim said, in a whisper meant just for me, "It's the most beautiful thing I've ever heard. Other Honors played music or sang, but she . . . she's different." There was awe in his voice. Awe all around me, like a cool, shifting fog.

Beatriz sang a long time before she paused. Since this wasn't a concert, I got up and headed over to her. Following my impulses had gotten me into more trouble than I could list, but I hugged her anyway—the kind of hug you give when somebody surprises you with a gift so special you never even knew you wanted it until you opened it.

She let out a little squeak, and then she squeezed me back. "My *vó* would be pleased with me. For bringing her music to the stars."

"Your *vó*?"

"My grandma. She was an opera singer at the Teatro

Real," Beatriz said. "Very famous, in her day. She sang to me all the time, and I studied music as well—but I was always afraid of being onstage. So I've always sung just for her. And for me."

"Nadim should broadcast you. The whole universe should hear that gorgeous voice."

She gave me a smile so radiant that I understood at once how different she must be back home in Rio. "I don't know about that, but thank you. The acoustics in here are so perfect, I might not sound so wonderful somewhere else—"

"Don't even," I cut in. "You're special. Get used to it."

"She's right, Beatriz. Thank you." Nadim sounded soft, warm, almost shy. "I've never heard anything like it."

Beatriz, I noticed, raised her head when she was talking to Nadim. "You built a pool for your last Honor. Did you design this place for me?"

"Not specifically. Marko played piano here. I altered the space a little for you."

"Yeah, about that," I said. "You made a pool. You made a concert hall. How, exactly?"

"The pool was easy. I can grow or shrink open chambers within my body, and the filtering of water was just a special organ I grew for that purpose. Like creating and filtering the air you breathe."

"Okay, fine, you grew a room—" Weird as that was. "But you didn't grow the chairs!"

"No," he agreed. "Those I requested from Earth. An accommodation for you."

Beatriz laughed. "I don't even care how you did it! I didn't have my own stage at home. I worked on music in my room and sang in the shower."

"Then I hope this is better?"

"This is magnificent. It's a little . . . overwhelming." From her tone, I didn't think she meant it in a bad way.

"What was that, the first thing you sang?" I asked her. Because I'd never heard anything like it.

That turned out to be the magic question. Beatriz was into opera, and she elaborated for a while about composers and history, more of a musical education than I'd gotten in school. Then she bit her lip, seeming as if she was about to confess to some shocking secret. "Sometimes I dabble with my own arrangements. I did a jazz adaptation of *La Bohème* for fun last month."

That sounded impressive as hell. And it sparked my curiosity, because I'd noticed a few different qualifications that stood out among the Honors over the past few years. More recruits had a musical background. Marko did. Now here was Beatriz, who sang so brilliantly.

There has to be a reason they picked her. And me. Since we were bonding over music, I kept the questions coming. "Do you have a favorite opera?"

"*Norma.* You ever heard of it?" she asked me, and when

I shook my head, she said, "Nadim, do we have a music library on board?"

"Of course. Each Honor has added to it. What would you like to hear?"

She enjoyed Caribbean fusion, insanely dramatic opera, reggaetón, Afro-Cuban jazz. While I didn't love everything she called out, I could *feel* Nadim soaking up the input, registered the moments when a particular cluster of notes gave him pleasure. Nadim especially liked the merry blare of horns, and I knew that because it washed in an irresistible flush of pleasure that cascaded over to me. Like emotional overflow. I wondered if I could control that. If I should. *Sure, this feels good. But what happens when it goes bad?*

Beatriz distracted me. Her expression animated, she asked, "What do *you* like, Zara?"

"Well, I don't know much, but . . . there was this old-time singer, Billie Holiday? I relate to her music, I guess. And her story. You heard of her?"

"*Claro.*" She grabbed my hands in her excitement. "She was a legend. What's your favorite song of hers?"

"That's a tough call. But I guess . . . 'Summertime.'"

"I have it," Nadim said. "Shall I play that one?"

"Please." Normally, the word didn't come easy, but I'd revealed an important part of myself; my mother and Kiz and I had all listened to Billie Holiday together. This time,

I didn't feel scraped raw over it, because I wasn't listening alone.

What started out as Music Appreciation 101 evolved into a proper party. Beatriz taught me dance moves to the beat of some of Nadim's favorite jams. The girl definitely had rhythm, and soon I was executing complicated steps that could've been on a stage backing up some auto-tune diva. The sheer joy of it took me over—and not just me, I noticed. Nadim too was soaking up our enthusiasm, our happiness, our energy. It seemed like a good thing.

If we could join together this way, I felt solid about our chances at making this partnership work.

Beatriz finally wandered off to bed, and even though I was tired, I lingered behind.

"That was fun," I said, more to myself than Nadim. It had been. Better than anything except a few times back in the Zone, and that made it impossible not to think of Derry. I had some shit times with him, some outstanding moments too. Now I also had the bitter memory of the way he'd burned me.

It cooled me down, got me steady. My natural defenses came back up again. I had to be practical, even if I didn't need to be ruthless. That meant I had to wonder if Nadim and Beatriz would do me the same way Derry had, eventually. I'd liked Clarice for a hot second back in rehab, and look where that had got me.

The memory of rehab, and of the dirty purity of the

Zone, crept back in. *That* Zara wouldn't have held a dance party. *That* Zara would have grinned and slipped away to rip off the marks while their defenses were down.

I wasn't one of them, I had to remember that. Beatriz had trained to be an Honor. Nadim . . . I could feel a lot of what went on with him, but how could I really know what he thought or felt? He was *an alien*. It might feel like I knew him, but I didn't. I couldn't.

It surprised me when the alien suddenly spoke up and said, "You and Beatriz are . . . brighter than Marko and Chao-Xing."

"Brighter?" That was weird. "You mean smarter?"

"No. I mean—you have more light inside. Both of you."

It was the opposite of how I'd been trying to feel. Darkness was cover. Darkness was safety. "Yeah, probably just adrenaline or something."

A pause, as he was probably thinking about how to respond. Or if he even should. "No. It's dimmed a little now in you, but you are still bright. Marko was the closest, kind but somber. He was always a little muted. You and Beatriz are different."

"So no dance party with Marko and Chao-Xing?"

"Definitely not."

With Nadim talking as I walked, it felt like he was seeing me to my room. *I don't need watching over*, I wanted to tell him, but at the same time, it felt good. Safe. "Okay, well, I'm out." Because I was at my door. And I suddenly realized I was bone-tired anyway.

Nadim said, "Sleep well. I'll see you in the morning, Zara."

I fumbled with the panel. The life I'd chosen in the Zone didn't grant privacy; freedom had its price. I'd gotten used to sleeping in overcrowded dorms or public squats, with people doing whatever all around. I hadn't really thought about it, but now I realized that privacy felt like isolation. "So you don't come in here without an invitation, right?"

"No," he said. "Unless you are in medical distress."

"Well, you're officially invited."

"As long as you're sure. You can tell me to leave anytime."

I sat down cross-legged on the mattress, fiddling with a pillow. I left the door open, through some bizarre notion that it made it easier for Nadim to get in and out. "I didn't want to freak Bea out; she seems to be finding her peace and I don't want to blow that. But you need to explain some things to me."

"Such as?"

"Why did you pick me?" I immediately rephrased. "Okay, I know *you* didn't pick me. Why are the Elders all of a sudden yanking crims out of rehab?"

He didn't answer for so long I didn't think he was going to. I had an impulse to pull the pillow in closer, and instead, I put it down and waited.

Finally, Nadim said, "The Elders began by choosing

scholars and mathematicians, and for a while, that was what was needed. But now they think we need different strengths."

"Different how?"

"I don't know why they picked you, Zara, but you clearly have many qualities that will be of use."

So now they need tech-savvy and a scrappy attitude? Sure. "I'm a good mechanic, but you could get that anywhere. What else?"

"I can only tell you that when the Elders find there are gaps in our knowledge, in our needs, we seek those that can fill them." He seemed uncomfortable now. His tone had gone flatter, and the warmth of his presence had dialed down to room temp.

"You want to hear what I think? I think there's more to this than cultural exchanges and bullshit like that. You're picking our brains. My question is, why? Why do you need to learn from *me*?"

"What's wrong with you?"

"I'm not hearing a denial, Nadim."

"I wouldn't ask my partners to do anything that wasn't for the greater good."

"Psht. Maybe in Leviathan speech that plays better, but let me tell you, back on Earth, a ton of humans have murdered for the *greater good*. And I'm not here for it."

"I suppose then the question is: Why *are* you here, Zara?

If you don't believe in the mission of our partnership?"

"Because—" I hesitated, and smoothed the fabric of my uniform over my thigh. There was a scar there, one of many from fights in the Zone. Reminders that safety was an illusion. "Because it's a way out."

"Out of what?"

"Everything that shuts me in."

Nadim was quiet for a moment, and then he said, "I don't understand that. I don't think I can. My whole life has been seeking contact, not escape. And I live in . . . a very large space. In that way we are quite opposite."

"Good. This would get pretty boring if we were all the same."

I felt that flutter of amusement again, a kind of unfiltered delight that made the pull of artificial gravity feel lighter. Too much of that, and I might lose my own weight. I resisted the lure of feeding his feelings, and the delight faded. Then Nadim said, very seriously, "I can't tell you what waits out there for us, if that's what you want to know. We call this year-long voyage the Tour; we take you to predetermined places where you will gather geologic and biologic samples and evidence of defunct civilizations for your scientists to analyze. For us, we chart the regrowth of the destruction and hope to someday witness a civilization rise again. But this route is familiar to us. Safe. I've told you before that I'm still in training. I'm not to deviate from our itinerary until I am released for the Journey."

"Okay. So if all this is preparing you for the Journey, then what happens on the Journey?"

Silence fell, and it seemed heavier than before. Emotional gravity, shifting again. Finally, Nadim said, "The Journey is a mission that lasts a lifetime. And I won't know what it is until I am ready."

"So you trust them that much."

"The Elders would not betray us."

I didn't tell him that on Earth, it was our elders who sold us out all the damn time—that the young were sacrificed for whatever cause, whatever war our old leaders thought important at the time. I'd trusted my father, once. I'd ended up pinned to a table, with a crazy woman holding a scalpel.

Trust your elders didn't cut it with me.

After all, at this point, whatever hurt Nadim would mess me up too—during the Tour, but still. I had to make him realize that trust had to be earned, not just given.

Part of me pretended it was just self-interest, but deep inside, I also had to admit that there was something so unguardedly honest about Nadim that I just . . . wanted him to be safe.

"Sure," I finally said. "But you know the old Russian proverb, right?"

"I do not."

"When the storm comes, pray to God, but row for

shore." A nicer way to say *don't be a mark.*

He thought that one over. I put Billie Holiday on my H2. She was singing a different song this time, and I had to explain what it meant to him. Explain the shit my people had gone through and still did sometimes. He didn't comment, but his mood shifted, soaking up the buried outrage, sadness, and horror hidden in the notes of the music.

Nadim and I listened to her voice, and sometime in there, I stretched out on my bed and drifted off, and I forgot to tell him to get out of my room.

I slept the best I ever had on the soft, warm mattress, with the whisper of Nadim's presence like a mist near me. I'd learned how to sense him, whether he was paying attention to me or not. It felt a little like a memory I had of my parents watching over me. Of sleeping with my crew in the Zone, knowing they were there if anything kicked off.

Safe.

I dreamed of stars.

Like Nadim, I drank the light and felt their radiance on my skin. Unchained from my flesh, I flew like a Leviathan—stars and galaxies spun around me in a kaleidoscope of colors—and the pleasure that roared through me nearly cracked my skull.

And then I felt alone. So alone. It was a void that sucked all the life and love out of me, a dark longing so profound it *hurt.*

Trembling, I woke with morning light streaming in my window. Damn, there was no morning. No window. Nadim must have turned the lights up in my room. At least he hadn't banged the alarm gong this time.

I felt breathless and strangely sad. On the verge of tears. And, oddly, I didn't think it was Nadim, or at least, not completely. Following my first instinct, I fumbled for the intercom. "Bea?" The short form of her name slid out, and she didn't object. "You okay?"

"I'm . . . here. Just got up."

"You sound . . ." I didn't know if I should say it, but her voice came across tremulous. "Have you been crying?"

"A little. I'm sorry."

"Don't be. What's wrong?"

"There's a word in Portuguese, *saudade*, it doesn't translate well."

"What does that mean?"

"It's like nostalgia, only . . . more. Longing for something."

"Something that's gone away?" I guessed. I knew that feeling, *saudade*. During that dream, it permeated me from head to toe, which was batshit. I'd felt it. And so had Beatriz.

"Yes," she said. "How could you know that? Are you saying you felt it too?"

"I think it's coming from Nadim. Sometimes I can feel what he's feeling." *Crap.* I should have said that before now; I hadn't been keeping it from her deliberately, but in a sense, I'd relished it being a tiny secret, too.

"You—you what?" She sounded less offended than baffled, which was good. "We're not supposed to do that, Zara. They said—"

"Yeah, yeah, I know all that. I look like some tight-ass rule follower to you?"

She just shook her head. "Why is Nadim sad?"

"No idea. Nadim!" No answer. I put my hand to the wall by the bed. "Nadim!"

"Good morning, Zara." He sounded all right. Probably *too* much so, as if he was working at it. "It's time to get up."

"Are you okay?" I asked. I felt his answer coming through the wall, into my skin, a wave of emotion, of sadness, of loss. It made me shiver. "Nadim?"

"I'm well," he said. "Thank you." He was pretending to be fine so hard that I could feel the strain of it vibrating through his skin.

"You don't have to put on an act," I told him quietly. "Not with me. Not with us. What is it?"

He was silent a long time, so long I thought he'd gone away except that I could still feel his emotional presence. He finally said, "I'm fine, Zara. Beatriz, please don't be alarmed. I had—what you would call a bad dream, I think. So we will put that behind us now." His tone sharpened into briskness again. "Now. Zara, you've completed your tasks for today, which is why—"

"Hey, if I didn't have work you could've let me sleep in." Right now, acting like I didn't know something was up with him was the best gift I could offer to keep him on track. I was an old pro at pretending to be okay.

"—why I have reconfigured your schedule," he finished. "You'll be learning navigation today. In the event it falls to either of you to pilot, you must be able to back Beatriz up."

"Don't you pilot yourself? I mean . . . it's who you are, right?"

"In case of *emergency*. Please get ready. You are due on duty in one hour."

The H2 on the table next to me chimed and scrolled with instructions. With a scowl, I picked it up. "Really? A full day on navigational drills? You're a jerk," I said, and he laughed, a bright silver burst. I felt the pulse of his amusement run from the crown of my head down through my toes, in a singular shiver. "You understood that? Who taught you slang, anyway?"

"You all do," he said. "I learn from each one of you. Some more than others."

"Yeah, I'm colorful as shit. Nadim?"

"Yes?"

"Get out of my room."

The shower was phenomenal, better if I didn't think too hard about the filtration system. My Honors haircut hadn't grown out, so I freshened my curls with some leave-in conditioner and finishing oil. The WHSC had stocked the stores up with everything I'd need for the year, so I didn't even need to skimp to make it stretch. I moisturized my brown skin too, no getting ashy in space; the lotion was perfect, and it made my skin feel like it was sighing in relief. Finally, with a faint flicker of pride, I dressed in my uniform and met Bea for breakfast. For her, a double espresso, and I made a bowl of oatmeal.

As we ate, we compared lists. I was supposed to learn how to accurately chart a course using the data interface by the end of the day, with various goals to measure my progress. The prospect was daunting.

"Do you feel prepared?" I asked Bea. Because hers had something to do with attending to some experiments that were going to be underway during our journey, courtesy of various Earth labs and scientists. It all looked very complicated.

Her laugh came out tinged with panic. "Not remotely."

"We got this." It was becoming second nature to reassure her, and I didn't hate the feeling when she smiled and offered me a fist bump on her way out. I didn't understand it. *I'm not a trusting person.* So what, she could sing, she was nice, she made a good cup of coffee. I wasn't used to sharing my space with anyone I didn't know well. What was making me befriend her? I kept coming back to Clarice.

When I turned my back on Bea, was she going to slip a cord over my head?

Why would she? some calmer part of my brain asked me. *She's got no beef with you. Just be normal for a while.*

Normal. Sure. Or maybe this wasn't normal at all. I could feel Nadim's moods. Maybe that closeness was bringing down defenses I'd spent years building, brick by brick. *Got to fight to keep your distance, Z. If you let him in any more, you'll have no defense at all.* Because why would I trust an *alien*? A ship who could get in my head, mess with my moods? One who could, if he got really angry, blow me out into space? I depended on him for air and water and food. That was one hell of a lot of trust to ask me to give.

So I made it a mission to ignore Nadim for the day. Completely. I threw myself into the data console like it was a game I was determined to win. I was crap at 3D math, but I was good at visualization, at least. It took me four hours to develop the ability to *see* the course in 3D space, and then another two to figure out how to enter all the coordinates.

Then levels of difficulty started up. First, varying gravitational influences from close-in stars. Then a hidden black hole. Then fuel warnings; Nadim wasn't infinitely powered, he needed regular infusions of starlight to be able to keep moving. He had to keep his courses close enough to star systems to angle his solar sails and catch the energy, or he'd go dark, like he'd shown me in the video.

So plotting courses wasn't as simple as getting from one spot to another. It was more like tacking with the wind on an ocean, judging just how far your food and water would take you.

The last level of simulations put us through a meteor field, and I couldn't keep the images out of my head of the Russian girl on the bridge, of the fog, the choking coughs, the blood. The whispering, silky rope of air fraying away into space, and Nadim waking up somewhere injured and alone with his dead.

I couldn't get the sim right. I tried and tried, pushed myself until it was clear I wasn't *going* to get it right, and then I shoved back from the console and let out a frustrated yell. I wanted to punch a wall, not Nadim. So I hit the metal side of the console, which hurt me a lot more.

After a long, panting silence, Nadim said, quietly, "Your heart rate is quite elevated, Zara. Do you need help? Shall I get Beatriz?"

"No," I snapped. "Leave me alone."

I grabbed the H2 and checked to see what was next. One level I hadn't conquered wouldn't matter much, I hoped. I was scheduled for a tour of the medical facilities, which were mostly automated and featured a doc bot that could be activated for emergencies. When I went in, Beatriz was coming out, wearing a mischievous grin. I didn't ask what that was about, just worked my way through the entire rotation, making sure I knew where every drug was kept, every medical instrument. I didn't activate the doc bot. I remembered how they worked from med clinics in Paradise, and my hand wasn't that bad. I was used to punching things.

I joined Beatriz for dinner, and she first proposed we watch a holo. Afterward, we played a combat sim game. Once I'd soundly beaten her two out of three rounds in the sim, I said I was tired and went to my quarters.

I'd just opened the door when Nadim said, "What am I doing wrong, Zara?"

"Nothing," I said. "Look. Just let me be, okay?"

The pain I caused him wasn't something he intended to share. I could tell, because it was just a brush, a whisper, quickly gone. But it was breathtaking.

I stopped on my way into the room. I didn't apologize, because I couldn't; I just put my hand slowly out and touched the wall. "Nadim . . . I feel like you—*this*—is changing me," I told him. "Making me forget to be who I am."

"I don't know what you mean."

"I'm not friendly. I'm not trusting. I don't *like people*."

"But you like me. And Beatriz."

"That's my *point*!"

"You think I'm doing something to you," he said. I didn't deny it, and I felt that hurt again, distant and almost hidden. "I'm not. But still, you don't trust me."

"I don't trust anybody." *Not true. I trusted Derry, once.* But look where that got me.

"Then how can you live, so alone?"

The question hurt, because it sounded so bewildered. It made me want to fire back an angry justification, but I swallowed that and said, "Safe. I live safe."

"But alone."

"I thought Leviathan traveled alone most of their lives. So what?"

"We're never isolated. Not completely. The stars sing. Even planets sing. And we sing to one another, across the long reaches, for comfort." He fell silent for a few seconds, and then said, "If you want me to stay away from you, then I will. It's difficult, because you are so—"

"Bright?" I said, a little bitterly.

"Loud," he clarified, which made me smile a moment. I deserved that. "I'm not changing you, Zara. You were a seed, surrounded by hard shell and stony ground. Now you can grow any direction you wish. I will leave you alone until you see that."

Alone suddenly didn't have as much appeal. I imagined walking through this space and *not* feeling Nadim around me, *not* talking to him or having him talk to me. I wondered how Chao-Xing did that for a whole year. It would break me.

"I don't want that either," I said. "And I don't know why."

"I think there's something in you like me," Nadim said. His voice was quiet, and I felt he was *looking* at me. *Seeing* me. "Like tuned strings, we vibrate to the same frequency."

Music, again. And it felt right to hear him say that. "Yeah, well, probably the biotech patch they put in my head when I was a kid. Right?"

"That's possible."

"It's just that I need to stay myself. Make sure what I'm feeling is really me. You get that?"

"Yes, Zara. I do. I—" He hesitated, and I felt the uncertainty again. "I don't know how much communication with you is too much. Is this?"

"No." It felt a little too good, a light, gentle flicker of emotion, like light against my skin. I imagined him turning down a dimmer switch on his broadcast. "That's okay. But when I say back off—"

"Then I will," he said, and instantly, he *left*, and I was drowning in cold silence. I hadn't realized how accustomed I'd gotten to the sense of his presence. His absence was . . . shocking.

I pressed my hand on the wall. "Nadim? Come back?" He did, and it felt like some anxious knot in my chest eased. I didn't invite him into my room again—it seemed wrong—so I went outside and sank down against the wall and sat there, legs out blocking the corridor. "How did your people ever learn to get along with us? Did they teach you in school?"

He sighed. Actually *sighed*. "Zara, we are not *like you*. We don't have a homeworld. We don't have buildings where we learn. *This* is my school. Here. With you. I learn by making mistakes. Don't you?"

"So many," I said, and leaned my head back against the wall. "And I'm going to make a hell of a lot more."

"As am I," he said. "But perhaps we can learn from them together."

"When do we get a day off?" I asked on Day-I'd-Lost-Count of work. Working *sucked*. I'd discovered that in the Lower Eight, where I occasionally turned my hand to honest labor. It hadn't taken me long to figure out that I'd rather lift a purse or a wallet than scrub toilets. Up here, though, there were no shortcuts.

There was, on this day, a seemingly endless list of repairs to make to the equipment of the human-built section of the ship.

"Days off are a human concept," he said. "Careful of that part, please. It's delicate."

Putting the thin, breakable data module down, I cursed under my breath, and he asked me what the words meant. I told him. Somehow, it wasn't as satisfying when you had to explain the mechanics of it, and all Nadim said about my definition was that it seemed strange. I guessed it would, to a being without sexual organs as humans understood them.

I was on my back inside a console, checking circuits to make sure everything was working properly, since Nadim had reported a glitch in the interface. Well, what he'd *actually* said was that one part of the console had gone deaf. But I interpreted that to mean something had burned out. It took me an hour of patient testing to find it, which was ratshit nonsense; diagnostics hadn't caught it at all and should have. I was still cursing when I crawled out from the dark, cramped space and braced myself against the wall to stand up.

"You did that on purpose!" I didn't think about the accusation—well, I hardly ever did—but more than that, I didn't know *why I said it*. Just that it was true. "What was that, a test? Did you screw the diagnostics too?" Without thinking, I sent the question out like a wave, trying to find out.

I got a shock back. It felt like a thin electric zap, nothing to damage, only to surprise. I snatched my hand away from contact with the wall—with his skin—and Nadim said, "That was just a reminder that you wanted more distance between us." He *could* hold a grudge. Interesting. "And I didn't do anything to the diagnostics. Why would you think I had?"

"*Such* a jerk."

"I've made you angry," he said. "You burn so . . . *warm*." There was something about the way he said that word that made my breath hitch. It was something I noticed about *him* . . . the tone in his voice, the heat of the walls within him. *You're reading into it*, I told myself. But I remembered the dream that had so unsettled me—Nadim's nightmare of being sealed alone in the cold, a lonely and desolate scream in the night.

No wonder he longed for warmth. No wonder I did too. All those long nights out in the Zone, running from my own nightmares and believing I was free. Weird, to come all the way out here into the black and find someone who understood me so well. Who wasn't even human.

Without even thinking about it, I blurted the next thing that occurred to me. "You *did* mess with the console."

There it was, an unmistakable pulse of surprise. And guilt. "How do you know that?"

"It's not my fault you're thinking so hard you're leaking into my head!"

"Zara, I wasn't thinking about it at all," he said. "That's the problem. You are . . . difficult to keep out. And I'm trying."

My mouth went dry, suddenly, and I rubbed my palm against the nu-silk of my uniform. "But—"

"It's difficult for me to keep things from you. I don't know why. I've never had this problem before."

"So I'm a problem."

"It's not the same thing, Zara."

Sure. Like I hadn't heard that one a million times.

I put the handheld tester back into the toolbox and

had the satisfaction of slamming the lid shut. Not very many things around here I could slam. The sound echoed through the chamber, and I kicked the metal housing of the data console for good measure.

His voice flattened. "If you're finished with the repairs, there are other tasks on your list."

"I'm ahead of schedule," I pointed out.

I'd learned something from this exchange, at least. Nadim could lie. And I could tell when he did. Since I was good and pissed about that reveal, I headed to the VR room to burn some anger. I scrolled through a lot of the standard game stuff, quests, and puzzles, and stopped on the combat sims.

I tapped that, fast, and got a dizzying array of options, from standard martial arts to cage fighting to guns and knives and half a dozen more weapons. I hadn't looked at all the choices before. *Damn.* Somebody knew how to party. I suspected it was Chao-Xing. I started out on the midlevel, just to get warmed up, on the cage match, and ended up in a startlingly realistic VR sim that gave me convincing biofeedback on punches, chokes, and throws. No bruises or broken bones, and Nadim's spongy floor came in handy for a fall mat.

It felt madly great. I dialed up the level to expert and went at it. Then, when I'd won two and lost the third, I swapped for an opponent with a knife. Then one with a gun in a realistic street setting. The bullets, I learned, *hurt.*

But I didn't get killed. Not once.

Sim was just what I needed to clear the cobwebs and confusion, get me back in my own skin again.

Nadim didn't tell me to get to work; I showered and returned to task myself. While I was kicking ass and taking names, more orders had appeared on my H2, sending me back to the same workroom where I'd assembled the shock device. Without a word, I went there and checked until I found the project number. Another huge rolling bin, and it was subnumbered.

Since Nadim can't work with components like this, humans brought this tech on board at some point. Maybe Marko or Chao-Xing?

I stepped back and looked at the rows of enormous bins. This one was number ten of a series that stretched all the way to fifteen. When I pulled the tabs, the sides fell away to reveal another enormous, mysterious device— larger than the last, towering over me by a good two meters at its highest point. It reminded me of something I'd seen before, at a distance, but completely outsized. *Is it an engine?* No, that wasn't right, though it had some aerodynamic sweep to it.

Took me a few moments to figure out it was a weapon. Laser cannon, missile delivery, I didn't know, but whatever it was, it was *militant*. And from the size of this thing—it wasn't meant for any drone.

There are weapons here, and they're having us assemble them. No. They were having *me* assemble them. Beatriz hadn't set foot in here at all. Maybe this was the kind of shit that Gregory Valenzuela couldn't adapt to, and I wasn't down with it either. In the Zone, I had been great at crafting new gear out of parts I scavenged, so a picture of why they needed me was starting to form.

This time, I didn't ask Nadim about what I found. I just sealed up the device, rolled it back into place, and checked the task off on my list. I'd find out what this was about. Nadim wasn't the one with the answers. I wasn't sure who was; maybe I was going to have to beat it out of Marko or Chao-Xing. But someone, somewhere was going to tell the truth.

Because I wasn't going to put thing A into slot B until someone told me why Nadim needed to be armed.

As I finished up, a loud, shrieking signal rang through the whole ship. It reminded me of the lockdown warning that pealed through the Zone when the cops stormed in to arrest someone really dangerous. *Shit.* Maybe by refusing that job, I'd set off something.

"Nadim! What's happening?" I ran out of the assembly room, only to pause in the hallway because there were no guiding lights to tell me where to go. "Nadim?"

"The Elder approaches." Nadim's tone came across oddly flat, devoid of nuance. He cleared the ship's wall and showed me the dizzying expanse of space. I might never get used to the wonder of having the solar system appear in an instant, floating right before my eyes. Rather than the impressive view, however, Nadim meant for me to focus on a rapidly closing Leviathan.

"Typhon," he said.

Beatriz burst out of another room, busy dragging her thick hair back and securing it with an elastic tie to keep it out of her face. She swore in Portuguese when she realized she was heading straight for the now-transparent wall. When she grabbed at me for balance, I let her.

"What's happening?" she asked.

The alarm died away, leaving a heavy silence.

I pointed. Typhon was already a pale spot like a very bright star, and he got closer every second. Beatriz's fingers tightened on my arm as the Leviathan swept in, growing in immensity with every breath until it filled the view and slowed to a drift. *Elder Typhon.* The other ship had pale, broad scars like the rake of giant fingernails, all down the side that faced us. I saw other, deeper scars, too—blackened spots. Gouges. Typhon was *old.*

He had to be twice Nadim's size. And he had . . . plating, bolted over what I assumed were vulnerable spots. Dark metallic flexible plates that covered parts of his body. Armor? *You saw the holo of Nadim getting hit by meteorites. Probably meant to guard against that.* I wondered when

Nadim would get those upgrades. Clearly, those were manufactured.

We were supposed to rendezvous near Earth after the first week, but—

Beatriz beat me to the punch. "They've come for us early. What does that mean?"

Nadim hesitated a fraction too long. "Nothing good."

Interlude: Nadim

He blocks the stars so I can no longer hear their song and casts me in cold shadow. His mind is vast, infinitely colder than the lack of suns, and I try to twist away, find the light again.

He is faster. *Stop*, he tells me, in booming shuddering waves that I know my Honors can feel but not understand. It hurts, these frequencies. He intends it to hurt. *This is the last of your chances. You understand this.*

I gather strength, though it is difficult, and reply, *I understand.*

Fail, as you have failed before, and you go into the wild. Alone.

Fear washes through me in a gray wave. *Alone.* I dread emptiness, running cold and desperate in the silences. Never hearing my name again in a song. Failure means exile, means a life of crippled solitary travel in the wastes. Others will avoid me. No Honors. No future. No great Journey. I will hear the songs, but they will never hear mine.

I will be cast out, and I feel the hard icy satisfaction in Typhon at the thought. *Weak*, he flings at me. *You are disorderly. Prove yourself.*

Prove yourself now.

CHAPTER NINE

Breaking Ranks

TYPHON DIDN'T SPEAK. At least, he didn't speak to us, though what he said to Nadim could have been private; a strange cold rumbled through our Leviathan that left me badly unsettled. Nadim seemed very still and quiet, none of the joy and enthusiasm I'd felt when we first came aboard. It reminded me of standing at attention at the wilderness camp, not daring to show weakness because weakness just meant vulnerability. Predators liked that. They smelled it.

That's your experience, I told myself. *Not Nadim's*.

But it felt the same.

Nadim finally said, "A shuttle is coming. Typhon's Honors will inspect your progress."

Beatriz and I looked at each other. She raised her fine, perfect eyebrows. I raised my pierced one in response.

"Nobody said there'd be a final exam," I said. "I hate tests."

I waited for Nadim to reassure me, but he didn't. I wanted to comfort him, which was stupid as hell because they were coming to evaluate me too.

Screw it. I wasn't about to salute. I pictured all the judges I'd been in front of, usually by remote-view sentencing. Severe old farts who barely even looked at me before pronouncing my sentence and sending me off to another rehabbing opportunity.

Somehow, I doubted there were a lot of Camp Kunas out here in the black.

Something echoed through Nadim's skin—a feeling, a shiver really, and then a quick pulse of shock mixed with anxiety. I didn't know why he felt that way as he said, "Typhon's Honors are here."

I exchanged another look with Beatriz, who still stood in a sort of awkward parade rest by the data console. I made myself comfortable on the couch, stretched out as lazily as I could with my hands behind my head.

A stern voice said, "I told you she had no respect. Just look at her."

Zhang Chao-Xing stood in the arched doorway with Marko Dunajski. But they didn't look the same. The familiar blue Honors uniform had been replaced by bloodred with black trim, lending them a foreboding air. There were no other details, no buttons or brightness, just sharp lines and ominous shades.

But it wasn't the clothing that made the difference. It was their eyes.

Marko's eyes . . . I'd seen kindness in them, humor and concern. Now his eyes were simply black, with pupil, iris, and sclera occluded. Chao-Xing's were the same. My gut impulse was to bail; there was nothing human in the void gazing back at me. But I'd faced enough walking sharks to know it was fatal to show fear.

"Marko," I said. "Hey. You're early."

He snapped, "Get up. Now."

I sat upright. Before I could think better of it, I blurted, "What happened to you?"

His unnerving eyes just stared at me, through me. *Like people on the streets in the Zone*, I thought. High as satellites. Except this didn't feel like chem.

"Stand to attention!" Marko ordered.

Bea and I both made a good attempt. A chill bit my skin, and for a moment I was back at that damn camp, trying not to show my fear. In less than a week, Typhon had transformed Nadim's former Honors from human beings into automatons. Per various science fiction holos, I should check them over for neural implants or possibly a parasite that might be controlling the host. I'd never thought of those scary vids as instructional before.

"We will review your records." Chao-Xing stepped to the console and began calling up data with efficient, mechanical, nearly inhuman precision. Even her body language seemed totally different. This was way off. They'd told us we had a week to complete our second training phase, so why were they changing the timetable? Her dead eyes kept me from demanding answers.

Funny thing. Chao-Xing was processing our info, but Marko was the one who stepped closer to me and said, "Honor Cole. You are dismissed."

"Wait a second! What did I do wrong? Come *on*, I checked off all your damn boxes, didn't I?"

You didn't finish the work, a little voice said.

They can't fail me, they don't know that.

Before all this had started, before Derry's betrayal, I might have felt a thrill at the idea of running wild back to the Zone. Now that I had some distance, that old relationship didn't seem so much fated as sad. The Zone's desperate freedom paled against the backdrop of red giants and white dwarves, of black holes, pulsars, and binary stars.

"You are dismissed because you passed," Marko said, and for a second there was a flicker of . . . something . . . in his expression. A ghost of personality. "Leave, Zara. We're done with you."

To cover the enervating rush of relief, I crossed my arms and glared. It was tough, but I managed. "Yeah? Well, maybe *I'm* not done. I'll wait."

Beside me, Bea stepped closer, pressing her arm against mine. Already she felt like somebody I needed to protect. As he registered our closeness, Marko's aspect warmed further . . . and then that hint of the old Marko melted like ice in an oven as his dead stare locked on to Bea. Who flinched, but held her ground. She raised her chin a bit, in fact.

Silence, as Chao-Xing scanned Bea's records. Nadim kept quiet, though I could feel his anxiety running through me like a raw, twitching current. There was nothing he could do. *If you don't want anything, they can't take it away*, I considered telling him; it was wisdom I'd earned in a lot of hard places. But I was a hypocrite, because I couldn't stop wanting, either.

The silence stretched an unbearably long time, with Nadim's distress coiling inside me. It seemed like her review took twice as long as mine.

Marko finally said, "Honor Beatriz Teixeira. Your performance is unacceptable. You will be dismissed and returned to Earth. A replacement will be selected."

She let out a breath that was as clear as a cry. Her lips were parted, her eyes wide, and I braced her as she staggered. That expression . . . like a child watching her house burn. Or more accurately, her future.

But she rallied. "If you'll just tell me where I need to improve, I will make every effort—"

"Waste of time," Chao-Xing cut in. "Not fast enough. Not bright enough. Unmotivated."

I found that hard to believe. What the hell were they testing for? Bea had aced the modules that gave me the most trouble; she'd been able to plot courses in record time, when I'd labored over that for half a day before narrowing in on it. She had a grasp of math that I never would. Sure, she'd been nervous at first, but she'd adapted just fine.

"That's some bullshit," I said. "Bea's as clever as they come. And Nadim likes her. Don't you?"

"Yes," he answered. I sensed how much it cost for him to say it. "I like Beatriz very much. I see no evidence she is unfit."

"I didn't ask for your input." Chao-Xing appeared to listen to something I couldn't hear. Her voice changed too, like I was hearing her through electronic distortion . . . or like Elder Typhon was using her vocal cords. "Nadim has no discipline. He is weak and emotional. Therefore, his preferences are insignificant. Honor Teixeira, you are officially—"

"Wait."

That wasn't me or Nadim. It was Marko, and it shocked Chao-Xing enough to cock her head. It was the most human gesture I'd seen from her since she'd stepped in the room.

"What?" she demanded.

"Wait," he repeated, and again, I saw the old Marko in

there, fighting to make himself heard. "We came early. A full two days early."

"And?"

"Give her another solar day to finish her training," he said. "She isn't far off. If we had kept the schedule, she might have passed."

Chao-Xing was suddenly her old self again too; I recognized that annoyed glare, even with the weird eyes. "Honor Cole didn't need such coddling."

"But I did," Marko said. "And Typhon chose me for the Journey. So dismissing her abilities out of hand might be a mistake."

They both went silent, and I had the eerie feeling that there was a conversation I couldn't hear going on. I wondered if Nadim could hear it. Or if it was put into words at all.

Finally, Chao-Xing turned to Beatriz and said, "You have one more day." She reached for an H2 sitting on a nearby table—next to a coffee cup I'd forgotten to clear away—and tapped it. It filled with a frighteningly long list, and she thrust it to Beatriz. "Begin."

Bea took it and glanced at me. I'd never forget that look—terrified, fragile, determined all at the same time. She nodded at me. "I won't let you down," she said, and I felt she was saying it to me and Nadim, not to Typhon and his Honors.

Marko and Chao-Xing began to walk in lockstep back toward the door they'd entered from.

"Wait!" I said. Chao-Xing didn't. Marko did, but it seemed like he was resisting some unseen undertow. "Your eyes. What happened—"

"It's nothing for you to worry about," Marko told me. "For the Journey, Honors are matched to our Leviathan in a different way. It doesn't hurt."

"But it does take away your free will. You can't tell me *that's* fine. What did Typhon do to you?"

He looked away, eyes scanning as if he was reading invisible text. "I'm not obligated to provide information simply because you ask for it."

"You didn't used to be such an asshole," I muttered.

"Word of advice, Zara: don't try to help Beatriz. We'll know."

His lack of emotion troubled me. I missed the old Marko. This grim stranger in his violently red uniform, with too-black eyes . . . I wouldn't have recognized him. Or liked him.

"Marko. Are you okay? Really?"

His head tilted just a fraction to one side, and a corner of his mouth curled into what was almost a lopsided smile. "If I'm not, what can you do about it?"

He was out the door, following Chao-Xing, before I could frame a response.

"What happened to them?" No answer. "Nadim?"

His eventual reply scared the crap out of me. "I don't know."

Beatriz worked like a demon all day. I couldn't help her and I'd be damned if I got in her way, so I called up every difficult, dirty maintenance task I could find, up to and including flushing out our biomechanical sewer system, which involved cramming myself into tight, claustrophobic tunnels and wading knee-deep in muck. Back when I was around fourteen or so, Derry and I had slept in a squat down a drainpipe. Took some crawling through awful to reach our hideaway, but that same filth kept us safe. People didn't want to brave it to get at what little we had stashed, and on the street, the grime made me invisible.

It gave me time to wonder why someone—Chao-Xing, especially—hadn't discovered I'd lied about assembling that weapons array. I'd checked it off my list, but surely they had some kind of audit, right? Otherwise, what was keeping any of us from cheating our way right on through this bullshit test period?

Oh, I realized. *Nobody's ever tried.* And why would they? They're stuck on an alien spaceship, isolated and unnerved, and until I showed up, they were all super achievers who'd never cheated a day in their life. It would never have occurred to them.

And since the Leviathan's experience of humanity got filtered through the Honors they interacted with, it probably never occurred to them, either.

I wrote a note on a piece of scrap paper and passed it to Beatriz during her brief lunch break. She looked hunted and haunted, but when she read it, her eyes widened, and she looked up at me in shock. "You don't mean this," she whispered. Like Nadim couldn't hear everything.

"I do," I said. "It works. Try it."

My advice was, simply, *cheat*.

For an answer, Beatriz—a super achiever if ever there was one—crumpled up my note, dropped it in a flash bin that incinerated it, and said, "Thanks, but I'll do it my way."

But she wanted to ask, I thought. She wanted to ask if I'd cheated my way through to get to this point. I hadn't—well, except for that last thing, and that was a purely moral objection—but I could see it was easy for her to make that assumption. I'd just cracked her trust. Maybe even broken it.

At least I knew Beatriz well enough to know that she didn't tell tales. Even if she failed out, she wouldn't rat on me.

I'd done what I could. I went to the console and tried to pull up information on all the bins that were stored in the assembly room—where they'd come from (which turned out to be Earth, not a shock) and full instructions so I could see the final products. Most were things I'd already glimpsed on Elder Typhon, like flexible scaling that would protect Nadim's skin.

But there were also weapons. Definitely weapons. Like the one I'd refused to build.

So I went back to my quarters and, with the door opened, said, "Nadim? I want to have a private talk. Inside."

I shut the door and locked it, and sat down on the bed.

"Yes, Zara?" he said, in a tone so neutral I knew he expected the worst.

"You have to know I didn't do that last thing I marked off on the list."

"I expected you would ask me about it."

I stayed quiet for a moment, idly drawing patterns on the silky bedcover, before I said, "You should have told Marko and Chao-Xing I cheated."

"You had no intention of cheating," he said, and he sounded sure about it. "This is part of the same objection to creating my alarm. You want to know how something is to be used before you build it. You don't like being kept in the dark."

"Yeah," I said. "It's what I hated about the whole world, back on Earth. All the rules you had to follow without knowing why, and if you asked, you got branded *difficult* and *damaged*. Well, I am difficult. I am damaged.

And I'm going to ask why."

"Why didn't you ask me?"

I debated that. I looked down at the patterns I was drawing. They looked like stars. "I wasn't sure you would tell me the truth, and I don't want you to lie to me."

"I would not, Zara," he said, and there was something in that voice that vibrated warm inside me. How had he put it? Strings tuned to the same frequency. I knew he meant it. "Please don't lie to me. I know it's something humans do naturally, but—"

"I won't," I told him. I wasn't sure it was a promise I could keep, but I *wanted* it to be true. "Why am I building you a weapon?"

The silence felt like forever, stretching and pulling and, finally, ripping when he said, "Because not everything in the universe is kind."

"Meaning what, exactly?" I raised my head and looked at a space on the wall like I was staring at him, even though there was no focus point. "Meaning you have enemies?"

"I—" He started, faltered, and started again. "I don't know everything about the universe, Zara. I'm still learning, just as you are. But I know one thing, from all these years of interacting with humans."

"Which is what?"

"Even the kindest of creatures has predators."

That rang so true that I felt it inside me. "So you don't

208

know why I'm building it, either. They haven't told you, have they?"

"Elder Typhon required us all to be provisioned with protective armor and at least one weapon," Nadim said immediately. "I did ask why. He didn't answer me."

"They never do."

"Are you going to build it?"

I leaned back against the bulkhead wall. Put my hand flat against the warm surface of his skin. "What do you want me to do?"

"I don't want weapons," Nadim said. "But I want to protect you and Beatriz. So would you please assemble it? As a favor to me?"

"I'm all for a good defense. And since you asked, yes. But if I find out you're hiding something from me, Nadim—"

"I'm not," he said. "If—if you want to look inside my mind and make certain of that, you can."

I thought about it for a moment. That felt like a cliff I wasn't ready to plunge off, not yet at least. I said, "Just don't let me down."

I went to assembly and worked for a few hours—good, detailed, sweaty work that took my mind off what Beatriz might be doing, or failing to do. I had a hundred asks for Marko, which was probably why he'd retreated to Typhon. He must know I'd never shuttle over to grill him, even if the giant Leviathan Elder would allow me to come aboard. Marko's parting rhetorical question burned a circle in the center of my brain. It made me think he was going through something, not entirely of his volition, and that heralded bad shit down the line. For me and maybe for everybody.

In frustration, I finally slammed into the combat simulation room. Each punch, each kick carried weight, and I experienced the visceral satisfaction of smashing somebody's nose. Even the crunch of cartilage and blood spray seemed right. I went straight up to expert-level street fighting, no rules. There were ranks. I started at one. Too easy, so I scaled up. Six opponents this time, a mix of bareknuckle and melee weapons. If you could get a degree in street fighting, I'd have a PhD. *I'm with you, Bea. I'm fighting too.* The VR learned my style, adapted, and eventually, I got my ass handed to me at rank five. Not bad, considering I was up against fifteen foes.

When I emerged at last, drenched and exhausted, the view on Nadim's transparent wall revealed that we'd arrived back home. The sight of the giant blue-green ball of Earth came as a shock. I'd gotten used to seeing Mars, and Saturn, and Jupiter, and Venus as Nadim cruised by them, but now we were home. Ready, I realized, to kick any unsuitable crew back down to the surface and take on an alternate. There were a few silvery, sleek Leviathan orbiting too . . . young ones, like Nadim, each escorted by what must have been Elders twice their size. Adults. All of those bigger ships looked scarred, their skin dull and rough where it wasn't plated in metal.

I'd rather give myself a lobotomy with a rehab shiv than travel on a ship like Typhon. I tried to imagine touching the Elder's emotions up close, and a cold shudder rolled over me so that my skin prickled with goose bumps.

I leaned closer to the clear skin of the viewscreen and put my palms flat on his skin on either side to brace myself. *Ahhh.* That felt better. We snapped together like magnets, and I breathed a long sigh of relief. I preferred it when we weren't at odds.

"How's Beatriz doing?"

"I can't tell you, Zara."

"Oh, come on. I'm not interfering!"

"I can't."

"Fine, let's talk about where we go from here. The Tour. Will we get to meet any little green men?" Maybe that ancient SF turnip hadn't made it up here, so I tried, "I mean, alien life forms? Besides you."

"You're alien to me too, you know."

"True."

"No," he said. "You will not meet any little green men. Not on the Tour."

"Is that why I'm really building the weapon for you?"

"No," he said, quickly and decisively.

"What about *after* the Tour?" I hadn't missed his quali-fier. "Any little green men then?"

He was silent. Very silent. Wary. I could feel it through our link in waves of gunmetal gray. Funny. This one was like a shield, flickering to life between us like a force field.

"Wait . . . you're not *allowed* to answer? Is that what I'm getting here?" I asked.

"Zara—"

"If you tell me about it, will they still let you go on the Journey?" I felt the shield grow spikes of white ice. Fear. Real fear.

"I can't talk to you about this," he said.

"Because of Typhon?" No answer. Paranoid curiosity burned a hole in my head, but I had to give in. I couldn't push him. He'd shut down completely on me. "All right," I said. "I won't ask."

Warm, orange gratitude burst within me like fireworks, sending tingles down every nerve. I found my fingers mov-ing slowly over the wall, and I could see the whispering warmth of it lingering on his skin. I wanted to ask him if it felt good to him, but it was obvious it did. Maybe too much for comfort. Closing my eyes, I let the strange sensation wash over me, while at the same time fighting the irratio-nal conviction that I'd been lost and angry my whole damn life because I hadn't had *this*. A real, cell-deep connection to someone else.

212

Maybe the Leviathan DNA in me that had fixed my brain had, at the same time, given me an aching kind of loneliness I'd never recognized before.

With a faint shiver, I stepped away and struggled to separate myself, put myself back into my own skin. I still tingled all over, and there was a flushing warmth to my body that mirrored what I'd felt from him.

We weren't in each other's heads, exactly, but it seemed we couldn't avoid being in each other's nervous systems. I wanted to ask if that was all due to my Leviathan DNA patch, but I didn't. Some things were too fragile to say out loud.

Nadim said, "I have to go. Typhon is calling," and I felt him—or his attention—leave me.

It felt cold. Very cold. That was both his withdrawal and a ghostly image of the icy calm he had to put on when facing his Elder. I went in search of Beatriz. By that time, almost seventeen hours had passed since she'd gotten her lists, and she was just finishing up in the equipment assembly room—finally, she had her turn in the box. She looked dirty, exhausted, and triumphant under all that as she pressed her thumb to the last item to mark it complete. I watched one of the massive bins roll back to its assigned spot and wondered what she'd been asked to assemble.

I wondered if it was another weapon. And if she'd even asked.

"Done?" I asked her.

Most of her hair had been tied up in a thick mane behind her, but she used the back of one dirty hand to swipe some loose curls away from her face. "I think so. I could use a long shower—"

We both staggered, because Nadim rocked hard on his side. We hit the wall, and I braced myself against it as he rolled back to the normal axis. Physical contact clicked us together, and—

His pain was so overwhelming that I cried out, and then I went down, smothering in the anguish, in the rage.

CHAPTER TEN

Breaking Faith

"Z? Z, WAKE up! *Please!*"

For a fuzzy second, I thought it was my mother's voice, but then a sharp, pungent smell jabbed into my nostrils, and I jerked back to reality.

Reality was me lying flat on the floor with Beatriz kneeling next to me, a snapped capsule in her shaking hands held close to my nose. I ached all over. It felt like I'd been burned in a flash fire . . . and then it faded, slowly, to nothing. I mumbled something incoherent, and Bea dropped the capsule and helped me sit up. It took me a second to remember why I was on the floor, and another to remember the pain, panic, and rage. I shook her off and stumbled to my feet to lay hands against Nadim's skin.

Nothing. *Nothing.*

"Nadim!" I said. No response. "Nadim!"

And then he was there. Faint and far away, but there. He didn't speak, but I felt him.

"Is he all right?" Bea asked anxiously. "Are you?"

I was. Just barely. If he was blocking us deliberately, I knew why.

The sledgehammer of pain had knocked me unconscious. He didn't want to risk that again. He was suffering in silence, alone, to protect us.

"Typhon," I said. "Typhon hurt him." The surety came as a wave, not my memory but Nadim's, and I didn't question it. I was angry enough to chew nails and spit bullets, not that it would make any difference to a Leviathan. "Bastard *hurt him.*"

"But—how?"

I didn't know. The red aura of the impact stayed with me, and it woke instincts that I thought I'd left behind on Earth. Instincts to *hit back.*

"We're here," I told Nadim. "Please. Come to us."

Beatriz sucked in a sudden breath, and I knew she felt him, just as I did: a sudden, echoing stab of shame and pain, darkly mixed with anger. I knew that feeling so well.

Abused kids were all the same, deep down. We blamed

ourselves. We hurt. We swore it wouldn't happen again. We swore we wouldn't *deserve* it again because that was how screwed up we felt. How screwed up our abusers made us.

"It's not your fault," I said to Nadim. He didn't believe me. I knew because I could never believe it myself.

It still helped saying it, and hearing it: some of the edge bled away from him, like Nadim might return to us. Tentative and wounded, but him.

"Honors," said Chao-Xing from behind us. Startled, Bea and I both turned and found her and Marko standing there in their dried-blood uniforms and their blackened eyes, watching us. "Step back. It is not wise to attempt to bond with your host at this time."

"Because your Elder slapped the shit out of him?" I asked. I was ready to try it with Chao-Xing, for sure. "What the hell?"

"Don't," Marko warned. I didn't know if he was talking about my attitude or my intentions, but I could hear some hint of humanity in him. "Honor Teixeira, the Elder has approved your work. You may remain for the Tour."

"How gracious," Beatriz snapped, which from her was like shouting in his face. Sarcasm. I liked it on her. "Thank him for me."

They let that pass without comment, and Chao-Xing suddenly broke from her spot beside Marko and walked directly up to me. In my face. Up close, her eyes were inhumanly different, unreadable. "You are here to learn about the galaxy in partnership with Nadim," she told me. "Not to question. Be careful not to dig so deep that you dig your own grave."

She left, and in the chilly silence, I said to Marko, "She's a charmer."

"She always has been," he said. He seemed more himself. Maybe Typhon had cut the connection with them. As I watched, Marko's pupils slowly shrank down to normal size, and he blinked hard, trying to adjust his vision.

"Hello, Marko," Nadim said. His voice sounded bland. "I'm sorry I didn't greet you earlier, but you were not free. You'll begin your Journey soon."

"Tomorrow," Marko agreed. "We came back to say our good-byes to our family. And to sign off on your new Honors, of course."

"Of course. I wish you well, Marko. You were a pleasant companion."

"And you—" For a moment, Marko's calm broke. He looked down. "I'm sorry. I can't do this right now."

"I understand," Nadim said as if he really did. "I will think of you with fondness."

Marko didn't say good-bye. He just . . . left. Walked away, and in a moment, I felt the whisper as the shuttle departed Nadim and made its way back to Typhon.

I also felt the continued, muted burn of pain from our ship. Whatever Typhon had done to him had hurt enough to leave marks.

"Nadim? Are you all right?"

"Yes, I'm fine," he said. *Liar*, I thought. "I didn't want Marko and Chao-Xing to go, but I didn't have a choice."

"You mean you didn't want them to go to *him*," I said. "Right?"

He didn't answer, but I was on target. He disliked Typhon. He feared him. He also longed for the Elder's approval. It was a sad, familiar story, and I hated that we had that in common, even if it explained why I understood him so well when I hadn't been with him long.

The quiet startled me when I realized I was completely alone with Nadim. Bea had gone for her shower and probably to drop exhausted into her bed. Even Typhon had withdrawn, presumably pleased with the discipline he'd delivered. It bothered me that the Leviathan didn't seem to know better than humans in this regard. Some might crack under sufficient pressure and pretend to comply, but others, like me—and maybe Nadim—would fight until we broke our backs. On a deep breath, an old memory washed over me.

I was six years old, maybe, and my teachers found me hard to handle. Intractable. Incorrigible. They were already saying that about me, and my odd medical problems didn't make me easier to deal with. My father accused me of faking the headaches like I was some kind of a criminal mastermind in elementary school.

The first time my father hit me, he kept saying, "If you cry, I'll stop. If you cry, then I'll know you're sorry."

For what? Being born? Having pain that the doctors couldn't diagnose fast enough? I remembered clenching every muscle in my body, especially my jaw, until my teeth ached, echoing into a feedback loop with the awful throbbing in my skull. But I never cried. I never fucking cried.

I refused to give him that victory or let him imagine even for a second that I was sorry.

It had been a long-ass time since anything could compel my tears; I considered them trophies, and I didn't yield them often. But I could almost weep for Nadim, for the way Typhon had brutalized him. I wasn't exactly sure why it had happened, but part of me wondered if it was because I'd demanded answers he wasn't supposed to offer.

"You're so sad."

My breath hitched. "Sorry."

"Because Beatriz left you alone? I don't think she meant to upset you. She was just tired."

"I'm not alone. I'm with you." I flung that out, not a gauntlet exactly, but more of a distraction.

"But I'm not . . ."

Human. A person? Whatever he intended to say, I cut it

off by sprawling flat on the floor, bare hands, bare feet. It was like being held safe against my mother's chest, only it was thrilling too, the first kick of new chem. Our points of contact warmed, and as I held still, the quiet thrum of his energy was countered by my pulse. By the lightning jolt of his surprise, nobody had ever done this before.

"You're so strange," he said, and vanished the ceiling so I was swimming in stars. How he knew I wanted that before I did . . . it was perfect.

For a moment, I considered making Nadim angels on the floor. If he mirrored my movements with brightness, as he did when he wanted to direct us somewhere, the pulses of light and color would flutter from my skin to his and back again, a language only spoken by the two of us.

"I want you to know . . . I won't punk out like that again. I wasn't ready, and Typhon hit us with a sucker punch. I promise not to leave you to deal with that on your own again."

The heat of his happiness washed over my hands and feet, giving lie to his words. "You're not meant to bear my pain, Zara."

I smiled. "Just you watch me."

The next evening's official ceremony, thankfully, wasn't held on Earth; it was a broadcast, and we could watch and respond when our turn rolled around. Each country called their own Honors, praising the ones who had graduated and were hand-picked to go on the Journey, along with the young recruits who'd made it past their testing week and gotten confirmed. It was bizarre when Gidra contacted me on the console.

"You're up in ten minutes," the press liaison told me. "Do your makeup for God's sake and find a fresh uniform."

Briefly I considered flying my slacker flag, but that might shame Nadim, and I cared more about his image than my own. So I hurried to my quarters, borrowed some of Bea's cosmetics, since I didn't own any, and donned formal blues so crisp that they damn near cut my shins. I got back to the console seven minutes later, pretty good, I thought. Bea got called up before me, and for a few minutes I thought she might choke up at the sight of the holo view of her brothers, sisters, parents, and that opera-singing grandmother all waving to her from her home in Rio. But she got through it and said a few words thanking the world for this opportunity: first in Portuguese, then Spanish, English, and, finally, German. *Hot damn, she speaks four languages. And they almost dropped her?*

In the background, Bea's grandmother couldn't stop crying—proud, happy tears it seemed like—and the camera cut away as the extended family offered a long-distance group hug. On Earth, I thought, Beatriz had a whole tribe; out here, there was only me. I resolved not to let her down.

"You'll be fine," Nadim said, reminding me that I was nervous and my turn was coming up. I was standing by, but not prepared, when they connected to my console. *What do I have to say to the world?*

"You're on in . . ." Gidra flashed three fingers, two, and then one.

Showtime. I had nothing planned, so the words surprised me too. "I'm dedicating this voyage to everybody in Detroit's Lower Eight. Maybe they said you'll never get out. Well, I'm sending a shout-out to folks who feel alone, who feel like hope is something they can't afford. Your shot is out there somewhere, so reach for it. Stay strong. Zara out."

I saw my mother and sister sitting together on Mars, looking beautiful even while they cried. I saw my father, in a separate image, trying to get a microphone, because of course he would. And then the media cut to a panoramic sweep of the Lower Eight. People stood on buildings, on cars, shouting and holding signs. Some had nothing to do with me, but I read enough congratulations that my shriveled heart sparked a little. Audio popped a few seconds later, and the only intelligible word I could make out was my name, chanted in unison, by strangers who, on a good day, struggled for life.

"How was that?" I asked Beatriz, not really expecting an answer.

She threw her arms around me. I froze, because hugs

were not something I was used to getting. "Amazing. Inspiring."

"Now you're just messing with me." I set her firmly back and looked up at the ceiling. "Nadim? What's next?"

"In four hours, we depart, and you won't see Earth for a year. Will you miss it?"

"Yes," Beatriz said, at the same time I said, with exactly the same conviction, "No." And we both laughed. "Maybe a little," I amended. "But my life wasn't exactly roses."

"No one's is," Beatriz said. "But won't you miss the sky? The clouds?"

I shrugged.

"You should rest," Nadim said. "I'll wake you both in a few hours when it's time for departure."

Beatriz left, yawning and stretching. I went to the galley and made myself some coffee, curling up on the sofa as I sipped it.

"Zara? Aren't you tired?" Nadim asked.

I'd only just begun to listen to how he said my name. Zah-ra, with a faint trill to the R. It wasn't how most people did, usually from reading it off forms. Generally, they rhymed it with Sara. Nadim's pronunciation made me feel like a reigning old-days queen.

"I should be. But I'm not, really. So much has happened. I can't believe that in a few hours, we'll be . . . gone."

"Freedom." His voice had gone low and quiet and warm,

and it felt like a blanket wrapping around me. "Except it isn't freedom, Zara, only the illusion of it. We will still be required to do our duties on the Tour. And we aren't free to go anywhere we like."

"You're bored," I said.

"Am I?" He sounded taken aback. "I don't see how that could be true."

There was some subtext I didn't quite grasp, but I pursued another line of inquiry instead of drilling for more. "You told me that you hear the stars," I reminded him. "It must be hard to resist heading out there. I heard it . . . when you dreamed."

"I don't . . . !" His denial trailed off, possibly as he recalled telling us that he'd had what we'd call a bad dream.

I sipped my coffee. "Am I bothering you?"

"Nothing about you bothers me," he said. "Even when you're angry. I like the way you shine when you're angry."

I laughed. I couldn't help it. "*Shine?* I do not!"

"Burn, then. Is that better?"

"Whatever." For some reason, I blushed, an actual hot flush that traveled up my neck into my face. With my free hand, I touched my cheek, more or less in disbelief, because I once watched a couple from my old Lower Eight crew go at it up against a wall without even blinking. *Yep. What is wrong with me?*

The blush intensified, and suddenly it was hard to

breathe. My fingers flexed on the wall, and then I felt the pulse of his life force. I went lightheaded, because it seemed like I was drinking Nadim through my skin cells.

I pulled away. Sipped more coffee. Tried to slow my breathing.

"I'm sorry. This is different than . . . anything I have known. Beatriz—she fits here with me. But not the way you do."

I knew what he meant, and that filled me with equal measures of fear and delight. It was blowing my mind that in such a short time, we'd be out of the Sol system. Sayonara, ISS. Bye-bye, Moonbase Alpha. Farewell, Mars Colony Roma. In what world did two teenage girls get to go joyriding on a sentient ship? A future so strange I couldn't have imagined it.

We're a team. And in an odd sort of way, Bea and Nadim had already become family. I would fight anybody who tried to hurt them or take them away from me.

Including Elder Typhon.

Nadim might believe his elders wouldn't do anything shady; I had no such illusions. And maybe my chary nature could save us when the shit hit the fan.

PART III

PART III

Over the years, people have attempted basic explanations. The Leviathan seek companions for their travels; they are sentient and feel loneliness. But the truth is never so simple.

Per compelling data compiled by leading scientist Hermann L. Schulz [null citation], they have a pattern. They seek out civilizations on the verge of annihilation and offer aid. Those who accept flourish. The ones who do not often perish. However, there is no proof to substantiate fringe claims that the Leviathan herald or precipitate extinction-level events.

Based on my evaluation of Dr. Schulz's work, I offer the following thesis regarding human and Leviathan interdependence. Consider the existence of the wax worm. It lives within a bee colony, tunneling, which protects the larva, while it eats wax, pollen, honey, and excrement. This keeps the colony clean while the bees hide the worms from predators. This is an example of a beneficial parasite.

We are the wax worms. They are the colony.

Further exploration into the Daedalean mystery as to why the Leviathan truly seek human allies reveals an interesting secret. In the course of my research, I discovered the memoirs of Moriah Krull, an early Honors selection. Most of her story has been suppressed, but I acquired a copy from the underweb, and what I learned . . . brace yourselves.

Humanity is not the first. Other sentient life forms have traveled with the Leviathan. But what became of them? How did we replace them? And why?

To find out, order my book, *True Symbionts: The Real Reason Leviathan Seek Us Out*.

[purchase information redacted, **TRUTHSEEKER** mod warning: DO NOT USE THIS FORUM FOR SELF-PROMOTION]

CHAPTER ELEVEN

Breaking Molds

I DIDN'T SLEEP. I was still up, staring out at the rotating Earth below, when Beatriz came out to join me. She looked wrecked, so I made coffee the way she liked it, Brazilian style, and she drank it curled on the couch next to me.

I'd expected some big send-off, fanfare, something like that. Instead, Nadim just said, "We're leaving."

And then, the Earth slowly turned out of sight, behind us. Bea whispered, "Nadim? Can you make the viewport larger please? I'd—I'd like to watch until it's gone."

He made the entire wall transparent. Beatriz sucked in a breath, then let it slowly out and nodded. Her eyes found and fixed on the Earth, and the only sign of her distress was the paleness of her knuckles as she gripped her coffee cup.

"Breathe," I told her quietly. She sent me a quicksilver smile and nodded. There were tears in her eyes, but they never fell. She blinked them away.

We sat silently in the lounge with the entire wall turned window, the entire ceiling transparent, as much a part of the stars as we could be while still having chairs and oxygen.

It was mesmerizing. Not just the spectacle of passing worlds, but the school of Leviathan who traveled with us. In view, we had at least twenty, both young ones like Nadim and Elders who resembled Typhon, the silvery shimmer of them picking up and shedding color like the scales of fish as they swam the emptiness.

We glided past Saturn. It was the farthest we'd been before, and we kept going. Light was fainter here, and the Leviathan were fading except in shimmers; I might have imagined it, but it seemed they were growing darker to match the weak ambient light from our sun. Stars burned hard, but they were far away, and as we passed the outer limits of our system—our home—I could only make out the other Leviathan when they blocked other lights.

At this diaspora, I thought of all the live ships that wouldn't return to the Sol system, or if they did, it wouldn't be during my lifetime. The Journey meant being willing to follow your Leviathan into the unknown, away from your home forever. Talk about a tough call. Nadim didn't speak, but I felt this was something special, this moment of parting . . . and then, a sound hummed through the floor. A low, throbbing rhythmic pulse that I felt in my chest, like boosted bass at a party.

"What was that?" Bea asked. Still not quite past her nerves, I could hear that.

"It's a song," Nadim said. "I suppose you'd call it a good-bye. Those going out on their Journey sing it to us."

I didn't have any idea how sound could travel through space—that was supposed to be impossible, wasn't it? But maybe it wasn't sound, it was resonance. Resonance the Leviathan were attuned to hear, and we couldn't under normal circumstances. It vibrated through Nadim's body.

The pulse amplified and I gripped the arms of my chair tighter. I shut my eyes, and I felt what Nadim did: proud, defiant, sad, relieved. Such a profound and complicated mixture of emotions.

Through my connection with Nadim, I also felt Typhon, at a far remove, like calling into a canyon. Not his emotions, but a kind of empty pressure, like the frozen bubble of a massive explosion. Terrifying and dark. No singing from him. No sound at all.

Then he was gone. Marko and Chao-Xing with him.

Nadim dimmed the transparency of the windows and ceiling gradually, rather than cutting us off at once—that was an adjustment I appreciated. It made it less traumatic for me, and especially Bea. We still sat for a moment, just breathing, and then she reached over and grabbed my hand.

"So," she said. "We're doing this."

"Damn right. Nadim, what's our first Tour stop?"

"We are on course for a planet that we refer to as Firstworld."

"Firstworld. You mean, where you're from?" Beatriz asked him.

"We are from a galaxy so far from here that it would takes years in human time to reach it," Nadim said. "This is the first world where Leviathan gathered and made contact. Once, long ago, there was a civilization."

Beatriz raised a brow. "You mean . . . there are people?"

"No. The indigenous race is gone. But it is a beautiful place. One day another intelligent species will rise, but it's fallow now. We visit often, to observe the changes and record them."

"Why?" I asked.

"When sentient life evolves, we must withdraw, continue observation from a distance, and strike that planet from the Tour. It would be wrong to offer aid before they reach a certain technological level."

"Is it dangerous?" That was Bea, of course. I'd never have thought to even ask. Everything was dangerous; that was my default position.

"There are some lower predatory life-forms," Nadim said. "But they avoid the ruins, which is where you will take readings and gather samples. It should be quite safe."

"Hey," I said, as if it was a logical segue. "So, do you have weapons for us?"

"There is a weapons locker. I will open it for you. You should take sidearms down with you. But please, damage nothing. Take nothing but the designated samples. This is a revered site for us."

"Sacred." Beatriz nodded. "We understand. We won't disturb anything."

I could hear Derry's response to that, whispering in my ear. *Yeah, right. If I see gold, I'm lifting it. Screw sacred.* I'd have agreed with him, before. I'd thought freedom meant breaking the rules, stomping on other people's ideas of what shouldn't be done. Hearing Beatriz say *sacred* made me think maybe freedom didn't mean wrecking shit. It meant not doing it too. After all, no cops out here. No rules. Just respect.

"How long until we get there?" I asked.

I could've checked our course on the console, but it was easier to ask. I liked hanging out in the hub, where most of the human-friendly tech was installed. The equipment and screens, the chairs, all of it reminded me of what humans had imagined a ship's bridge would look like in old science fiction vids.

"Not long," he said. "Now that I can move at real speed." Meaning, of course, that flying around Earth's solar system had been like being trapped in a tiny room. I could feel the energy coursing through him now.

"What's it like down there? Hot? Cold? What about—"

"I've put climate data on your H2s, as well as historical information, and visual records that will help you understand the context of what you're examining. We have a record of what it looked like when the Biiyan were still here."

Bea eagerly grabbed the H2 and began scrolling. "What happened to them?"

Nadim chose not to answer that. I picked up my own H2 and searched for a hint. Nothing.

Whatever ended these Biiyan, I thought, it seemed like Nadim didn't want to discuss it. That was . . . unsettling. "Nadim? Did the Leviathan kill them?"

"No!" That was the sharpest tone I'd ever heard him use, and the pulse of emotion that accompanied it was very clear. Outrage. Disappointment that I'd even think of it. "Of course we didn't."

"Then why won't you say what did?"

"Because—" He was quiet for a moment, and I felt him

struggling against his own better judgment. I'd done that a time or two or thousand. But, like I always did, he surrendered. "Because they were wiped out in a war of their own making, one we couldn't stop. We tried to convince them not to enter into it, but . . . they didn't listen. And we lost them. It's a difficult thing for us. A failure."

I mumbled, "Sorry," and let it go. Then, as if it was an afterthought (it wasn't): "Just for clarification . . . what kind of weapons in the weapons locker?"

Nadim sighed. "Fine, Zara. I'll give you the code."

He rattled off a series of letters and numbers, so fast that he probably thought I wouldn't catch them. But I hit record on my H2 the second he said *code*. There was a smug amusement in his tone when he added, "Did you get that?"

"Damn right." I was grinning when I hit play.

Holding the unit overhead like a trophy, I swaggered to the armory and played the file. The lock disengaged with a satisfying hiss, and I dug in, pulling out various weapons. Some were standard ballistic guns, others looked more bizarre, and the rest I couldn't figure out at all, despite turning them over in my hands, inspecting them from all angles.

"You have no idea what that is," he observed.

"Seriously, how is this a weapon?" "This" was a perfect black cube with no switch I could detect, no pressure plates, no barrel. It looked like plastic, but felt heavier and more durable to the touch. I'd never encountered anything like it, but the sinister heft in my palm sent a wicked chill through me.

"You don't know?" His tone was grave. "Then put that back. You should only use it if we're threatened by something worse than death."

Eyes wide, I set the object back in the locker. "Seriously?"

Nadim laughed. His delight ran down my spine in liquid trills. "That's just a weight. Sometimes you need ballast on low-gravity worlds to keep your other gear from floating away."

"I see how you are," I said. "Messing with the new girl."

"You don't like it?"

Truthfully? I did.

My first view of Firstworld came at 3:17 a.m. Iceland time, though out here, there was probably no point in keeping track by that standard anymore. Nadim called me portside and in teasing increments opened the viewscreen. The relatively monochromatic hues of our local planets hadn't prepared me for the vibrant colors that swirled together on this planet like a sand painting. Violet, brown, deep green, and cerulean, all discernible from this distance, so it must be incredible on the ground.

"It's beautiful," I breathed.

"You'll need to wear scrubbers, as the atmosphere is

mildly toxic to humans. And the vegetation grows on ultraviolet rays, hence the difference in coloration."

"Can we lose the lecture mode?" Teasing Nadim already came natural, but I was too enthralled to soak up all the information. I just wanted to gear up and get down there.

"Proceed to the docking bay," Nadim said. "I'm in stable orbit."

Bea met me there, vibrating with equal measures of nerves and excitement. She was already dressed, and she handed me the mission suit, much thinner and more formfitting than the old days. The fabric reminded me of a dolphin's skin, hard to describe, but I'd touched one at an aquarium over ten years ago. The suit's color was dark blue, nearly cobalt, but when I touched it, my fingers reacted with the surface, resulting in a kind of starfish ray effect. Startled, I almost dropped it.

She laughed. "Isn't it fascinating? It seems to be biosensitive, though I'm not sure if it's the heat or electromagnetic stimuli."

"Both," Nadim answered. "It can also blend with its surroundings, detect radiation, and the mask will purify the air so you can breathe it."

"Does it go over our clothes?"

"It's a skinsuit." That answer came from Bea.

Giving her a thumbs-up, because obviously she'd memorized all the manuals on our reading list that I'd ignored in favor of time in the combat sim, I stripped without a second of hesitation. No lie, it felt a little creepy as I pulled what amounted to a second skin over mine; it seemed to melt around me, for lack of a better description, until it fit to perfection. No denying that it felt like walking around naked, though, and that was both weird and strangely wonderful.

"It's nonconductive and offers a good amount of protection," Nadim added.

"Is it bulletproof? Laser resistant? What about—"

"Zara." Clearly he was ready to move on.

"Fine, I'm putting on my mask."

It adapted to my curls, shaping to my head naturally. I expected some vision impairment or a sense of claustrophobia, but I could see perfectly, just . . . not with my eyes. It was like there were tiny cameras all over, beaming information to my brain. Freaking disorienting, but after a few turns, I got the hang of insect vision. Gloves, check.

Fortunately, I got ass-kicking boots with weights in the heels instead of stilettos. Once I put those on we were good to go, and Bea had raced through her mission prep and was now bouncing beside the shuttle. I grabbed our gear bag, as we'd also be taking various readings on the surface in addition to visiting Nadim's so-called sites. Doing the Leviathan's scientific measurements for their records.

We were going to see alien ruins. If I'd said that six months

ago, squatting over a meal of street food in a ruined building in the Zone . . . Well. I'd have either been laughed out
of the neighborhood or checked into Benny's for a psych
eval.

"This might be a dumb question. . . ."

"There are no dumb questions, Zara," Nadim said.

"Really? That's not what my fifth-grade teacher said."

The pause told me he wasn't sure how to respond to
that. "Whatever it is, ask."

"Are you going with us?"

"I can't enter the atmosphere. Gravity would crush me,
culminating in lethal impact. That's why we have shuttles,
Zara."

"Shit. No. I mean . . . I want you to see what we're seeing." It wouldn't be the same to try and describe things to
him on comms. Besides, I also wanted his company, but I
couldn't just say so.

Bea beckoned to me, eyes shining. "Hurry up!"

I held up one finger, telling her to wait. Nadim still
hadn't responded, which made me think this was a weird
request. All the other Honors really did treat him like a
thing, huh? It was impossible for me to wrap my head
around that because he was so much of a person that I had
a hard time focusing on anybody else if I had even a glimmer of his attention.

"That is an unusual request. We can communicate

through the shuttle comm. But . . ."

"You know what I'm asking. There's no way to jury-rig something so you can, ah, come down with us? See what we see?"

After a little more hesitation, he said, "You can attach a remote unit to your skinsuit."

Bea came over to investigate the holdup, and she helped me with the installation. "This . . . and . . . here we go."

Half an hour later, presto—Nadim-mobile.

He was weirdly quiet, and I didn't know why. Bea powered up the Hopper—what I called the frog-like short-flight craft reserved for planetary excursions. Human tech for the interior, Leviathan biotech for the exterior. She'd done better than me in navigation and piloting, and there was always the auto-nav if she got in trouble. Theoretically, we should be fine. Still, a frisson of fear-excitement (fearcitement?) jolted over me.

"Good to go?"

Once she checked all the instruments and we strapped in, she got us in motion, not perfection but smooth enough for her first flight. Nadim opened the hatch; then we were away, swooping out of him and yet still with him. That was the best part.

Finally, he spoke. "I've never seen myself before. Not like this."

"What?"

"The attachment to your skinsuit . . . I can see myself with your eyes." He expressed a strange mix of delight and horror. I made sure to linger as we flew past. He should get a good look from head to tail.

"Nobody ever did this for you?" I'd suspected.

"No. Both you and Beatriz talk to me more than other Honors. The rest were content to complete their checklists, they never really thought of including me. They never thought to be so . . . interactive. This is unsettling. I'm here . . . and there also."

"If it feels too weird or distracting . . ." I started.

"It's just new. I know you will disengage if I ask."

That much trust did funny things to my stomach. So I just nodded and held on as Bea figured out how to compensate for gravitational pull, lift and thrust, X and Y axes. With some help from the auto-nav, she nailed entry and pulled up just a little rough, so my lunch rolled around but didn't come up.

"Great job, Bea. You okay?"

"A little shaky. That was a lot of pressure. The only reason I didn't panic was because I knew we had a fail-safe."

She set the Hopper down in a field of golden grass. Okay, maybe that was the wrong word since this was tall and frond-y, but it was the closest equivalent I had. The thrusters burned a circle, and I imagined natives venturing out to marvel at the pattern once we took off. *Wait, no,*

Nadim said there's nobody here, not anymore.

There should be fanfare for a moment like this, flags to plant, but Bea just opened the doors and we popped out. Despite the mask, the filtered air still carried the acrid tang of whatever was making it toxic. I snagged the gear bag and got out my scanner, which told me the exact components of the gas. Methane, hydrogen, right. I could have probably brought along logs that gave statistics on the ranges that were normal for Firstworld. I'd transcribe readings when we got back.

Bea bounced a little on her feet. "That's not *grass*. This isn't *air*."

I sucked in one processed breath, two, and took an experimental step. This was light gravity compared to Earth, so even with my weighted boots, I bounced like the dirt was half trampoline. A shriek escaped me as I came down, and then I heard Nadim laughing. Though I couldn't sense his joy, just hearing it felt like eating an ice cream cone.

"This is *amazing*." I shout-sang it.

For a while, we played, but eventually we got down to business and took our readings. Bea dictated detailed holos and notes on flora into her mini-H2 while I handled the mineral samples. We were supposed to collect these and log them, compare to stuff that had been hauled in before, with the goal of seeing how long it would take for the planet to return to the state they'd recorded before the war. Sounded boring, but I found some real interest in it; being an alien geologist pretty much rocked. Pun intended.

Now and then Nadim offered commentary on things that puzzled us, and our progress took us across an open field toward the ruins that rose like jagged teeth in the distance. With my eyes half-closed, I could almost, almost imagine the disaster that had shattered what might have been a temple or a coliseum.

We were nearly there when I heard it—the sound of footsteps behind us. I didn't hesitate. In an instant, I had a weapon in my hand. Whirling, I took aim at the blur of motion.

"Don't!" Nadim called out.

And I froze, caught between his urgency and my fight instincts. I'd never backed down in my life.

CHAPTER TWELVE

Breaking Silence

THERE WAS NOBODY behind me. Nothing at all.

"Please don't discharge your weapon. You might disturb the native fauna." Nadim's tone all wrong, too anxious, too urgent.

But I knew damn well I hadn't imagined somebody behind me.

The wind whispered through my skinsuit mask, tanged with the alien mix of gases. I scanned twice, once with my eyes and next with my equipment. No signs of life popped on the screen and I lowered the weapon. I didn't put it away.

Beatriz patted my shoulder as she set off toward the ruins. "I never expected you to be jumping at shadows, Z."

"You're hilarious," I mumbled.

In my mind's eye, I tried to process what I'd seen, but it had happened so fast. Nadim said there was no intelligent life, but Earth-wise, the lines got blurry around whale and chimpanzee. Could be that Firstworld had some native creatures, big enough to shake me. Whatever it was, it didn't want to get close to us, which did suggest wildlife. Yet—

"Nadim," I said, low. "Come on, tell me the truth."

"It was nothing." Clearly he didn't want to have this conversation dirtside. Damn, but I was getting tired of secrets. I wanted to trust him, but it was getting harder. Our connection couldn't change the fact that I'd seen *something*, and he wasn't going to talk me out of it.

My skin crawled the whole time we trekked through the golden grass; the suits we wore shifted to a lazy whisper of colors that blended perfectly, but I could still feel someone watching, and it wasn't Nadim. I kept turning and scanning behind me, searching for any sign of trouble.

I didn't see anything. Just the alien plants bending in the breeze.

I'd had this exact feeling in the Zone when somebody was trying to decide whether to start some shit or not. No matter which way I looked, I saw only alien landscape, painted in unnatural colors. And then it occurred to me . . . *What if what's watching us blends in too? Like our skinsuits?* The thought pulled my muscles tight and my nerves even tighter. If there *was* something out here, I needed to be ready. I couldn't let anything happen to Beatriz.

She pointed things out, and I kept nodding, but my attention was on the perimeter, scanning like a bot on patrol. Every so often, she paused to collect samples of plants. I did the same with minerals, but only because Nadim kept murmuring that I had a job to do. The dirt was an interesting mix of colors that probably told a fascinating story to somebody who knew more. I'd analyze it back aboard and let our equipment do the heavy lifting for some professor in Paradise to delight over once the digital information reached his desk.

It occurred to me that where humanity had, back in its late golden days, sent out machines to other planets to drill core samples and wander the landscape of another world . . . that was us now. We were humanity's arms and legs and eyes, but only partly its brain.

I didn't much enjoy the comparison.

Since the ruins were the only landmark, it was impossible to get lost. As we approached, the jagged stone teeth resolved into broken pillars, cut from some mineral that shimmered blue-black against the smooth surface of what might have been a raised platform. Red and brown earth filmed the steps leading up to the monument, but I didn't miss the fact that there were lines in that dust. Not footprints like a human would leave, but some strange thing had moved through here, not long ago. That put me on guard, again, and I faced back out, watching for anything that wanted to come at us.

"Look at the carvings, the bas relief, and the . . . what is this? Is it writing?" Bea peppered Nadim with questions, breaking the uneasy silence. I glanced back at the pillar she was scrutinizing. It did look like writing, all swirls and dots, but it could just as easily be decorative.

As usual, Bea was right, because Nadim said, "Yes. I have translations if you're interested."

"Of course!" I couldn't see her face under the mask, but the tone left no room for doubt that she had lit up like New Year's Eve.

"Please understand, this is imprecise, as it has been shifted through many languages. 'Here we sing to the stars. Deep in the dreaming, we have come and gone for many evers. Until the joining. Until journey's end. Sing back to us when you come, so that we may know the silence is never eternal. Our sun, your stars, their gods, they have sailed in other skins, far beyond the dark and into the hollow, where all light sleeps.'"

As he spoke, I had an eerie kind of vision. I had no idea what this alien race had looked like, so my imagination put them in robes, all gathered in a circle while they chanted beneath strange and forlorn stars. Firstworld had a sky utterly unlike Earth's, radiant with colors we got only at sunrise and sunset. A permanent aurora borealis streaking the sky, and a world full of life and color and desolation.

For some reason, a little shiver went through me, as if Nadim had incanted a magic spell. The superstitious kid in me expected a puff of purple smoke and a dragon or a demon to appear. But there was only the disquieting wind, whipping over me in greater gusts, so that the golden fronds in the distance bent nearly double as if performing reluctant obeisance. We stood for a moment in silence, and then Bea dropped to her knees. Normally, I wasn't the reverent type, but it seemed wrong not to do likewise.

"I don't know what that means, exactly," she whispered. "But I feel it. Zara?"

"Me too." I wasn't sure what was happening here, and it made me both wary and entranced. But there was *something* still in this world. A memory, maybe.

She bowed her head first. I followed suit. Then she astonished me by lifting her voice, doing exactly as the writing said. I was no singer, but I tried to follow, offering lower tones to harmonize with her gorgeous soprano. And her voice echoed, swelling in the crystals that remained in the shattered columns. Flickers of light pinged back and forth, trying to send a signal, trying and failing, but dear

God, it was exquisite, with streaks of light trembling in the heart of stone. Something in the air changed—charged—and it raised all the hair on the back of my neck, like being trapped in a lightning storm. Even the scent of the breeze changed, that smell of electricity burning up the air.

When our voices fell quiet and the glow died, the silence stretched and stretched, paper thin, then a filament of spider-silk, broken at last by Nadim, in a lovely, shattered tone. "I have never seen this. This has never happened before."

"Really?" I got to my feet and dusted off my knees.

"There have been no lights on Firstworld since . . ." In his silence I sensed uncertainty, a span of time so long that it was impossible to estimate without carbon dating, maybe. "I've heard stories. . . . The whole world used to shine, sparking one stone to another. It was one reason why my people came here. For the songs."

I nudged Bea. "You did this. How incredible are you?"

By her tone, I guessed she must be hot-cheeked beneath her mask. "I only did what they asked. Anybody could do it."

But if the other Honors hadn't brought Nadim along, they might not have had the translation. Even if they had read it, I had a hard time imagining hardcore science types singing to a bunch of ruined rock.

Their loss.

The light was dwindling by then, the violent colors fading to pastels that passed for night on Firstworld. Though we had climate control in our skinsuits, I had no desire to test out how good it was under extreme temperatures. Or to be out here in the dark. Now that the awe had faded, my paranoia was creeping back.

"We should wrap it up and get out of here," I said.

There were no arguments; as gorgeous as that display had been, there'd been something eerie about it too. Like ghosts whispering across time. We didn't speak on the way back to the Hopper. Beatriz seemed to be thinking about her impromptu performance while Nadim had to be trying to decide how to explain away what I'd seen in the fern meadow. I didn't intend to give him a chance to bullshit me.

As Bea booted up the ship, I asked, "Do we have enough fuel for one last sweep?" The Hopper could hover like a beast, and I was curious enough to ask.

"Definitely. Cells at eighty-four percent," she said after checking. "But what are you looking for?"

"Just checking out the view."

And searching for aliens.

We skimmed over the ground, and I peered hard at the changing landscape. Just before the grassland yielded to what would be considered forest on Earth—though these were weird-ass, almost sentient-seeming trees that looked like mushrooms, fleshy and leafy at once—I saw it. Bea didn't spot the dark patch hidden by waving fronds, but it was similar to the circle our thrusters had made. I didn't mention it. But I felt a hot little burn of confirmation.

Native wildlife, my ass. Somebody else was *here.* If it was another Leviathan crew, I'd almost shot another Honor.

Shouldn't have been sneaking up on us, then.

I said, "Okay, let's go. I'm good."

"Thank you for taking me with you to the surface," Nadim said, gentle and uncertain. "I have much to consider."

Like how to handle me.

This time, I didn't attempt to talk to him about it, which probably made him wonder what was up. When we returned, I was meticulous about putting the samples away and replacing my gear, once I'd cleaned it properly. Then I went to my quarters for a shower. I was hungry too, but this conversation would go better if we had it in private.

It was possible that was the longest I'd gone in a while without talking to Nadim, because he was the one who spoke first when I rapped on the wall. "Zara . . ."

"Yeah?"

"I'm sorry."

"For what?" Maybe I was being petty, but it wouldn't hurt him to say it.

"Lying to you. I said I never would, and I'm sorry. It caught me off guard."

"Then are you ready to level with me? About what I saw down there."

When he didn't reply, I tried to imagine that my brain had an off switch and flipped it. I locked him out, tighter than I'd ever done before. Then I closed my eyes. *I see nothing. Hear nothing. Feel nothing. I'm not even here. I don't even exist.*

To my surprise, severing that hard link with Nadim rocked me with feedback, so that my head burned with white noise . . . no, *dark* noise. If silence was a pit that you could fall into, I had one growing in my skull like a black hole.

"Zara! Stop. Please stop!" He sounded frantic.

When I got my head right again, I discovered that I'd bitten my lip hard enough to bleed. "Nadim . . ." I didn't even know what to say.

"Don't do that," he said softly.

"I won't. But you have to tell me what was down there! I'm not gullible. I know something—someone—was with us on that planet."

With a faint sigh, he surrendered. "Most likely, it was a pilgrim. They are not supposed to be there during the Tour. I'm not sure what happened, why our paths crossed. But if you had injured one, the consequences would have been—"

"Bad?" I supplied.

"Unthinkable!"

"So what's a pilgrim, then, when it's at home?"

"Zara—"

"It's not from Earth, that's for damn sure."

"I can't tell you."

"Then let me say it. These pilgrims . . . they're not human. That's obvious. Except for the Tour, there are no humans out here."

The air was thick with his struggle to be honest with me, and at the same time, to play by the rules he'd been given. I didn't really expect to win that battle; I'd just gotten here, and Nadim, I knew, had been earnestly following his orders his whole life.

So I was taken aback when he suddenly said, "Yes."

It caught me cold, and I sat down, very fast. "Uh . . . wait. So there *are* other aliens out here. *Living* aliens."

"You're on board one, Zara."

"I mean, other than Leviathan!"

"Of course. I told you that we've come in contact with other civilizations—"

"Dead ones!"

"I omitted certain information for the good of your species." That sounded arrogant. And rehearsed. "Humanity is not ready to interact with other civilizations we have encountered in our travels."

"Why *not*?"

Nadim sounded a little impatient with me now. "Zara. You know why. Billions of your people lived in pain and terror. You had eradicated most native species on your own world, and unlike some of the species we encounter, you brought ruin on yourselves."

"So we're not fit to meet the neighbors, is that it?" I bristled all over. If I could have grown spikes, I would have. "Punks and criminals, our whole planet?"

"I never said that. But as a species, humans have been *thoughtless*. Our participation was meant to teach you how to manage your needs more effectively. And the Honors, the Tour . . . that was originally meant to acclimate Earth to the idea that it was one of many civilizations. We thought . . . we thought that we would begin slowly."

"What happened?"

"There was a death," he said. "And the other species . . . no longer wanted to interact with humanity. It is regrettable."

Someone had been quick on the trigger of a weapon. No wonder he'd been so terrified I'd shoot wildly down on Firstworld. "Was—was the human who did that one of your Honors?"

"No," he said. "That was before I began the Tour. But it doesn't matter. We all feel a burden for what occurred. We're hopeful that, as Earth becomes more peaceful, you might be able to try again to become part of the larger universe. Until then . . ."

"Until then, we paddle around in the little puddle you let us have and pretend it's ocean."

"Zara, it's for your *safety*. . . . What is that?"

"What?"

"Are you *happy*?"

I was. Not for any reason I could explain at first, until I let myself really feel it. Then I laughed. "Yeah. Yeah, I guess I am."

"Why? I thought you would be angry!"

"I should be," I said. "I mean, really. You think of us as a bunch of violent, angry fools. But honestly? I'm just kind of excited that little green men exist."

"They're not—"

"So. Besides these pilgrims, how many more are there?"

"None."

"You're a terrible liar."

"Thank you," he said. I think he meant it.

Over the next two weeks, I pestered the shit out of Nadim.

We had to finish analyzing all the data before we could go on to the next stop on the Tour, which for me mainly boiled down to prepping samples, making minute logs of the times and places we'd taken them from the surface, and sending on the results. We were far from home, so it would take—according to Nadim—a year for the signal to reach Earth. Everything had to be packaged properly and stored. The physical samples would be transferred once we came back at the end of the Tour.

Added to our routine maintenance, it left surprisingly little time for unrelated tasks, like, say, imploring a sentient ship to spill the remainder of his secrets. Since he'd confirmed that there was one race of aliens thriving enough to conduct galactic pilgrimages, it stood to reason there would be more.

The one thing I didn't do was cut off contact with him again. Maybe it would've gotten me what I wanted, but since I knew it frightened Nadim, that would make me no better than Typhon, whipping him to get my way.

No better than my father. And damned if I'd ever go down that road.

Tired of failure, and just generally tired, I trudged down the corridor to Beatriz's room. It was late in the evening, or the Icelandic equivalent, so I didn't know if she'd be up. I rapped twice, and only went in when she keyed open the door. "Can't sleep?"

I shrugged. "I should probably work out more. What're you doing?"

"Recording a personal log." She seemed slightly abashed to admit it.

So far, I'd only done one, and it was like ten seconds long. Mostly I felt like a jackass talking to myself when I could be learning every humanly accessible inch of Nadim. Privately I admitted I might be obsessed. Slightly. Okay, a lot.

"Do you mind if I come in?"

"No, please." She stepped back, and I came into a room that was nothing like mine.

Not only did her room feel warmer, it smelled better too, faint hints of dark chocolate and cinnamon. She'd brought some small, colorful pillows and a picture of the Rio skyline at night. Those touches made it . . . personal. "Nice."

"Make yourself at home."

I read that offer as sincere and collapsed on her bunk. "You can finish the log if you want. I won't make any noise."

"If you're sure."

She went back to the table, where she'd set up her H2, and resumed. Since she was speaking in Portuguese, I only caught the occasional word, not enough for a ballpark translation. Certain phrases echoed close to Spanish, which I'd heard a lot of in the Zone. That took me back to listening to old ladies haggle in the street market.

To entertain myself, I studied up on Nadim's circulatory system. Being a human doctor wasn't my dream, but Leviathan physiology was considerably more intriguing.

When Bea fell silent, I asked, "You done?"

"For now. I have a lot of thoughts."

"Me too." I decided on impulse to test the waters, see how she'd react to what Nadim had told me. It wasn't like he'd sworn me to secrecy, and maybe if I enlisted Bea's help, we could coax some more information out of him.

There could be terabytes of forbidden knowledge taunting me from behind a firewall. "You remember how I flipped out that day on Firstworld?"

"How could I forget?"

"Well, when I asked you to sweep, I spotted a second burn circle in the flora." At her questioning look, I added, "Where another ship likely put down."

Her eyes widened. Her mind went in the same direction mine had. "Did we cross paths with another Honor? Good thing you didn't shoot them. Try explaining *that* in your personal log."

I laughed. "That doesn't make sense, though. If they were human, why run? Why not say hello?"

"What are you trying to tell me?"

"I got Nadim to admit we weren't alone down there, Bea." She just stared at me. "Whoever was down there with us, they weren't human."

Since she was bright, it didn't take her long to come to the right conclusion. But she didn't take it well. She bounced to her feet and paced, rubbing her hands together in what psychologists liked to call a self-comforting gesture. Mumbling in Portuguese, she eventually settled on, "Are you serious?" in English.

"From what I gather, it wasn't supposed to happen. Are you game to find out more?"

She was already shaking her head violently, which

surprised me. "There have to be reasons we're kept in the dark. It's . . . security clearance, or on a need-to-know basis."

"So? They didn't hurt us, we didn't hurt them. Help me talk Nadim into opening some of the files to show us what these aliens look like?"

"No. Leave it, Zara." That was sharp, coming from Beatriz, and after a moment she said, "I'm sorry, but I just . . . I need to rest."

Didn't take a genius to figure out that she wanted me gone. It was possible she'd change her mind in time. Space travel hadn't immediately enraptured her either, but she'd come around. With those silent reassurances, I said good night and headed for my room in low spirits.

"You're upset," Nadim observed.

He hadn't spoken to us in Beatriz's room, which made me think she hadn't invited him in, and therefore, he hadn't been listening to what we said. I'd counted on that. He did follow into my quarters, however; I felt him in a warming swirl, prickling over my skin. Normally I would have found that relaxing, comforting, more than a little thrilling.

Not just now. "Don't worry about it," I said. "I'm all right."

"You told Beatriz about Firstworld."

"So you *did* eavesdrop on us!"

"No. But it's obvious you would want to involve her in trying to find out more, and I think from your mood that she rejected your offer."

"Damn. Why are you so perceptive? But she's happier just doing her job."

"You aren't."

"What?"

"Happy."

"Eh, I can be happy in some ways but not in others. I'm complicated like that."

He seemed to consider that for a moment, and then said, almost hesitantly, "Would you let me share something else with you?"

"Always." The response popped out before I could stop it.

"You should make yourself comfortable first."

A little shivering breath gusted out, but I curled up on my bed. Hell, I even closed my eyes. Before Nadim, I never took instructions, but these days, it was hard for me to imagine him asking me to do anything that would hurt me.

"Okay, I'm good."

"I don't know what you did that day at the pool, but do it again. If you can. Or this might not work." He hesitated. "Call this . . . an apology. I want you to see what I see."

I didn't even ask what he intended to do. Before, I'd closed the door on him; this time, I threw it wide, and it was like having my mind drawn into a breathlessly fast whirlpool. Silent currents carried me straight to him, and as we had before, we clicked in, two missing pieces, and then there was no *I*, as everything of *him* became *me*. The new thing, the sweetness of *we*, moved with growing confidence. My mind opened like a flower so we could feel the cool, distant starlight streaming in an incandescent glow. Everything expanded. I was enormous and minuscule at the same time. Joined.

Bonded.

A flutter of fingertips, and we leapt forward. But it wasn't enough. There were no words anymore, just the endless loop of emotion—joy, excitement, euphoria—and it echoed until we couldn't contain it. Notes that I (the smaller *I*) only sensed before they burst into starsong, humming along our hull-skin, glittershot, thrumming, hopeful, all cadences in light and sound, simultaneous and eternal and exquisite. Roaring repeat, call and icy chorus of distant stars—

Pop.

I tumbled into my skin, and I felt like I was choking, trapped in a small dark place, alone. I felt myself flailing and couldn't control it, and then I was sickly falling off the bed. Laying on the floor, I panted, hard. My head hurt like it hadn't since I was a little kid. "N-Nadim . . . ?"

"I'm here, Zara." He spoke warmly, quickly, and I heard the deep concern. "You're showing elevated heart rate and respiratory distress." Such a scattershot voice, pinging me with the pink of his panic. "Do you require medical intervention?"

"No. Just . . . give me a minute. That was hard-core."

"Hard . . . core?"

"Being you. I heard the stars. Tasted them. Or . . ." I had no words.

"And I felt your heart beating, your blood rushing, the flicker of your nerves and skin. It was . . ." Apparently, this was new territory for Nadim too. "That was my fault. I only meant to show you a little of what I see. Not everything. Not yet. I didn't mean—"

"To do what?" Put that way, he made it sound like we were doing something forbidden, and for me, that was like a catnip mouse on a string.

"Deep bond."

Why did that sound so alluring? Despite my exhaustion, I immediately wanted to do it again. I ached to feel that freedom, to explode out of my tiny, fragile skin into the exultation of starsong. "That was amazing. Would we get in trouble if anyone found out?"

"Yes. It isn't meant to be done on the Tour. I think it happens on the Journey."

"Then it has to be our secret." Right then I made up my mind, I wouldn't even tell Bea. From general conversation, I'd gleaned that her impressions from Nadim were superficial at best, only glimmers of what I felt. She was more hesitant about connecting with him and she didn't have a boost of Leviathan DNA, either.

"I just . . . I wanted to make it up to you." He didn't even need to explain what he meant. I could tell that Nadim didn't like holding out on me. It chafed like a sliver of glass beneath his skin. I twisted onto my back and flattened my palms on the floor, then bent my knees so I could use the soles of my feet too. Not only did it ground me after that wild ride, it also offered four points of contact. It occurred to me I might prefer sleeping on the floor in contact with him to sleeping on the bed, as it carried the same emotional resonance as snuggling in somebody's arms.

Where we touched, warmth blossomed. With my eyes closed, I could feel what he felt, the energy flow back and forth as we adjusted as separate things once more, falling away from the *we*. Before I realized it, he had me tracing patterns with my hands and feet, following the subtle trail of pulses. The sleek, hot delight of it spiraled in secret art that only we could see, only we could create. Nadim's peace washed over me as if I'd survived a shipwreck.

I finally said, "If you ever bullshit me again, you'll see some Lower Eight wrath."

"Consider me forewarned." I sensed what I would have called a smile. His voice dropped to a slightly lower pitch, and the floor beneath me warmed. I could see the tendrils of color pulsing beneath me, like an aura. "Then . . . I should be more candid. The first time, at the pool . . . that was accidental. This was not. I wanted to share with you."

My mouth went dry, and I closed my eyes, listening to him. He was nervous, I thought, waves of yellow and cool green and little spikes of orange like goose bumps.

"Share what?" I asked.

"Everything." The word came like a fall of light, warm as summer. "Being with you is different, no awkward words, the way others flinch when I touch. You aren't afraid of me. Of this. I know it isn't time, Zara. Our rules say a deep bond is only for the Journey; not every Leviathan can find such a partner. But—"

"You didn't want to wait," I cut in. "I'm not good at rules either. Maybe that's why you picked me."

"I didn't. Typhon did," he reminded me.

Disquiet prickled to life. From what I knew, Typhon was a bastard, and maybe Nadim was grown in his image, only smoother, capable of making me forget my anger with a single glimpse of the stars. I didn't like feeling like I'd been . . . handled, and I was still uneasy when I drifted off to sleep.

Biggest mistake of my life.

CHAPTER THIRTEEN

Breaking Laws

I WOKE TO sunlight and birds twittering in trees, which was *the* most annoying way to wake up. The only birds I'd seen in the Zone had been seagulls, loud scavengers that would sooner shit on you than not. Birds didn't make me think of open meadows and forests—more of trash piles.

"Hey," I said, sitting up and running my fingers through my uneven hair. "Could you make the alarm do, um, water instead? Rain? Or maybe the ocean? Birds aren't my thing."

No answer. I flopped back down. "Nadim?" The floor beneath me was still warm—he'd increased the temperature to keep me comfortable while I slept—and I stayed huddled there beneath the thin blanket for a moment before I said his name again. Worried, this time. "Nadim? Are you there?"

No answer, again. I jumped up, didn't bother with niceties like showers and deodorizers and hell, even uniforms. I was still in my thin, silky underwear when I left my room at a run, heading for the data console. "Nadim!" I shouted. "Answer me, dammit!"

Only silence came back, even when I stopped and pressed both hands flat against his skin because physical contact boosted our basic connection. He was there, I could feel him, but he was . . . drifting. Barely there, distant as the stars. Imagining my thoughts as silver tendrils, I reached for him, *reached* and opened my mind until the effort hurt; he was too far. Despair and fear curled through me in gray and bloodred waves. I yelled his name again into the darkness.

Nothing.

Beatriz stumbled out of her quarters, equally disheveled. "Something's wrong!"

I stepped back from the wall and almost fell. She grabbed and shook me. Hard. "Zara! What should we do?"

Suddenly a shudder went through Nadim's body, an ominous shiver that brought with it a low, silvery flash of what felt like pain. *Please, Nadim. . . .* I remembered the video I'd found, the one he hadn't wanted me to see, of the grim third voyage where he'd lost his Honors and nearly his own life.

Oh God. He's gone dark.

This is why I built the alarm, I realized, and felt immediately better. Quickly I ran diagnostics; it had all looked good before, and still did; shouldn't it have buzzed him awake by now? I checked it again. Diagnostics said it was fine, but it wasn't responding.

I tried inputting the backdoor code I'd created but it only turned the alarm off, when it was allegedly on already. The shock part wasn't working. . . . *What the hell did I do wrong?*

It came to me with a rush of horror what Nadim had so off-handedly said: that it would be installed before he went on the Journey. *But we weren't on the Journey yet.* Right now, the thing worked, but it wasn't *installed*. And it wasn't doing a damn bit of good sitting in the assembly bay.

He was supposed to be safe on the Tour without it.

I grabbed Bea's hands. "Manual controls! Go!"

Her lips parted, but she didn't waste time asking questions; she turned and ran down the corridor, around the curve. I followed on shaky legs, feeling more strikes and shivers in his body, like needles driven into my own skin.

As I got to the hub, Bea was cursing under her breath in rapid-fire Portuguese, staring at the data readouts as her fingers flew, touching controls, swiping, spinning. I headed for an adjacent data station to check on Nadim's condition, but a speck of darkness caught my eye on the viewport, occluding a cluster of stars. Then it was larger, huge, and I involuntarily ducked as it slammed brutally into the wall a few meters over my head with an enormous, shuddering impact. I expected glass to crack and expel me into space, but the thing bounced off and rolled away into the dark.

Another sharp, silvery pain beneath my skin. Nadim's nerves firing warnings to a brain that was no longer receiving.

"Bea!" I shouted.

"I know!" she called back, and finally, *finally*, something she did worked. I felt a lurch inside, and a tugging, drawing sense of deceleration.

We were slowing down, here in the darkness between stars, and as we did, I saw we were in the orbiting graveyard of a pulverized planet or moon—debris everywhere, from dust to pebble-sized fragments to enormous islands of rock. If we'd gone farther into it and hit one of those floating mountains . . . The one on the port side had to be the size of the entire city of New Detroit. Maybe an Elder could have survived the impact, but I didn't like to even think what would have happened to Nadim.

We slowed, still bumping into fragments, creating an open wake behind us until the collisions bled enough of our momentum that we hung silent and still, trapped in the middle of this dead debris field. It was moving too, driven by whatever long-ago forces had acted on it to blow it to pieces. As I joined Bea at the console, I realized she was manually controlling our position and speed relative to it. We were moving. Just matching our speed to the cloud.

"Can you get us out of here?" I asked. She took her hands off the controls long enough to wrap her hair into an untidy knot at the back of her head.

"Not until I make sure I have all the other pieces' vectors mapped," she said. "I might be able to, a little at a time. But it's dangerous."

"So, we stay here?"

"Just as dangerous. Everything's moving, Z, at different speeds, different angles. He'll keep getting hit, I can't avoid everything. Sooner or later, one of the big ones that are moving around out there will crash into us." She looked up at me, dark eyes fierce. "What's wrong with him?"

"I think he's asleep." I hesitated for about two seconds, then nudged her aside and started the vid of Voyage Three on the console screen.

She flinched and covered her mouth by the end, and gave me a horrified look as I shut it down. "What *is* this?"

"Nadim lost his Honors," I said. "Early on. He's got a kind of condition—a very deep sleep, like a coma. He only does it when he expends too much energy and is too far from stars to recharge properly. It wasn't supposed to happen on the Tour. Part of my checklist was building him a kind of alarm clock to wake him up if it ever happened again. But there weren't any directions to install it, just to build it."

"But he was fine yesterday!" Somebody else might waste energy getting pissed over being out of the loop, but Bea was all business during a crisis, checking our position on the star charts. "How close does he need to be to a star to refuel?"

"Closer than this, or he wouldn't be drifting," I said. "What's our nearest option?"

"There." A star chart flickered to life all around us, glorious 3D. She pointed. "This is a red giant. So we shouldn't have to go more than half a day at his normal speed to reach a significant amount of light and radiation coming from it."

I had a terrible suspicion as to why Nadim was hibernating. For all my contempt toward rules, I was starting to think that the Elders' restrictions about deep bonding might have been in place for a reason. Maybe he'd used too much of his strength last night. Guilt tapped at the edges of my brain, but falling into a pit of remorse wouldn't help. Only action could.

I swallowed hard and said, "How can I help?"

Beatriz switched back to the screens that showed the dizzily moving field of debris around us. "Take the biggest pieces," she said. "Calculate their speeds and trajectories. Be careful, we need to know exactly where they'll be to chart our path. I'll take the medium-sized ones."

"I should have said something, Bea," I said as I took my place. "I'm sorry. I didn't think this would happen."

"We should have both been told," she said. I heard the grim tone of it. "Never mind. First we have to get out of this. All of us."

We both started in on the calculations, the same kind of exercises that the checklists had been drilling us in since we'd started. I was grateful for the hard training now, under pressure, with our lives on the line. This was what we had going for us that his long-dead Honors hadn't on that fatal voyage. We weren't necessarily smarter or better, but at least we had training.

Of the two of us, I'd taken the more intensive interest in Leviathan physiology, an offshoot of my fascination with Nadim. So I called up the system that monitored his physical condition. It was basic, and the diagnostic did show me the location of the debris projectiles that had penetrated him, but it gave me no sense of scale.

"Can you find out more?" Bea asked.

"Not through the console."

I'm doing this to help, I told myself as I sat down and closed my eyes, flattening my palms on the floor. That contact resonated between us, so the thrum of his energy trembled through me. Something sparked in my head, and the vibration passed between us in a feedback loop of theta waves like the tap of a tuning fork with each moment that I focused. Matching frequencies, he'd said. I quieted my mind, blocking out everything else.

Nadim, asleep, was a haunted house. I could sense him somewhere on the fringes of my awareness, a shimmering silvery light, but here, in his skin, everything was shadows.

And in the shadows, blackened wounds that bled smoke.

"He's got two large injuries," I heard myself say aloud, but it sounded like someone else's voice. "One above us, on his dorsal side. It goes down through the skin and into muscles. The area's exposed into space. He's bleeding."

"Bleeding?" Her voice seemed fainter, farther away as I mentally moved closer to the site of the wound. Splitting my consciousness like this, it was more than disorienting; my head hurt like back in the old days, though maybe that was an echo of Nadim's pain too. Ghostly flickers of anguish crawled over my skin: side, sternum, ankles, shoulder, off and on like a water tap.

"It's not as bad as I thought. I don't think he can control his right side until those muscles heal and the tear closes up. But it's mending on its own. Leviathan bodies can heal faster than ours."

"And the other wound?"

"It's not as large," I said, "but . . ." My mind drifted, pulled by the shimmering afterimages of pain that still lit the nerves, and saw a foreign object lodged inside him. In the strange vision I had here, it looked like all spikes and angles, but I thought it was one of the jagged pieces of planetary debris.

Worse, it was stuck very close to a thick, throbbing membrane that served as filtration for his respiratory equivalent, according to the studies I'd been doing. I came out of my trance for a moment and accessed the data console again.

Leviathan didn't have a single pumping mechanism for their blood, but they did have critical junctures. This was one of them. Damage to it would be very dangerous. Maybe fatal.

I had the eerie impression that the organ was moving. It sat within a large, empty space, but I could sense it steadily expanding to fill that space. If it shifted much farther, it would jam up against the sharp rocks that had never seen the softening effects of wind or water. And those edges would slice that membrane right open. Maybe, in time, softer tissue would form, pushing the foreign matter out, but it wasn't happening yet, and it couldn't happen fast enough. Not if we intended to try to fly Nadim out of here with any kind of precision.

We might kill him if we tried. Or even if we did nothing.

Dropping the connection left me weak and dizzy. I stammered my findings to Beatriz, shivering as if I'd crawled out of a cold river. She grabbed a blanket and put it around my trembling shoulders.

"Well. That was something they didn't cover in the manual."

"I . . . we can talk about it later. If we survive."

Her mouth compressed. "This isn't the time, but yeah. We'll have words."

I remembered how Nadim had kept me warm through the night and wondered just when he'd dropped off to sleep. Maybe our very closeness had lulled him into it. Guilt had an ugly rust-red color to it and a bitter taste on my tongue.

As I shivered, a warning flashed on the console: *EMER-GENCY INTERVENTION REQUIRED. Follow Leviathan care protocols set forth in Appendix A-17.*

This time, I didn't even need to reach for my H2 to understand my mission.

"We have to get that rock out of there," I told her. "It's below us, off to the left. I can find it, but . . ."

"But what?"

"It's not one of the areas he's let us go into before. Not fitted out for human habitation." I struggled up to my feet. "I'm going to need a skinsuit."

Bea didn't argue about it; she ran and got one, and I stripped down and put it on. It melted onto me, gray and then swirling with colors, as if it wasn't quite sure how to camouflage me. I settled the hood and mask on and felt a momentary panic as it molded to my face before starting to process air in a cool, constant flow.

"How are you going to get to it?" she asked me.

"The waste system," I said. "It links up after the filters with natural venting, and then I can get from there into his circulatory system. I think I can fit through the waste tubes. But—" I didn't like the idea, but I said it anyway. "I'm going to need the medical kit. I'll have to cut into his blood vessels." Quickly, I activated a holo of his full biosystem. Lines of light appeared, a complicated 3D maze that twisted and wrapped around itself, branched off into sections and groupings. Each blood vessel seemed large enough for a human to pass through. That didn't mean it was safe. "I'll get as close as I can to the site before I get into his bloodstream."

If Nadim were awake, he would have been able to adjust the atmosphere inside himself, maybe even eject the rock fragment on his own.

But Nadim wasn't awake, and he needed me to do this.

Beatriz stopped me as I picked up the portable med kit. I thought she wanted to talk strategy, but she grabbed me by the arms and looked me right in the eyes. "Zara, this is dangerous—"

"Better for me to go. I can—I can feel my way better than you can right now."

"Because he's connected to you," she said. "In a way he isn't to me."

"Doesn't mean he doesn't care about you, Bea."

"I know. I can feel he does. But—not like he cares for you."

I wanted to stop and tell her about the sensations from the time I first came on board, about the Leviathan DNA grafted into my own to stop my brain from destroying me. About the joy of it, and the terror, and *everything*. But I couldn't. We were all going to die—all three of us—if we wasted time right now.

So I hugged her close, and she hugged me back, and I said, "I'm coming back, and when I do, I'll open up on all counts. I swear."

"You'd better."

I flashed her a grin. "Come back?"

"And tell me everything," she said. "I'm holding you to it."

"Keep us alive until I get there."

She stepped back and nodded, and I saw the Beatriz she'd become these past few days—calm, steady, relentlessly capable.

I wished I had her focus. All I had was nerve, and now, I was going to have to use it.

Med kit and H2 attached to my suit, I began the long, dirty crawl through the waste tunnels. We'd done a good job of keeping them clean, so it wasn't nearly as bad as it might have been, plus the skinsuit insulated me from the smells and tactile nastiness of it. I unlocked the filters, slipped through, and Beatriz, who'd followed in her own biohazard suit, replaced them with a whisper that I thought was a prayer.

That left me crawling alone in the dark through incredibly narrow tubing that flexed when I pushed at it. It was exhausting and slow; I had to keep fighting my own clumsiness and checking the map. I had no sense of direction here, and Nadim's injuries echoed loud inside me. I had to close him out; his pain threatened to drain what little energy I had left.

It seemed to take forever before I reached a spot close to the damage. I took a laser scalpel from the med kit, turned it on, and made one quick, cauterizing cut to slice open the tube.

Red-edged pain shot through me, as if I'd taken the scalpel to myself, and I had to bite my lip not to yell; I didn't want to panic Beatriz, and answering questions would distract me. I could feel—even though I'd muted the connection—that the problem of the sharp, protruding rock so near Nadim's fragile organ was growing more urgent, the damage more severe. No time to waste.

I slithered through the wound I'd inflicted. I'd intended to close it up with the same cauterizing laser, but there was nothing to stand on beneath, nothing to hold on to; coming out of the tube, there was just a long, sloping organic wall curving into the dark.

I had no choice. I let go, bounced, rolled, and landed in something thick, gooey, and—when I lifted my gloved hand to the light—silvery, with weird oily rainbows shimmering on the surface.

Nadim's body suddenly shuddered, hard, but it didn't feel like another impact; I didn't sense anything hitting him or injuring him again. It was more like a reaction to me being here, where I wasn't supposed to be. He had antibodies, the way humans did, and they'd detected me. Would the bond we'd made protect me? I couldn't be sure.

"Nadim," I said aloud. "I don't know if you can hear me, but if you can, I'm trying to help you, okay? I swear, what I'm doing is to make you better. So please, uh, don't kill me. All right?"

I so badly wanted to hear him say, "Acceptable," in the dry, amused tone he so often used to respond to my attempts at humor. Yet there was nothing but the echo of my voice through a vast, dark chamber, and the knowledge that he was depending on me.

I trudged on through the dark, trying not to step in the rivulets of silver again, and then quite suddenly, the floor dropped off and down another sharp slope—into a lake of the silver stuff. Well, a pond, anyway. How deep, I couldn't tell.

I checked the H2 again on its wrist mount, then closed my eyes and tried to figure out where I was relative to the rock that needed to come out. As I opened them, I realized that the wall opposite me, shimmering pearl pink in the light attached to the side of my mask, was moving. Slowly expanding toward me, pushing the silvery liquid in front of it.

I was in the right place. This was the membrane I'd sensed, and somewhere under that liquid was that damn rock. If I didn't move it, right now, it would slice through that wall like a laser scalpel, and . . .

Nadim would die. Then we'd be trapped aboard a drifting, dead ship, all systems down until there was nothing to breathe or the cold got us first. Three frozen corpses, drifting on into the dark.

Kicking off, I landed on my back and slid down the wall, straight into the silver fluid. I hit it with what I thought would have been a splash, but it was thicker and heavier than water, more like liquid mercury. I disappeared underneath the surface without a ripple.

For a second I panicked, because I was sure I was going to drown in Nadim's blood, but the skinsuit, though it seemed to tighten hard around me, coped with the change. Air continued flowing, less than before, or maybe I was just breathing too fast. The liquid felt heavy. I wasn't buoyant, like I'd have been in water; moving was a huge effort, and I couldn't see a damn thing. The light on the side of my mask provided a dim, ghostly glow, but it didn't even penetrate past my nose. If I wasn't careful, I'd never figure out which way was up, much less where I needed to go.

Calm down, I told myself, and shut my eyes. I could visualize myself now as a weird shadow over the misty shape of Nadim's insides. Ahead of me, maybe twenty meters away, I could see the denser, sharper shape of that rock.

The moving, expanding tissue came terrifyingly close to those cutting edges. I had to move, and I had to do it fast.

I pushed off, struggling against the thick, muffling liquid. One step, another, another. Then I reached out my hand and brushed something solid.

Something that cut cleanly through my skinsuit, and Nadim's thick blood glided in. Cold. The cold quickly turned into a burning sensation, and I was afraid of exactly what this stuff would do to me, but there was no time to think. I was swimming in it and the debris was a hand's breadth from cutting into a major circulatory junction. I wrapped both hands around it and heaved, hard.

It came unstuck from where it had embedded itself in his skin and muscle. Heavier than I'd expected, and yes, sharp, so sharp that I was bleeding as it sliced through skinsuit and skin alike, and the crippling, searing cold of Nadim's blood made me shriek wordlessly, then pant in agony. The debris had blown in through his thick outer skin to lodge here, and I could feel the wound track still grooved in the flesh near me. I pushed through the blood, weight clutched in both hands. When I reached the wound track where it had entered, I realized his body had already started healing and sealing up the hole.

The wound was too small to push the fragment back out now.

I couldn't feel my fingers, and trying to find the laser scalpel was hard enough. But then turning it on and using it to slice open a wider hole would be far worse.

I braced myself, took in a deep breath, and ignited the laser. *Fast, do it fast*, I thought. Then the laser made contact with Nadim's healing flesh, and the pain roared and dragged me under, a red tsunami of anguish that made me scream and shake and *keep cutting*. Mercy wasn't an option now; the only way through this for either one of us was to bear it, scream through it, try to stay conscious under the numbing impact of the knowledge of the pain I was causing him.

I shut the laser off when I had a rough hole hacked all the way through to the thin membrane that covered the outside of Nadim's body.

I shoved the rock into it, still screaming. My throat felt raw, and I tasted metal. I was hurting myself, but I didn't care, because at least we were hurting together.

The rock's razor edges sliced the membrane, and it tumbled through, even as the vacuum of space sucked a bright

spray of silvery blood after it—with some red human drop-
lets that froze instantly—out into the black. Ruby jewels,
frosting with ice crystals, mingling with still-liquid Leviathan blood out here in the ultimate wilderness. Nadim
shuddered, and the pain flashed in such a spike that I lost
the ability to scream at all.

Vacuum pulled at me, but the agony drove a wave
through the liquid at staggering speed. I slipped, and the
slick silvery lake of blood flowed over me in a disorienting
flood.

CHAPTER FOURTEEN

Breaking Out

I DIDN'T KNOW where I was. I was down, floating, lost . . . and then, as the pain gradually began to recede, I heard someone talking to me. Just a voice at first, with no meaning.

Then Beatriz was saying in my ear, "Zara, *get up*, you have to try! Come on! I can see where you are, and you need to get up and out of there! Please!"

I fumbled around. There was no sense of up or down anymore, and I was floating blind . . . but then my shoulder brushed something. It was soft, and yielding, but it was also strong.

And it pushed me forward.

It took me a few seconds to get my brain operating again and to remember the pink membrane that had been moving toward the sharp edges of the debris. It was shoving me, and now, I felt a solid surface under my feet. I put my back against the membrane and let it push me on. The surface beneath my feet rose sharply in a curve, and I scrambled up, flailing for purchase. If I wasn't careful, it would crush me against the slope. I'd slid down this wall. Now, half-enveloped by Nadim's expanding tissue, I fought my way back up again.

As I came up out of the blood and rolled onto the flatter surface, I realized I still couldn't feel my hands. They didn't hurt anymore, at least.

Actually it felt like they didn't exist.

"Bea?" I gasped. "Bea?"

"I'm here! Zara, you did it, you got it out. He's going to be okay. But you need to come back now. You have to."

"I can't feel my hands." My voice was shaking. I didn't want to look at what was happening to me. What had already happened to me.

"We can fix that when you get back," she said, and her voice was calm, clear, just what I needed. "I'm going to guide you, all right? Can you see your H2?"

I clumsily lifted my left arm and tried to look. The screen was gummed with silver blood. I tried wiping it off, but it only smeared. "No," I said. I was so tired. I just wanted to sit down and rest. "I can't. I'm going to lie down now."

"Don't you *dare*!" Bea's voice thundered at me, and I remembered all the authority figures who'd ever yelled at me. Underneath all of that was my father's voice. I wanted to lie down just to spite them . . . and then the tone changed. "Zara, please. He needs you. *I* need you. If you quit now, you're not coming back, and you belong here. With me. With us."

That sounded like someone else now. It sounded like all the people who'd cared. Who'd loved me, despite all my cracks and flaws. My mother. My sister. Even Derry, sometimes.

It reminded me of Nadim too. And reminded me of just who Bea was, the angel who could sing stars out of the sky. I could hear music in her.

So I sucked in a shaking breath and said, "Help me."

"Okay, you can't climb back up. I want you to go straight ahead . . . now a little left . . . a little more : . . . Stop. Reach up, there should be a kind of ledge there. Pull yourself up."

"I can't. I can't feel my hands."

"You can."

Bea's certainty made me reach up, and I did feel . . . something. A distant pressure, maybe. My body remembered things my mind didn't. I went up. Then I kept going, walking blind, turning and twisting, an exhausted stumble into silence where Nadim should have been. At least he wasn't hurting anymore. But what did that mean? If he wasn't hurting . . . Panic chewed at the corners of my mind; I didn't let it take root.

I'm not supposed to be here. I hope I'm not contaminating him with my blood.

"Okay," Bea said. I could hear a change in her voice. Hope, and something else too. "You need to listen to me now, Zara. Don't move, okay?"

"Okay," I said.

"You're standing right on top of one of Nadim's main arteries," she said. "The blood in there is moving very, very fast. I need you to focus, all right?"

I could actually feel the hiss of the liquid passing underneath my feet, a purely physical sensation that made me feel dizzy and a little sick. "What do you want me to do?" But I already knew. I just didn't want to think about it.

"Use the laser scalpel and cut it open and get inside," she said. "It'll carry you part of the way. I'll tell you when you need to get out."

I didn't bother trying to tell her I couldn't, not this time. Surviving meant I had to. So I fumbled the laser scalpel out of my utility belt again; I was glad it was firmly attached, because I dropped it twice before I got a good grip. Focusing the light on it, I saw the deep slashes in my hands and fingers; no wonder I could barely feel anything. Shock must have clamped down hard, and the Leviathan blood had created a sticky rainbow film over the damage, sealing it almost like the skinsuit.

I sliced down with the laser scalpel—one decisive cut that opened up the tissue wide enough to allow me through. I braced for the pain, but oddly, it didn't come. This tissue didn't have nerves to damage. The thick wall of the blood vessel parted, and silvery liquid flooded out in a spray that nearly knocked me over.

I slid myself in feet first, hanging on to the rubbery edge as an irresistible tide tried to pull me free, and with my other hand used the laser to burn the edges together, right up to the edge of my grip. I hoped he'd be able to heal that relatively small tear quickly.

"In," I gasped to Bea. The pull of the current was intense, and I couldn't hold on for much longer.

"Trust me," she said. "I've got you. Let go."

It was like being blasted into orbit. I held myself as straight as I could and the tide carried me. It felt good to just relax, at least for a moment. Beatriz would tell me when to move again.

An alarm went off in my ear, and I flailed, turning in the current. I had to level out. If I blocked the flow of his blood, that would be worse still.

"What the hell is that?" I asked Bea, and for the first time, I sounded more like the old Zara.

"Oxygen alert," she said. "Your suit can't manufacture enough to last much longer, not under these conditions. It was never meant for this. Try breathing slowly, okay?"

"Sure," I said. "That sounds easy." Just the idea made me want to suck in another, deeper breath. Nothing like the threat of suffocation to make you want to gulp air. I felt a little giddy, which was probably the falling O_2.

"Focus, Zara. I'm going to give you a countdown from five. All right? Here we go. Five—four—three—"

The edges of the artery were brushing my shoulders now and still narrowing. I tried not to breathe too deeply. My vision glittered at the edges, and I felt dangerously light-headed. Bea's voice sounded far away. Was she counting in Portuguese?

"Now, Zara! Cut your way out now!"

I spotted a minuscule tear ahead. Twisting, I managed to hook a hand in it—and the effort nearly tore my shoulder from its socket. I didn't realize I'd been going that fast, but fighting the current and getting my other hand in place felt like lifting three times my body weight. When I pushed, the tear widened, and I wiggled out, shoulders, then hips, like a baby being born. I emerged in a forest of strange, thick filaments, and I squirmed through them, trying not to pull any loose. I was breathing deeper now, but it wasn't helping. My head hurt. My vision was fragmenting into strange sparkles.

Then I was in a wider tunnel, this one smooth and similar to the connective ducts. The skinsuit was barely breathing for me now, no matter how deeply I dragged the air in; I wanted to rip it off, but if it was still trying to feed me oxygen, that meant the atmosphere here in this tunnel was toxic. "Bea?" I managed to gasp out. "Where?"

"Go straight!"

I stumbled on and then slipped when I stepped in something slick.

The processed-waste flow.

It seemed to take forever to stagger to the end of the tunnel to the mesh that marked the beginning of the human-built sector, but eventually I slid under a flap and into the familiar sludge so comforting I almost wept.

Hard tremors set in as I half crawled toward our section of Nadim. The skinsuit had quit breathing altogether now, and my vision was nearly dark. I stripped the mask off as I splattered out of the hatch and onto the floor.

Air. Sweet, wonderful air. I dragged it in, out, long gasping, raw breaths, and finally realized someone was talking to me. Beatriz. She was frantically telling me she was on her way.

I collapsed in a puddle of ick. No idea how long it took Bea to find me, but she didn't bother with the biohazard suit. She was liberally splashed with muck as she rushed to my side in the narrow waste tunnel.

"Hey," I said vaguely as she grabbed my arms and started to drag me. "I made it."

She didn't answer; she was putting all her effort into moving me. I tried to help; by the time she managed to get me into a corridor, I rolled up to my knees and let her help me to my feet, and together, we stumbled to the med bay.

Medical intervention came in the form of an Earth-style bot, programmed with all the knowledge modern medicine and alien tech could devise, along with an impressive range of pharmaceuticals. The Emergency Medical Intervention Treatment Unit hadn't been built for beauty, so it was all boxy chrome, speakers, cameras, and spindly arms that could grasp, pull, twist, or inject with ease. I hadn't needed EMITU since we'd come aboard, so the thing perked up when I stumbled through the door.

"Honor Cole. You are injured. Processing severity." EMITU's voice had a definite old-school robo reverb, no uncanny valley there. The downside was it also couldn't manage empathy, so his cheer sounded like ghoulish delight. "Looks like we need to amputate. You will enjoy your new robot hands, manufactured by Jitachi, the industry leader in medical robotics."

My head was clearing, but for a long second I was almost sure I was hallucinating. Then I was sure I wasn't. I stopped cold and hid my butchered hands behind my back. "No way!"

"Only a little bedside levity. Are you not crazy entertained?"

From what I knew, EMITU wasn't supposed to have a sense of humor. I turned to glare at my companion. "Bea! Did you hack this thing?"

"It's great, right? I gave it some personality, over five hundred slang words, some I invented." She was using handfuls of medical wipes to clean the waste off her skin. "And you're in no position to complain, okay?"

I mumbled some choice Zone slang as Bea helped me out of my skinsuit. The med unit herded me into a decon shower, and the spray smelled overwhelmingly like the cheap pine cleaner they favored in institutions. It would have been reassuring if the mist had stung; I could see the damage to my flesh, but I couldn't feel it.

"Diagnosis: permanent nerve damage. Regenerative course required. Unless you want those robot hands?"

"Oh my God."

"Then please dress, Honor Cole. I'm not here for the booty."

Despite myself, I laughed. I put on the treatment gown and lay back in the chair. *Permanent nerve damage* didn't sound good, and the seriousness of it sank in fast. I realized I was breathing deeply, trying to make myself stay calm . . . and then Bea sat down next to me. "Hey," she said, and touched my shoulder. She was trying not to look at the mess of my hands. "I need to go back up there. We're good for now, but . . ."

"But you should keep alert," I agreed. I swallowed hard. "Bea, I'm sorry. I should have told you when I found out about Nadim's problem. But I honestly didn't think it would happen. I didn't."

"I know. And you were wrong." But her hand stayed gentle on my shoulder, and she smoothed my hair back from my face. "We're not out of this yet, Z."

EMITU told me to close my eyes, but the minute I did that, I thought that Mr. Personality would probably imitate a buzz saw. Beatriz walked away, so there was nobody here to check the thing if it went full horror show. I kept my gaze locked on EMITU, but it only prepped a syringe. Though I tensed, I still didn't feel any pain when it jammed the needle home in my hands. Not then. About thirty seconds later, the feeling came back in an excruciating rush, liquid fire from wrists to fingertips.

"Has sensation returned?"

"Yes." I hissed it through a clenched jaw. It was that or sink my teeth into my arm and chew off the offending limbs.

"I can give an injection for the pain, but I cannot expedite healing until the regenerative treatment runs its course. To attempt both simultaneously could result in a catastrophic shitstorm."

That was the best verbiage I'd ever heard from medical personnel. I imagined Beatriz cackling as she made her upgrades, and it occurred to me that she and I were two of a kind; she just rebelled in quieter ways. No wonder we got along so well. Most of the time, when I didn't screw it up.

"Understood."

"I am applying a protective sealant to discourage foreign matter as your wounds heal. Please return in twenty-four hours."

"Sure."

The stuff EMITU sprayed on my hands came out pink and looked like flesh caulk, basically. It molded over the gashes, at least, and while they still hurt, at least I didn't have to look at the gaping edges. Next I got an injection straight to my neck and my pain receptors all went on vacation. Such fast-working meds actually made the top of my head tingle. *Right, this is probably how Derry got hooked on chem.* My relief was so great, my whole body slumped, and I closed my eyes in the chair for a few seconds.

"You will live, Honor C. Get out of my office." The last sentence was pure Bea.

Now that it seemed like I would survive, and better yet, without pain, I mustered the last of my energy to get cleaned up, then stumbled to find her. When I got to the control room, she barely glanced up to verify proof of life. She was drenched in sweat; clearly we weren't out of the woods yet, and it had cost precious time towing my ass to EMITU.

I didn't speak as Bea flew Nadim on a complicated course to avoid the rolling, seemingly random paths of the big- and medium-sized chunks of rock, passing through the last of the debris field. Then it was just cold and dark and lonely, and I suspected neither of us had ever seen anything more purely beautiful.

Beatriz sat back in her chair and covered her face with trembling hands. She still had some crap in her hair and smelled like the waste tunnel. She quaked like an autumn leaf in a storm.

I put an arm around her. "Thank you. Thanks for saving us."

She elbowed me, hard. "It's your fault we're in this mess in the first place, and if you keep anything *else* from me, I'll kick your ass."

Normally I'd be like, *You'll try*, but she'd earned my genuine repentance. "Look, I really am sorry. But you know, if they'd leveled with us back in training, maybe I'd have known better. So it's maybe not entirely my fault . . . ?" I tried a coaxing smile that used to work on some of my counselors, the soft-hearted ones anyway.

With a sigh, she said, "Fine. I accept your apology. And . . . thanks to you too. I didn't crawl through Nadim's organs. You did. And look at you!" She lowered her hands and glared at my hands. "Is that the best EMITU could do?"

"It'll heal. And it doesn't hurt, which is all I care about right now." I flexed my fingers a little and winced. "Okay, it almost doesn't. Just feels weird as hell. Also, I love you, Bea, but you need a decon shower."

"I know," she said. "I also need to crawl into bed and pull the covers up and pretend this never happened, or I'll never sleep again. What are we going to do if this doesn't work?"

I just shook my head and used my newly useful fingers to chart a course to the red giant's glow—a glow that would wake Nadim.

I hoped.

That optimism died in the hissing, atonal light of the star we orbited for almost a full day, to no effect. I could hear the star—what Nadim would have called its song—but to my limited human understanding, it was a frightening, metallic hiss of roaring radiation. I knew because I processed the energy as sound through the console speakers. Couldn't take more than a few minutes of it before I shut it off, but I hoped it would be the healing balm that the Leviathan needed.

But Nadim didn't awaken. I sat up, staring at the screen until my eyes ached, listening. Pressing my hands to the wall. Calling his name out loud until my voice went rough and cracked.

I felt silent inside. Dark as the space between stars. *Wake up.* I wanted to scream it, pound on the walls until my hands were bloody, until he heard me. We were here. Around a star. And he wasn't coming back.

Bea brought me a cup of hot tea with lemon and honey. I couldn't remember how long it had been since I'd eaten or slept. Too long. I drank the tea too fast, and didn't care that I burned my mouth. Bea sank down on the floor next to me. "Anything?" It was just something to ask. She knew I had nothing to tell her. I just shook my head. "I did some reading. Maybe it just takes longer. Maybe the star isn't giving off the kind of radiation he needs."

"How would we know?" My voice sounded thin and rough, and I tried some more tea. More carefully this time.

"Without Nadim to tell us? Maybe we need to call Typhon."

I shuddered at the thought. "And say what, exactly? This is Nadim's last chance. If he doesn't graduate up to the Journey this time . . ."

"He needs to live, doesn't he? We can worry about the rest later."

I wasn't sure Nadim would feel that way, but Bea was probably right. We had to do something. Anything.

"I'm afraid we're losing him, Bea."

Nadim dying meant we died too. Maybe we could get a message off. Maybe someone would hear it. But honestly, neither of us could be sure.

She sank down to a crouch beside me, staring into my face. "Is he still bleeding?"

"No, the wound's clotted. I think this is just his . . . condition. He can't wake up."

"What about installing that device you built?"

I'd thought about that, but there were no instructions, not in the assembly room, not in the console. That, presumably, was information that would have gotten loaded later, before he went on the Journey.

Nadim had told me that he didn't need it on the Tour because he stuck to the approved routes. That he didn't take risks. So what had he done wrong?

Before he'd fallen asleep, he'd bonded with me. I couldn't shake the knowledge that this was because of *me*.

"We'll activate the distress signal," she suggested. "Maybe one of the other Leviathan will answer it."

Neither of us liked it, but there were no more options that either of us could find. We were probably ending Nadim's chance for the Journey; from what Nadim had told me, that might mean he'd be sent off, alone and exiled. We'd lose him. He'd lose us.

But at least he'd be alive.

And alone, I told myself. *He doesn't want to live that way.*

I didn't either, now that I understood how it felt to be a part of something bigger.

With clumsy hands, I fiddled with the console. I missed voice activation via Nadim. Hell, I just missed Nadim. *How long has he been out, now?*

"There may not be anyone in range," Bea said. "By the time our message reaches them, real-time, Nadim might have gotten the starlight he needs or—"

"There is no 'or.'" My entire body tightened just thinking about it. Past that point, we'd lose power to these machines. Nadim wouldn't be manufacturing breathable air for us or keeping us warm. Long after we suffocated or froze, Nadim would die.

"Okay." Her tone was gentle, like she was a doctor about to deliver bad news.

I didn't want to imagine any scenario where Nadim was dying or dead. Luck used to be my nemesis, but things had shifted in my favor lately, so why not roll the dice again? I didn't wait for Bea to locate any emergency procedures buried in Nadim's records, so while she scrolled and sorted, I activated communications and recorded a message that would loop, short and to the point. "Our Leviathan is injured. Requesting immediate support. Please advise."

Then I beamed it out wide into space.

"Zara! What if someone else hears that?"

"You mean, other aliens? I don't care, as long as they know how to wake a Leviathan. I'm on first watch, monitoring Nadim and listening for a response."

"But—there must be a reason that the Leviathan didn't tell us about any other ships, other races—"

"Maybe," I said, and met her eyes. "It's all we've got, Bea."

She didn't ask me to promise that we'd be okay. At that moment, I didn't have it in me to reassure her. Not with Nadim checked out and the memory of his former Honors screaming in my head. Bea kept me company, not talking much, just being there. I remembered long nights in the Zone, huddling with my crew for warmth and solidarity against the dark.

Eventually she said, "EMITU sent a message. He says you'd better get down there or he'll put you to sleep like a bad puppy."

"You got carried away with his personality profile, you know that, right?"

"Maybe. But he's not wrong. You need to make sure the treatments are working."

So I went to med bay. EMITU was sarcastic and ever so slightly concerned about my lack of ability to follow simple directions, but I responded in monosyllables, and eventually, it said that I was good to go after another pain shot. I came back to find Bea sitting quietly. Waiting. Listening to the sound of my message, playing on loop.

"I found the other distress beacon," she said. "It's on. Other Leviathan can hear it."

"Something will break soon. I have faith."

That was, maybe, the first time I'd ever said anything like that. I'd had no religion to speak of since my childhood, nor reverence, but Nadim had become my pillar of fire in the wilderness. Judging by the look Bea gave me, she thought I was losing my shit. I preferred to think of it as dedication.

"I'll check back later."

Don't think about failing life support. Don't think about the worst-case scenario. But I did, of course. The average time to failure of human-based systems in the event of a Leviathan's death was less than half an hour, which had been one of those statistics that they'd taught us in orientation classes. As I looked up more intel on the console, I found that human-based systems *might* be able to function for two to three days in the event that a Leviathan was unresponsive due to injury or illness. At that point, Nadim would start shutting down what his instincts told him were unnecessary systems—unnecessary to his survival—to save energy.

Where were we on that timeline? Better than halfway into it.

I didn't want to imagine Nadim finally coming awake and finding us frozen and dead inside him. But of course, I did. I role-played through his rage and grief and guilt. I wondered what he'd do with us. Take us home? Give us a burial in space? Send us into the red giant, a star for a funeral pyre? Morbid thoughts. I couldn't help it. That carried me along a dark road that led to my own role in this mess. Because I always wanted a little more, skated a bit closer to the edge, and so did Nadim. We'd tipped over that edge and now, my recklessness might end Beatriz, Nadim, and me.

Impossible not to wallow some in *that* guilt.

There was no telling how much time had passed when the comm crackled with a shocking burst of sudden, inhuman noise, which slowly resolved into English. Some translation protocol coming into play, I guessed, via the data console.

Holy shit, I'm listening to an alien.

"... responding. We heard your message—bond-name?" A lot of whatever was being said didn't translate, or maybe our translation system was one of the first things to start shutting down.

For a few seconds I trembled, and then I stumbled upright, two left feet all the way. "I'm Zara. My partner's Beatriz. Our Leviathan is called Nadim. Hello? *Hello?*"

A long silence followed, ominous by any token. "... your bond-name?"

"Excuse me?" Distance could account for some of the pause, and there'd been some of that inhuman wailing that didn't translate again, but I had the awful feeling I wasn't giving the right answer to a question I didn't even under-stand. It was downright frustrating, these time-lag stops and starts, but the response—when it came at last—nearly froze the blood in my veins.

"... without bond-name cannot—" A series of beeps and whistles cut into the audio stream, obliterating any hope of comprehension.

"Look, screw the rules! This is an emergency. We need help and you're the only other Leviathan in range. He won't wake up, and if he doesn't soon—" I swallowed hard to continue. "If he doesn't, we're dead."

I got nothing but static in response.

CHAPTER FIFTEEN

Breaking Even

BEA SCOWLED, PACING beside the console. "Was that a good idea? I *told* you I found the standard distress beacon. You have no idea who you were talking to . . . or what their intentions might be. I've never heard of a bond-name, what is that, a code? We don't know codes!"

"We're in the red zone," I said softly. "That means trying all angles to survive. If playing by the rules means waiting to die, I just can't."

Still, her sensible fear was rubbing off on me. Maybe I'd screwed up in a colossal way, announcing our weakness to somebody inclined to exploit it. I didn't have a monumental amount of trust in strangers, come to that. I didn't even trust most friends.

She seemed to be thinking along the same lines. "The Leviathan aren't all gentle. Remember Typhon? What if this one's . . . gone rogue? What if the crew are pirates or scavengers? I have a bad feeling about this, Zara."

The continued comm silence felt ominous; that was for damn sure. Because I couldn't just stand still, I got to work on the console. Maybe I could at least get a decent tracking on the approaching ship. With some searching, I located their signal. We watched the trajectory for a while.

"They're coming in," Bea said, and looked up from the console at me. Our eyes met and held, and I nodded.

"Let's try the comm again." I sent two more messages. No response at all this time. Panic wouldn't help, so I considered why they might not answer. "Maybe they're having technical problems?"

"You think?" Bea sounded dubious.

On the third try, we got the same sounds I couldn't process before. "Damn, what is up with this translator?"

"Low-power mode," Bea said. "It's pretty worthless right now. The sounds have a pattern, but I don't have the experience to translate this. Do we have anything in our database . . . ?" She started searching frantically, but we only found logs and Honors material, nothing related to exo-translation. Probably deliberately, since the Leviathan didn't want us ugly, violent humans messing up foreign relations.

"They're coming in fast," I said.

We couldn't manually vanish walls or ceilings with Nadim out of it, but I watched their Leviathan close on the console screen. I let out a nervous breath.

Then a little blip split off from the main bulk.

"Their Hopper's been deployed. Zara—"

"I know, I see it."

"What should we do?" A light came on, messages scrolled, and a warning tone sounded. "They've overriding our docking bay doors!"

More alien chatter came across the comm, but we had no idea if it was an offer of help or a demand for surrender. "I'll go."

"You'll need a skinsuit. Life support's already down in the docking area."

Yeah, that was a hot, fresh reminder of how screwed we were and why I'd beamed an SOS in the first place.

My suit was still being repaired, so Bea offered to get hers, but before she could, the console warning tone got louder. An automated voice said, "Interior breach, docking bay. Unauthorized personnel detected." The computer went on about how we should respond to the intrusion, but we'd already activated our distress beacon, and Nadim was still out.

None of the standard protocol helped.

This is what you get for breaking the rules in deep space. Guilt and remorse had no place in what was about to go down, though, so I sealed those emotions away. Bea grabbed my arm, thirty seconds from a meltdown. I shook her off and defaulted to what I did best, sprinting to the weapons locker to grab a few options at random. Whatever was coming, I needed to face it full-on.

Squaring my shoulders, I took a deep breath. I was about to meet an alien, and all my bravado aside, I wasn't ready. This wasn't a Leviathan, after all. I'd grown up knowing about them from countless holos. This was coming face-to-face with the unknown . . . and I'd invited it in. I knew how bad that could be. I'd seen the old horror vids.

When I got back to the hub, Bea was peering at the console, her hands shaking. "It's heading this way!"

"How many?" I asked.

"Just one? I think? The reading is—yes, it's one."

I confirmed that with a glance at the biothermal signature and relaxed a touch. If it had bad intentions, at least the odds were even, though I was assuming it didn't have tech that could melt my brain or disperse me into atomic dust. Turning to Bea, I said, "Find some place to hide."

She gave me a doubtful look, but I shook my head. Bea was great, but if this went sideways, she needed to survive to protect Nadim. She paused to give my arm a squeeze, a last, wordless message of good-bye and courage, and then she took off.

It didn't take much studying of the console to figure out that our intruder was heading straight for us. I realized that the lights were getting dimmer. Normally Nadim's natural bioluminescent glow provided sufficient light for me to navigate; when I checked the console, I saw we were operating on auxiliary power now, conserving resources to keep our life support on longer. Nadim was starting to ration his resources.

Great. Darkness *and* an unknown trespasser.

I intercepted the alien just outside the hub, and it was big. Topped me by at least a meter, and it was far wider. More importantly, it wasn't remotely human.

My brain went on strike and refused to make sense of what it was seeing; to reconcile the number of limbs, the configuration, with something in our human database. I forced myself to calm down and slow my rapid breathing.

The creature, whatever it was, wore a skinsuit and a mask, though in its case the mask was more like a mis-shapen helmet. Its head was elongated, and not even the skinsuit disguised that it had a multiplicity of eyes behind that visor.

Below that, it was a nightmare of tendrils, tentacles, nothing like arms or legs I could recognize, all contained in individual little skinsuit extensions. The suit didn't seem to know what color scheme to take; it cycled wildly between matching the whitish color of the room around us and a deep eggplant purple that lightened to red and whirled to white again. I had no idea what it meant.

If the alien had come to help, I didn't want to start some shit, but it was hard to stay calm when I had no training, no frame of reference for any of this. *This is why Nadim said humans aren't ready. Because we aren't. At all.*

The strange speech I couldn't interpret on the comm didn't make any more sense up close; the frequencies were ear piercing. Another noise; then the swaying of the tentacles increased. So did the patting of the little filaments. It adjusted something on its suit, and since it wasn't attacking, I tried talking.

"I'm Zara. Our Leviathan—"

A screech that seared my eardrums cut me off, and it performed more multitentacled gestures I couldn't interpret, then blew past me to fiddle with our console.

"What are you doing?" I yelled. "Stop!"

I tried to tell myself it was here to help, but truth was I had no idea why it was here or what it was doing. Fear negotiated with uncertainty, and I clutched the stunner I'd pulled from the weapons locker, palms sweaty. So far, it hadn't attacked me, but I didn't get a good vibe about the way it just came aboard and started messing with our stuff. If only it would *say something* I could understand . . .

It paused to adjust the tech affixed to its suit as I said, a bit more forcefully, "Hey. You. What the *hell* are you doing?"

The alien thrashed, like it was in the midst of a convulsion, all its tentacles twisting and flailing the air, filaments rising straight up like a ruff around its head. It made an absolutely chilling howl, tentacles flaring wide, and it looked so much like the posture of a snake before it struck that I didn't even think about what to do.

I fired my stunner.

Wasn't exactly a considered decision; my mind went blank with gibbering terror. The beam caught the creature where a human neck would have been, between the head and the explosion of tentacles thrashing at me.

It collapsed into a limp sack, tentacles still flapping, and I nearly shot it again before I got my shit together. It was making some weak whistling noises, but hell, I didn't speak Tentacle, and apparently neither of our translators was helping.

"Zara!" Bea's voice came from the corridor. "What happened?"

"Um."

She looked properly appalled. "Did you kill it?"

"I don't know."

I edged forward. No idea where to check for a pulse on an alien or even if it had one. I tentatively pressed my fingers to the neck, and instantly, half a dozen filaments whipped out to wrap around my fingers, hand, and wrist. "Not dead!" I squeaked, and tried to yank free. It took effort. "Really not dead!"

The creature burbled at me. It sounded angry. A tentacle raised and slashed at me, and before I could duck, it connected and sent me spinning out across the floor. Strong, I thought through a fog that wasn't entirely due to the hit.

I rolled to my feet, bouncing and ready for a fight. The alien made a roaring sound like water as it thrashed around on the floor, slapping tentacles. Not coordinated yet, but it wouldn't take long, and then what was I going to do? We needed help. Maybe I'd already screwed that up, but I wasn't even sure how to start apologizing.

So I just started. "Uh, look, we got off on the wrong—" I was going to say *foot* but how would that translate at all, if his translator was working? "I'm sorry. I was just asking what you were doing!"

Apology was not accepted.

It was *fast*. I watched it writhe toward me, filaments stiff and jutting like knives around its head, tentacles slapping the floor with angry emphasis as it came at me. I clutched the stunner and considered firing again, and before I could, its limb wrapped around the barrel and wrenched it decisively out of my grip to crush it into sparks.

"Doing?" Finally, it produced a word I understood. "Not hellfire damnations?"

I had no idea what it meant; something must've gone badly awry in its translation matrix. "Yeah, doing. You." I pointed, hoping it wouldn't take that as a hostile gesture. I had a huge bruise forming where it had slammed me into the wall. I didn't want a repeat.

More tinkering with what I took to be a translation aid. "Reading. Learning starsign. Yours need . . ." Alien chatter. It played with the settings again. "White dwarf."

A deep, groaning sound rushed through me; it came from outside, echoing through flesh and metal and rushing on past us.

That was a Leviathan song. I was sure half of it wasn't within the range of my ears, because the floor under my feet vibrated. My bones too. What I could hear of the sound was keening, sharp, and decidedly unmusical.

Definitely not Nadim. It's the other ship.

"Angry," the alien said. "Try to calm. Soothe. Sing." It extended two tentacles toward me in a whiplike motion. They wrapped around my arms, strong as steel cables, and yanked them hard out to the sides. "Do not make me _____ you." That important verb was replaced with a harsh gurgle. The concept of what they were going to do to me *simply didn't translate.* That was terrifying.

"Hey, easy," I said to cover my trembling. "Those don't

grow back. I made your ship angry when I stunned you?"

That made sense. *Nadim would be pissed at the way this dude knocked me around too.*

Pure alien sounds—the translation matrix failed again. To me, it seemed like they—somehow, the intruder had settled down to *they* in my head—didn't have any more experience with humans than I did aliens. Which was maybe why they'd tried to take my head off over a simple question, even if I did swear at them. With a wonky translation, maybe it had sounded like a threat of violence? I had no idea what they were trying to say now.

Something hit Nadim hard enough to send us tumbling. Gravity disappeared, and we slammed around like dice in a cup. The alien wrapped their many limbs around metal braces and grabbed me too, holding me as Nadim spun and twisted. The other Leviathan must have rammed Nadim again, this time from the other side.

You asshole, I wanted to scream, but I was too occupied trying not to bash my head against the console. Tentacle Alien had a good grip on me, but whiplash was a bitch, and I could feel new marks where Nadim was hurt in the dark, throbbing stars erupting on my skin.

The spin slowed and stabilized, and gravity melted back in. My weight sagged toward the floor, and Tenty—I had to call them something—gently lowered me down. The filaments were waving in agitation around their helmet.

It said something, maybe a good-bye, flared tentacles at me, and then raced toward the docking bay while I tried to get myself together. I'd done exactly what Nadim had been afraid I'd do: I'd shot the first alien I saw. And what had we gotten out of that? I had a fresh set of bruises, and so did Nadim.

And he still wasn't awake.

But Tenty had said something, I realized. Something important. *They mentioned a white dwarf.* At least the shitty translation gave us that much, even if it had failed in every other conceivable way.

The console was still reporting that we had an unauthorized intruder on board. I slapped at controls until it shut off, along with the droning alarm. I tracked Tenty's progress on the console screen; they went straight back to the docking bay, no detours. I watched the alien Hopper swoop out, and as soon as it was gone, I hit the lock button and sank to my knees against the hub wall. Delayed shakes. My head hurt. My back and right arm ached where I'd hit the wall.

What in the blazing hell had just *happened*?

"Bea?"

"Here," she said faintly, tiptoeing to my side. "Are you okay? I thought—"

"Whatever you thought, it's probably worse," I said. "What's happening out there now?" It was easier to ask than to haul my exhausted body upright to look.

"The other Leviathan—it attacked us, didn't it?"

"Sure felt that way."

"It's circling us. I don't like this, Z."

Nadim was helpless. This other ship could *kill* him in his weakened state.

"Bea, can you pilot?" I asked.

"Do I have a choice?"

"Not really."

"Then chart a course to the nearest white dwarf star and get us out of here!"

I put my head in my hands, and after a moment I felt the rush of acceleration; she'd really punched the speed. I couldn't blame her.

A few minutes later, I felt well enough to get up and leaned in to check the console, not wanting to distract her. "Damn. They're following? No, they're breaking off."

"I've found a nearby white dwarf. At top speed, it won't take long. We're okay. We'll be okay."

Sure. The lights were dimmer now. It felt cooler in the room, and I shivered. Bea's assurances had to be a litany of wishful thinking. I crawled over to the seat nearest to the console and shut my eyes. When I did, nausea came back with a vengeance. If the alien had meant to kill me, I'd be meat paste on the wall, so I counted my blessings. I was a mess of bruises, damaged hands, and phantom pain from the beating Nadim took. I guessed I could call it a win.

Whatever the hell had just happened, I hoped it was worth it.

It was exactly half a day until we detected the white dwarf star's radiation. I put it on audio for Bea, and together, we listened to the starsong. A strange, eerie chorus, full of rising and falling hums and hisses, clicks and ticks. An alien choir singing in keys humanity had never imagined, but there was something organized and beautiful about it too. It felt more vibrant than the atonal hiss we'd heard coming off the red giant. This seemed . . . younger, somehow. More vital.

"Well," I said, "it doesn't have much of a hook, but maybe we can jazz it up with some samba beats."

"That isn't funny." Beatriz was holding my still-healing hand—which, to be fair, EMITU had done a fabulous job of repairing. The caulk was mostly absorbed now, and the swelling had gone down. "What if that thing had killed you?"

I had been trying not to think about that, or what the consequences might be for making unauthorized first contact. I did my best. My best had ended up violent, and I had to think hard about that for the future. Fear and action, back in the Zone, had been a survival trait. But here? Maybe I had to learn a whole new set of rules and instincts.

"It didn't," I said. "I admit, that encounter could've gone better, but I'm pretty sure nobody picked me for my diplomatic skills. Maybe next time, you do the talking. I'll be the badass in the background."

Beatriz drew in a steadying breath. "Is Nadim—"

"Awake?" I shook my head. I couldn't feel any difference, not yet, and the lights were still down to a faint, eerie glow. "I checked to make sure that the beating the other ship gave him didn't do more damage. Just bruises. He'll probably be sore when he wakes up."

If he wakes up, I thought, but I didn't say it because Beatriz was already on the glassy edge of panic.

"They never told us," she said softly.

"What?"

"That the Leviathan hurt each other. They always seemed so benevolent, you know, the way they talk about them back home? But first Typhon, and now this one beat Nadim up when he was down and then just left us to fend for ourselves!"

Call me cynical, but I'd always assumed that everything they taught us about Leviathan back on Earth had been propaganda. Candy coated for sure, if any of it was even true. "Nadim told us they're not social, really. They don't seem to harbor much affection for one another, that's for sure."

With a sigh, she made a gesture that said she was tabling

the question because talking would burn more energy than we could spare.

It felt cold. I checked the temperature on the console readout, and our baseline environmental had slipped down by almost twenty degrees. Still falling. He was withdrawing power from our section to keep himself alive.

Wake up, Nadim. We don't have long.

"I'm afraid," Bea said simply.

I couldn't blame her.

The radiation from this star roared and sang, plenty strong and loud, and if it was the kind he needed, then why was he still drifting?

We had to drag him back, somehow. I'd pretended I wasn't scared to the best of my ability to keep Bea from freaking out, but there was so much weight on me, I could hardly breathe. This whole thing might be my fault, mine and Nadim's together.

In that dizzy metal darkness, something the alien had said came back to me. *Soothe. Sing.* He'd been talking about calling off his own Leviathan, but if Nadim heard starsong, maybe he heard human music more strongly.

The epiphany sparked like a Roman candle.

I turned to Beatriz and said, "Do you trust me?"

From the archives of the **A'Thon**, *amended from mathematical song for human translation.*

Bright the stars always, dark the space between. We fear. But we trust the Vessel to carry, one bright to the next. Trade ensue peace. But Vessel tell us not of Other. This break bright, sorrow sing, trust drown. Many generations spin. Vessel comes again. Trust again.

But now comes war.

And death.

CHAPTER SIXTEEN

Breaking Off

BEA DIDN'T HESITATE at all. "What do you want me to do?"

"Sing," I said. "That first song you did for Nadim. He loved it. I think he might—"

"Come back for it?" Her face lit with understanding. "I'd been wondering why the Honors had so many musical talents. I thought it was to make us more compatible, but maybe it's something else. Maybe this could reach him. That's what you're thinking?"

"It might not work."

"But it could." She bounced up and ran toward the

media room. I followed. By the time I reached the door, she was already on the stage, taking in a deep, slow breath.

Then she began, the notes rising like pure silver in the air, echoing and enveloping me in light. Oh *God,* she could sing, and right now, she sang like her life depended on it. I calmed myself because that was what the alien had emphasized. While Bea serenaded, I sank to the floor and made contact, first with my injured palms and then with my bare feet. This time, I was careful and deliberate.

Nadim.

I framed his name in the shape of music, thought-singing, in accompaniment to Beatriz, so that the notes floated out of me and into him. Every note, every echo my siren song, more relentless than any alarm. At first he gave back only low rumbles too inchoate to be called thoughts, so I followed the bass line and drummed with my hands and feet, until his rhythm shifted to follow mine. Hard to say if it came from Bea's singing or our connection. I guessed it was some combination of the two. A rush filled my ears—no, my head—sort of like that eerie wind that Bea summoned back on Firstworld. The same flicker of lights flashed behind my eyes, and then I sensed the shift.

I felt *Nadim.*

He wasn't quite awake, but he was stirring. We'd touched his dreams, and they were aching. The grumble of his pain whispered through me, reverb of loneliness spiked with something else—an unspeakable yearning. Realization dizzied me; dark sleep wasn't the same as when humans winked out for a few hours. This was something else, more like he was *lost*, and he needed something to guide him back to the path.

With that in mind, I painted a mental picture, so that each of Bea's notes hung over the dark road that connected us, buoyant as Chinese lanterns set aloft carrying wishes for the future into the New Year. Music passed through Bea to me, down my hands and feet, and became a winding path framed in brightness.

"Come to me, Nadim. Just a little farther."

"Zara?"

The hesitant, desperate touch sent a shiver of pure relief through me. Even confused and in pain, he knew me. "I'm here. Take my hand and we'll go." Though the scale didn't make any sense, I imagined leading him like a balloon on a string. As he grew stronger, more present, he leapt in bounds from pool to pool of liquid song. For the Leviathan, this was like being born. Intuitively I understood, probably from the DNA that linked us, dark sleep brought with it a kind of maturation, like going into the cocoon as larvae and coming out a butterfly. Now I couldn't rid myself of the question of what Nadim might be when he woke up, if he'd be brutal like Typhon or furious like the kin we'd just met.

It took a long time, and no time at all, inside my head. The only way I really knew that hours had passed was that Bea began to sound more and more ragged. She was hoarse and breathless now, but we were so close. With hands and feet, I renewed my percussion on the floor with a frenzy that I knew in some distant corner of my mind wasn't good for me, but he was close, close enough to touch and hold and keep. When I pulled him out of shadow, Nadim's great body vibrated, toppling me sideways, and I was too tired to get up. I let my cheek stay where it was, pressed against the warming floor. I'd lost feeling in my lower limbs again, from sitting in one place for so long, but sensation burned back in.

"He's awake!" My voice came out hoarse.

Bea didn't seem to have much volume left. By the way she was shaking, she had been performing that damned aria for hours, and my poor hands were swollen again, badly bruised from all the drumming, and the fragile skin at the seam where my toes joined my foot had split in two places. She bent over, gasping, and collapsed on the stage, sprawled in an exhausted, dramatic X of limbs and a spreading pool of curls.

"I'm sorry," Nadim said quietly, and the warm, familiar voice washed over me like summer rain. "I didn't mean to."

I was too tired to pretend to be okay. "I was so scared. That you were dying, that we would, and it would be all my fault. Thank you. For coming back to us." Tears burned at the corner of my dry eyes, but I didn't let them fall.

"I'm sorry," he said again. "It was my fault."

"Our fault." Guilt and regret threatened to drown me.

"Nadim, I'm glad you're back," Bea said. Croaked, really.

"Your voice!" He sounded horrified. She weakly flopped a hand in the air.

"I'll be fine. My *vó* sang herself hoarse many times in her day." She levered herself up to a sitting position with a groan. "Are you all right, Nadim?" She pressed her palms against the floor—an embrace. A connection.

"Yes." That, at least, sounded decisive. Then his voice turned hesitant. "You—you saved me. Both of you."

I raised my head, finally, and exchanged a look with Beatriz. We were exhausted, sweaty, trembling with the aftermath, but that made it worthwhile. Bea fairly glowed.

It gave me the strength to push myself to a sitting position with my back to the wall. *Ow.* My body was starting to protest, and it had a lot to complain about.

"I'm glad to hear your voice, Nadim," Bea said softly. "Don't go again. Please."

"I won't," he said. "I'm sorry I distressed you. I am bringing all your life-support functions to optimal levels."

The lights were coming up now, and I could feel the warm air pouring in to diffuse the bitter chill. Life, returning.

"Can you manage now?" I asked.

"Yes. I'm in some pain, but the damage will heal." He paused. "I feel that things happened while I was away. Will you tell me?"

Beatriz sighed. "Later. If you don't mind, I desperately want a shower. And a few hours of sleep."

"You must be burnt." I reached up to grasp her hand as she got up. "Maybe see EMITU for the backache and the throat?"

She shook her head. "Sleep will fix me. I'd rather not be fuzzy." She bent to whisper, "You're staying awake?" I nodded. "Good. Don't let him go out again, okay?"

"I won't."

She hurried off to her room for privacy, maybe to sob in relief in the shower that we'd survived this challenge. She wouldn't want me to see that, much less Nadim.

I wanted to feel victorious. It was like winning the Olympic gold in space hurdles, only there would be no fancy ceremony, no medals. Our only reward was currently performing some kind of self-inventory, with little purrs of curiosity.

"Fascinating," Nadim said.

"What is?"

"I can dark run now." Together, those words made no particular sense, though I understood each of them separately.

"Which means?" I studied the damage I'd done to my

feet. Blood trickled from the splits in the skin between my toes. *Ow.*

"I told you that I go into deep sleep—dark sleep—unexpectedly."

"Which is why you need the alarm, which by the way doesn't do a damn thing until it's installed."

"Yes," he said, and sounded chagrined. "I'm aware of that. I never thought I would need it on the Tour. That was my error."

"Pretty sure it was *our* error."

"Yes." There was something both warm and regretful in that word. "That's true. And we must be careful."

"You were saying . . . ?"

"Dark sleep is a natural process that allows our bodies to rapidly develop and mature. It's similar to a . . . human growth spurt, but normally, we control it and enter that stasis when it's safe."

As analogies went, it wasn't bad. "So what does 'dark run' do?" *Sounds ominous.*

"I can vanish from sensors. Hide myself."

"You have a *stealth mode*? Cool. But . . . you feel conflicted about it?" His ambivalence whistled through me, jarring as a train signal that just wouldn't stop.

"I went into dark sleep before I should have," he told me. "This was different than before. It seemed . . . deeper. I haven't just slept. I've . . . changed."

"And that's bad?"

"It's . . . unusual," he said. "It's not supposed to happen until I am on the Journey. I think . . . I think this is why there are rules about sharing deep bonds with others before the Journey. It triggers . . . changes."

Lord, this was starting to sound a hell of a lot more complicated than I'd thought. Maybe deep bonding was like sex: while it felt great, you needed a certain level of maturity to handle the consequences. And the consequences changed you.

"I don't want to . . . mess up your development, Nadim. Or hurt you." I took a deep breath. "You almost died. *We* almost died. That shouldn't happen, no matter how good it felt in the moment."

"I know." He was regretful, that ambivalence in full force. The *wanting* was still there, but so was a new, quelling caution. "The Tours . . . the Tours are supposed to accustom me to light bonds. But it didn't work. *I* didn't. I will know better now."

"Hey, maybe share a little of that knowledge too? Because lack of it nearly got me and Bea killed."

I felt his contrition in waves of sad blues. "Yes. I will make more information available to you. I am sorry, Zara."

I heaved myself upright, and my sore feet left smears of blood. It was so little in comparison to his massive bulk that he shouldn't have sensed it, so it startled me when he said, with an urgent edge, "You're wounded. Please seek medical assistance."

"How can you recognize that? Blood, I mean?"

"It's—" He seemed to consider that for a moment. "It's mixed with mine, but I don't know how that happened." I did. I'd been wounded and bleeding while inside his body, fixing him. "I can sense it now. How odd. Are you badly injured, Zara?"

"Nope. I'm fine." I immediately winced when I took a step, and slipped my shoes on. It didn't help, but at least I didn't leave bloody footprints limping to the med bay.

I got a sarcastic lecture from EMITU and flesh caulk on my hands and beneath my toes, plus some kind sticky balm for my bruised palms. The treatment left me walking weird, trying to balance on my heels, and it also left me realizing how bone tired I was. I couldn't wait to lie down.

I was heading for the data consoles, though, when Nadim said, gently, "You don't need to keep watch. I won't slip away again. Please. Go and rest."

I trailed my fingertips over the wall in silent thanks. As I hobbled to my quarters, Nadim asked, "Is now a good time to share what I missed?"

I did—in general terms, at least. He listened in silence until I got to the part where I'd gone deep-Nadim-diving. His startled reaction nearly knocked me flat. "You went . . . to the heart of me?"

Putting it that way made it seem so intimate when I hadn't been thinking like that at the time. Nothing sexy about crawling through waste and getting my hands sliced to ribbons in the process. "I guess. It was the only solution we could come up with to keep you safe."

"I don't know how you survived that." He sounded dazed again.

"Skinsuit, a little luck, a laser scalpel, and a lot of running. And Bea talking me through it. She was brilliant."

"You both are. You keep doing the impossible, Zara." An unidentifiable sound escaped him. "Now that I'm searching, I can feel the path you carved into me. Like a physical reminder of you."

"Oh God, did I damage something?" If so, I wondered how the hell I'd get up the courage for another repair run. I didn't have the stamina at the moment.

"No. But . . . it is . . . unprecedented?" He seemed to struggle to find the words, and though I wasn't trying to feel what he did, it was more like I couldn't *help* feeling it, as if we'd turned some corner, and that yearning loneliness I'd sensed in the dream swept over me, heavier this time and more irresistible. Sometimes it felt as if the more I gave him, the more he would absorb, and I should have been frightened.

But I wasn't.

I paused in my walk and leaned against the wall. My

feet needed the rest. "Unprecedented?" The little prompt slipped out before I could stop it. After all the terrifying silence, I was so hungry for Nadim's words.

"Without more training, neither of you should have been able to wake me. That is what the shock device is designed to do. Yet somehow, you did."

"Because we are just that good. There was no way we were losing you."

His response was grave. "This is why there are always two Honors, one starsinger and one pilot. Both of you were well chosen. I have no right to say this, but . . . thank you. For staying alive."

Beatriz had to be the starsinger, so that meant I was the pilot—but I was nowhere near as good as Bea at that, either, so how did that track? I had so many questions, and this time, Nadim *would* address them. While he might still be healing, that was no excuse for avoidance.

"You're welcome. But you owe me all the answers, got me?"

"That is fair," Nadim said.

"Okay, first off, I want all your databases unlocked. Everything. Including files on alien races. I don't want to be caught like that again."

"Understood, Zara."

"And what was it that Tenty said about a *bond-name*?"

"Tenty . . . ?"

"Octopus tentacle thing from the other Leviathan. Answer the question."

"When we are accepted as worthy to undertake the Journey, we are renamed. I think you might understand it as . . . a baptism. Some choose a name formed of ship and pilot."

"So we'd be like . . . Zadim or Nara?" I was mostly joking with that, but he seemed to be considering it seriously.

"I would prefer Zadim." He *wasn't* joking. He also seemed sad. "But it is unlikely I will be able to choose my final pilot and starsinger. The Elders choose who we are most compatible with."

That reminded me of Elder Typhon, and the momentary distraction of humor burned away. I got serious again. "Right. Next, you're going to tell me what the *hell* was going on with Marko and Chao-Xing and Typhon. He was using them. Is *that* some kind of . . . deep bond?"

He didn't want to answer this one, I could tell. "An imperfect one," he finally said. "Imbalanced. Typhon takes what he needs from them. Commands. Controls. It is very difficult to find the ideal bond. Typhon had that, once. But he lost them. Since, he has not been—not been the same."

Suddenly I understood the look that Marko and Chao-Xing had, all pupils and dead man's stare. "You lied to us." The words came out quieter than I meant, but they had hard, cutting edges. I pushed off from the wall and limped the rest of the way toward my room. Not far now. "About what the Honors program really is. It isn't just cultural exchange and learning, is it?"

"No," Nadim said. "But at the same time, it *is* those things too. We are beneficial to humans, and humans to us. That isn't a lie."

"You don't tell people about the bond. About how it can take away our *minds*! Our humanity!" Fury crackled through me, realizing that Marko and Chao-Xing had gone off to their new ship expecting another voyage like what they had with Nadim. Instead, they'd gotten jumped. "You sure as *shit* should have said something about that!"

He went silent, though he didn't draw back from me; he just didn't seem to know what to say. I didn't want to sleep anymore. I wanted to pace, even though it hurt, but common sense took over; I opened the door to my room and sat on the bed. I felt Nadim come in with me—a sense of him right beside me, an almost physical presence, so strong that I fixed my gaze on the space where I felt he stood.

"I can't change what Typhon does," he said. "One human is not responsible for the actions of all humans, isn't that true?"

"Sure."

"Then please understand. Typhon is not . . ."

"What, they're all like *you* and he's the outlier? Is that

what you're telling me?"

"No," Nadim said. "I'm saying that we are all different. Please don't think I would ever do that to one of my Honors!"

"What's the Journey, Nadim?"

"I don't—"

"You know. Don't try to tell me you don't! I can give you a pass on the shock device, but the weapons? That isn't just shit you come up with because it looks cool. You develop it to protect yourself!"

"I never said the Journey would be safe," he said. "No one has ever promised that. We're taking precautions—"

"Shut up!" I yelled, and stood up. "Come *on*, you know better than this! Something is *wrong* and if you don't know what it is, then you're being lied to just as much as we are!"

I felt him draw back that time, as if I'd slapped him. I wasn't sorry, either. Sometimes a wake-up call was necessary. "Stop shouting at me!" Now *he* had lost his temper too. Good. "I haven't done anything wrong! I'm not responsible for what Typhon does, any more than you were responsible for your father—"

The rage bubble burst inside of me and drowned me in a flood of fire and ice. "Get the hell out of my room."

It was impossible for a living ship to slam a door on himself, but Nadim did his best to try. He disappeared, and the sudden chill of his absence was breathtaking. I froze in place, struggling for breath. It physically hurt to lose him in this way. I wondered if it hurt him too. I couldn't tell, because there was absolutely no way I was going to check on him. I hadn't told him about my father. About any of that. Angry as hell, I slammed out of my room, blocking him from my mind as I rushed back to the console. Called up my own personnel file, which I hadn't done before because why would I?

It was full of my sealed treatment records. Everything from my therapists. Everything that I'd thought would never be revealed to anyone else. Not even Camp Kuna had seen these things, but here they were.

It was all in the files that the Honors Selection Committee had sent to the Leviathan. All my damage, all my violence, all my wounds, laid bare.

Nadim knew.

The anger rushed out of me as if someone had pulled a plug. I staggered and instinctively reached for a wall, flinching when I felt the warmth of it, but I stayed in contact anyway, because I needed the support.

When I breathed in again, I had to take a convulsive gulp of air to clear spots from my eyes.

"Zara?" Nadim's voice came from all around me, and it was sharp with alarm. "Zara, what's wrong?"

"Everything," I whispered. I felt something wet on my cheeks, and I swiped at it in disbelief. Not sweat. Tears.

He said my name again, this time pleadingly.

But when I closed the door, he stayed outside. *I don't cry*, I told myself. My father had tried to crack me. I'd learned to turn off tears long ago.

But the need to cry this time was overwhelming. *No. No, I won't.* And I didn't. Exhaustion finally closed in.

Just as I was about to doze off, my bunk rocked hard enough to tip me onto the floor, and Nadim's agony split my skull into a thousand pieces, so all I could do was writhe and scream. Since I'd promised not to leave him alone in his pain again, I did *not* pass out.

CHAPTER SEVENTEEN

Breaking Hearts

I MADE IT to the data console without succumbing. It was like he'd been hit with a shock baton. I knew that feeling. I'd been stunned plenty of times back home—rehab, the Bible camp, even in the Zone a couple of times when the enforcement troops had come in to clean up the place.

It had been a hit designed to keep him in line and unable to fight back. The quarrel we'd just had paled in comparison to this new situation. Mentally I called for a truce.

"Nadim! I need to see!" I shouted.

Hopefully he'd get the need to cooperate too. The wall

opposite the data console shimmered into transparency.

Typhon filled our sky, massive as a living moon, pitted with dark scars and thick with armor. There was grace in other Leviathan, and beauty—like luminous fish in dark water. But not him. He looked graceless and brutal, and most of all, he looked three times Nadim's size. I'd never felt as scared of him as I did in that moment. That was partly because he was just that badass, but also because I could feel the raw fear vibrating inside Nadim like a drum. This had taken him completely by surprise. He wasn't good at hiding the feeling, and somehow, I knew Typhon would be able to sense it.

Bullies always could.

I hit the comm. "Bea! Get up here *now*!"

I heard a confused flailing on the other end, and the clear sound of her feet slapping the floor. The first part of her question came out in Portuguese before her brain caught up, and then she translated, "What? What is it?" She wasn't waiting for an answer. I could hear her pulling on her uniform.

"Trouble," I said, and switched off. Explaining would only make her more anxious and solve nothing. Besides, I had things to do. Nadim's pain was passing, and I sensed his defenses coming up. "Nadim! Why is he *here*? I thought the Elders went out on their Journey and we never saw them again!"

"Almost never. But he didn't go." There was a strain in his voice, as if it was hard to think past the suffering and stress.

"What do you mean, didn't go? He left, we saw him go!"

"He didn't sing."

Ah. Of course. I remembered that; the other Leviathan had sung their beautiful, mournful good-bye when they'd darted out of sight, gone on their Journey to distant stars. Only Typhon had remained silent.

"Are Marko and Chao-Xing still on board?"

"Yes. They are his deep-bond partners."

"So they can't leave."

"They can, with his cooperation. But—you saw how he treats them." His attention narrowed in on Typhon. That tightened our connection to a trickle, so I only got glimmers of what Nadim heard and felt. But fear, Nadim had an ocean of it. Through him, I sensed that Typhon was a black hole of a presence, radiating grim menace.

And then he was talking. Not to me, of course. Elder Typhon didn't deign to talk to insects. I felt the booming waves of vibration that rang through Nadim like a shout, and his involuntary flinch, as if he was afraid of being hit again. I put my hand on the wall beside me, trying to send him comfort and support, but I didn't know if he felt it. His focus was all on the other Leviathan, and for good reason. I was still shell-shocked from before, but that didn't matter right now. Outside threats mattered more than my feelings. Always would.

Beatriz arrived at a run, tying her curls behind her head as she slid to a halt beside me. She didn't ask questions, just took in the intimidating view from the window and then scanned the console. "Can we lose him?" she asked.

It was a sensible question, but I knew from my training that even at his best speed, Nadim wasn't fast enough to outrun Typhon.

I shook my head. Nadim's dread seeped into my head, making it hard for me to be logical. Bea didn't seem to be feeling it as much.

"Then can we fight?"

"With what? Near as I can tell, Leviathan fight by ramming each other, and Typhon's big enough to crush Nadim. I don't think anything we have in our weapons locker will be more than a flea bite on him." I thought of the weapon I'd assembled for Nadim, on the day that Bea was trying so desperately to finish her qualifications. *If only we'd installed that . . .* but it might not have mattered. At all.

She hummed a little in the back of her throat, gaze intent on the console. That was her thinking mode, an absently musical one as she analyzed.

Bea pointed to the star we were orbiting. "Do you think Nadim's fast enough to get on the far side before Typhon can catch him?"

"Maybe. What good will that do?"

"It's cover. Even Leviathan have to avoid flying too close, and surely it blinds them. Maybe not their eyes, but the noise it produces—"

"Yes," Nadim said, suddenly very interested in what we were saying. "If I can get very close, the starsong will baffle his senses. Not for long, but maybe long enough."

"Did he track you? Or did that other Leviathan who responded to our distress call tell him about what happened?" Bea asked.

"Likely the latter would be the case," Nadim said. "According to Zara's account, you frightened his Honor. He would have sought help."

"Look, the guy had a million tentacles," I said. "Don't pick a girl who shoots first if you don't want her to, all right?"

You know how I am. That's on you. Or the Elders. I knew it was on me too, but still.

Bea brushed that aside. "Doesn't matter. If Typhon didn't track us, and he was told where to find us, then we might be able to lose him. True?"

"Perhaps." Nadim sounded relieved. "But I should be sure of what he wants before we run. It—it could be more than just punishment."

"I still think we should run," I said.

"Zara." My name sounded gentle from him, and it

relaxed some of my tense wariness. "Typhon is harsh. But he is not irrational. He won't hurt you or Beatriz."

"But he'll hurt *you*," I said. "And I'm tired of you getting hurt."

"I have to speak with him. I will try to be brief."

Typhon, as far as I was concerned, had nothing that I wanted to hear about, and imagining Marko with those dead-black eyes again, stranded aboard, made me sick. *Unequal bond* was the same thing as Typhon playing with human dolls, and Marko deserved better. Hell, I might not like Chao-Xing, but she did too. It was sickening.

And there was nothing I could do about it.

Nadim and Typhon had some Leviathan-level exchange; I could feel the rumbles through my boots. With my hands on the human-built console, it was harder to sense what he was feeling. He was being very careful to keep it all buttoned up tight just now.

Beatriz put in a course that would swing us under the burning ball of the sun at the closest safe distance, then vector us away into the dark while Typhon's senses were confused. It might work. Maybe. Her fingers hovered over the controls, and she was listening, just as I was, for the slightest hint of trouble.

But it didn't come as a hint.

Our comm activated, and both Bea and I jumped in surprise. Chao-Xing's calm, measured voice said, "Honors. Lie flat on the floor. Do it now."

"What?" Bea blurted. I hit the button to reply.

"Why?"

"We wish to avoid unnecessary injury to you. You have five seconds to comply."

"Punch it!" I yelled to Bea, and she reached for the panel. Just as she touched the activation button, the entire data console shut down. Powered off completely, like someone had pulled an emergency switch. Not Nadim's doing—I could feel his surge of astonishment, and then grim determination.

"Please lie down," Nadim said. I heard the fatalism in his voice. "I was warned that if I broke rules on this Tour I would not have another chance to make amends. This is my punishment."

"That's insane! We can run! Get away!"

"I am about to try. But you must prepare yourselves now."

"Nadim!"

"Please, Zara." My name was almost a caress. "Beatriz. Please comply. I will try to protect you as much as I can."

I grabbed Beatriz and pulled her to the floor. We accelerated as Nadim dived for the blazing curve of the sun . . . and I glimpsed a flash as Typhon flipped with eerie agility outside the window and slapped Nadim with stunning force with the ventral surface of his tail. Normally, it fanned out into what looked like a delicate structure designed to catch starlight. He'd folded up that fan, and what hit us was like a whip, full of devastating power.

It sliced through Nadim's skin, crushed fragile tissues, cracked whatever passed for Nadim's bones. It was a full, cruel blow, a fist to a child, and I screamed into the muffling surface of the floor.

Run, Nadim. Before he destroys you.

But he couldn't. The blow knocked him off course, and though Nadim dodged and tried again, Typhon was not only faster, he was so much larger that he cut Nadim off easily and knocked him tumbling again, a strike to the injured dorsal side, the fresh scar he'd earned in the debris field. That scar broke open with a hot, wet rush, and I *felt* Nadim bleeding, smoky silver pouring into the darkness. The newly healed muscles beneath were crushed by the blow.

It was a good thing we were on the floor, but even then, Nadim's uncontrolled spin sent us rolling, tumbling clumsily around and banging hard into the unforgiving metal of the console. I rolled over the transparent window and for a heart-stopping moment I was gazing into the universe itself and felt it looking back with an intent, uncaring focus. *If this membrane ruptures . . .*

Typhon hit Nadim again. *Again.* The strikes were vicious, and Nadim was already weak. This had to stop. Ignoring the danger, I grabbed hold of the edge of the console and hauled myself up with all my strength to slap my hand on the comms control. "Marko!" I shouted. "You have to stop him! He'll kill Nadim! *Stop him!* Marko!"

Another shuddering impact flung me into Beatriz, who clutched me tight as we cowered together, wedged into a small alcove as the beating continued . . .

. . . and then suddenly ceased.

I raised my head and looked at the transparent window. Typhon's enormous bulk hung there, momentarily still. That lethal tail was still bare of solar sails, and I realized it wasn't only a whip, it was now *barbed*. Like the tail of a scorpion. It could stab as well as crush. But he hadn't used that. Yet.

"Nadim?" My cry echoed back from the walls. When he didn't reply, Bea let out a little sob and let me go. The ship was still spinning, but slowing down now. Gravity stabilized beneath our feet. "Nadim!"

I felt a trickle of something. He might have meant it as reassurance, but it wasn't that at all. It was so fragile, and it made me think of a long-ago friend in the Zone, beaten to death but still flashing me a bloody grin through broken teeth before he'd breathed his last. The memory terrified me. I pressed hard against the floor. Pressed my cheek to it. Reached for him.

"All right," Nadim whispered. Even the synthesized

voice sounded raw, hardly even understandable. Something groaned deep inside him, and I felt another bright hot-pink spike of pain stab through me. I winced and stumbled, bracing against the console. "Marko stopped him—"

Marko had intervened, somehow. Not quite the human doll after all, which was what I'd so desperately hoped. "Nadim, can you move?"

"No." I read the desperation in it. "If I try and fail, he will hit me again. It might hurt you."

"*Screw that.* Run! Do it!"

I turned my head in surprise, because that was Beatriz saying it, not me. Her hair had broken loose to riot around her face, and her eyes were ferocious. I'd have stayed out of her way if I'd crossed her path in the Zone.

I held up my hand, and she clasped it, our fingers knitting together tightly. "Yeah," I said. "Nadim—you said you could go into stealth mode?"

If he'd been human, he might have drawn in an audible breath. He'd forgotten that. He'd never even tried it yet. "Yes," he said. *"Yes."*

"Do it!"

"I can't. I'm not strong enough."

"I am," I said. *"We* are."

I felt the wild surge in him, and his mind reached and opened to me, and I fell, and it wasn't *I* anymore, it was *we*, spinning in a vortex of black fear and red pain and stars,

stars, the pulsing beat of Typhon's rage pummeling our body, vital fluids streaming into the dark, so much hurt, so much, but we clicked together in pieces made to fit and *there*, there it was, a shimmering pearl of power greater than either of us could ever be separately.

We disappeared. Typhon's surprise flared like a dying star. We dove, stiff and awkward with the pain, the damage, and skimmed barely past the stabbing thrust of his barbed tail, drinking thick starlight and whispering by, not even a shadow, not even a ripple. Turning now, gliding, the sun so hot it hissed and burned the wound on our dorsal surface black, turned the blood to ashes drifting on solar clouds, and we ran, racing up and out into the dark.

Escaping.

Behind us, Typhon's rage exploded with the heat of a supernova, and I felt something grab at us, *yank*, like a hand around a trembling heart.

Nadim spun, caught like a fish on a line, and I fell out of the bond, slamming back into my body with suffocating force. I tried to get out of my skin, back into *us*, but he wouldn't let me in as he twisted and struggled against the pull. He was doing it to protect me.

I clung to the wall and cried for him as he fought, and fought, and lost.

Interlude: Nadim

We come apart. It feels like cutting, like the bleeding holes that the Elder has gouged in me, and though I reach for her, I am now just *I*, and she is just *Zara*. There is no *we* now, no protection, and I am glad for that small favor because in this I am alone, must be alone. She should not suffer for me, though I know she would. There is a bright hot star in Zara, a heat I orbit and drink and wish with all my instincts to share. It is a fierce kind of bravery, a kind I do not possess. I am not made for battle. And like Zara, I am not made for rules, though I know they exist for a reason.

The Elder teaches me this error again, with cold fury and colder precision. In blood and pain, I learn I am not fit, not strong, not *ready*. I have failed. I will never take the Journey. I will be forced to surrender my Honors. I will be cast out, alone.

These are the threats he beats into my body. But I endure.

I feel Zara, distant starlight on my skin, feeding me her strength. I shut out everything but the faraway warmth, the tiny crack in the wall between us that spills her light into me.

It keeps me alive, but more, it keeps me alert, and under

Typhon's red waves of rage, I sense something else. Something I do not expect to find.

I sense that he is *afraid*.

He knows I sense it. His fear grows. He inflicts more pain to hide it, but I *see*. Zara and Beatriz have given me the understanding of these things, and as I drift and fight his hold and lose, lose, always lose, I know one pure thing.

I will find out why he is afraid.

I will find out what he is hiding from me, and I will survive to hurt him in turn. Not for myself.

I will hurt him because he has hurt my Beatriz. My Zara.

He will never hurt them again.

So I endure in the twisting, bitter net of agony, and I listen to their ragged, sobbing songs, and I *hold*.

CHAPTER EIGHTEEN

Breaking Loose

NADIM'S ANGUISH WAS a river, draining into me as water returned to the sea, but I wasn't infinite. It spilled the banks of my mind. He wasn't trying to hurt me, I knew that, but deep bonding had cracked something open between us that could never be sealed off. Not pair-bonded, like Marko and Chao-Xing; we weren't quite *Zadim*. We were still two, but a nebulous umbilical tethered us, and we both *hurt*, too much to bond again.

The punishment that Typhon inflicted on Nadim was precise and personal. I'd never known rage like this before; this was a whole new spectrum of violence that Typhon had introduced, a kind of calculated cruelty that steeled my resolve to make this bastard pay. Nadim couldn't hate like this.

But I could. I did. I *would*.

That hatred, I hoarded it at the core of me like the pit of a bitter fruit. With each lash, I remembered my father, every supervisor, warden, and rehab officer with a cruel streak. My father even said, once, that something about me made people want to force me to show respect. *Bow your head, girl. Don't give me that insolent glare.* But nobody had ever been able to command my regard; it couldn't be taken. It could only be earned. By treating me like a person, by listening when I spoke.

A lifetime in the Zone had taught me that pain always passed. I only had to ride it out. The worst came from knowing that Nadim lacked my experience. He was good. Gentle, even. I'd stake my soul on that. His bewildered anguish pared me to the bone, so that it felt as if I was all raw meat and exposed tangles of nerve. He kept trying to push me away, to shield me from those sensations. How long the punishment lasted, I didn't know; Beatriz held me as I screamed. She, at least, was spared most of it.

"Zara, you have to stop!"

It was all I could do to keep from biting my tongue. Despite the suffering, I didn't want to disengage. "Worth it," I gritted out through clenched teeth.

And he heard—Nadim *heard*—so his surprised joy diffused the despair for one beat, two, not quite enough to shield him. If there were tricks or techniques in the deep bond, I hadn't learned them yet, so we only held together for a sparkling heartbeat and then we both plummeted, back into the red-black depths, a bloodstain of an eternity.

My head went fuzzy and I heard Beatriz shouting. "Stop it! Typhon, *stop*! Marko, Chao-Xing, you have to make him stop! If you don't, *I'll kill you*!"

Bea's fear had metastasized into a rage that made her incandescent. Through foggy eyes, I admired the avenging fury Beatriz had become. *She loves me? Us? Us.* The fire of vengeance burned in her now too. Typhon was trying to shatter us, but we wouldn't let Nadim go.

Zara . . . The faintness of Nadim's call tasted of the ocean, of bittersweet farewell, and I locked on to my denial like a rope. Trembling from head to toe, I held on with bloodied, slippery hands to keep him with me. I sang to him in a wordless, broken melody. Bea harmonized with me. Together, we sailed down the river that bisected the banks of hell.

Hell froze.

Our torment ended.

He'd almost drifted away, but for us, Nadim came back. Tired. Beaten. But present. Still caught on the end of Typhon's line, trapped and terrified, but *present*.

I collapsed and felt the misty presence of him form around me. It was the closest we could come to an embrace. I wasn't going to let go. If he died, I died. We'd both spiral into the dark.

There was a sudden tug, a sense of motion. We were moving. No, *Typhon* was moving. We were pulled along like a toy on a string.

"Where are we going?" Bea was working on the console, trying to bring it back up.

"Gathering," Nadim murmured.

"What does that mean?" I asked.

"He is summoning the others. They will judge." Nadim seemed too tired to volunteer information, but we couldn't wait for him to recover fully, so I pressed on.

"Judge *what* exactly?"

"My crimes."

I was struck silent. Me, Zara, the smart-mouth, the one who flipped off enforcement agents and laughed in the face of courts—because Leviathan laws were different. I knew they were. The worst I'd ever get was rehab, maybe in a for-real prison if I tried hard enough back home, but even those were humane.

Somehow, I didn't think the Leviathan scale of justice tilted that kindly.

"What can you have possibly done?" Beatriz asked, and I wished she hadn't. Because I didn't want to face it.

Nadim didn't answer her, but she'd keep at it until she got the intel, so I told her—everything. About the deep bond that had triggered his dark sleep. How that was against the rules.

She didn't seem surprised. In fact, she waved it off. "Oh, that. I could tell you two connect in a different way. It's not better, not worse. Just different. Right, Nadim?"

"Yes," he said, and sounded faintly cheered. "You and I are music together."

"And you and Zara are something else." Bea raised her perfect eyebrows at me. "How is that a crime?"

"I should have waited for the Journey," he said. "There are rules."

"Rules." Bea rolled her eyes. "Since when does that merit *this*?"

"Multiple rules," Nadim told her. "The first was the deep bond. The second was failing to recognize within myself that I was slipping into dark sleep. The third was allowing humans contact with other races—"

"You didn't *allow* shit," I said. "That's on us. Besides, what else were we supposed to do, let you die?"

"None of it was *intentional*," Bea protested. "What's the worst that can happen at this Gathering? They'll tell you never to do it again?"

Please say yes, Nadim. Please.

"It's already been decided," he said in a lightless voice

that held no hint of hope. "I am unfit to continue. The Gathering will silence my voice. I will be driven out. I will be alone."

I felt cold, colder than when our life support was beginning to fail. What he was talking about . . . for a Leviathan, it meant being *mute*. Never speaking again, never joining the lonely songs across the dark. Listening, but apart.

Silence, to a Leviathan, was worse than death.

"No, you—you won't be *alone*," Beatriz said. "We'll be with you, Nadim!" Even to me, that sounded weak. She might not get the full picture yet, but she was glimpsing the edges.

And I wasn't surprised when Nadim said, "No. You won't." I still heard that extraordinary compassion in his voice. As if he was trying to shield us from the worst. "They will send you home, to Earth. Back to your people."

"No! No, they can't do that. We'll tell everyone what—"

"They'll do something to us," I said flatly. "The way they did to Gregory Valenzuela. They wiped his memories and sent him home half-crazy. But that's the point, right? Even if we remember something, nobody believes us."

Nadim didn't answer that. But I knew I was right. Most probably Valenzuela's Leviathan had been exiled, the way Nadim would be, and he'd not only been damaged but *grieving*. Suddenly I wished I had been kinder to that stranger. It seemed to me that Nadim must be a lot like me, knowing that shit could go disastrously wrong yet unable to comply with rules he didn't agree with or understand.

The silence was profound, broken only by a faint hiss of the static interference from the stars . . . starsong, even here. I tried to think of something to say. Something that didn't contain a scream or a sob.

Finally, it was Beatriz who came up with just the right thing.

"Then we don't play," she said. "We get away before we arrive at the Gathering. And we avoid Typhon until you're strong enough to stop him."

Of course, that was a great goal, but it wasn't exactly what I'd call a *plan*. Plans had steps, and we had to start from scratch. First: How could we help Nadim heal faster from his injuries?

I looked up at the curving ceiling. "Nadim. How long until we reach the Gathering?"

"A few days at most, in your time."

"And . . . how long until you heal from your damage?"

"Five days," he said. "At least."

"Can't we speed it up? With EMITU, maybe?"

"Your robot can't help me," he said. "But perhaps you can."

That, it turned out, involved music. We started blasting recordings through the ship, loud enough to vibrate;

according to Nadim, the songs helped accelerate his healing process. At least six times a day, Bea sang. When she slept, we played a recording of it back on a loop and kept earplugs jammed firmly into our ears to avoid going crazy from the repetition.

I felt the damage to him slowly knitting together. It would have been faster if we'd stayed in orbit around the white dwarf, but Typhon towed us away into the black, and even with his fins spread wide, Nadim's energy levels began to slip.

He sacrificed nonessential systems, closed up spaces we didn't need, cut his power outputs to nearly nothing. And he healed.

Whatever it cost, we would make sure Nadim didn't go out like this.

Three long days into the trip to the Gathering, I remembered to ask Nadim about Typhon's barbed tail as I got ready for bed. Turned out, that was aftermarket, grafted by another alien race humans had never met. It wasn't the Elder's only body modification, either.

I'd been angry over making a weapon for Nadim. Come to find out, Typhon already had them. *Lots* of them.

"He has weapons that fire sublight projectiles at very high velocities," Nadim clarified. "Telling you this is another crime, by the way."

"I'll add it to the list. So, we call those rail guns. How many?"

"Six, I think."

I whistled. That was an impressive armament system. The Mars colony only had one, meant to take out incoming asteroids. I'd seen the vids of rail guns firing and it was terrifying how accurate and destructive they could be. "Where are they on his body? I can't see them."

"The dark patches," Nadim said. "They are grafted beneath his skin, into special chambers. He has many modifications. Do you remember asking me about space lasers?"

"Oh, crap, *Nadim*, he has those?"

"I was truthful in telling you that *I* didn't."

"Well, points for that. But *shit.*" Our chances of breaking loose from Typhon couldn't have looked worse. Out here in the black emptiness, there weren't even stars or nebulas to use for cover. This was a wasteland. "Why didn't he use any of it before?"

"He didn't need to," Nadim said. "Physical force is enough to subdue me. Also, we do not use weapons on one another."

I thought about that. My fingers tingled, and light pulsed around the outline of them in his skin. It was a healthy gold, which meant he was feeling far better now.

"One more question?" I asked it very quietly. I felt the silent pulse of his assent. "If the Leviathan don't use those weapons on each other, then who are they meant for?"

He went still. *Very* still. And his answer was more ominous than anything I could have predicted.

"We're only told they are necessary for the Journey."

What was truly chilling was that I knew, through the link we shared, that he was telling me the absolute truth.

I rolled onto my side, but sleep was impossible. My thoughts churned in a single direction—escape. If there were aliens, there should be a space equivalent to the Zone, where refugees could elude the authorities. If there was a civilization, there *had* to be those who wanted out of it or didn't fit in; that was just part of natural selection, wasn't it, that nature was always pushing out to the edges? It was critical that we get free before the Gathering.

Eluding Typhon presented a monumental challenge, but evading a whole pod of Leviathan? Impossible. We'd be obliterated.

I dozed fitfully and dreamed. Nightmared, really, about being strapped down in a shadow-blurred church by an angel in white, of my father's hands holding me down for the knife. Of running, always running. Of suddenly stumbling into Derry—thinner, eyes dark-ringed and dull. His fingers jittered like he was shooing invisible insects. He gave me a hollow grin that didn't strike me as handsome or charming anymore.

"You'll be back soon, Z. You can't quit me. You know that, right? The Zone is the only place you'll ever call home."

With no transition, we were standing in Conde's shop, and he was holding me, and I heard the whirr of the drone overhead, and then everything was burning. Derry was burning, his face peeling away to become a bloody skull. But he was still holding me, no matter how I screamed and fought to get free.

A cold sweat bathed me when I woke, like the Lower Eight had spectral fingers wrapped about my ankles and could tow me back down. But it was Nadim caught on Typhon's hook. My head felt scrambled, like somebody had stirred my brain with a stick.

"Who is Derry?" Nadim asked.

Shit. My mental shields came up with a decisive, instinctive slam while I tried to figure out how to respond.

"In our time together, you've asked many things that I couldn't answer . . . or didn't want to. You've never refused to answer me before." He sounded . . . puzzled. Not hurt.

"Why are you asking about Derry?"

"You were speaking to him."

"Well, he was important to me. For a while."

"Not anymore?" Nadim asked.

"No." I'd let go of Derry for good when he sold out to Deluca; for old times' sake, I'd saved his life, but that was all. Forgiveness wasn't my strong suit in the first place, and he sure didn't deserve any, after how he'd played me.

"Ah." That sounded . . . neutral.

I decided not to follow up. With a groan, I checked our status—still tethered and unable to flee. After a quick shower, I had some food and did a few rounds in the combat sim. My inability to impact our dilemma made me especially ferocious; I beat a new level of difficulty by dislocating my shoulder during a particularly brutal hold, and I was still sore from putting it back in place when I went looking for Beatriz.

Found her, under the console, *again*, trying without much luck to get it back online.

"We're going to need full capabilities," I said.

She squirmed out and stared up at me. "I *know*," she said, and knocked what looked like an expensive laser soldering tool into the metal top of the console in frustration. "Convince Elder Typhon to turn the energy tap on. I can't wire around a problem I can't even reach! I don't know how he's done it, but the power just won't flow. It's in the cables, but there's some kind of bio-interference that's inhibiting it from reaching the human components."

"But the air and lights are on."

"Kitchen's got full capability; so does the media room. I've checked. But this? No. I can't understand how he's done it. It's like a Leviathan version of malware, sealing up a very specific function. I can't slice it, and I can't work around it. There's nothing I can do." Her voice faded, but her eyes went bright and distant.

I knew that look. Sometimes, if I talked to Bea about the problem, she talked herself right into an answer. So I waited, and she thought.

Then she smiled. It was a delighted yet purely evil sort of expression.

"What—"

She held a finger to her lips and pointed up, circling it around. I understood what she meant; it was possible—probable, even—that Typhon had his Honors listening in. She dropped the soldering gun back into a portable toolbox and took out another tool: a simple wrench. Under the console again, working fast, and I caught the component—the main input screen—as she loosened it. Bea twisted up and grabbed it and ran out of the room. I took the toolbox and dashed after her. No idea where she was going, but it still came as a surprise when I found her in the kitchen.

She gestured impatiently for the toolbox, and I set it on the counter and watched in bemused fascination as she pulled out connections and rapidly connected the data input screen into . . . the reheater? "I'm hungry," she announced. "Do you want something?"

"Um . . . sure?"

She gave me a silent nod, grabbed a food packet at random and shoved it in the reheater, and pressed the button. It began its work.

She quickly touched the input screen.

It booted up. Bea did a silent victory dance, hair whipping, and then shut it down again as the reheater *dinged* for attention. She grabbed the food and tossed it to me. Ugh. Meatloaf. Not my favorite.

I got it, then. She'd tapped into a power source, but in order to disguise that the input screen was live, she needed to run something else on the line at the same time. Not necessarily the reheater, just something that Typhon didn't consider a threat.

I mouthed *media room*, and she grinned and unhooked the screen as quickly as she'd put it together. Leaving the food, we managed to wire the input screen in series with the vid player. I queued up a marathon playlist, and as it began, she turned on the data input.

We were into the database. Nadim had unlocked it for us, and now we had a way in.

We bumped fists while the opening credits of an old movie rolled over the screen behind us, and got busy.

Nearly six hours later, we sat in the lush seats, watching the end of a movie we hadn't so much as glanced at until now, and passed the reheated meatloaf back and forth, taking small bites. I pulled out my H2 and quickly wrote, *Do you think it will work?*

Yes, she said, with five bouncing icons for emphasis. Good enough for me.

I wrote, *Nadim, are you following?*

He wrote *Yes* on my H2, and then, on a separate line, *I don't like this. I can't help you there. It's too dangerous for you.*

I love risk, I told him.

I know. That's why I don't like it.

I almost laughed. Instead, I wrote, *It's our shot. We have to take it.*

He didn't approve of that, but he accepted it. Now, all we had to do was make it work. And that depended on all of us working together.

Just like it was meant to be.

PART IV

CHAPTER NINETEEN

Breaking Vows

"MARKO? ARE YOU there?"

I had been trying to hail the other vessel for the better part of an hour. It was so annoying to contact somebody you knew damn well was listening and was choosing to ignore you. If he thought I'd give up, however, he didn't know me at all.

Into the third hour, his furious face finally appeared on my comm screen. "We have nothing to discuss, Zara! We are not interested in excuses or justifications."

There went my first pretext. Time for Plan B.

"I need medical treatment. You already know I'm partially

deep-bonded with Nadim, and that beating messed me up. EMITU isn't working properly. I might die if you don't do something." I leaned over and groaned, took a mouthful of red juice offscreen from a bottle, then coughed up a stream of it at the holocam. That had to look gross. "But I guess that's just fucking *fine*, huh? You don't care?"

"Get out of the way." Marko was shouldered aside, and then Chao-Xing appeared. "We don't have time for your bullshit. Have EMITU fix you."

"It's not working." I moaned and clutched the wall. "Don't believe me? Come with me to medical." I picked up my H2 and went mobile with the call.

All my years of truancy paid off in my performance. I hacked, I stumbled, making sure to give them plenty of shaky cam. When I got to medical, EMITU was offline, courtesy of Beatriz. "Please help me," I begged the inert droid.

No response.

"Try resetting it," Marko said.

He seemed slightly concerned now, so I milked it, pitching forward so that I almost dropped the H2. From that angle, I'm sure it looked like a full face-plant. I lay there for a few seconds before rolling onto my side with a gargle. I fumbled around at the back of the machine and nothing happened. I rasped out, "Never mind. Probably easier if I die."

If they could monitor my vitals remotely, then we were

screwed. Plus, I was gambling everything on them still having souls. A muffled argument raged behind me, but I didn't dare move. *They have to send someone. They have to.*

It would be inconvenient if I died in the Honors program, but there would be ways to spin it, probably. A sudden aneurysm in my brain, some other hidden health defect? Such a tragedy; she was so young. Same way those two Honors on Nadim's long-ago voyage had just . . . disappeared.

Suddenly this didn't seem like that great a plan.

Finally, Marko said, "Hold on, Zara. I'm coming. But you'd better not be pulling anything."

Success.

I lay on my face until Marko arrived. Bea made her entrance just as he did, crying out, rolling me over, babbling questions at me and him in a mixture of English and Portuguese until he waved her off. "Not now. I'll update you when I know something."

"She's been so sick since—" Bea was actually *crying*. The Teatro Real was in her blood. "I think there are internal injuries, I thought she was resting."

"All right, calm down, I'll take care of her."

She caught her breath on a sob. "How do I know you won't just—"

"Beatriz." Evidently her terror registered as sincere because Marko paused. "Am I a murderer? *Am* I?"

Even I got chills when she whispered, "I don't know."

"*Psia krew!*" I'd heard that swear in the Zone. Still Marko sounded weary more than offended.

First he tried to get EMITU working, but Bea had hacked it good. Now he sounded legit worried. Playing possum took incredible self-control when I wanted—needed—to see what was going on.

Eventually, Marko lifted me and carried me toward their Hopper. *Yes. I'm on my way.* I made sure I was dead weight in his arms and that spurred him to careless haste. Once he deposited me in the passenger seat and strapped me in, I risked a look through my lashes. Marko checked the instruments with a scowl; he looked way older than he had that day he'd pulled me out of Camp Kuna, with all the girls sighing over him. He looked ragged and tired and ill. And yes, I felt sorry for him too. For being bonded to a bastard like Typhon, for being caught like an animal in a snare. And most of all, for the way I was about to play him.

I let him take off and fly back to the Elder Leviathan. My timing had to be perfect. There might be signals I didn't know about and Typhon would probably realize the instant I made a move. If he knew, Chao-Xing would also. They were both deep-bonded, distinct frequencies, but similar strength. Pilot and starsinger, like me and Beatriz.

The second we landed, I saw the difference. Although it had a similar design, Typhon's docking bay was bigger than Nadim's—with curves you wouldn't find in a mechanical craft like the ribs inside of a whale. It almost looked like an organic cathedral. I took a good look at the arched ceiling with its cut ridges. There were no teeth, but fangs wouldn't have surprised me, either. Chills broke out as Marko opened the Hopper doors. The walls were tinted grayish-white, which might have been a sign of age or an aesthetic choice, but the space gave off an institutional vibe. The lighting inside was harsh, a fluorescent glow that stung my eyes.

Marko retrieved me and slung me over one shoulder; not the most careful handling. If I'd had spinal damage, I might have never walked again, but his proximity to Typhon chilled his humanity, his empathy, and I became a female-shaped problem instead of a person.

As we reached the internal docking entrance, I pulled the stunner I'd concealed inside my uniform. Considering how exhausted he looked, I didn't expect Marko to move quickly, but he blocked the hit and twisted my wrist so hard that I dropped the weapon. He tried to wheel me in for a behind-the-back arm lock, a move they'd used to subdue me at various rehabs, so I was wise to it. I dipped my shoulder, tucked my arm close to my side, and surprised him by spinning toward him with my other hand, striking his solar plexus hard enough to steal his breath.

"What're you trying to accomplish?" Marko wheezed.

"Saving Nadim." I grabbed the stunner off the floor and

fired, and he went down hard. Out.

Diving past him, I rolled clear before I got locked in. I made it, barely, though the heavy doors caught my foot. When I pulled free, I lost a layer of skin and would have a deep bruise. They couldn't vent the hangar bay with Marko on the other side, so I had a little freedom. For now.

Or so I thought.

As I oriented myself, a rosy mist puffed down all around me. It smelled like bitter chalk. Almost immediately, my eyes blurred, my knees weakening. "Damn you, Chao-Xing."

"Told that idiot you were faking. Want to know a secret, xiao Zara? I was *just* like you once." The last thing I heard was her mocking laughter.

However long later, I woke in lockup, a five-by-five cell with a blanket and a bucket. Nadim didn't have holding cells, and there were lockers on the other side, so this was probably a storage room. A blue, shimmering force field prevented me from moving farther. Both Marko and Chao-Xing stood before me in their bloodred uniforms. Their eyes were black again, full of Typhon's presence.

I played my part to the hilt. No point in pretending to be innocent, and nothing gained by cowering. Bravado was more my style.

"Hey," I said. "How's it going?"

Staring into Chao-Xing's eyes was like falling into an

abyss. No, like getting a glimpse of Typhon's soul. A shiver trembled through me, and even through the nu-silk fabric of my blue uniform I felt the chill. It *was* cold in here. Colder by far than Nadim kept our environment. I suspected the cold was comfortable for Typhon or he just didn't care and kept it at the bare minimum that optimized the performance of his Honors. I could almost see my breath in the air.

Bravado didn't seem to work, so screw them, I wouldn't speak again. If they'd come to interrogate me, they could get on with it. On impulse, I brushed my fingertips over the wall—Typhon's skin—and got an icy shock. He didn't want me here. Well, that made two of us. Since I didn't like his dismissive power play, I pushed a little harder, and a shock baton fried my brain as he rejected my attempt at contact. Forcefully.

"Zara," Marko said finally.

Just my name, in a tone ominous enough that I imagined him intoning it at my funeral. *We are sorry to inform you that Zara Cole was lost in deep space. America mourns.*

Somehow I twisted that dread into defiance. "It's freezing in here. Got a blanket? Or a shot of tequila. I'm fine either way."

Marko, impatient, said, "Tell us what you were trying to accomplish with this stunt."

"Your ship beat the hell out of mine. And now you're

towing us God knows where. Don't you think I ought to *do* something? Anything! You're not exactly reassuring us that everything will be okay."

"It won't," Chao-Xing said, with a frozen smugness, though she was probably channeling Typhon. "Nadim has always shown weakness and impulsivity. Since you and Honor Teixeira came aboard, you've encouraged this behavior. We gave you tasks to complete and you deviated from them. Nadim knew the boundaries. You have failed to comply and broken regs. Now he'll pay the price, and you will be returned home in disgrace."

The hell we will.

"I don't even know what rules he broke!" I said. "You could at least tell me that."

Okay, so that was a lie. I just wanted to keep them talking. From this side of the force field, I had no hope of mounting an escape. Stalling was a time-honored tactic for coming up with Plan C on the fly. With all my heart, I wished I had some way to contact Beatriz. She must be worried. By now she must suspect that things had gone wrong.

Marko answered. "That is not our responsibility. There is no more to say." At the very edges of my awareness, I felt Nadim stirring. Starting to fight a little on the end of his tether. That distracted Typhon, and he let go of Marko and Chao-Xing; their body language shifted, just a little, like they were waiting for a blow they couldn't avoid. Both blinked rapidly as their eyes adjusted again, and Chao-Xing stretched, as if she had been forced to stand in an unnatural position for too long.

Flesh puppets, I thought.

Marko slumped against the wall. *He's clearly exhausted. He's fighting it more.* Chao-Xing was more wholly in Typhon's grip.

"You shouldn't have done this," Marko told me quietly. "He won't let you go. Keeping you away from Nadim—Typhon knows it hurts."

"Marko, what's going to happen to Nadim? The Leviathan won't beat him again, will they? That was—"

"Awful," he finished for me. "I'm sorry. I'm sorry that I couldn't stop it sooner, but—the bond—"

"You're deep bonded," I said. "I know. What's your pair-bond-name?"

"You're not supposed to know about any of that."

"So he didn't tell you what rules we broke?"

Chao-Xing said, back still rigidly turned toward us, "The Elder is under no obligation to tell us anything."

"Then that's not much of a bond, is it? I mean, two-way street and all."

She didn't answer. I wondered if all her humanity was gone already and what it took to do that to a person. A shudder rolled through me, contemplating it.

"We don't choose who we bond with," Marko said. "What's your point, Zara?"

"My point is that he eats your soul and doesn't even think of you as *people*," I said. "Is that how the Elders work? How the Leviathan *really* work?"

"You don't know anything about it."

"Of course I don't, because you're keeping those of us on the Tour in the dark! Well, guess what? We're turning on some lights and looking around. If you're smart, Marko, you'll do the same before it's too late."

"If you want to talk yourself into worse treatment for your Leviathan, keep going." Chao-Xing folded her arms, but I didn't miss the faint smears of moisture on her cheeks. She'd wiped away the tears without eliminating the evidence. *Something I said moved her. If only I knew what . . . I could dig at that fissure.* Maybe we couldn't win this battle with a frontal assault, but I'd already infiltrated their fortress. The whisper of an idea scratched at the edges of my mind, not ready to emerge in the light just yet. I'd give it time to germinate.

"Worse than death?" I asked softly. "I'm not letting you take his voice away and drive him out to die alone. I can't. And I can't believe you'd let that happen, either."

I thought for a second they'd keep talking, but then Marko shook his head. He and Chao-Xing exchanged a look. "We have duties," Chao-Xing said. "And there's nothing to be done. Nadim's fate is already decided." She hesitated after a couple of steps and looked back. "I'm sorry."

She actually was. A little.

"Marko—" I called out after him.

"I can't," he said. "I'm sorry."

Nothing to pass the time in here, just silence and my own thoughts. For the first time since I came aboard, I couldn't feel Nadim, and the emptiness chewed at me. Based on what Marko had said, it must be the same for him. He'd be half-mad, wondering what they were doing to me. That little crack in the wall between us had been sealed tight, probably by Typhon.

Don't let them hurt you again. Keep healing. Stay strong.

With every moment that ticked away, Typhon towed Nadim closer to the Gathering. Taking a breath, I shored up my flickering resolve.

No prison was escape proof, and this one was more of an improvised closet. Carefully I scanned every centimeter of my surroundings, but I didn't find anything that could help me. Just the bunk . . . and the bucket. They probably expected me to use it as a makeshift toilet, but I had a better idea. I already knew that Leviathan were susceptible to music. Marko sang, so Typhon must respond to lower registers. My voice lacked range, hovering around a husky alto, but I'd make do. I had one advantage that perhaps Typhon didn't know about.

I had Leviathan woven into my body.

The worst that could happen was that Marko or Chao-Xing would tell me to settle down, or I supposed they might gas me again. I'd survived it once, right? I'd seen street performers make music out of what most people would call trash. Bin lids and broken bottles, rusty ladles and upturned pails. There was a whole troupe of them who worked the Zone, and I'd admired their skill more than once. Now my life—our lives—depended on me matching them.

I started slow with gentle raps on the bucket, and Typhon didn't register the sound until I brushed the wall, trying to make it seem accidental. Suddenly I had all his attention, and it was like being drenched in ice water. Despite fingers that wanted to tremble, I went on with my quiet rhythm, not enough to make him think it was purposeful. When you tried to coax a wary cat into your lap, you had to pretend like you didn't even notice it slinking around. Basically I felt like ten kinds of a fool drumming alone in my cell, like this would do any good. It didn't matter how I looked or what anyone thought. My dignity was nothing compared to Bea and Nadim, so even if this turned out to be a colossal waste of time, I wouldn't be sorry for trying.

After a while, I added a soft rendition of a song my mother sang to me when I was very small. *Hush little baby, don't say a word.* Papa never did buy me a mockingbird, or much of anything, for that matter. There weren't many lyrics, and they made no damn sense, but it was a relaxing melody. Added to my slow taps and thumps and hissing brushes of fingers, the music I made had a soothing, hypnotic quality. I nearly nodded off a time or two.

At first I thought it wasn't working at all. Typhon's attention drifted away, and it seemed like it was just me, singing to myself like some old-school jailbird. I just needed a mouth organ to make the picture complete. Except as time wore on, I noticed my cell warming by such minuscule degrees that I didn't even think the Elder was aware of it.

I took it slow. The next time I brushed the wall, I lingered just a little, and the spark I got back from Typhon wasn't all death-lightning and *GET OUT* written in blood. I wasn't sure how deep bonds worked, but he was clearly responding to my song. If Chao-Xing caught me at this, she'd put a stop to it. Then again, she probably didn't feel about Typhon the way I did Nadim.

Even if I wasn't supposed to.

Singing this song on loop summoned thoughts of my mother. For the first time, I wondered how hard it must've been for her, having a child in pain that she couldn't save. I couldn't imagine giving somebody life and then having that person walk away as if it meant nothing. I did love her. But I'd never understood how she felt before, not really. And I'd never regretted hurting her this much, either.

I didn't know if my new softness was the key, but the

next time I touched Typhon, he opened too—a rusty creak, like an iron hinge that had been sealed for years. The Elder didn't seem alarmed by what I was doing. In fact, some of the darkness had washed away with the song, like an ocean of peril at low tide.

What I found, deep in the heart of the Elder Leviathan, surprised the hell out of me.

CHAPTER TWENTY

Breaking Barriers

WEARINESS. ISOLATION.

I'd expected to find a monster hiding behind his cold walls, a fiend that feasted on violence like it was wine and meat. Instead, I encountered a lone soldier, poised on ancient battlements, overlooking a war. One he was losing. Knowing he'd fight and die, yet he could not lay his weapons down. It was terrifying, and I wasn't sure if what I sensed was literal or metaphorical. The top of my head tingled and I couldn't get my breath.

Never expected to feel sorry for Typhon.

Somehow, I was in the Elder's consciousness in a way he didn't permit Marko and Chao-Xing to be. He suddenly noticed me and rumbled a threat that shook the whole ship. I didn't advance or retreat, just kept singing softly.

A few moments later, I heard Typhon directly for the first time. Not aloud, as Nadim spoke, for courtesy's sake, but like thunder in my mind. *Honor Cole, you dare too much.*

You're so tired. So alone.

I didn't mean it as an accusation, and Typhon knew that—of course he did. There could be no dodging a truth with that much weight. *That does not concern you.*

More avoidance. More secrets.

With some effort, I pictured the Elder as that lone soldier, not the enemy who hurt Nadim. It took everything in me, all my self-control, and then I relaxed into Typhon, still singing. Echoes of wrongness pricked at my brain, needle sharp, but I ignored those frissons. The shock that reverberated through him told me he wasn't used to this unfiltered sharing; he was used to taking, commanding, not receiving from the humans he bonded with. I scooped up a few of his memories like collecting fish from a pond and realized that the two Honors he carried now were certainly not his first deep-bonded crew.

Why do you settle for such a bleak existence? Did you forget it could be more?

Sudden pain nearly blinded me. Not mine. Not Nadim's, either.

I didn't forget. We can't forget. Another tide of memory,

and it carried me along to when Typhon was young and eager, like Nadim, soft and sweet. His first pilot wasn't human—an alien race whose name I didn't know—but those emotions, the warmth of the sharing—that was the same. His pilot gave him everything, even unto death.

It hurts too much, I realized, not trying to hide it from him. Tears gathered in my eyes. *You treat them like things so it doesn't wound you as much when they die.*

It is not your concern, Zara. It didn't escape me that he was using my name now; I'd become a person to him at last. His tone shifted as well, no longer ominous thunder, but more like funeral bells heard at a distance. The Elder's inner voice filled me with melancholy. *But . . . you speak the truth.*

It doesn't have to be like this. I can comfort you. The offer had to feel impulsive. If it seemed calculated, I'd lose all the ground I'd gained. *You're going to send me back to Earth, without any memory of why, so it doesn't matter what you show me. I can be your friend for now, at least. You can share your burdens with me.*

This felt all kinds of weird. Though Typhon still didn't seem to notice, my cell had warmed to the point that it felt downright cozy. My song was working on him, touching notes of pathos and home that he probably couldn't defend against. Not with weapons, anyway.

There's no profit for you in helping me, and I do not trust altruism.

But the fact that he hadn't slammed the door shut between us spoke volumes on how much he'd missed this, how he ached for that long-lost alien Honor. In the end, he didn't deep bond, but he wanted to, enough to be distracted by the tantalizing possibility. And that was exactly the rule of the con. Misdirection, make them watch your left hand while robbing them with your right.

The best con of all? Believing it yourself. And I *had* to believe this, had to feel it, because he'd know if I was holding back. Minds couldn't lie. It would have been so much easier if I didn't care, couldn't feel his pain and be sorry for it. But this was my price. Pain and guilt.

While Typhon resisted the lure of opening to me fully and soaring as one, we bobbed together, dreaming in that lullaby sea. Drifting, drifting, until he eased and went from listening to rocking, borne aloft on my mother's music. My taps slipped into strokes and my voice softened. I had the patience to do this forever or until one of two things happened—we reached the Gathering or his Honors noticed his emotional shift.

With Typhon as a conduit, I sensed Marko and Chao-Xing on the other side of a mental barrier, faint and fumbling, but I couldn't feel what they felt; that was how well the Elder had blocked them. A lazy pleasure spiraled through him and into me. He was enjoying this—it was just enough that it felt good—not enough that it seemed dangerous. I was just a tiny, caged bird, singing in my captivity. What possible danger did I pose?

It took an eternity of whispered song, soft drumming, but then, finally it happened.

He drifted to the edges of dark sleep, lost in memory, a weary soldier nodding off on the battlements.

The lights dimmed, and the blue curtain of energy in my cell flickered and went out.

I sent the bucket spinning as I dashed for the opening and felt the harsh clash of the energy slamming back into place behind me. I hit the floor rolling and came up on my feet, pushing from stop to sprint in record time. I also slammed the mental barrier between us shut with conviction, because no matter what else Typhon was, he was also the asshole who had hurt Nadim.

If Leviathan couldn't forget, neither could I.

I popped open the door before they locked the ship down and then searched the lockers. Exultant, I pulled out a bulky old skinsuit; it wasn't the latest model, but at least they wouldn't catch me with the gas trick again. I scrambled into the suit and yanked the mask over my head just as the pink mist drifted down. My suit sealed and filtered just in time; though I was little dizzy, I held on and kept moving.

Okay, next stop, armory.

I didn't want to fight Marko or Chao-Xing, but if they

tried to stop me from freeing Nadim, then we'd throw down. As of now, that was my new goal. Free Nadim. Run like hell. Not much of a Plan D, especially when Typhon had such scary weapons, but I still had the idea of finding a space version of the Zone in the back of my mind. We'd hide out, perform a training montage, and come back ready to fight. So maybe I'd watched too many sci-fi vids, but in desperate moments, it was all I had.

As I raced down the corridor toward the armory, I nearly tripped on the prone figures of Marko and Chao-Xing. *Holy shit, they weren't ready for the gas?* That must've been Typhon's doing, not theirs; he'd overreacted to my betrayal, big-time. He probably would have loved to turn the atmo toxic, or blow me into space, but some part of him still cared for his crew, even if they were just tools to him.

I hurdled their unconscious bodies and pounded the armory door with frustration when I realized that the Elder had locked me out. Beatriz could hack this *and* fix a broken toaster oven in the time it would take me to key in two password guesses. Weapons, weapons, the other Honors probably had some. I searched them quickly and took two stunners and a hypodermic, probably a tranq.

"I don't want to kill you, Honor Cole. You remind me of my first pilot." Damn, Typhon was talking to me, out loud. Shit must be serious. "But if you continue, I will vent all decks, all corridors."

"That'll kill your crew too!"

"There will be more Honors next year and the year after that. And so on. Your people have so many bright young minds to spare." That had to be the most optimistic threat I'd ever heard.

"I don't believe you care nothing for them. Plus, you must have a boss, too. The Leviathan you're gathering to judge Nadim will probably be curious why you had to kill your own crew to deal with me."

The cameras on board meant he couldn't explain this away without giving context, and instinctively I knew he wouldn't want to reveal that moment when he'd let his guard down with me. Typhon rumbled in rage, rolling hard enough that I almost fell over. Forever ago, I ran through a funhouse, part of a carnival, where the floor was constantly tilting, shaking, and sometimes dropping out altogether. My run through Typhon's depths felt about like that. It had to be driving him crazy that he couldn't just smash me, but he could still lock me out of everything, essentially herding me like a rat in a maze.

When I slammed into Beatriz racing around the next corner, I held on for dear life. I'd recognize her anywhere, even in a skinsuit. "What're you doing here?"

She grabbed me back, talking so fast I couldn't follow at first. "Are you okay? They claimed you were really sick and ordered me to come over to help. I suspected it was probably a trick, but I wasn't sure. Then the lights went out, they went to check on you, but—"

"Breathe," I said, giving her a little shake. "I need your big, sexy brain. Come on, Bea. We need a Plan E."

"You must have already used Plans F and U." She got out with a touch of sass.

Love this girl. We hugged each other tight while she thought, then she whispered in my ear, "I need an H2 and five minutes. Make sure I have both."

"Understood. Don't take your hood off. We might need the scrubbers. Or oxygen. And if you feel a breeze, hold on to something and try to grab Marko and Chao-Xing if they fly by."

Laughing at her horrified expression, I hugged her again and ran off. First, I had to make sure that the other two couldn't interfere. The gas wouldn't last forever, so while they were still unconscious, I fashioned makeshift bonds out of their socks and belts and fastened them at wrist and ankle. To the Elder, I'm sure it looked like I was running aimlessly after that, but I didn't want him to guess what door I needed to enter and lock it down.

My feint paid off. Plainly he wasn't used to dealing with con artists. Gravity issues aside, Typhon wouldn't last long down in the Zone. At the last moment I dodged into Marko's quarters and wedged the door so he couldn't lock me in. Luck was with me; he'd left his H2 on the table beside his bunk. Snatching it, I raced back to Beatriz, who was tapping a foot near the console. There was no way to seal this room down as it was the heart of the ship with corridors ranging off in four directions.

"What are we doing?" she asked, taking the tech.

"Think of it as boosting a car."

"Nadim is not a car. Besides, I've never stolen anything." Despite the worried tone of her bitching, she was already working on the H2. "There's a conduit in the stern. I need to route some things there, and I need you to wait. I'll see to the timer. When I get everything set, it's imperative for us to hit this simultaneously."

"We're not, like, turning keys for a self-destruct sequence, are we?" That was too far, even for me, though part of me wondered exactly what I wouldn't do for Nadim. Or Bea.

She snickered. "Don't be ridiculous. Just trust me. I'm going to distract him. It'll take too long to explain."

"Okay. I'm on it." I tossed her one of the stunners. "You never know, right?"

"Be careful." With that, she ran off down a corridor, leaving me to pace.

"This is your last warning," Typhon thundered. "I *will* kill you if you leave me no choice."

"You can try." Beatriz had reached a comm, wherever

she was. It wouldn't be long before she was slinging code into his systems, screwing with all his software and Earth tech. "We're not afraid of you!"

She'd become a *much* better liar, and I laughed so loud that it hurt my throat. I'd wondered when he would speak up again. If I had an inkling how he thought, he'd been scanning for something, anything, that would eradicate Beatriz and me without hurting Marko and Chao-Xing. Two human lives might not amount to much in the grand scheme, but that failure would probably tarnish his reputation. Eventually trust would erode in his leadership. How long before other Elders decided Typhon was unfit to serve? Of course, this all might be bullshit human rationale, and I couldn't hope to unravel the tangle of their politics.

Numbers came up on the console in front of me, counting down, just as she had promised. This was some kind of crazy-ass New Year's Eve—with all our lives hanging in the balance. Finally, the timer clocked to zero, and as it did, I felt a shudder move through Typhon's body. Nadim was fighting him; we'd been gone too long, both of us, and he must be terrified. He couldn't win, but that didn't matter. He'd be enraged at the idea of something happening to us.

Especially when that something involved Typhon.

Bea came back on comms. "When the numbers come

up, I need you to key them in, Z. Timing is critical. Don't screw it up."

Shit, I'd never been a twitch-gamer. But this was a contest we simply could not lose.

Taking a steadying breath, I matched each flash, stroke by stroke, until the sequence was complete. Then I felt the lurch. At first I didn't understand, but as the star charts flowered beneath my fingertips, I realized the monumental scale of what Beatriz had done. I broke out in chills, no, full-on goose bumps. With nothing more than an H2 and an access panel somewhere in the stern, she'd *hacked an Elder Leviathan.*

"And you wanted to wash her out!" I shouted with an air punch.

But if I knew anything, it was not to celebrate too soon. I took control of our course and sent Typhon in the opposite direction from the Gathering. I wouldn't have control for long; the console wasn't designed to fight for supremacy against a noncooperative Leviathan, but that wasn't the point. It forced Typhon to split his attention yet again. We'd given him so many problems to untangle. Damn, I hoped it took long enough for us to get clear, and even as I piloted him off course, lights were popping red on the console.

"What are you doing?" I asked Beatriz over the comm.

"Screwing up all his systems," she said. "Distracting

him. If he focuses too much . . ."

My mother used to say, *mention the devil and the devil will rise*, and just then, Typhon decided to cut to the chase and try to get his nav back. I felt the crushing weight of his attention and knew he was seconds from changing the course again.

Not if I lock him out.

Bea wasn't the only one with bright ideas. I dove under the console and fired the stunner directly into the weak point—the power conduit, the same one that Typhon had blocked on Nadim. It shorted out the console completely. Now we were even. It'd take time to repair that, the course was locked and he'd have a hell of a time unlocking it, his Honors were down, and Nadim was struggling with everything he had to break free. Typhon was fighting too many battles.

I was frightened for Nadim, though. If he kept that up, he might tear himself apart trying to save us.

"Head for the docking bay." Bea still had the intercom. "By the time you get there, I'll find a way to release the tow the Elder's got on Nadim. See if you can raise him on the Hopper."

"We should go together," I said.

But she couldn't hear me. All around us, Typhon roared like a mad beast, shuddering so hard that it seemed he might split at the seams. It must be maddening for him to be locked on autopilot, but he'd override the Earth tech or his Honors would work free and perform repairs. Otherwise, he couldn't stop until he reached the destination I'd selected, a dead planet on the other side of a distant system.

That would take time. I'd tied Marko and Chao-Xing up pretty damn well. On my way to docking, I grabbed a knife from the commissary and dropped it at the end of the corridor. It would take a while for them to inch down that way; they were awake and glaring when I raced by, but I didn't pause to talk. No instructions either. With sufficient time and effort, they could grab the blade and free each other, hopefully not soon enough to let Typhon catch up.

Defense mechanisms kicked in that I didn't even know Leviathan had. He unleashed drones first. They zoomed after me, shooting with grim precision. Laser fire spattered the walls and floor, singeing Typhon's interior. Running like hell, I dodged and rolled until my lungs burned with exhaustion. *Can't keep this up.*

I didn't know if my stunners could fry the electrical components, but I whirled and fired. *Time to find out.* The drone sizzled and sparked, but it didn't drop, so I took aim again. This time, the electric burst shorted it out and it smashed to the floor. By the noise in the distance, I could tell that more were on the way. I couldn't linger.

As I rounded the corner, I took a glancing shot across

the back of my arm. *Damn, not a stunner.* Typhon was no longer inclined to play. On the plus side, the laser burn cauterized my nerve endings, so it didn't hurt after that first white-hot burst.

I must be getting close to the docking bay.

Abruptly, the floor dropped out from under me, plunging me into the sublevel. The hard landing knocked all the wind out of me, and I wheezed on my side for a few seconds. They probably thought that would contain me, but I'd likely memorized more Leviathan physiology than they expected. It was dark as hell, but the drones couldn't get to me either. I'd crawled through worse with Derry, but not being able to see did screw with my head. My own breathing sounded extra loud, echoed by my heartbeat.

It would be so easy to get lost. I made a few wrong turns, stumbled into walls, and into a pile of . . . I didn't know what. Something broken that Typhon had hidden. I sliced my fingers on the metal scraps and ended up pulling a piece loose to use to feel my way forward. No more face-plants, no more smashing my nose into walls. Like that, I crept through the dark, trying to keep my bearings. *If I'm right, then . . .*

Here.

I felt around for the catch and breathed a word of thanks when I found it. Crawling on all fours, I came out into the hallway to hear sounds of combat in the distance. Were the drones targeting Bea? I had to trust that she could handle herself and would meet me as promised. *Still have to get there.*

Outside the docking doors, I found a patrol bot waiting for me. It hadn't spotted me yet, so I took a knee, aimed, and fired. The stunner shot bounced off its shielding, and I spat a curse. Tranq darts would be useless too, and I wasn't strong enough to beat this thing into pieces with my bare hands. As it unloaded on me, I tucked and rolled, the heat stinging my skinsuit while I took cover. Smoke rose from my feet and legs, though the smart-clothing saved me from more serious injury.

All or nothing, I told myself.

While its energy cells cooled and cycled, a failsafe to prevent overheating, I charged with everything I had and jammed the metal shard into its power core. The resultant shock blew me backward, slamming me into the wall so hard I saw stars, but the bot was worse off, juddering and frying with blue sparks and dark smoke. When the thing cooled enough, I crawled toward it and ripped out its manual command input panel. I might not be as good as Bea, but I could use the bot's security codes to override the docking door.

They're sending more drones. Hurry.

A minute later, the doors disengaged and I limped into the docking area. Shakily I keyed the bay shut and locked it just as something exploded against the metal blast door. Too close. It took the last of my strength to hobble to the

Hopper. I hadn't been running for my life on Nadim like I had in the Zone, and the last thing I'd eaten had been those greasy bites of meatloaf. How long ago was that?

Trusting Beatriz to cut us loose as promised, I opened the door and climbed into the pilot seat. Like any good getaway driver, I should have our ride prepped and ready to jet when she rolled up, so I checked all the panels and started the engine. I got the Hopper computer connected to the docking bay, just a simple override that meant I could open the doors for her in a crisis. Necessary when shit was chasing you. Worry flared, and I rubbed the fresh burn on the back of my arm, fiddled with the scorched bits of my skinsuit.

She'll be okay, right? She's fast. Smart.

As I opened a comm channel, the big Leviathan rocked again, Nadim straining himself to death on that tether.

It would take too long to go private, time we might not have. I opened up a channel. "Steady, Nadim. I'm here. Bea's fine. We're both good."

At this point, it was irrelevant if the Elder heard us. It wasn't like we had state secrets to hide, more the other way round.

Typhon knew we planned to run, and it was his job to stop us. No matter the cost.

CHAPTER TWENTY-ONE

Breaking News

"ZARA. ZARA . . ." NADIM said my name like a prayer, all desperate amazed sweetness. "You're alive. But how—"

"I'll explain later. We're going to get you loose. You need to catch our Hopper quick and then take off, top speed. It may take some slick maneuvering to execute. Are you up for it?"

"For you and Beatriz? Anything."

"Then stand by, stay calm, and wait for us."

"Yes, Zara."

Letting out a slow breath, I tapped the comm. "Bea, you're on the way, right?"

"Thirty seconds out, coming in hot!"

That had to mean Typhon's defenses were on her, so her life hung on my timing. But I wouldn't let Beatriz down. Not today. I counted, slapped the control, and opened the door just as Bea slid inside, followed closely by a drone. I was a shade too slow to destroy it with the closing of the heavy blast door. She took cover behind some piles of gear, and I vaulted out of the Hopper. We didn't have any time to waste, but fighting for my friend would always come first.

Grabbing a metal pole that was likely a repair tool of some kind, I swung for the bleachers. It fired; I dodged. The bastard drone could hover just out of my range, and if it blasted me, I'd be crispy meat chunks instead of a person.

"Get to the Hopper!" I shouted. "I got this!"

Bea sprinted for the shuttle. The thing wheeled to fire on her, and I whipped the pole at it and clocked it so hard, it spun into a stanchion. As it righted itself, Typhon listed to starboard, and I realized Nadim was trying to help, actually ramming the Elder. The knock tumbled the drone hard enough to screw up its axis, allowing me to hit it again and again. My last strike bent its firing barrel, so that when it tried to shoot me, it went up in a hail of sparks and shrapnel. Tumbling forward, I thought I dodged the worst of it, until I scrambled into the Hopper and Bea's eyes nearly bugged out.

"Zara, you're on fire!" She beat at my arm—the same

one where I got shot earlier, so no wonder I didn't feel it.

"Just get us out of here. Nadim's waiting." I pounded the button for the external doors and waited for them to open.

Fear nearly crippled me—maybe Typhon had his systems back by now—but no. His Honors must still be crawling like inchworms toward the knife I'd left them, cursing me all the way. With excruciating precision, the docking doors fanned open, and finally Bea could swoop the Hopper out. As promised, Nadim was waiting, battered and beautiful, and Beatriz had totally come through, because he was free. His doors opened, and he dipped to catch us in a twisting move so graceful that my heart skipped a beat.

We're home. We have to keep one another safe. We can't rely on anybody else.

Nadim and Bea were my imperatives. She helped me out of the Hopper, and together, we limped toward the main deck. Nadim threw the doors wide for us in welcome as Beatriz said, "I have to ask. How did you get out of the cell?"

"Magic?" I offered.

"Seriously, tell me. Or I'll drop you." She moved as if she meant to take away the shoulder I was leaning on.

With a sigh, I gave her a concise version of events, and Bea stared at me, wide-eyed. "Holy shit, Z. You seduced *Typhon*? You're like a damn Leviathan whisperer or something."

"What is *seduce*?" Nadim asked.

Oh God.

Bea studied me. Then, with an evil-pixie grin, she answered, "When a human and a Leviathan love each other very much—"

In a rush I covered her mouth with my palm. "Don't say that to him!"

"I'm confused." He did sound bewildered, which tugged at my heartstrings.

"To distract Typhon, I bonded with him. A little." It was stupid when we had so many other problems, but I worried how he would respond.

But Nadim only said, "I'm surprised he permitted that." Then I could feel him leaping, putting all his speed and strength to use as he ran from Typhon, from everything Typhon represented. We were *running*.

We were *free*.

Nadim suddenly wrapped himself around me in a warm rush, exactly like a desperate embrace. I fell through him, into him, blazing like a star and meeting his brightness with a collision that blew apart everything else, every hurt, every regret, every fear. Pure and perfect, no rough edges or pieces that clashed.

Zadim.

I felt his laugh, saw it shimmer in silver and copper around me. Felt the joy of it flare in every nerve. I could see the stars burning hard around us, hear the sweet chorus of their songs that twined and twirled into a vast symphony, intricate as precision clockwork I could only dimly comprehend. Each galaxy, singing. The universe, shouting its life, its power, its fierce beauty.

I felt small as an atom, and large as a sun, and most of all, I felt *right* for the first time I could remember.

I was not *I*.

We were Zadim.

And we flew.

It took practice to walk in Zara's body with half my mind flung out among the stars; being flesh felt clumsy and impractical, full of flaws and leaks. *Leaks.* We could see, looking down at it, that the body had damage—a scorched, wide burn on the upper right arm, and even more reddened skin from the drone's fire. *Must be repaired*, we thought in perfect agreement, and split again, though not apart exactly, to inhabit Zara's form. Selfish, perhaps, to hold together so hard.

When Zara's eyes opened and focused on Beatriz, we recognized the shock, the flinch. We made Zara smile. "It's all right," we said, Nadim's music and modulation, Zara's energy and voice. "We're all right. Don't freak out, okay?"

"Your eyes . . ."

"Black?" She slowly nodded, a frown grooved between her perfect eyebrows. "Chill. It's us. Zadim."

"Zadim?"

"What? We can't have a cute couple name?" That part of us was pure Zara Cole, and we laughed. It relaxed Beatriz, who had good reason to be wary.

But it was not a trivial thing, as Zara's tone had implied. This was a bond-name. We had chosen it. Become it. It was *ours.*

We also knew it was time to stop. Zara was weak and tired. Nadim nursed injuries and hunger. So we let go, drifted apart, and . . .

I—the smaller *I*—fell.

The breath I dragged into my lungs felt alien and tainted, but I needed it to clear my head and get myself straight. My eyes ached. I blinked hard, fast, and remembered Marko and Chao-Xing doing the same thing. My pupils must be contracting again. Everything seemed slightly bright, slightly blurry, and then it was better.

Though I didn't exactly remember leaving the docking area, I was about halfway to medical, still leaning on Bea's shoulder.

"Graças a Deus," she breathed, and steadied me when I stumbled. "You need treatment. Now."

She was right. My arm ached, a screaming burn that made me want to curl up into a ball. Bea hurried me to the med bay and cursed when she remembered we'd deactivated EMITU. With a sigh, I sank down on the soft, squishy med bed as Beatriz rewired the bot.

It came alive with a sudden rush of motion, rotating arms and sending her ducking for cover as it rolled forward toward me. "Honor Cole," it said. "You come here often?"

"Way too," I said, and bit back a groan. "Arm."

The bot leaned forward, examined it, and said, "Congratulations. You've achieved peak barbecue." While it was sassing, though, it was also working fast with a cutting tool. My uniform sleeve slipped off, revealing a spectacularly burned expanse of skin, and I winced and looked away. EMITU let out a mournful little whistle. "Blue ribbon, Honor Cole. Shall I whip up a sauce?"

"Only if the sauce is the kind that *stops it from hurting*."

By the time I said it, the bot was already treating me with needles and sprays. A cool blessed relief slipped down my spine as I let out a long, satisfied breath and closed my eyes.

"Honor Teixeira! Bring plates! Tonight we feast like kings!"

Really got to reprogram that damn thing.

I should have been worried as hell. That Typhon would follow us or we might not be able to run fast enough. Should have tried to figure out what we'd do next and where we would go.

But I couldn't stay awake a minute longer.

403

I woke to find Beatriz sitting beside me, reading. Somehow, I'd known she'd be there. "Hey," I whispered. "Where are we?"

"Somewhere off Centaurus A," she said. "No sign yet of Typhon." She hesitated and fussed with a corner of the sheet covering me. "Nadim was singing to you. I could hear him. I think he was trying to help you heal. I tried to tell him it doesn't work like that for humans, but . . ."

"I think I heard him," I said. I had a dim memory of it. Also of a sweet, soft humming. "And you."

EMITU suddenly jerked out of the recharging unit and charged across the room to my bedside, where it used a tiny laser to slice bandages and check the healing beneath.

"Hmmm," it said. "That doesn't seem right."

"What?" Alarm blared through me, and I raised my head to look at a perfect, smooth, uninjured arm. "Good job, Doctor Sarcastic."

Whisking the bandages away, EMITU checked my arm, and despite the terrible bedside manner, it did so gently. "You've been asleep for four point seven two hours," the bot said. "This should not be healed. It should be *healing*. Note my tenses."

"You're making *me* tense," I said. "What are you going on about?"

"I have no information for you. You're healed. Get out."

"Rude!"

"Get out, please?"

That was so purely Beatriz's tone that I had to laugh as I swung my legs off the bed. I felt good. *Really* good. The bot was dead right. Four hours of sleep and some pain chem shouldn't have done that, but I felt like I could run every corridor on the ship and still have energy to burn. In fact, I grabbed Beatriz out of her chair and danced her around the room in something that was half salsa, half stumble.

"You," she said with mock severity, "are *high*."

"I'm not," I said. "I'm fine."

We walked to the kitchen and made a meal. Nadim, I realized, hadn't spoken, but I felt him there, calm and assured at the edges of my awareness. I brushed fingers over the wall, and light followed in a lazy streak. Pulsing gold. My brown skin was beautiful against the blushing pallor of Nadim's.

Bea watched me, then hesitantly reached out and put her palm flat on his skin. A flare of color streaked away—purple, not gold. It zipped back and exploded in a corona of color around her fingers, and from the smile, she could *feel* that. "My favorite color," she said, and stroked the wall just a little. "Thank you, Nadim."

"You're welcome, Beatriz," he said. "Is there anything you need?"

"I—I'd like to hear the stars sing. The way you hear them."

I could feel Nadim's surprise and his pleasure that she seemed willing to take this step. "Close your eyes. I promise, I won't take you deep."

It was strange, watching her go away, disappear out of herself and swim with Nadim . . . shallow, as he'd promised, but the sensations I felt from her were familiar. Delight. Wonder.

He let her go just a moment later, and when she opened her eyes again, they shone brighter than ever. "Oh," she said faintly. "I see. Wow." She let that hang for a few seconds in silence, then said, "I—I'm not comfortable with the idea of losing myself. You understand that, don't you?"

"Of course. But you won't. I'm not Typhon."

Typhon wasn't Typhon, once upon a time, I thought. That haunted me, the memory of that young and hopeful Leviathan bonding so exultantly, so freely with his pilot and starsinger. Broken and mutilated by grief. But I didn't say anything.

More to the point, I couldn't stop thinking about the glimpse I'd had of Typhon as a lone soldier. If the Leviathan were fighting some unknown enemy, it explained the need for weapons. Maybe we needed to worry about something other than Typhon?

I dug into my pancakes. "Hey, Nadim?"

"Yes, Zara?"

"Where are we?"

He linked with me just enough to show me a vast star field with a giant white arrow pointing to a tiny speck moving through it. I laughed, because he spelled out *YOU ARE HERE.*

But the humor faded fast, and I said, "What about Typhon?"

The star field collapsed into darkness. "I don't know," he said. "I can't feel him anymore. We've left him behind."

"Good." But it still bothered me. Typhon wasn't one to give up easily, if at all, and he considered it a mission to bring Nadim in for the rough justice of the Leviathan's Gathering. So why wasn't he on our track? He was quick and angry. If he had to quarter the galaxy to find us, he would. Leviathan didn't forget.

"Nadim, I was thinking . . . back on Earth, I lived in the Zone. You know, with the fringers. People who couldn't fit into the perfect society. Anything like that exist out here?"

"A complicated question," he said. "There are thousands of civilizations scattered through the stars that we visit. Most are well advanced, some are not. Some are barely controlled chaos, like your Earth."

Bea and I both burst out laughing. We were trying to imagine casting our clean, straight streets and orderly houses as chaos. "Okay, so . . . are there places we can hide? Aliens who could grant asylum or something?"

"It's possible. The younger Leviathan who embark on

407

the Tour, who bond with humans, we are not told of these things either. We're . . . sheltered for *your* protection. But Zara has queried me so much that I had to question things too."

"Like why I'm building you a weapon," I said. "Which you never answered."

"Because I didn't know. I still don't," Nadim said. "But I do suspect."

A vid screen opened in midair. It showed us a series of images.

Typhon. Covered with scars and spots of damage.

Typhon's wicked barbed tail, gleaming hard black under starlight.

Typhon's skin peeling away, revealing bio-grafted weapons.

Nadim said, aloud, "I believe the Elders may be involved in some kind of intergalactic crisis."

That lined up perfectly with what I'd glimpsed in Typhon: the lonely, fatalistic soldier, weary and afraid and unable to hope. Glimpses of death and horror, all too fast for me to understand.

"Don't hold back, Zara," Nadim said, gently. "We have to trust each other."

I gave in and let him share those memories. With her heightened connection, Bea saw them now too. She bounced right out of the link, shivering in her skin, hands held to her mouth as if she might vomit, but it was more shock than sickness.

Nadim was rocked too. "*Typhon* showed you this?"

"Yes," I admitted.

No Honor ever came back from the Journey.

And maybe, just maybe, we'd figured out why.

CHAPTER TWENTY-TWO

Breaking Ties

"TYPHON IS ARMORED up like a tank and carries *six rail guns*. I don't think he went through all that bioengineering for fun. You might carry one gun for fun—well, I would—but *six*?"

I could see the whirl and crash of thoughts behind Bea's eyes. "Maybe that's why their Honors choices have changed. More military officers have been chosen. Maybe they're trying to learn how to fight better," she said.

That hit me hard, for some reason. Typhon had once been a gentle soul, like Nadim. He'd been twisted by what he went through. Maybe violence didn't come naturally to the Leviathan. It wouldn't, to a species that hadn't evolved in the competitive hothouse that humans had.

"If they don't use their weapons on other Leviathan, then they have to be squaring off against an alien species," I said.

"There are few we've encountered who could hurt us," Nadim replied. "Most species who develop that level of technology in conjunction with sufficient aggression have used it to destroy themselves. As humans were bent on doing, before."

"So you don't even have a guess?"

"My records are incomplete."

I hated that the Leviathan suckered humans into some private struggle, but the idea that they dragged their younger kin into it without warning—that was another level of disgust.

"Nadim needs to be armed," Bea said then.

"I'm not allowed to have them yet."

She was implacable. "So what? Were there instructions on how to attach that weapon you were making, Zara?"

Nadim answered, reluctantly, "I was able to take some of the data from Typhon. Including the plans for how to install the weapons. And my . . . alarm. But perhaps we should wait."

I wasn't having that. "If there are enemies out there who want to kill your people, you need the ability to fight them.

No arguments, Nadim. Whatever you've got in storage, we are going to install. Now."

Bea said, "I'll take inventory and see if there's anything we can scrap to build something we can use for defense. Or offense. Nadim, I'd be grateful if you'd line up any details on the weaponry that the Elders use."

"I don't have much," he said. "But I will."

"I'll be on the supply deck," Bea said.

No point in wasting time. I got to work too. There were complicated instructions for attaching the weapon to Nadim's exterior; he'd have to reroute some nerve endings to control and power the device, but we needed to position it and clamp it down first. Nadim would then graft skin around it, integrating fully with his body.

The self-powered cart glided effortlessly ahead of me into the airlock, and I stood beside it in my skinsuit while the atmosphere cycled out. When the outer door opened, it did so without a sound, and suddenly I was . . . *there*. Drifting in the stars, just like Nadim.

It took all my concentration to pull myself away from the dizzy expanse and focus. The mass of the weapon made it dangerous once I had it out in space, but Nadim altered his speed and trajectory to help me maneuver it within a fraction of a centimeter to its assigned spot, which meant all I had to do was activate the biotech seal between his skin and the base of the weapon. I'd have to wait a bit for the connection to take, so I allowed myself to really look around.

This was my first spacewalk. The enormity of it, and the lonely smallness of my body, took my breath away. We were in a bright, busy part of the Milky Way galaxy, thick with stars, and it was hard to imagine that Nadim's home was so vast, so cold, so beautiful. So many stars. I could feel the life of them all around me—and even though I wasn't currently deep bonded with Nadim, I could *hear* them. Not clearly. Not the way he did. But when I closed my eyes, I could still make out the positions of the burning points of light, the ancient swirl of slow movements. Dark occlusions of planets.

My awe was interrupted when I felt a bright, hard stab of pain. Not mine. Nadim's. "It's all right," his voice said in my suit comm. "That was the nerve connection being made. There is some discomfort as the grafting begins. The technology is not completely compatible, but it will work."

"Okay," I said. The red wash of feeling ebbed. Now it just felt like a bad bruise. "So, do you want to test it while I'm out here? In case you need me to, ah, adjust something?"

Nadim fired the cannon at a nearby asteroid. I don't know if he meant to use that much power—from the shock that flashed through me, it seemed like he hadn't—but it damn sure *worked*. Energy blew out of the open end of it in a thick plasmatic stream, bright as the stars, so bright that even though the skinsuit darkened the goggles to save my vision, I couldn't blink away the afterimage. No sound, of course, except my surprised yelp and fast breathing. The energy cut out in another second, and Nadim said, "That . . . feels . . ." He didn't finish. I could sense what he did, and I didn't know what words to put to it, either. There was a wave of almost visceral thrill, and then horror at having this kind of power. Then his exhaustion swept over me; this had drained him somewhat.

"It taps your star energy," I said. "So try not to use it, okay?" Last thing we needed was to get into a running gunfight and have our ship *fall asleep* in the middle of it. "Maybe I can find something else we can use."

"Zara," his voice said. I drifted back toward the opening in his skin, trailing my fingers along the thick, resilient flesh of it, and I realized that when I touched him, patterns of light followed. "It's time to install the alarm too. It can help keep me awake even if I run low on power."

"I'll keep you awake. I can be super annoying."

"You don't like it. I know. I don't either, but this is why I asked for the device. I *need* it."

"It's going to hurt you."

"If it preserves your life, and Beatriz's, then it is worth the discomfort it might cause me. Please, Zara. Do this for me." My H2 chimed where it was strapped to my arm. I tilted it and found that the instructions for installation were right there. Unlike the cannon, this would be different. It would have to be buried deep inside him, near a nerve cluster.

I was going to have to cut into him. Again. Much deeper this time.

"I can't," I said quietly.

"I can't do it to myself," he said. "It's necessary. Like—the DNA you had spliced in to repair your own damage."

"That's not fair."

"No. But it's true. Please. Do this."

I hesitated, surrounded by the stark beauty of the universe. My touch sparked glowing comets on Nadim's skin.

We listened to the stars sing. Just for a moment.

I found Beatriz deep in the supply deck, rummaging through boxes of spare parts.

"We don't have anything that we could use to build more weaponry, so we're limited to the one gun," she complained.

"Okay, time to pivot." This was where I shone, no false modesty. I'd spent my life jury-rigging tech out in the Zone. "If we can't build additional guns, what about a shield?"

Bea stared at me like I was out of my mind. Or a genius. Quite possibly, the two shared common ground. "Are you serious?"

"When I was on board Typhon, they locked me up with some kind of energy field for a wall, right? Nadim should have the same basic tech. And if we can generate a small version inside, theoretically, we'd just need parts and power to replicate the effect externally."

"Damn, Z. You sound so pro right now."

I grinned and pretended to dust off my shoulders. "I wasn't asleep when you were talking all that science, okay? And making something out of nothing is where I live."

Nadim weighed in for the first time. "I'm not sure how well it would work against rail guns or lasers, but it would help with ramming attacks and defend against ballistic projectiles."

"That includes debris, like passing through an asteroid field," I added.

"If we can do it, it would be a choice upgrade." Bea wore a pensive expression, studying the inventory list. "But . . . there's no way to avoid a lengthy, external installation. That may be dangerous."

"I'll do it," I said straightaway. We needed to cannibalize some of the sensors and cabling, and while we were about that task, I added, "You know, I've been wondering. . . ."

"That never goes anywhere good," she mumbled.

"For real, Bea."

"Okay, let me hear it."

"Why did Typhon have all those internal defenses he

sprang on me when I was on the way out? I mean, drones? Traps? He's strapped to the gills. But—"

"The only reason he'd be so prepared otherwise is if there was a chance he might be boarded by hostile forces," she finished.

"So we're definitely not looking at another race of sentient ships," I mused. "It's probably something . . . what, smaller, right?"

"I agree with your curiosity, but we should get busy, don't you think? Typhon's still out there. We'd better get this done as soon as we can."

If it delayed the surgery to implant Nadim's internal taser, I was all for that.

With the help of more automated dolleys, we hauled parts Bea selected to the nearest hatch. Bots could help me with the installation to some degree; she was busy programming the cleaning units to assist. Meanwhile, I suited up again and fed the oxygenated umbilical back into my mask.

Despite the gravity of the situation, I couldn't stifle repeated frissons of excitement at the thought of my next spacewalk.

Half an hour later, Bea left the pressure chamber so I could open the outer door. It was awkward dragging the dolley out with me, but once I stepped out, gravity ceased to be a factor and it grew exponentially easier to guide.

After that, it was monotonous but not difficult. Since I was still touching Nadim, feet to hull, I felt him following my progress.

Zara . . .

You're not using the comms. Why not?

I was testing. The abashed tenor of his thoughts made me smile.

To see if I'd answer?

No. If we could still touch—with you beyond my walls. That's good. It means our bond is deep and strong.

You got that right. Now stop distracting me or this will take forever.

My hands felt clumsy as I installed the hardware and inched along his skin. The power units needed to fire at regular intervals so the force field could spread to cover his whole body. In theory, it had sounded easy. In practice, I would need to make multiple trips out here, working each time in eight-hour shifts.

I worried when you sang to Typhon, he said, and it felt sudden, like he'd been compelled to get it out.

Why?

Because you might . . . He didn't finish the thought. I understood, though.

You thought I might like him better? Come on. Typhon's a monster.

But you felt sorry for him. I know that too.

I had. I'd been forced to reach out to him, to understand him. *I'm not going to leave you*, I told Nadim. *Not ever.*

I felt his relief, and I moved to set up the next unit in rote motion: drill, drill, bolt, bolt, clamp, power on. Nadim was right: I *had* felt something. I'd exploited Typhon's loneliness, used his private sorrow against him. But I didn't let remorse linger long. That asshole wanted to kill Nadim, who I'd protect to my dying breath. The thought drifted through Nadim, and he purred, a low vibrato that I felt through the soles of my feet, even past the skinsuit, and deep at the base of my spine. To this, I had no coherent response, only visceral emotion that streamed to him and back again in a feedback loop so exquisite it left me dizzy. Not the best state when working in zero gravity on a ship's hull. I squatted to ground myself and tried to be stern. *Remember when you asked Bea, What is* seduce? *It's exactly what you're doing right now.*

You did that to Typhon.

Hard to tell if he was teasing me. I thought so. There was a thread of humor, undercut by a layer of wildness that hinted he wasn't quite as gentle and understanding as he wished. Maybe all Leviathan had some of that cold brutality, held in reserve. Maybe Leviathan and humans had that in common. But the moment passed as he quieted, becoming a gentle hum in the back of my head.

For hours more, I progressed along the hull, until I just

couldn't continue any longer. Part of that was exhaustion, but more to the point, I had no more parts. Continuing would require me to go inside, load up the dolley, and make another trip. I didn't have the fortitude today. *We have time, right?* But Nadim didn't answer, so he must be feeling the pressure too.

Bea was waiting when I stumbled through the hatch. She helped me out of the skinsuit and handed me a flask of water. "You're bent, you know that? Nobody meant for you to work nonstop, no breaks, no meals."

"I don't know, I guess I feel like we're on the clock . . . and it's winding down."

While life might shake out to rose petals and moonlight for everybody else, I pretty much had a road paved with C-4. Usually, when stuff seemed to be going well, that was when everything went to shit. Like me scoring the sweet bag off Torian Deluca's daughter. Sure, it had all looked good upfront; then Conde's shop had exploded, and that was right about where I stood. Waiting for the big boom.

Possibly I'd developed a bad case of paranoia. *I hope it's that.* Still, I couldn't help asking Bea, "We're shielded here, right?"

Her tone was patient. "As much as we can be. Per my readings, Nadim's signature is masked to long-range sensors. Obviously if another Leviathan stumbles across us, we're screwed. But what are the odds when space is this vast?"

I really wished she hadn't said that. In vids, whenever someone asked, "How could it get worse?" all hell would immediately break loose. But Bea continued eating calmly and nothing broke down, no alarms went off.

Maybe I just needed to relax.

Food and sleep helped a little, then I went back out to work on the shield. For almost a week, Iceland time, Nadim drifted and concealed himself while I installed the rest of the shielding. My knees and shoulders were sore as hell. Probably an actual work crew could've done this in a day.

I was almost done when it went wrong. I was tired, rushing with the end in sight, and I lost hold of the dolley. It drifted, and hell, I leapt for it, thinking only of losing the last of our spare parts, except I had no plan for getting back.

The skinsuit didn't have propulsion. Neither did the dolley, really, just little hover jets and no guidance at all. Pure visceral terror slammed through me as the umbilical stretched. If it snapped, I'd choke and die. *How long do I have, again?* And I still had three units to install, dammit. It added insult to injury that I might bite it without finishing what I'd started. The shield would protect Bea and Nadim, even if I couldn't. Panic beat me about the head and neck, just like a rich old lady whose purse I'd tried to lift once; she was sprier than she'd looked.

Lock it down. Don't let—

Zara?

Too late. Nadim was stirring.

"Nadim, *stop moving!*" I said out loud. "I can do this."
Maybe. In thirty seconds, I'd be testing the limits of my
tether.

Zara! This time worried, more emphatic.

I'm fine. With prejudice, I slammed a mental shield
between us. Nadim had a short fuse where I was concerned,
and it wouldn't help if he started freaking out, adding his
fear to mine.

Think fast. What would Beatriz do?

The first answer was, *be more careful.* Then I had it.
Quickly I checked the straps on the remaining supplies and
angled the dolley—no gravity, no problem—so that the jets
were facing away from Nadim. I hit the button and they
fired; I jerked forward, like it was a vertical surfboard. Not
enough, but I was closer, and it kept me and the dolley
together. Short, controlled bursts. Easy now. Easy. The last
time I hit it, I was so close I could practically touch him.
Once more . . . and—

I'm home.

My weighted boots hit the surface and I dropped into a
grateful squat, wishing I had arms big enough to hug him.
I settled for a quick pat and dropped the wall between us.
Immediately Nadim's presence spilled into me like a wave.

What happened, Zara?

Nothing serious. Minor hiccup. I'll tell you later.

With trembling hands, I continued my work, counting down the last units. Three. Two. One. Moaning, I couldn't even summon the energy for a victory shuffle, so I crept along the hull toward the hatch. It was quite a long walk and being out here no longer felt exciting, just precarious.

Bea wasn't on standby; she must be working on repairs elsewhere, so I stripped down and went to find her. She glanced up with a smile, blissfully unaware of how close I'd come to messing everything up.

"Done," I said. "Are we ready to fire up the shield?"

"Almost. I'm running diagnostics. I had to piggyback on some other conduits and jury-rig a few connections, but in thirty seconds, we'll find out if this works."

Her excitement made up for my numbness. I forced a smile. "I'm crossing fingers and toes."

Zara, you're not fine.

Not now, I told Nadim silently. *After the test, okay?*

Silence. Great, now Nadim was pissed at me. But I just didn't see the point of making a big deal out of a mistake I'd corrected. For the first time ever, I momentarily wished that Nadim could just hug me.

"You want to do the honors?" Bea asked.

This time, my smile felt more real. "Pun intended?"

"Oh God. No."

"Then go ahead."

She hit the button, and the lights flickered from the

additional power draw, but from the satisfaction that rippled through Nadim, I didn't need Bea to interpret the readings. We had done it. Bea cheered wildly and I gave a weary thumbs-up. Hopefully they thought my weariness was from a week of nonstop hull crawling.

"We're done," I said.

"Not quite," Nadim said. His tone sounded quiet and sober. And then I remembered what I'd been trying really hard to forget.

I still had to install the alarm.

Beatriz kept her head down as she worked the console, fingers flying. "Zara, EMITU wants you to check in. He was worried about the healing on your hands."

"My hands are fine."

"I'm just relaying the message. Five minutes, then you can relax."

I did want to rest. Desperately. So I went down to the med bay, sat down on the treatment bed, and glared at EMITU as he powered up and wheeled over to me.

"Great," I said, and held my hands out for inspection. "See? There's nothing wrong with me."

"No," he agreed. "There is not. Which is why this will make you so angry. Please do not shoot the messenger."

And before I could ask him what the hell he was going on about, one of his sneakier appendages jabbed me with a needle, and before I could yelp, I was falling backward onto the soft mattress. I felt him tut-tutting and dragging me into place and covering me up with a sheet and blanket. Fussing with my pillow. I wanted to ask *why*, but my lips were too heavy, the word was too heavy, and last thing I heard was Nadim saying, inside my head:

Forgive us, Zara.

CHAPTER TWENTY-THREE

Breaking Open

I WOKE UP pissed, with a drug hangover, and EMITU trundled out of my way when I staggered out of bed. "Thanks for staying with us, Honor Cole!" it said cheerfully with a little wave of all its attachments. "I hope your enforced rest was pleasant!"

"Screw you," I snarled, and lunged for the corridor. I didn't bother with the comm units. I just yelled. "Bea! *Beatriz!*"

She met me in the hub. She looked tired, paler than usual, and she had her hands clasped together like some little schoolgirl, but her gaze was steady and calm. "You're mad," she said.

"Hell *yes* I'm mad, what the hell? You sandbagged me?"

"Technically, *I* didn't. . . ."

"You ordered EMITU to drug me."

"Yes." She bit her lip. A little bit of a tell that she felt guilty and anxious about more than just this. "I had to. Otherwise, you would have . . . insisted on doing it yourself."

"Doing what—"

But I stopped, because I suddenly realized who was missing from this conversation. Nadim was very quiet, and though I could sense him, he was distant.

Still, I could feel the ragged red pulses of pain coming from him.

I glared at Bea. "What did you do?"

Nadim was the one who answered. "It's not her fault. I asked her to do it," he said. "You were too close to me for this to work, Zara. I couldn't give you such pain."

"I don't feel it as much as you do," Bea said. "So we put you out and I did the install on the, uh, alarm clock."

"What did you use, a chain saw? Do you know how much he's hurting?"

"Stop, Zara!" Nadim's sharp tone caught me off guard, and I took a step back. I'd been looming over Bea, I realized. "She followed instructions. I will heal. We agreed that you didn't need to be involved."

"You should have asked me!"

"Told you," Bea said. Not to me. To Nadim. "She's not going to get over this any time soon."

"Damn right," I said. I took in a long breath and let it out. "Okay. So. What's our situation?"

"Two Leviathan have come close. Neither have detected me." The implied *yet* hung in the air. "They are singing my name. Searching for me."

"I guess that's the Leviathan version of a citizen alert," I said. "All right. How long until you're healed enough to move on?"

"A day," he said. That sounded optimistic to me. "Zara—"

"Later," I said. "Right now, I want to shoot something."

Combat sim got the cobwebs out and blood moving and expended the anger that would have been pointless to level at Bea and Nadim. Afterward, I raided the weapons locker, because if we were really on the run, I damn sure planned to look the part.

Time to mend some fences.

When I found Bea in the lounge, I struck an action pose in my jacked-up skinsuit. I'd added multiple belts, two nicely lethal guns, a couple of knives, and something that Nadim had assured me was a sonic weapon, nonfatal to any species. I looked like a damn space pirate. I loved it.

"Well?" I asked.

Bea cocked her head. "Don't you think it's a bit—"

"Fantastic?"

"Frightening?"

"That's the point, Bea. We're not Honors anymore. We're—I don't know. Rogues."

"I don't have any idea how to be a rogue."

"First rule: more belts. Second rule: no more rules. Except one: we don't let Nadim get caught." I reached out to her, and she took my hand. "Deal?"

"Yes," she said. More lip biting. "Zara, I'm sorry. About—"

She was cut off as a strong electric pulse zipped through Nadim's body, followed by six more, then a pause before starting again.

"What is that?" I asked. No immediate answer, and I didn't think it was because he was still irked at me. "Nadim?"

"It's a distress signal." He sounded distracted. "A long way off."

"From?"

"From a Leviathan," he said. "I can't make out which one. The song is . . . confused."

Bea shook her head. "Trap."

"Trap," I confirmed. "Nope. Thanks for playing, Elder."

"But—" Nadim seemed surprised. "If it's genuine—"

"Nadim. Typhon wants to destroy you. Don't you think he'd fake a distress signal and hope you come running? Because I'm betting that would be your first impulse."

"Of course," he said. A yellow wave of anxiety fluttered

in him like a trapped butterfly. "This doesn't feel like Typhon. I think one of my kin needs help. Right now."

"Well, there's a Gathering, right? Plenty of Leviathan out there to help. Including Typhon. We're fugitives. That means no helping unless we practically trip over someone in our path, okay? We're trying to find a place to hide, and we aren't running some intergalactic hero service!"

"*Zara.*" Mournful green disappointment crashed over me. "We can't be so selfish. Didn't one of my cousins come to help when I was drifting in dark sleep?"

That was an accurate little guilt missile. He was getting to know me too well. "Yeah, but—well, I screwed that one up. What do you call the guys with all the tentacles?"

"You mean, the race of people? We can't fully pronounce what they call themselves; we don't have the vocal range. The closest is Abyin Dommas. That is a description from another language. It means—"

"Singers in the deep," Beatriz said, which shut me up. How did she know? From the look on her face, she wasn't exactly sure. "They—they are purely musicians. It's their entire life. They're born singing."

"Yes."

"I'd like to hear them," she said wistfully. "It must be—"

"Amazing, sure thing, but let's stay on target. Music appreciation later. So, I kind of stunned one of the Abyin Dommas and we broke all those rules and I'm not so sure

430

your Leviathan cousins are all *yay Team Zadim* even if you do a good deed now. You understand? It's a risk. A big one."

He did, of course; he didn't need all my spoken words to do that. It just made me feel better.

I hadn't changed his mind, though. "Risk or not, someone calls, and I have to answer. I have to. It might be deception, but if it is, we can still run. If it isn't—what if that Leviathan is drifting? What if his crew is calling for help, as you did? They could die."

I thought about it, all my instincts telling me *screw those people*. Nadim couldn't turn away. He couldn't put himself ahead of the needs of his helpless kin.

I put my hand against the wall. Bursts of gold formed around it, and then streaked away down, then back. Exploded out in a silent flash.

Beatriz put her coffee down and did the same thing. Purple fireworks behind his skin.

We were saying yes without saying a word. His relief was tangible as he changed course, looping sinuously to intercept the beacon and then accelerating, a sense of urgency driving him.

"Come on," I said, pulling Beatriz by the wrist.

"Where're we going?" she asked.

"Weapons locker," I said.

"You don't have enough?"

"I think *you* don't."

When we got there, I kitted out Bea with dual stunners and something with lethal kick to it. I wasn't about to let Typhon hook Nadim again. If he wanted a fight, he'd get one. We'd lose, probably, but I intended to give him some new scars in very tender areas.

We sped on, driven by starsong, to find the Leviathan calling for help.

Halfway there, hours into our quest, the beacon went silent. No pulses, no responses when Nadim sent back his own signals. I pulled up a starmap and looked it over; Nadim wasn't in any mood to do handy *YOU ARE HERE* graphics, but I could tell where we were and that we were heading for Cosmos Redshift 7.

I ran the timeline back, so I could see the historical track; in reverse, Nadim headed farther toward the nearby galaxy, and then curved on a different path, moving backward. I overlaid the two maps and analyzed the course patterns.

We were headed back in the same direction.

It *was* a trap. Our first instincts had been right.

"Nadim!" I said sharply, and reached for our bond. He blocked me. "Nadim, you need to stop!"

"Trust me, Zara."

"He's going to kill you! Don't you get that? You can't go running headlong in there!"

"Typhon would not lure me with a distress call. No

Leviathan would. I know this puts you in danger, and I am sorry for it. I will do everything I can to protect you. But we must try to help."

"I disagree," I said flatly.

"I don't," Bea said. She was standing in the hub now, looking half a pirate, tying her hair back. "We have to go. If Nadim's sure, we have to do it."

"But—"

"Zara." Her eyes locked on mine, and what I saw there made me shut up. "We're going."

The pings came again. Both of us turned to look at the console. Nadim said, "It's not Typhon."

"What?"

"I analyzed the harmonics. It isn't Typhon sending that signal; he's an Elder, their range is different. It's a ship younger than I am. One carrying Honors on a Tour, not a bonded ship. Otherwise there would have been a bond-name. . . ." He sounded anxious and distracted, and he wouldn't let me in. Maybe because he was afraid I'd try to make him do something he didn't want to do, like turn around.

"I won't stop you," I said. "But you have to be prepared, Nadim. Stay alert!"

"I am," he said. "You and Beatriz need to be at stations, in case something happens."

There was a new and resonant timbre in his voice, a

determination that hadn't been there before.

In the end, this was Nadim's decision. His people, calling for help. In the Zone, the "honor among thieves" code might be bullshit, but out here, maybe we needed some code to live by. Even if we weren't Honors anymore.

I let Beatriz know what was up, and together, we stood watch in the console room, staring at our steady progress in the 3D star charts. We'd already passed the point where we'd broken free of Typhon, and Beatriz was keeping a sharp lookout for any sign of the Elder's presence, but it was ghostly empty out here. A binary star system hung on the outer edges, with a cluster of planets frying in their orbits; if anything had evolved there, it had to be fireproof. I speculated what they might look like. Asbestos bunnies? Snakes made of shimmering steel scales? Maybe they were liquid and ran in rivulets down channels on the planet, built vast lakes for cities and fountains for towers.

I was afraid, I realized. My healed hands were cold, and when I flexed them, the joints felt stiff. *Get centered, Zara. You are badass.* I was rocking heavy armament, tight pants, and a glorious crown of curls that would have killed in the Zone.

Ready as I would ever be for whatever was coming.

Beatriz said, quietly, "Contact."

Nadim slowed. I felt the shift, though it wasn't hard

enough to throw us around; I still braced myself on the console and stared hard at the charts as they magnified, zeroing in on Nadim's position.

Debris field. Not again. I remembered the sweaty fear of being caught in that last one, of dodging rocks the size of buildings and trying not to get squashed between them. Bea had saved us on that one. Now, she looked both alert and deeply wary. She touched controls, a graceful dance of fingers, without looking away from her screen. Then she grabbed the screen image and threw it up for a 3D visual so I could see it.

It still looked like a debris field to me, but Bea was trying to tell me something.

Nadim got it before I did. A wave of dull gray shock shot through him, streaked with the scarlet of anguish. I pressed my hand quickly to his skin, and the power of his emotion nearly knocked me off my feet. No. No. I couldn't make sense of what he was feeling. Why would a debris field make him so—

Beatriz tapped the image screen and zoomed, and finally, I understood.

We were looking at shredded pieces of silver flesh, floating limp in space. Blackened at the edges.

Pieces of Leviathan.

Nadim hung silent in space, grieving, horror stricken, and I couldn't move. Finally, I wet my lips and asked,

"How many—" I couldn't finish the question. This was a slaughterhouse.

Bea didn't answer. I glanced at her and saw she was silently crying, shaking with the force of it. Like me, she was battered by Nadim's grief, but it was more than that. "The Honors," she whispered. "Nobody could survive this."

The scale of it silenced me, still. I thought about that beautiful silvery display of ships around Earth, glittering and shimmering in our yellow sun, welcoming young humans to the stars. I thought of the handsome, well-dressed Honors dancing at the ball. Then I thought about Tenty, an Honor too, a singer in the deep far from his home. A thousand civilizations, Nadim had said. Thousands of Honors, traveling the universe, hopeful and determined. Leviathan carrying them on.

How many lives had been snuffed out here? I couldn't calculate. I couldn't bear it.

Nadim was wailing. It was a low, discordant sound of anger, grief, and devastation. I felt it vibrating inside me until tears fell, when I hardly ever cried for anything that wasn't my own pain. But there was so much here. Grief wasn't a big enough word for this.

"Typhon," I whispered, and turned my head toward Beatriz. "Is he dead too?"

Something flashed in the corner of my eye—not on the screen, but in the transparent window. I whipped around and saw an Elder, dark as an extinguished star, block out the distant binary suns an instant before his guns began to fire.

On us.

How the hell did he hide?

Even linked lightly with me, Nadim saw and reacted faster than I could have imagined. He twisted, flipped, and sped away, dodging pieces of dead ships with a precision that was born of desperation. We had one gun, but it would be suicidal to square off with such limited weaponry.

"Zara!" he shouted. "Dark run!"

I dropped into *we*, and together, *we* became the dark, drew it around us, vanished from the attacker's senses. Zara fell away, and Zadim went deep, deeper than before, crushing depths of power and motion and senses and star-song cacophonous around us like a chorus of mourners at a funeral, screaming stars, everything warping at this speed into smears and moans because the other ship was fast, so fast, and though he couldn't see us he fired in mercilessly accurate patterns at places we might be next.

We twisted again, curled, flashed like a speeding shark between the corpses of the ships. We were using them for cover, though the disrespect of it woke a sick, gray, discordant wave of horror in us . . . and, at the same time, we began to see flashes of thought from our attacker. Flashes of cold and hunger and blood raining silver in the dark.

Could this be Typhon? Has he gone mad? We both thought it, but the Elder was difficult to even glimpse. His song was all discordance and ruin and screams. We slipped and twisted through a blown-open corpse's ribs, out another wound, reversed and glided under, then raced for the shelter of another dead body as the one where we hid shuddered under a wave of hits.

We had one single glimpse of the Elder, silhouetted clearly against a distant star.

It wasn't Typhon.

Dead Leviathan shattered as the attacker's guns fired on us. The dark run wasn't working against whoever this Elder was; he was still tracking us somehow, and it was only the dead Leviathan shields that kept us alive. We darted behind a rolling, twisted tangle of skin and organs, something so purely horrific that even a glimpse of it made us both flinch, and gathered ourselves in one shimmering second. *We have to fight.*

We slammed against the next corpse and pushed it ahead, keeping it between us and the other Leviathan's massive bulk. More fire poured down on us. Some got through as it chewed up soft tissue and spilled fragments in silvery waves.

Our bond suddenly tightened, drew the two of us together, and forged us into one bright, burning spark. Greater than both. *Now.*

We felt one shot graze our flank in a deep, ugly, rip-ping gouge. Felt the cooling rush of blood whispering out into the dark. We called to Beatriz, and she opened in fre-quencies and song, showing the way. Twist, rise, fall, twist, spin . . . We held on to the shelter of the dead Leviathan as long as we could and came up fast underneath the Elder's lightly protected ventral side, the side that our starsinger showed to us.

We fired the cannon and felt the cold spread inside, energy drained away. Flesh seared and burned, turned to ash. The Elder's surprise roared through us, over us, pain and shock and surprise, and he rolled.

Now. Now!

We hit full speed at the point where a barbed tail was bio-grafted to him, and ruptured the skin; it tore away and sent a froth of silvery blood spinning out into the void, mingling with the blood from so many others. It didn't come cheap, this small victory; we sustained crushing injuries, and more wounds from his guns before we sped free, turning and arc-ing and twisting back.

He fired at us again but still couldn't see us through the pain and Beatriz's singing reflecting back at him. Couldn't hear us. Couldn't feel us.

We were tired, though. The dark run and firing the weapon had drained us fast, left us cold and clumsy.

Nadim pushed me free of the bond just as the last of it

flickered away, and he was left exposed, an easy target in the glow of the suns. Beatriz had collapsed. No more song to baffle the Elder's senses.

I staggered to the console and slapped the panel. *Shields.* Nadim shuddered and the power dropped still more—but the shield soaked the hit that could have broken him in two. But we didn't have the power to absorb another of the Elder's massive attacks. It gave Nadim time to wheel away from the onslaught, so instead of it annihilating us, we only took damage.

Only.

The Elder went to his guns, and though Nadim lithely rolled, he couldn't quite avoid the shot that blew part of his solar fin away. The pain made both me and Beatriz scream. I hit the floor without even realizing that my knees had given out. When I opened my eyes, I spotted Bea clinging to the edge of the console, swaying, but she still stood, like she was never leaving her station. Bravery and defiance in every line, every curve. I got the hell up and joined her. Shoulder to shoulder, soldiers on the battlements just like I'd seen in Typhon's mind.

Except our war wasn't his. We were fighting for Nadim. And we would never, ever surrender.

Nadim didn't have enough energy to fire. Our shield was gone. We needed a thousand generators, maybe a nuclear fusion core, or we'd have to harvest a star to have enough power to survive this fight . . . I could've cried. All that work . . .

There was no victory here. Nobody to left to save in the wasteland.

Run, I pleaded through the bond.

Nadim complied, diving close to the twin suns, twisting a narrow course between them, and I felt the heat even through his insulating skin; the Elder was waiting for him and fired again. Nadim fell back, close to the sun's surface, so close I could feel his skin cooking before he plunged out again, vectoring to put the sun between him and the other ship.

I turned on the comms. "Calling any Honors aboard that ship! What are you doing? *Stop him!*"

Nothing. We should have felt the Elder's massive, powerful essence, but there was nothing coming from the other ship at all.

He was a void of cold, arid destruction.

Had his Honors died? If a human could go mad with his ship, did a ship go mad without his Honors? *It isn't that. Can't be.*

I'd once thought of Nadim as a haunted house when he was in dark sleep, but this Elder felt like a real one, inhabited by a bloody, savage ghost who craved nothing but death.

Nadim faltered. He was running out of power, unable

to feed properly due to damage. We were too far from the right stars, the right songs.

I dove, clicking into the deep bond, leaving my skin behind to stand motionless and black-eyed at the console, and braided my strength, my resolve into him. *We must get away and spread the word. We have to stop any other Honors from being dragged into this. . . .* But we were too damn far to contact Earth directly. The best we could hope for was that they'd receive our signal someday, long after our fates were sealed.

Nadim told me, with surprising gentleness, *We won't get away. I am trying to sing to other ships what has happened.*

That was when I heard Bea lifting her heartbreaking, beautiful voice, rising and falling in harmony with the vibrations and pulses that Nadim was sending out. Singing with all her strength and adding it to Nadim's. The Leviathan could communicate across huge distances. Maybe somewhere, someone would hear.

Unless they've all died, I thought on a tide of despair. *Unless Nadim is the last.*

And that was when the rushing, screaming, ice-cold presence of Typhon blew in, coming in a heart-stopping rush from out of the void. Seeing him and the other Leviathan Elder together, I didn't know why I'd confused them even for a moment. It was clear that Typhon was even bigger, bristled with even more weapons.

What was also unmistakable was the rage that rushed out of him when he took in the shattered corpses of the other Leviathan and Nadim's damage.

Comms activated with a burst, and I heard Marko shouting something.

Typhon came on with screaming speed. I melted into Nadim again, and together we rolled out of the way, and Typhon slammed the other Leviathan, wrecking his shit in an epic crash that sent pieces of broken guns scattering, fire erupting from energy cells buried deep, lighting the dark side of the planet beneath where Nadim dipped and curled to avoid the destruction as two titans clashed in battle.

What the hell is this thing trying to destroy us? It looked like an Elder, but it acted like it wasn't a sentient being anymore, just a beast of boundless violence.

Zadim watched as Typhon's tail flexed, lifted, and drove with brutal, stunning force deep inside the other Leviathan. It did huge damage, but the enemy darted away. Its weapons mostly hung useless, scraps of metal trailing loose from open sores.

"Zara!" Beatriz was shaking my body, and I dropped out of the bond to respond.

I scrambled after her to the comm. The roaring of two Elders shook Nadim, making it almost impossible to hear or concentrate, but I caught some of what Marko was saying. "—escape, get Nadim out of here, *now*, he's too close, when it spreads—"

I had no idea what he was warning us about, but I agreed; we couldn't stay. Typhon was locked in a vicious struggle, behemoths colliding and crushing like galaxies going to war, and we had nothing useful to add. We needed to go. Now.

Nadim was willing, but weak; the damage done to his solar fin was not just painful, but debilitating and healing far too slowly. We were close enough to the binaries that he was able to fly on, but he wouldn't get far from this battlefield. The next star was hours away. I wasn't sure he could make it, injured as he was.

We'd only gotten as far as the next planet out when the battered, silent Elder ship spun free of the battle and hung silent while Typhon backed away. The battleground swam with drifting trails of blood, eddies of wreckage. Typhon had been hurt too. Badly. I could sense the maroon agony pulsing from him, and the raw determination too. A wounded soldier, facing the enemy with a bent sword and no hope.

Something happened to the other ship. It seemed to rock in space, side to side, as if it was being hit, only there was nothing I could see near it. Then I saw that it was . . . pulsing. Swelling. And then the other Leviathan's skin peeled away, spinning off in strips. Blood geysered from severed arteries into a floating cloud of silver around it.

It swelled again. Pulsed.

Exploded.

And out of the corpse came a black rush of . . . things.

CHAPTER TWENTY-FOUR

Breaking Bad

"BEA! DROP ALL power to nonessential systems. Drop *everything*! Get our shield back up." I was already running for the nearest hatch.

Nobody had to tell me that this dark swarm was why Typhon had internal defenses, all the traps and gases and sectioned-off corridors. They were like onyx needles, visible only from the hissing violence of the binary stars as the light shimmered on sharp edges. These were some nasty weird-ass space pirates, and I wasn't letting them commandeer either of these ships.

This idea has to work, it has to.

If it didn't, I had nothing else.

Leaving my body at the hatch, ready to fight in case we were boarded, I leapt for Nadim with no hesitation. He was scared and in pain, and when we locked in, it nearly overwhelmed us. We fumbled for a second until the Zara part remembered. The dark cloud was nearly to Typhon; we would save him, we *could* save him.

Typhon, grapple! We sang it, as both an order and a plea. The irony might amuse in better times, since we'd fought so hard to get free of his hook before. We had no choice but to ally with him. We still didn't trust him, but that didn't mean we'd leave him to . . . this.

A rumble of disapproval mingled with reluctant admiration. Typhon thought we meant to stand and die with him. Then the Elder latched on, not just the tow line from before, but a full docking tube that connected us hatch to hatch. Symbolic acceptance, *we are one, we share the same fate.* A significant commitment, but events were not going to unfold as he expected. We hoped.

As the swarm neared Typhon, we lunged, and our shield came up with exquisite timing. We could not go weapons hot. We would *be* the weapon. Our shield let us slam into Typhon's side without taking additional damage, and he was so much bigger that the impact did little more than bruise. But the crawling things caught between the two ships?

They died. Crushed.

We swung in reverse and slammed into his other side, smashing more, but others survived, swarming up, up. And our horror grew as we watched them stab, chew with diamond-sharp mouths, trying to penetrate Typhon's armored skin.

This is how they take us.

Our energy shield bewildered them, so they crawled along the docking tube with awful dexterity. Hard to say how many; we could not count them. Soon, they would breach Typhon's hull. Already, his thrashing had slowed, movements sluggish, and the blood trail sang of dying stars, of so many who had gone before. Of those lost in the Gathering.

Time to fight.

We—I—dropped back into my skin, and I took a quick inventory. No intruders—Nadim was still clean. "Status, Bea?"

"Some damage, shields holding for now," she came back.

"Okay, I need you to keep them up and start towing Typhon away if you can. I don't know if we have the strength for it."

"I will find it," Nadim said as if it was as simple as deciding to do it.

"Excellent. I'll be back soon." Without waiting for possible objections, I cracked open the hatch. "Two seconds, bring the shields down, then back up."

"But—" Nadim sounded shocked. "You will be outside their protection!"

"That's the idea," I said. Before he could talk me out of it, I dodged out as the shield sizzled away. It was rock steady when it came up again. The shields wouldn't let anything in now. Not even me.

I checked my skinsuit as I ran down the boarding tube, weapons at the ready. A black-edged *thing* dropped down on me, too fast for me to get a good look, and I shot it in the face, right in a rotating ring of fast-moving teeth. I didn't use a stunner, either. Its head evaporated, leaving an arachnid body that ran five steps at me before falling down. A deep shudder rolled over me so hard, I almost threw up.

And the smell—

Indescribable.

It was worse inside Typhon. There were multiple breach points, and though I'd only bonded with him once, his revulsion and agony nearly swept me at the knees. I stumbled, catching myself on the wall. Huge mistake, because it clarified the contact even more. Quickly I yanked my hand away, wondering how the hell Marko and Chao-Xing were even functioning.

He's protecting them, I realized.

His coldness and cruelty keeping them separate from him had a point after all; it might save their lives during an attack like this.

I tried my comm and hoped the ones inside Typhon were still working. "Marko! Chao-Xing! Where are you?"

Marko's voice came back in a rush. "Midships, near the central hub!" That was a long way. I broke into a run. The corridor ahead of me curved, and there were signs of fighting—cuts and dark splashes on the walls, two black-shelled bodies lying on top of each other at the next bend. I leapt over them and hoped that they weren't just pretending, that they wouldn't reach up and grab me, horror-movie style. They didn't. I landed and kept running.

I found Marko pinned down and half-mad with Typhon's pain, shooting wildly; the hall between us was filled with black-armored intruders. This corridor had been fitted out with some control boxes, and I quickly took shelter behind one. Multiple electrical conduits were fried, so the lights kept flickering. We wouldn't have oxygen much longer if this kept up. It wouldn't all escape at once, of course, but—I cut that thought short. One problem at a time.

Taking a knee, I aimed and fired, nailing an intruder in the back. But it only whirled and raced at me in an awful, arachnid crawl. This thing was like if a lizard had a spider's babies, and then ate them and then threw up and wrapped the vomit up in knives and then—hell, I ran out of ideas. *Awful.* That was the only word for what was trying to kill me. How many eyes were there? Instead of counting, I shot it.

That made the others turn, and I picked a couple more

off while Marko settled enough to take one. Typhon's training was supposed to harden him, but he only looked worn to the bone. There was only so much wax in the candle, after all, and burning it at both ends for too long was a bad idea.

I took out every intruder between us and skidded to a stop next to where he crouched.

"Zara! What're you doing here?"

"Dumb question. I'm saving your ass, obviously. Where's Chao-Xing?"

"I'm not sure. I lost track of her." He tried to stand and his knee buckled.

Belatedly, I caught sight of the dark blood trickling from beneath his torn uniform. I threw his arm over my shoulder and hefted him. He wasn't a small guy, but I was motivated. We needed to get the hell off Typhon and trust that his automated defenses would take care of any creatures that had burrowed through.

I was about to suggest the comm when he activated it on his own. "Chao-Xing, are you there? Do you copy?"

"Busy!" she shouted.

The sound of weapon fire rattled the air, along with the bizarre clicks and hisses that seemed to pass for speech among the attackers. I took the comm away from Marko. "Can you get to the docking bay? We'll help you clear a path."

"I'll get there or die trying."

Pulling Marko along with me, I got moving. "Either's okay with me, C-X."

"Call me that again, and I'm going to kick your ass!"

"Yeah, right." I wasn't scared of her at all anymore. Compared to these . . . creatures, she was a huggable bunny.

"Do we have to worry about these things hacking Typhon's nav system?" I asked Marko. If they took over, it would be bad. Even if we saved these two Honors, we might not be able to save the Elder.

He shook his head. "Not until they've destroyed us. Then they'd have to burrow into his brain and take it over. They have built-in imperatives."

"Say what?"

"First, destroy organic resistance. Then infest and occupy the vessel. Then core out the host's mind."

"Shit," I said. "So, we're the organic resistance?"

"Exactly."

"Well, I've been called worse. Let's move."

That explained why they were so focused, though, running at us like machines. They didn't show fear or hesitation, no matter how many we killed. If they'd had greater numbers, if we hadn't smashed so many outside with operation Scylla and Charybdis, we would've been overrun. As it was, I used all my energy packs and had to holster both lethal guns. We left a trail of stinking corpses behind us, easy enough for Chao-Xing to follow.

By then, Marko was dragging his leg like it was dead,

and his weight slowed me down. I didn't consider leaving him. But as if he sensed the slant of my thoughts, he asked, "Why did you come back? You were clear to run."

"Nadim," I said. "He's not the type to abandon his friends."

Marko smiled. "And you are?"

As we neared the docking bay, we hit one last pocket of resistance. From the other side, I heard the sound of Chao-Xing's weapons firing and the explosions from automated defenses, bots and drones working hard to purge the invaders.

Typhon boomed with frustration, anguish, and fury. Then he managed to force his message into words. "Go. When you're clear, I can vent atmosphere."

"Copy," I said.

With a ferocious cry, I charged into the knot of aliens and scattered them with wild stunner shots because that was all I had left. A few twitched and fell down, others shook it off. It didn't matter because I wasn't trying to kill them, just clear a path. It took all my strength to push through with Marko leaning on me, and my skinsuit tore in three places, claws or fangs or I didn't know what. The stunner vibrated and died. Now it was down to knives and street fighting.

I grabbed the nearest limb and twisted; horror nearly drowned me when it *snapped off* in my hand and the creature didn't even slow down. It latched on to my arm, about to bite, and I dislocated my shoulder in the maneuver that had saved my ass more than once. That gave me the time I needed to kick it away and slash. The knife didn't do much harm; it skidded off the armored skin of the thing. As the rest lunged at me in mindless unison, Chao-Xing unloaded on them with a viciously accurate salvo from behind and a wicked battle cry in Mandarin.

Alien goo splattered Marko and me. I hurt in so many places, but I still got a happy chill when I turned to look at her because she stood with her weapon cocked, scanning for additional threats while covered in the blood of her enemies.

"You'll never know how cool you just were."

Somehow, she didn't even crack a smile. "Trust me, xiao Zara. I know."

With her help, I got Marko on board the Hopper. Chao-Xing took the wheel since she was the more experienced pilot. He was drifting in and out, maybe poisoned? I didn't know if he'd been bitten or if those creatures had venom. The way they looked, I could believe it. I had their blood on me. It felt unnaturally cold, contrasting with the fire in my dislocated shoulder.

As soon as we strapped in and opened the docking doors, a boom rolled through Typhon like thunder. He was jettisoning everything that wasn't bolted down with enough force that some of them might be killed if they smashed up against Nadim's shield, best-case scenario, and with Nadim towing hard, we were moving away from the swarm, the few that struggled weightless in the void. They moved slower in isolation, faster as the group. Surely they'd die if they didn't eventually find shelter? It was hard to imagine otherwise, but maybe they could go into hibernation or something—dormant until a likely target appeared. They could latch on to a passing ship like a tick, burrow in, take over.

That must have been the fate of the other Leviathan. These things had killed the Honors, gutted the brain, and worn its skin. They had multiplied inside, like a virus, before bursting out on us.

With a skill even Beatriz couldn't match, Chao-Xing glided the Hopper out into space. We weren't far from Nadim's docking area, but something in the wreckage caught my eye. I didn't ask her; I just scanned.

Two life signs, faint and flickering now, but holy shit, somebody had survived that horrific battle, maybe even Honors we'd stood onstage with.

I tapped Chao-Xing's shoulder. "Detour. We've got survivors."

"We should escape while we can," she said.

"If we'd said that, you wouldn't even be here."

Her fulminating silence only lasted a few seconds, felt longer. Then she switched course, dodging Leviathan debris with a celerity and grace that filled me with admiration. I could learn so much from her. Soon, we had visual confirmation; I'd expected pods like I had seen in old vids, but these were more like membrane pouches similar to the sac that protected a human fetus during pregnancy. Shapes were moving inside.

"That stuff must be stronger than it looks," I said, doubtful.

"It is. Get to the back. You'll have to find a way to haul them in."

There was room, barely, for the two, and it took precious time we might not have because I was struggling to catch and pull while Chao-Xing reverse-thrustered toward them. The rescue op was slow and tedious, and we had to avoid floating pockets of the dark swarm, struggling feebly toward us. Impossible to make out who we'd saved, but I breathed better once we had them aboard.

"Okay, let's go. Open a channel to Beatriz."

"Where the hell are you?" she shouted the minute the comm pinged.

"I'm on Typhon's Hopper, incoming with Marko, Chao-Xing, and two others. Marko will need EMITU, so have him on standby, okay? And tell Nadim I'm fine."

"You have to stop doing this!"

"What?"

"Running off without talking things over with us first. Nadim is out of his mind, and it's making me want to climb the walls. This bond stuff is bullshit, absolute . . ." Bea lapsed into Portuguese, still ranting.

A sound came from Chao-Xing, one I didn't recognize. Laughter. So much that she could hardly pilot the Hopper. I gave her a dark look. "This is funny to you?"

"Hilarious. And you wonder why we almost failed you both."

"Hey, I passed, remember?"

Chao-Xing smirked. "Did you?"

No matter how I pestered, she wouldn't elaborate. We sped up, and I got my first look at Nadim towing Typhon, both bleeding starlight. It was like those old tugboats hauling a giant barge down the river, small in size, mighty in power. Nadim slowed and dropped shields long enough for us to swoop inside, and then he locked everything down again. Maybe it was safe to relax, but I wouldn't let my guard down until we put some distance between us and the remains of the horde.

There was so much shit to sort. Thankfully, Bea was there when we piled out of the Hopper. She'd put EMITU on rover mode, and it immediately locked on to Marko. "You're all kinds of jacked up, son." Then it ran the scanner over him and jabbed him with a hypodermic.

Chao-Xing swiveled her head so fast, I was surprised it didn't pop off. "You altered our medical unit?"

"Uh, *our* medical unit," I said. "He's awesome now."

We got Marko onto a gurney and Bea hurried off,

presumably to supervise EMITU. "Hey, C-X, we're pretty far past worrying about minor infractions. Right?"

"Don't call me that."

"Okay. Warbitch?"

She ignored that, but a faint smile tugged at the corner of her mouth as she wiped blood from her face. "I don't care about your mods. Those shields saved our asses. And I don't mind saying, your battle strategy was not bad for an amateur."

That shocked me so much, I tripped on my own feet. "I . . . what?"

"That's a compliment. Say thank you and then shut your hole." Chao-Xing still looked stern, but I caught a hint of a twinkle that time.

She'd said before, *I was just like you, once.* Maybe she really meant it, and like me, she wanted people to think she was quite the hardass, but the truth was, it just took a while to earn her respect. I could relate to that on all levels. Anyway, I liked her better when we were on the same team.

"Your shoulder needs to be fixed," she said then.

"I know."

"It's going to hurt. A lot." The relish in her voice made me take two steps in the opposite direction, but that didn't stop her from grabbing me.

Her hands were brutal and efficient, and they slipped the joint back together. I ate a shriek and then stopped wanting to die. There were levels of pain, and compared to the migraines I used to get, this was a five at best. I breathed through it and eventually managed to whisper, "Thanks."

"You did well," Chao-Xing told me.

It felt like a hug.

Honor Cole. The deep voice startled me because it wasn't Nadim. It was Typhon. Technically, we were bonded through him, as the boarding tube still connected the two ships, but I didn't realize the Elder could do this, especially at such a remove.

I answered hesitantly. *Yeah?* Then, *How are you talking to me right now?*

There is something in your brain not like other humans, he said. I suppose he meant my Leviathan DNA patch, to cure the headaches. I didn't like the implications. *And you touched my mind before. I have the right to speak with you.*

Last time you do it, Typhon. We're not friends.

No, he agreed. *We are not. But if you had not returned, all would have been lost.*

For obvious reasons, I had to ask, *Does this mean Nadim is safe?*

Soul-deep weariness enveloped me. *From judgment? Yes. There is no Gathering now. I owe my survival to him.* Typhon paused before going on with great care. *I am old. It is still possible to be a warrior with a living heart. Nadim has proved that.*

While that didn't entirely make sense, I thought I had

the gist. But Nadim was done with standing by while I communed with Typhon. He enfolded me in warmth that also sent the Elder away, efficiently severing our contact. Nadim's relief buoyed me up, but he was still citrine and crimson with fear and restrained violence.

"Are those creatures still a threat?" I asked. First question, most relevant.

"We are outpacing them," he said. "They are going quiet now. I don't know if that means they're dead."

"Do you know anything about them? Anything at all?"

"Only what you saw," he told me. "But the others will know more."

I had so many questions, but we needed to tend our rescued Honors first. "Okay. Shall we see who we've brought aboard?"

Chao-Xing was already on it, slicing the membranes with assurance. I kept one hand on my weapon in case this was a trick and something came out that needed to be shot. But when she dug her fingers into the slimy goo and scooped it away, the movement revealed a human face. Male, a little younger than Marko, dark skin, luxurious braids. Brown eyes opened and the man lurched upright, hacking up a spate of liquid.

"I lived?" He sounded none too sure, but I recognized his uniform. Definitely an Honor, but not one who'd come up with us.

"It appears so." Chao-Xing gave him a hand and helped

him climb out of his space placenta.

Figuring why not, I slashed the next one open and only recoiled slightly when I got a tentacle face instead of an earthling. Abysmal Hummus? I couldn't remember the alien species name, but it looked just like the one I shot. Gingerly, I poked it—the skin felt like a manta ray, but thinner and more delicate—and then I launched backward when it scuttled at me.

History does repeat.

Only this time I didn't fire, and it stopped just short of touching, writhing a bunch of tentacles at me. "Thanks this you for salvation."

"Uhm. Sure. Could you, uh, back up?" I asked. It slithered away, blinking all its eyes at once. "Nice. Good."

"Good," it echoed. "Good?"

"Good."

"Good."

I didn't know what he *thought* he was saying, and I glanced desperately at Chao-Xing. Who produced an H2 from her belt pouch. "What're your birth names, and bond-names if you had one?"

"Yusuf," said the human. "I served on Xolani for my Tour and later bonded with Artemisia for the Journey. Together, our name . . . is . . . was . . . Temiyus." He seemed to process the tense then. Realizing his loss. His knees buckled, and he dropped to the floor, so stunned it hurt to see it.

I made an unconscious move, maybe to comfort him,

but Nadim whispered, *No. There is no help for him. Only time. And waiting to see if he is strong to bear it.*

I couldn't, I thought.

You must, Nadim said, bathing me in steely determination. *If it comes to that. There must always be a you, even without me.*

A breath that was almost a sob gusted out of me. *And if I say that back to you?*

Nadim had no reply.

Ignoring the tragedy she couldn't change, Chao-Xing made a note and turned to the Abysmal Hummus. "Report your details."

Like before, there were weird stops and starts in its speech, likely due to processing. "My . . . name is . . . He who Sings the Star Current. I . . . sailed with . . . Ship of Breakwater. For Tour. Deep bond with Hail to You, My Goddess. Bond-name, Star Current Goddess."

"We need to repair your translation matrix, stat," I mumbled.

The alien flashed me a couple of tentacles. "Good!"

"I really don't know if you get what that means."

Chao-Xing sighed. "We'll just call you Starcurrent for now, if that's all right?"

"Good," said the tentacles.

Appearing satisfied, she turned to the other man. "What do you prefer?"

"Yusuf," he whispered. "I am only Yusuf now."

Chao-Xing was uncomfortable, somewhere behind that blank look. And I had so many questions. Not for Starcurrent; we'd probably end up repeating words back to each other in an endless loop. Not for Yusuf, who was clearly in no shape to talk.

Let us care for the weak and wounded, and then ask. Nadim seemed a bit different now, more assertive. Maybe Leviathan changed after their first battle too.

I helped Yusuf up. "Come on," I said. "Let's get you somewhere safe."

There is no safe, Nadim whispered to me alone, and an instant later, Chao-Xing said, in precisely the same tone, "There is no safe. As you have seen."

Much later, when everyone was tended, when we'd eaten, when we'd put light years between us and that awful carnage, untethered Typhon and Nadim and set them cruising around a nourishing star, we sat together in Nadim's lounge. Starcurrent fidgeted, poking at this and that like he expected the furniture to poke back and fluttering tentacles when it didn't. Marko, sedated and limping, got settled full-length on the comfortable couch.

I went over to him. "You okay?"

"Not really," he said.

"Lot of that going around."

"But . . . thank you for saving me."

That wasn't something I ever expected to hear from the polished person who hauled me out of Camp Kuna. "What can I say? Nadim made me do it."

I should've known Nadim wouldn't let that stand. "Untrue. I was wholly opposed to you risking your life."

We touched silently, mind to mind. Nadim ached with the remembered misery of my reckless decision, *and* he still wasn't healed from installing that damned alarm. He needed solid starlight and rest. Beatriz had already chewed me out, so he let me feel the aftermath—his fear cooling to a low hum of dread. In apology, I opened to him and filled him with all of the strength and reassurance I could muster. His delight swelled in response. A look from Beatriz said she *knew*, but she didn't join us.

Chao-Xing paced, lost in her own thoughts. Yusuf sat silently in a chair, staring at his hands, his whole body slumped and loose.

Leaving Marko to rest, I sank down on the floor next to Beatriz. We were dirty and tired. I'd scrubbed the worst of the filthy alien blood off and changed clothes, but I still felt the ghost of it on me, cold and destructive. *What if it can soak in?* I wanted right then to scramble up and run to have EMITU check it out, but I was beyond exhausted. If I was infected, I'd still be infected in half an hour, and I'd be better able to deal with it.

"Well?" I asked. Nadim was silent, but his presence was everywhere around us. Typhon's massive chill hung beyond him, almost comforting now. Sometimes, having the bully at your back could be an asset. You just kept him pointed away.

Chao-Xing gave us both a wry, shaded look, grim with a touch of graveyard humor. "Congratulations, Honors Cole and Teixeira. You're the first humans in history to graduate to the Journey without first completing the Tour. You've met the enemy. We call them the Phage. And now, you are at war."

I understood at last why I'd been chosen. Why I'd been plucked out of the grim and struggle.

I'd always been at war.

ACKNOWLEDGMENTS

To all those reaching for the stars. Someday, the stars will reach back.

ANN:

Thanks so much to those who listened and supported me while I was working on this project. Obviously I'm starting with Rachel Caine, because without her there would be no book. Major thanks to Justina Ireland as well. I'd also like to thank Bree Bridges, Courtney Milan, Rebekah Weatherspoon, Molly O'Keefe, Melissa Blue, Kristen Callihan, and Karen Alderman. Each of these phenomenal women played a role in bringing this story to fruition, and I'm so lucky they share their wisdom and insights with me. I definitely thank my family also, particularly my husband, who has been my anchor for nearly twenty years. I hope I'm lucky enough to give him twenty more. Finally, thanks to our readers, who believed from the start that this ship sails itself.

RACHEL:

All the love to Ann Aguirre for immediately seeing the potential and agreeing to jump in and fly with me. My husband, Cat Conrad, has put up with my flights of imagination for twenty-five years, and it's never been more difficult than these last couple of years, so *extra* love to him. Lucienne Diver placed tremendous faith in this crazy idea . . . and thanks also to Claudia Gabel, for taking a chance on an unconventional OTP. Special thanks to Justina Ireland for helping us see what we could not see, and to Sarah Weiss-Simpson, for somehow fitting reading this into her incredibly busy schedule, again. And thank you, always, to teachers and librarians, who labor so hard for so little, all for the love of books and readers. You shine.